Immaculate Deception

Stephen Leonard Lancashire

AuthorHouse™ UK Ltd.
500 Avebury Boulevard
Central Milton Keynes, MK9 2BE
www.authorhouse.co.uk
Phone: 08001974150

© 2009 Stephen Leonard Lancashire. All rights reserved.

No part of this book may be reproduced, stored in a retrieval system, or transmitted by any means without the written permission of the author.

First published by AuthorHouse 12/2/2009

ISBN: 978-1-4389-9138-2 (sc)

This book is printed on acid-free paper.

DEDICATIONS

For my eldest son, Marc, who truly understands The Power of Words.

For my youngest son, David, who truly believes them.

For my wife, and harshest critic Gaby, who patiently reads them,

And, finally to my Mum and Dad who suspected nothing but knew all along.

ACKNOWLEDGEMENTS

Acknowledgements with thanks go to:

Friends of Merseyside Police – They know who they are!

All at the Coroners office in Liverpool

The forensic toxicologists at the University Hospital Liverpool

The friendly Father at the Catholic Church who wishes to remain anonymous

Friends of the Police Service of Northern Ireland

To Bryan Waterson, friend and confidant, thanks for all the words of encouragement

To Sue Dodd @spotlight on writing, thanks Sue for your help, advice and patience

And finally when all else failed

Google.

Thank you.

Chapter 1

*August 1980.
Belfast, Northern Ireland.*

Sharon Byrne got the taste for whisky when she was just twelve years old. She could remember it as if it were yesterday. It was her twelfth birthday and she had just received another severe beating from her father. She was in her bedroom crying.

The sounds of drunken rowing from the living room had died down completely. All she could hear was the muffled sound of a late night talk show coming from the television downstairs. It was late and she hadn't had any tea. As she tiptoed quietly through the living room, her eyes were drawn towards her parents. They were both crashed out on the sofa. She stood perfectly still, staring at her sleeping father. Beside his feet was the whisky bottle. It was almost full.

On its side underneath the coffee table was another whisky bottle, empty. She returned her attention to the first bottle, staring at it for a full minute before moving closer to pick it up. The pungent scent of the cheap whisky drifted around the mouth of the bottle. The fumes burnt her nostrils and made her eyes water. *How could anybody ever drink bottles of this stuff?* She decided she was going to find out. She held the bottle in both hands, raised it to her lips and tipped it. She took a swig from the bottle without taking her eyes off her sleeping parents. She tried to stop but it was too late. The whisky slipped past her lips, into her mouth and hit the back of her throat. She tried to breathe and swallow at the same time. The vapour scalded her lungs, causing her to gag and retch.

Streams of whisky and saliva dribbled down her chin. In her panic, she nearly dropped the bottle, but caught it just before it smashed on the glass coffee table. Standing absolutely still in case either of her parents woke up she tried to catch her breath, her throat burning. Neither of them budged an inch. Gradually, the taste in her mouth became less sickening. The whisky she had swallowed began to glow inside her and she felt the gentle heat as it rose through her chest. Any thoughts of having something to eat vanished. *So this was what it was all about.* She had come down the stairs for food; instead she had discovered the reason her parents drank.

She took another two swigs. There wasn't so much as a peep from her mother or father. Having lost her appetite, she decided to go back to bed. By the time she reached the top of the stairs she was already drunk. That night she slept more soundly than she had done in a very long time. No dreams, no nightmares.

When she got up her mother and father had left for the pub and would more than likely be there all day. She waited until her breakfast of toast and beans had settled before she went to look for the whisky bottle. It was on the coffee table, just less than half full. One or both of her parents had obviously had a good slug at it before leaving the house. Taking the bottle, she unscrewed the top and without hesitation took a good long swallow. There was no gagging this time; she drank it as if it were milk. Fifteen minutes later she went out to look for something to steal from the shops. She would sell whatever she stole and find someone to buy her a bottle of whisky.

Two years after that first bottle of whisky, Sharon was walking along the High Street near Nutt's Corner a few miles from the city of Belfast. She had just sold her body on the back seat of a punter's car for the second time that day. With the money she bought herself enough whisky, lager and cigarettes to see her through the next twenty-four hours. Any more money she made that day would be a bonus.

Sean, her father, had been killed a year before, caught in a bomb blast outside the "Tinkers Arms" in the Shankhill Road. The day after the bombing she stood next to her mother staring at a painted mural on a brick wall less than a hundred yards away from the pub. The mural depicted two members of the IRA, dressed in black combats with black balaclavas over their faces, standing either side of a scroll with a message on it, *Lest We Forget*. Her mother couldn't fucking wait to forget and had taken her opportunity to escape from her miserable shitty world. Sharon hadn't seen or heard of her since.

Fending for herself had come easier than she'd expected. There had been no shortage of punters willing to part with their money for the pleasure of spreading the legs of a pretty young girl. She had no problem finding men willing to buy her all the alcohol she needed, either. Her regulars now brought whisky as a down payment.

Loaded up with her carrier bag full of lager and two bottles of whisky she was heading back towards the flat she squatted in on the outskirts of Belfast. She heard the music coming before she saw the car. The sound of Billy Joel's *It's Still Rock and Roll to Me* was playing loudly enough to cause the speakers to rattle. The driver slowed to a halt a few yards ahead.

The occupants of the car took a good look at her. The car pulled up to the kerb and Sharon stood on the pavement staring at the young lads inside. The one in the front passenger seat wound the window down and switched off the radio. He turned towards her, leaning his head on folded arms, eyeing up the carrier bag full of booze, and spoke in a broad Northern Irish accent.

"Is that a private party you're going to or c'n anybody come?" he said, winking. He was good looking all right and he knew it.

"It depends on who the anybody is," she replied, smiling.

The young man flashed an even bigger smile back at her. "Well, I'm Brian Murphy and these are me mates Mickey, Sean and Alex," he said, pointing to each of the others as he spoke. "We're not just anybody by the way. D'you fancy coming for a ride?"

She thought about it, weighing up his two mates in the back of the car. "I might do. Where you gonna take me?"

Brian turned and gave his orders. "Shift your arses up you two, this lady's coming for a ride." He looked back towards her. "We're goin' to the seaside, probably up Carrickfergus way, if you fancy it?"

Fits of laughter broke out from the lads in the back "Fuckin' seaside, Carrickfergus? Y'can hardly call that the fuckin' seaside, it's the Belfast fuckin' Lough for fuck's sake."

Brian glared at Sean and Alex in the back seat. "Shut the fuck up you two, it's beside the fuckin' sea isn't it? Then it's the fuckin' seaside."

Alex and Sean promptly shut the fuck up. Sharon saw, it was obvious who was in charge here.

Fourteen years old and she had never been near the seaside; suddenly she fancied the idea a lot. "Sounds great. I'll provide the booze if you lot chip in for the food?"

Brian gave her the thumbs up and winked, it wouldn't be a problem. Quick as a flash he got out of the car and opened the rear passenger door.

"Alex, get in the front with Mickey. Sean, move over yer fat bastard!"

The fat bastard moved over as far as he could until he was pressed up hard against the door. Brian turned towards Sharon and held the door open for her.

He smiled and bowed like a chauffeur as she climbed in. "There you go darlin', we'll have you there in no time at all. It'll be burgers and chips and ice cream all round."

Sharon didn't see the look on the faces of Mickey and Alex in the front as they glanced at each other, each silently confirming what the other one thought. Their leader had plans for the afternoon all right, and food wasn't included. As Sharon climbed onto the back seat, the radio burst into life with the sound of Gary Numan's *Cars*. Tyres screeched as the car pulled away.

Chapter 2

*December 2004.
Merseyside Police Headquarters
Canning Place, Liverpool.*

Detective Inspector Frank Carroll stared through the window of his eighth floor office at Canning Place in Liverpool city centre. On a clear day, he could see from the MIT base right across to the Albert Dock, overlooking the River Mersey.

Today he couldn't see anything, not even the old shipyards at Camelairds. The rain was lashing up against the windows of his office with such ferocity he thought they might cave in. The wind was howling and blowing hard enough to pick up the tips of the waves from the grey old River Mersey and carry them the full half-mile or so before throwing them against the windows to his office.

There would be no walk along the riverside for him today. His daily forty-five minute walk was something he did to keep his exercise levels up. Without a single grey hair on his head and still in possession of all his own teeth, he reckoned he was in pretty good shape. Not like one or two of his DC's he could mention. During his walks he was able to think more clearly, focusing on current cases and future plans. He made most of the important decisions in his life walking along the banks of the River Mersey.

Standing at the window, he remembered the first time he took that walk during a weekend trip from Ireland as a teenager. That was when he made one of his most important decisions, the decision to leave Ireland for good as soon as he was eighteen. After he left Ireland and settled in Liverpool, he continued his walks along the river. Once, he walked for hours pondering over the decision to join the police force. Other times; whether getting married at the age of twenty-three was a good idea, could he afford to buy a house, should he agree to let his wife choose the name Cram for their son.

The one decision he regretted most, of all his life changing decisions, was the one that led to his divorce from Hilary and losing custody of Cram. Now he was making up for lost ground and had made some improvements in his relationship with Hilary. She had agreed it was okay for him to have Cram for the occasional weekend. When it suited her of course.

Walking along the banks of the Mersey, he was also able to concentrate on his strategies for solving serious crimes. He'd solved murders; serious villains and crooks had been caught and locked up within hours of completing his daily walk. Once when he got back off a walk, he was greeted in the car park by several members of MIT in a car with the engine running, handcuffs at the ready. "Where to boss?"

Piss taking bastards! Only a few that knew him well enough, would know when it was safe to risk this kind of cheek with their DI. He also had a reputation for his ruthless single mindedness. If anyone or anything got in his way in pursuit of the truth, there were serious repercussions.

He didn't mince his words either. A young DS on detachment from a visiting force had upset him once and brought on a classic quote from his repertoire, one of many he had picked up from his dad's years in the army. "You do that one more fucking time and I will ram the toe end of my boot so far up your arse you'll be fucking spitting boot polish for a month." The visiting DS had got the message.

Frank was still staring out of the window when another vicious blast of sleet hurled itself against the window, bringing him back to his thoughts of missing his walk. He glanced at the mountain of paperwork on his desk, his eyes focusing on the photograph of his parents. Memories and this picture was all he had left of them.

After his dad was killed in the Falklands, Frank's mother Kathleen had gone back to Ireland, still not forgiven by her parents or anyone else who knew her for marrying a British soldier. In the early hours of the 1st of January 2000 she died, aged 53, killed by a drunk driver coming home from a Millennium New Year's Eve party. In the six months following the death of his mother, the arrest rates for drunk drivers in Merseyside increased by 80 percent.

There was a knock on the door. Frank looked up. Despite the frosted windowpane, he could see it was DC Rob Turner, known amongst the lads as "Rob the Bob" because he was always "bobbing" out for something. When asked if he were all right, he would usually reply with, "Bob on, Boss," meaning no problem. It was a Scouse thing. Bob was a local lad, and a Red through and through.

He spoke very quickly and had a tendency to run words together. It had taken Frank a while before he could talk to him without an interpreter being present. Looks-wise he was a bit on the podgy side, but he was, "*werkinonnit*", as Bob had informed him when they first met. Frank checked his watch; it was brew time. "Yeah come in Bob."

The door opened a bit at a time to reveal Bob doing a balancing act with a pie in one hand and a pasty in the other, with a cup of coffee balanced between the two.

He was trying to open the door with his feet without spilling the coffee. It was Thursday, well past lunchtime, and the lads knew if Frank wasn't going on his walkabout he would have something to eat in his office.

"Steak'n kidney pie or Cornish pasty, Boss?" said Bob, without taking his eyes off the coffee. Frank chose the pasty and took the coffee gratefully.

"Everything okay Bob?" Bob was nursing a minor scald from the hot pasty.

"Yeah, Boss, bob on…just thought I'd let you know there's some Irish feller downstairs at the front desk, says he's a mate of yours and wants a word."

Frank was already tucking in to the pasty and juggling a hot piece of meat round inside his mouth. "What's his name?" he said, between huffing sounds.

"Says his name's Father Maloney, he's piss wet through, looks like he walked here in this shite weather from the church at the topperUpperParly."

Frank's on-board translator took over. UpperParly was short for Upper Parliament Street. Topper meant top of. Frank had learned fast. He coughed and spat the mouthful of scalding pasty into a serviette on his desk. "Fuckin' hell, Bob, get him brought up here straight away! And leave the pie while you're at it!"

"Right, Boss, bob on." DC Bob Turner left a lot more quickly than he had come in.

Frank put his pasty down on top of the pile of paperwork on his desk and stared at it, a million and one thoughts going through his head; fuck, that pasty's hot; Bob must have nuked it in the microwave before bringing it in. The other million thoughts surrounded his friend, Father Ted Maloney.

Frank and Ted were more than just mates; they had played, fought, laughed and cried together in the same street in Carrickfergus, Northern Ireland. As kids, they had shared dreams of a better future, away from the troubles on the streets of Belfast. Back then, they were practically brothers. They had made a pact to leave Ireland as soon as they were eighteen, to come to Liverpool in search of a job and a new life.

Frank had tried one or two Mickey Mouse jobs, as Bob would have called them, before eventually getting accepted into Merseyside Police. Ted had arrived with high grades from school and was planning to go to University and study Law.

Later he got the calling to study a different kind of law, the law of God. Two years later, at the age of twenty, Ted joined the Catholic Church as a Curate. Now, like Frank, he was serving the public, but in a different capacity with a completely different mission statement. Father Maloney, or Ted, as Frank would usually address him, was the Reverend Father at the Holy Church of Trinity at the top of the hill on Upper Parliament Street.

Frank paced his office wondering what on earth had possessed Ted to walk all the way from the church to the station in this weather. Not even a phone call to alert him he was on his way or check that he was in? An unscheduled visit; something was wrong. The last time they had met was two years ago just before Christmas; sadly, the demands of their jobs had caused them to drift out of touch. He sat down and waited, staring at the scar on the palm of his hand. There was another knock at the door.

It was almost three o'clock in the afternoon when Bob, carrying another cup of coffee, ushered Ted into the office. He put the coffee down on the desk and left with a nod to his boss. Ted, looking as if he had been for a dip in the Mersey, walked in and held out his hand. Frank's eyes were drawn to the identical scar.

"How're ye keeping Frank?" Fifteen years since he and Ted arrived in Liverpool, and not a sign of a dent in Ted's Irish accent.

Frank shook his hand. "You know, busy," he replied, checking out Ted's appearance. His white hair was uncharacteristically long and, even more unusually, he clearly hadn't shaved for a day or two. Ted was as tall as Frank but weighed at least two stone more. Right now, he looked to be carrying a heavier burden than that.

"Grab a seat, Ted." Frank pointed to the seating area in the corner of the office. Ted sat down. Frank grabbed the coffees and food from the desk and joined him.

By the time they finished talking and said their goodbyes it was pitch black outside. The rain had stopped. Every surface was frozen over. The rest of the people in the offices of Canning Place had gone home. Frank sat back at the table and stared at the skin that had formed on the surface of his coffee. He picked it up and downed it in one. The untouched food was stone cold.

Chapter 3

Carrickfergus 1980

As Sharon was climbing into the car, miles away in the town of Carrickfergus two young boys were freewheeling on their bikes along the Marine Highway. Frank and Ted were heading for the ruins of an old Keep that lay on a large section of swampy land just off the old coast road towards Milebush and Eden. The boys lived next door but one to each other in a row of brown and red-bricked terraced houses known as Woodburn Villas. For their lunch, they had packed lemon soda, malt bread and jam butties in a battered old school satchel.

The Keep had become one of their favourite playgrounds. It was a bit like an old church but without the steeple. Inside was a maze of stairs leading to more floors above and below. The rooms were damp and smelled bad. There were dark passageways leading off in all directions to more stairs down to the cellars. This was where the scary monsters lived. It was spooky, but so much fun when you are nine years old and imagination is unlimited.

Frank looked up to the sky, clear and blue as sapphire. It was hot. Hot enough to melt the tarmac on the road making it sticky. He raced along, enjoying the feel of the warm wind on his face, eyes watering and tears streaming. Racing down the hill, he felt like he was going a hundred miles an hour.

The onshore wind blowing in across the Belfast Lough had dried out the wetter parts of the marsh surrounding the Keep. The last time they came here they had got up to their knees in mud and been given the almightiest of bollockings when they got back home. Today, they left on the understanding that if they came back filthy they would never be allowed to go again.

Ted's mother had watched them go, shouting after them, "Remember now what I told yez, don't you be comin' back here all covered in muck now, or ye'll have your backsides tanned so hard ye'll not sit down for a week."

Frank's mother had watched them through the curtains of her front bedroom window. "Bless the wee men, they're only havin' a bit of fun, and Lord knows they don't get much of that around here," she had whispered.

Frank and Ted reached the broken fence surrounding the marshy field. In the distance, they could see the Keep and their pulses began to quicken. They had decided to give the burnt-out cars a miss today; there wouldn't be time for that. Instead, they went straight to the Keep and parked their bikes so that they were hidden between the bushes. They were intent on playing their favourite "Who Dares, Wins" game, and it was Ted's turn to go first.

The first time they played the game, it had taken the best part of a day to find the courage just to climb in through the open stone window on the ground floor. It had taken less than two minutes for them to come running out again screaming, convinced that there was something really, really bad chasing them. They had laughed about it afterwards and called each other chicken. The game of "Who Dares Wins" had been born.

Every time they came to the Keep, they were getting braver and braver, as they got used to exploring the darkest parts deeper inside. The last time they had brought matches and a candle with them.

That was the first time they went all the way down the stairs and stumbled across the ancient underground cellar. Inside, it was so cold they could see their breath as it crept eerily around them in the flickering light of the candle. The place had a rich, musty smell; spidery cobwebs covered in dust clung in every corner. So far, neither of them had managed to stay down there for more than three or four minutes before they completely bottled it and ran for the stairs.

Today they had brought with them an old bicycle light and they were planning to go back down into the cellar, determined to stay down there for longer than five minutes. Full of anticipation and nervous excitement, they entered the Keep. They felt a lot bolder with their bicycle light and got down to the cellar quicker than ever before. They were having a good look around when, in the far corner, they found yet another set of stairs that led down to a much smaller room.

"What d'you think of that?" whispered Ted. Frank just shrugged. This was unchartered territory, a new challenge. Ted led the way. "C'mon, let's see what's down there."

Frank followed, reluctantly. The light from the lamp gave them confidence as they descended the stairs and stepped inside the small room. It felt harder to breathe this far down and it smelt so bad they could taste it. Even with the light, the room seemed dark; darker than any place they had ever been. To their left, they could just make out an arched doorway with a huge timber frame surrounding a solid wooden door.

The door was half open, hanging partly off its hinges. Behind the door they could see what looked like water reflecting the yellow glow from their lamp.

The water was black and shiny, like freshly melted tar. Mould and fungus grew around the water line and up the door. Cobwebs hung all over the walls and ceilings like dripping layers of slime left by the hungry beast living under the water.

They stood still, cold, too afraid to go any further. The lamp flickered, as the batteries grew weaker. They held on to each other, both gripping the lamp in case one of them decided to run for it and leave the other stranded in the dark. Too scared to turn their backs to the water, they edged their way backwards towards the stairs. They were slowly turning their heads to look for the first step, when they heard the noise.

They turned around just in time to see something moving towards them. It was big and moved quickly. Frank let out a piercing scream and the thing made a break for the water. The splash from behind the arched doorway was the final straw. They turned and ran for their lives. They did not stop until they were safely through the door and into the bright sunshine outside. They tumbled onto the grass their hearts beating like crazy and heads banging with the adrenalin. It took a moment for them to catch their breath. When they finally looked at each other they went hysterical with laughter, swearing that they would never go down there again.

"I'm starving," said Frank.

Ted shot off in the direction where they had parked their bikes. "C'mon I'll race yer."

They retrieved the satchel and sat out of the wind on a flat stone bank just inside the door of the Keep. They shared their butties and lemon soda, joking about how scared they'd been down in the cellar. They had almost finished their lunch and were wondering what they were going to do next, when Ted cocked his head to one side.

"Sshh...what was that?" he said. He turned to Frank with an anxious look on his face. "Did you hear that?"

Frank almost choked on his malt bread. "Aw yer just shittin' me ain't yer?" he spluttered.

"No, I swear listen."

Frank stopped chewing. "Yeah, I can hear it. Sounds like music," he said.

"It is, I can hear a car, it sounds like its comin' from a car."

They quickly packed up the remains of their food and ran upstairs to a small stone opening to the right hand side of the stairway where they would be able to see what was going on without being seen. The music they had heard was coming from a dark blue Ford Escort, racing across the waste ground with its engine screaming and wheels spinning in the mud. They had a clear view of the car as it careered towards them, sliding across the open ground, barely missing the other burnt out wrecks.

The driver of the car was doing his best impression of Jackie Stewart on a bad day, spinning the car around on its own axis, spraying mud everywhere. He was either showing off or was very drunk.

In fact, Mickey O'Hare was both, completely pissed and trying to impress the others inside the car. The car made a final wheel spin before the tyres took hold on more solid ground and Mickey drove the car towards the Keep.

Frank and Ted recoiled from the slot in the wall and stared at each other. They were more scared than they'd been inside the cellar.

The car slowed to a halt on the gravel less than a hundred feet away from the entrance to the Keep. Sean

Flynn was the first to climb out from the back of the car.

He sank to his knees and immediately spewed his ring up.

"What the fuckin'ell did you have to drive like that for you fuckin' idjit? I told yez I wasn't feelin' so good!"

The others got out of the car laughing, admiring the mud-spattered car and the tracks they had made across the ground. Alex was the first to look towards the Keep. Frank and Ted felt as though he was looking right at them. Instinctively they felt that trouble was on its way.

Chapter 4

Friday 18 December 2004
The Blue Bar, Waterfront,
Albert Dock, Liverpool.

Frank left Canning Place and walked in the direction of the Albert Dock. It was supposed to be a tourist attraction. From what he could see during his time in Liverpool it was past its sell by date. Back in the late 70's some whiz property developer had turned the empty buildings into shops and Museums for the tourist industry, but the boom in tourism was over except for the Beatles Museum.

The museum relied mostly on Japanese tourists standing around with their flash digital cameras and sporting Beatles style haircuts. Frank had made a conscious effort to avoid it like the plague.

As he entered the docks next to the Beatles Museum, at the opposite end of the dock he could see the Merseyside Maritime Museum, which as far as he was concerned was well worth a visit if you had fuck all else to do and it was pissing down with rain outside. The one and only time Frank had brought Hilary and Cram here, he was disappointed to find that most of the remaining shops were tacky little places with not much to offer other than sweets and ice cream; or the odd

Beatles poster and Tea Towels with a map of "The Best Pub Crawl" around the city.

He took the shortest route to one of the few cafes left with a decent menu. It was Friday lunchtime and starting to get busy, but Frank managed to grab a small table next to the window. A keen-looking waiter with greasy hair and acne approached him. "Would you like to order some food Sir?"

Frank studied the menu. "No thanks, I'll have a coffee" he replied. The place was filling up and people were looking for tables. The persistent ones were hovering about in the hope that Frank would soon be leaving.

Frank finished his coffee and was reluctant to order another before Ted showed up. While he was waiting, he tried to maintain a look on his face, one that said, "Don't even think about asking me am I leaving soon, and, yes, there is someone sitting there, so fuck off". So far it had worked. He would give Ted ten more minutes, but if he hadn't arrived by then he would leave, knowing there would probably be a fight for his table. Just as he started to think about it, Ted walked in, looking no better than when he had last seen him.

The only difference today was, he wasn't piss wet through. More significant was that this time he wasn't wearing his collar. He didn't do incognito. "Sorry I'm late." Ted greeted him, "Have you eaten yet? I'm so hungry, me stomach thinks me throat's been cut."

Frank knew how he felt. "Nope, I'm Hank Marvin." He replied, sliding a menu across the table.

The waiter was on them in a flash. "Can I get yous guys something t'drink?" The scouse accent still didn't quite fit with Frank and often he found himself hoping he didn't sound the same.

"I'll have another coffee and the chicken and cheese melt on ciabatta bread with salad and chips." Frank glanced at Ted. "My treat."

Ted didn't bother looking at the menu. "I'll have the same but tea instead of coffee, thanks." The waiter scribbled on his pad and scuttled off, grateful that he did not have to fend off any more questions from his boss about what was that guy doing sitting there and not eating or drinking.

"Thanks for coming Frank," began Ted. "I know you're busy. Sorry I couldn't meet with you before now."

"Don't worry about it. It's given me some time to mull over what we talked about," he lied. "I haven't changed my mind, what I said still stands."

Frank cleared his throat. "In fact I'm more certain now what I said was right. One, I am not prepared to take the risk, and two, more importantly I'm not prepared to let you drop yourself in the shit over this either." Frank often swore in front of Ted. It was an unwritten rule that he would be forgiven no matter what he said.

Ted looked at him scornfully. "Jeez, you were always the stubborn one, an' all, but I'm at me wits end. Honestly, if you don't help me with this, I've no idea what I'm going to do." He studied Frank's face for signs of a reaction. Nothing.

"Okay, so you're right, its a risk, I could get into serious trouble. But, I'm not going to ignore this, and I'm prepared to accept the consequences."

Out of the corner of his eye, Frank clocked the waiter approaching with the food. He leaned forward. "There's got to be another way for us to sort this, I just haven't thought of it yet. Don't worry, as soon as I do, you will be the first to know."

The waiter placed their food on the table with the tea and coffee then disappeared to fetch the condiments.

Ted sighed, nodded, sat back in his chair and got stuck into his chicken and cheese melt. The bunch of optimistic hoverers waiting for a table gave up and moved on.

Ted sat up, wiping his mouth with a serviette. "Not bad. You eaten in here before?"

Frank stared at Ted's empty plate. "Not that I can remember. You look as if you haven't eaten for a week the way you shifted that." He was barely through his own meal. "Did any of it touch the sides?"

"C'mon now, Frank, you know me. Remember that time in the Kebab shop when we first came over here?"

Frank remembered it vividly. Ted had been served before him and had walked out of the shop with a double chili kebab and salad. By the time Frank had got his change and walked outside Ted was wiping his face with a serviette.

"You goin to eat all of that?" he'd said, eying up Frank's Kebab.

Frank smiled. "I remember, happy days eh? I suppose some things never change."

"Amen to that. So, what're we gonna do?"

"Well first of all it would have been better if you'd called me before you came to see me at the office the other day. At least then I could have tried to talk you out of it. Apart from that the rest of the lads at the nick know me well enough to tell when I'm keeping something from them. They've started asking awkward questions."

"Like what?"

"I don't know, they just know something's up that's all."

Ted's face creased up with a grin that lit up his eyes showing a lot more wrinkles than Frank remembered seeing last time they met. "So what have you told them?" he asked, shifting uncomfortably in his seat.

Frank took a sip of his coffee, it was cold. "Not much, but they've got a nose for when something's up."

"What do they suspect?" asked Ted, eying up the dessert menu.

"Everything and nothing as usual, they know me by now. When I say I don't need anything or any help, they read that as, I want all hands on deck. If I ask them for help with something, they automatically assume I'm trying on some kind of new bullshit management strategy, so they completely ignore me."

Ted had summoned the waiter and was using his hands to describe how he wanted his baked Alaska cooked. The young lad shuffled off in despair.

"Keeps them on their toes doesn't it?"

"Yeh, and don't I know it. They know I'm meeting someone for lunch today."

"How?" said Ted looking worried.

"They just do. It wouldn't surprise me if they know exactly where I am right now and who I'm with."

Ted looked around beginning to suspect that anyone of the customers wearing a suit could be one of Frank's team. "You still haven't answered my question."

Frank looked at his watch. "The way I see it, everything this girl told you was during confession, right?"

"Right." Ted nodded. "She, by the way, is a woman not a girl, she's thirty three years old."

"I thought this was an anonymous confession?"

"It was, she told me her age I never asked her for it. I couldn't even give you an accurate description. She's..."

"Whatever she said during her confession is *absolutely* sacrosanct and can't be used in a court of law, in fact if you did you would be in big trouble with the church."

Ted nodded in agreement. "Ex-communicated more than likely."

Frank raised his eyebrows and looked at Ted concerned. "So therefore anything she told you can't be repeated to anyone, not even me, unless first of all she gives you her explicit permission. Correct?"

"Absolutely, excuse the pun."

"Then, as far as I'm concerned, until that happens I don't know anything."

The waiter returned looking pleased with himself. He'd brought Ted's baked Alaska, done to perfection. Ted had lost his desire to eat it and it showed.

"Thanks." he said sheepishly. The waiter looked crestfallen as he left Frank and Ted alone once again.

"You've already taken an almighty risk, Ted."

Frank's reference to the Almighty did not go unnoticed. Ted forced a smile.

"Don't you think I know that? I came to you for help because you're the only one I can trust. Put yourself in my position, what would you have done?"

Frank couldn't answer, but he knew Ted was right. Torn between a rock and a hard place. On one hand he had his religious faith and all the beliefs that went with it, yet on the other, he was prepared to forgo all of that to make amends for something that had happened a long time ago.

Something both he and Ted had ignored. A sin, for which although God may have forgiven them, Ted had never really forgiven himself.

Frank leaned across the table, clocking everyone within earshot.

"All right, here's what I want you to do. Give it a week; if we're lucky the woman will come back. If she does, do whatever it takes to get her to agree to meet you and repeat her story outside of the confessional. Then I can help, we both can."

Ted didn't look optimistic. "And if we don't get lucky? Or she won't agree to see me?"

Frank waved to the waiter and stood up to go. The place was nearly empty and the lad was waiting to see if he would get his tip before he finished his shift.

"I don't know! Give me some time to think about it and I'll get back to you." Frank instantly regretted the harshness in his voice.

Ted looked mournfully at the molten blob of ice cream on his plate and then up at the waiter. He rummaged in his pocket for his wallet before Frank had a chance to object. "Here ye go son, keep the change. That was lovely, thanks very much, compliments to the chef and all that."

He handed over twenty-five pounds hoping it would cover the bill. Frank put on his coat, watching Ted as he spoke to the waiter. The Irish blarney hadn't left him and his kindness and generosity were as sincere as ever. The waiter left. It had been worth the wait.

Ted turned back towards Frank, their eyes meeting as they shook hands.

"We agreed then Ted? Give it a week before doing anything, promise me?"

Ted placed his other hand on top of the handshake. "A week it is then."

Frank saw the torment in his eyes.

Together they left the warmth of the Blue Bar. The December chill bit hard as they leaned into the wind and headed towards the Southern exit of the Albert Dock. The shops and bars would still be open for another two hours, but the last stragglers were already rushing towards the exits as the dark clouds gathered overhead. Small boats tied to the dockside heaved up and down with the swell, straining to break free.

Frank and Ted stepped through the sliding doors onto the cobbled courtyard at the entrance to the Beatles Museum. As they turned into the wind, Frank recognised the sound belting up the stairs from the cellar ... *"and I do appreciate you being rou-ound, won't you please, please"* Frank knew he had no choice.

Chapter 5

The Keep, Carrickfergus 1980

Frank and Ted remained absolutely still as they watched the lads climb out of the car. "Do you think he saw us?" asked Ted.

"I don't know, shh... wait and see what happens," whispered Frank.

Not wanting to stick around to see what happened next, Mickey and Sean climbed out of the car leaving Brian on the back seat with Sharon.

Alex saw the anxious look on their faces; he knew what they were thinking.

"I don't know about you two, but I'm bustin' for a shite" He headed straight towards the Keep and walked in through the front door, forty feet below the point where Frank and Ted were hiding. He peered into the murky gloom inside; he had no fear of ghosts and no amount of scary monsters was going to put him off what he needed to do. He just about managed to get his trousers down before the contents of his bowels, loosened by the lager and whisky, splattered the ground where Frank and Ted had been sitting.

"Thank fuck for that." He groaned, relieved, because minutes earlier he was on the verge of letting it all go inside the car. The embarrassment alone would have been bad enough, but Brian at the time had been having a serious snogging session in the back of the car and he would have been furious. Alex had heard Sharon complaining that she was feeling sick and wasn't in the mood for sex, so far she'd resisted Brian's attempts to get her knickers off.

Alex knew, from the look of determination on Brian's face that they would have to hang around until he achieved his goal.

He looked around for something to wipe his arse with and found what looked like an old bread wrapper lying amongst the stones, greaseproof paper, perfect for the job. He picked up the paper and noticed that there were fresh crumbs and the remnants of jam smeared on the waxy surface. Someone had recently had a picnic here and left their litter behind. *Jeezus, some people have no respect for old buildings like this.*

The paperwork finished, he stood up, buttoned his trousers and headed back towards the car. Mickey and Sean were still hanging around, smoking, trying not to look towards the car.

"He not done *yet?*"

Mickey looked up. "Nah, she's givin' him a real hard time by the looks of it."

"I wish the fuck, she'd let him get on with it, then we can all fuck off back to Belfast. I'm supposed to be goin out t'night," Sean chipped in.

Alex was staring at the Keep. "Whose the lucky g…?" He was cut off by the sound of angry shouting, swiftly followed by screaming from inside the car.

"Ooww!! You fuckin' little bitch!" There was a loud slap and sounds of struggling. More muffled screams came from inside the car.

Alex clenched his fists and turned his head to the sky. "Uh oh! Its all going fuckin' pear shaped."

He looked back towards the car. "I FUCKIN' knew this would happen," he said, agitated.

Mickey and Sean looked at each other.
"I don't know why she doesn't just let him fuckin' do the business, she *is* a prozzy after all, fuckin' slapper!" screamed Mickey.
"And just how d'you know that then, Sherlock?" queried Sean.
"Coz it's fuckin' obvious from the clothes and the make up she's wearin, and where d'you think she got the dosh for all that booze, eedjit?"
They looked back towards the car. There was more angry shouting from Brian as he wrestled with Sharon. She was putting up a brave fight until Brian's patience finally snapped. Without warning, the rear passenger door flew open to reveal the girl with her skirt around her waist and knickers torn around her ankles. Mickey, Sean and Alex stepped away from the car.

From inside the Keep Frank and Ted stared, mesmerized by the events that continued to unfold before them. The older lad, wrestling with the girl, was bleeding from the cheek and holding his neck, his face was a picture of pure agony and hatred as he screamed at her.

"Right, that's it. Get out of the fuckin' car, fuckin' slag. I'll teach you t'fuck me around."

As Sharon struggled to get through the door, Brian leaned backwards, and using both feet, kicked her square between the shoulder blades and out of the car. Her head jerked backwards as she tumbled out, spilling awkwardly on to the ground.

The others stared, transfixed, as Brian reached for the Webley .455 in his jacket pocket. Sharon started to pick herself up and saw the look on their faces. Brian was scrambling towards the open doorway, reaching up to grip the upper inside edge of the roof with his free hand, ready to haul himself out. She saw the shape of the heavy metal object in his other hand, and, like the others, realized what it was.

Anger kicked in, blanking out her fear. She scrambled to her feet and launched herself at the door, throwing all her weight at it, slamming it shut. The door crushed Brian's fingers between the doorframe and the roof, trapped nerves causing his fingers to go into spasm, flexing involuntarily, like giant maggots wriggling from a corpse.

Alex, Mickey and Sean watched in awe at the look on Brian's face. He was in shock, face screwed up, grimacing with the pain. He glared out of the window in disbelief at what she had done to him. Sharon stared back; his eyes were black as thunder. She knew all hell was about to break loose. She turned towards the others and screamed at them.

"Don't just stand there gawking, help me you bastards! He's trying t'fuckin' rape me!"

They stared back at her, frozen to the spot, open-mouthed, unable to speak.

A loud cracking and the sound of breaking glass filled the air as Brian shattered the window with the butt of his gun. As Sharon turned to look, splintered fragments of glass showered all over her. Her fear returned and as her survival instincts took over, she turned and ran towards the Keep.

Brian pushed the car door open and jumped out. If he had been mad before, now he was absolutely fucking fuming.

"You bunch o' useless bastards, get the fuck after her!" he screamed at them.

Frank and Ted watched the whole scene unfold, gripped by fear as the girl ran towards them. They looked back at the car as the man with the gun was shouting his orders. Mickey was the first to react, his senses sharpened by the sight of Brian waving the gun around. He turned and ran after the girl for all he was worth.

The others followed. Sharon was almost at the entrance to the Keep by the time Alex caught up with her. He shoved his foot out and tapped her trailing leg bringing her to the ground in one movement. Mickey and Sean soon caught up; they were on top of her in seconds. They held her down; waiting while Brian strolled up holding his damaged fingers under his armpits, cursing with the pain.

"Drag her over here and hold her down." Brian waved his gun towards a small dip in the ground. "Alex, you keep watch. Sean, Mickey get a 'hold of her arms. And keep your hands away from her mouth, fuckin' cow bit me. And watch out for those fuckin' nails they're sharp as fuck."

Sean and Mickey could see the teeth marks on Brian's neck and the deep scratches on his cheek. They did exactly as they were told. Alex gratefully took up his position as a lookout. *At least he wouldn't have to watch.*

Brian turned his attention back to the girl. "Are yez ready for this now, bitch? Eh? You've had your bit of fun. Well fuckin' look out coz I'm about t'have mine. Teach you t'fuckin' bite me, you slag,"

He dropped his trousers and underpants revealing his erect penis. "See this?" he said towering over her. "This is my pussy hunter and yours has just been fuckin' hunted." He stood astride her, lowered himself between her thighs, parted her legs effortlessly and entered her without resistance.

Looking down from forty feet above, Frank and Ted saw the look of hopelessness and despair on the girl's face. She'd stopped struggling. *It was going to happen no matter what.* She gave up.

Resigned to her fate, her arms became limp as the tension left her body. Feeling that she was no longer resisting, Sean and Mickey momentarily relaxed their grip on her. The second Sharon felt their grip soften on her arms, she snatched her right arm free and grabbed a lump of rock lying next to her on the ground.

From their hiding place, Frank and Ted heard the splintering sound as she cracked Sean full in the face with the rock, smashing his nose. Startled, Sean rolled backwards holding his hands to his face. He fell to the floor; blood spurting through his fingers, running down his arms. Mickey automatically jumped back in shock. Now the girl had both arms free.

Brian had his head back, eyes shut, still frantically thrusting his hips up and down, grunting as he neared the point of no return. Almost at a climax, he was oblivious to what was going on. Now Sharon had both arms and her upper torso free, she sat up under him. Brian felt the shift in her position and opened his eyes just in time to see the rock flying towards his face. Instinctively he turned his head sideways; the rock glanced off his jaw and disappeared over his shoulder. He swore at her again and reached for the gun.

Sean and Mickey watched helpless. "Brian, please don't fuckin' shoot her, please." Said Mickey almost tearful. "Please, just finish what you're doin' and let's get the fuck out of here."

"I'll finish what I'm fuckin' doin' all right, as soon as I've silenced this wee mare."

Alex turned from his position as lookout. He did not want to watch, but he couldn't take his eyes away from the chaos unfolding in front of him. Frank and Ted watched from the second floor, faces pale, mouths dry, breathing shallow and pulses racing like trains.

Still inside her, Brian pinned the girl to the ground by the throat. He swiveled the gun, flipping the barrel into the palm of his right hand. He gripped the barrel tightly and extended his arm behind him, then in one swift movement brought his arm over his shoulder like a fast bowler in a game of cricket. The hand holding the gun swung downwards towards the girl's face.

Sharon saw it coming but could do nothing to stop it. She closed her eyes just before the butt of the gun smashed through her cheekbone. Sharon felt pain like she'd never felt before. Brian raised the gun over his head and brought it down again and again, smashing it into her face beating her face to a pulp. Each time there was the sickening sound of bone splintering as her nose and her lower jaw caved in. Her teeth were shattered and she was gagging on a bloody cocktail of broken teeth and shards of bone.

Sean, Mickey and Alex couldn't watch any more, powerless to stop it. Brian had the gun and with that came the power to do whatever he wanted.

The girl had become totally still. Brian carried on thrusting himself inside her until at last he let out a deep groan. His head tipped back like a wolf howling at the moon, eyes rolling upwards showing only the whites of his eyes as he climaxed. Finally, he'd finished with her. He raised his hips and rolled to one side, still breathing heavily.

Keeping a firm grip on his gun he waved at the others. "Away yez go boys, who's next?"

Mickey spoke up first. "I think we should be headin' off, Brian, we've been hangin' round here long enough now. Sean's got himself a date in Belfast tonight and the rest of us are still a bit too pissed to get it up" he lied.

"C'mon, lads, don't be shy now; she won't fuckin' bite yez. Least not now she fuckin' won't," Brian said, winking at them and then started laughing at his witty remark. By the time he had stopped laughing, the girl's heart had stopped beating.

Brian glanced down at the mess in front of him. Around the dead girl's neck, shining through the sticky gore, was a gold chain. Hanging from the chain was a heart shaped locket with a single diamond in the centre.

He reached down and snatched it from around her neck. "She won't be fuckin' need'n this where she's going." He stood fastening his trousers and pocketed the chain and locket. He told the other three to search the Keep for a suitable place to dispose of the body while he went to see to the car.

Frank and Ted had witnessed the whole event from their hiding place. While it was happening they'd kept absolutely still, trying not to breathe or move a muscle. The horrible sound of Brian's laughter had echoed throughout the Keep. That sound would haunt their dreams. The sight of the girl trying to breathe through the scrambled mess of her own blood and bone tissue would stay with them for the rest of their lives.

Sean, Mickey and Alex dragged the body into the Keep. Seeing how dark it was, they found some old rags and bits of wood to make torches. They lit the torches and went inside. Soon they found the stairs leading down into the cellar.

Sean held the lit torches while Mickey and Alex heaved the body down the stairs. Once inside the cellar they looked around to see if there was a suitable place to hide the body. Sean quickly discovered the second stairwell leading down to the smaller room where Frank and Ted had been earlier. Sean led the way; Mickey and Alex picked the body up and followed him down the stairs. It was darker and damper down there. The flames from their torches were beginning to die down. They stepped inside the room and discovered the perfect place, the flooded room.

Sean instructed Mickey and Alex to find something they could use to weigh the body down. In the far corner of the room they found some old wooden packaging crates. Hanging above the crates from a rusty iron hook on the far wall was a length of rope. Sean gave one of his torches to Mickey and left him and Alex with the body.

He carried his own torch over to the crates and inside found a pile of old gauze-cloth sacks used for bagging up grain.

He grabbed a handful, lifted the rope off the hook and took them over to Mickey and Alex. "Here, see what you can do with these." He walked back to the crates and left Mickey and Alex in semi-darkness. They were starting to get the jitters. Being down there with the dead body was freaking them out.

Alex shouted after him. "Sean where the fuck are yez goin with the torch? I can hardly see a fuckin' thing in front of me eyes over here. Sean?"

Sean was using his torch to set fire to the rest of the sacks and the wooden crates in the corner. The flames quickly took hold and the room brightened considerably.

"There you go boys, is that fuckin' bright enough fer yez? Now get a fuckin' shift on with them sacks before we all fuckin' choke to death down here."

Moving quickly they filled the sacks with as many rocks as they could find and wrapped them around the body, using the rope to keep everything in place. As the flames from the burning crates began to die down, the room started filling up with smoke. Groaning and coughing the three of them dragged the body to the entrance of the arched doorway. With a final shove they managed to slide the body into the water. There was a loud splash, followed by gurgling sounds, as the air trapped between the sacks escaped and rose to the surface.

The battered young body of Sharon Byrne sunk twelve feet to the floor of the flooded cellar, settling in the darkness amongst the mulm and debris that had lain undisturbed for over twenty years.

Mickey sounded relieved. "Good now let's get the fuck out of here this place is givin' me the fuckin' eebie jeebies."

With the last of the light from their torches they made their way back up the stairs out of the Keep. Throughout the time it had taken them to dispose of the body, four floors up, Frank and Ted had listened, straining their ears to hear what was going on. They'd heard the groaning as the men struggled with the weight of the body, dragging it down the first flight of stairs. The smoke from the torches had filtered up through the ruins to where they lay.

When they heard the splash they'd wet themselves, Ted was crying. Frank had done his best to comfort him, but he too needed comforting. They wanted to go home, wishing that they'd never been here. Ted's sobbing got louder as he went deeper into shock. Sean, Mickey and Alex were walking towards the car when they heard it.

Sean stopped. "Hang on a minute, listen, d'you hear that?" They all listened.

The crying sounded like it was coming from the rear of the Keep. Mickey almost pissed himself, his imagination starting to run wild. His first thought was that the sound was the voice of the girl dragging her way out of the cellar. *Maybe she wasn't dead?* He wanted to run but was frozen to the spot.

"Alex, come on, let's get round the other side of that place and see what the fuck is goin' on. Some fucker is in there and we need to fuckin' find out who. Mickey, you stay here, and what ever ye do, don't let Brian get back over here. If he starts headin this way, tell him we're takin' a shite or somthin."

Mickey was relieved to be staying *exactly* where he was.

Sean and Alex ran around the side of the Keep into the bushes and stumbled over the bikes. "Fucks sake!" said Sean, holding his knee. "There is some bastard in 'ere, look at these bikes, young kids fuckin' about probably."

Alex checked out the bikes, they were shiny and new looking. "You know, I was sure there was some bastard watchin me when I was havin' a shite in the doorway earlier on. I thought it was just me mind playin tricks on me like, but the paper I used t'wipe me arse on was brand fuckin' new."

They ran round to the front entrance and stood inside the doorway looking up at the double flight of stairs. They stopped, pausing to listen again for the crying. It had died down but they could still hear it and it was definitely coming from upstairs.

Sean led the way up, shouting as he went. "Okay, whoever the fuck yez are up there, we're comin' up, so just stay there, d'you hear me?"

Frank and Ted lay still, terrified. Sean and Alex reached the top of the stairs and saw the two frightened figures cowering in the corner with their heads covered. Frank and Ted were crying, clinging on to each other for dear life.

Sean walked right up to them and tapped Frank on the shoulder.

"Okay, sonny boy," he looked at Ted, "and you wee man, just fuckin' listen to me now." Frank and Ted lifted their heads opening their eyes just enough to see the faces of Sean and Alex glaring down at them, drawing little comfort from the fact that neither of them looked like grown men.

"You're not goin' t'kill us are you?" Whimpered Frank.

Sean just smiled at him. "See this face, and this smile, this is my bestest and most friendliest, *I'm not goin' t'fuckin' kill yez* smile. No fucker, is gonna kill no fucker, d'yez hear me all right?" The lad's breath reeked of stale beer, and whisky laced with nicotine.

Frank recoiled from him while Ted continued to sob uncontrollably. Frank pulled him closer, doing his best to comfort him. "Sshh...It's alright, Ted, sshh... it's okay, it's okay, they won't harm us Ted, they aren't going to shoot us, it's okay, ...sshh" Frank looked up through tear filled eyes at Sean and nodded to say that that he had understood.

Sean leaned towards them. "Now then, me friends, what'll be your fuckin' names?"

Ted was incapable of speech. "My name is F...Frank Carroll and he's...he's T...Ted Maloney," stuttered Frank.

"And just where would yez both be livin' then?"

"W...we both live in Www... Woodburn Villas, in Carrickfergus, ... we just come here to pp...play." Frank whimpered.

Sean knew the kid was telling the truth. *The two of them must have been having a fuckin' great time until he and his friends had arrived.*

"Well, that's mighty good of yez to say so. Now listen to me very carefully, the both of yez. Me and me mate here are riskin our fuckin' lives by letting yous two stay alive, knowin what yez know, and what yez have seen. Are yez gettin me meanin wee man?" Frank and Ted were *gettin his meanin* loud and clear.

"If, the big man yez heard doin the business with the wee girl, finds out about this, then we're all dead meat, the fuckin' lot of us. Now *none* of us wants that now do we?" Frank and Ted shook their heads, acknowledging that they didn't. They continued to listen as the stranger told them what they already knew. A girl had been killed.

Before the men dumped the body in the cellar, Frank and Ted had heard the threats made by the one with the gun to the other three. They both knew full well what *kneecapping* meant; they also knew the damage caused by petrol bombs. They understood all right, the threats were for real.

Sean warned them both that if a word of this ever got out, Frank, Ted and their entire families would be wiped out. As he finished explaining what would happen to them, there was a shout from Mickey at the bottom of the stairs.

"Are yez fuckin' comin or what? Brian's gonna set a fuckin' light to the car! The bizzies'll be here any fuckin' minute."

Alex ran to the wall and stared out through the small window overlooking the waste ground. There was a loud whumph, as Brian set light to the petrol he'd poured over the car. Sean could see the orange glow reflecting on Alex's cheeks as he stood watching the flames and smoke belch into the sky.

"Oh Fuck, oh fuck…" He turned back to Frank and Ted. "Right yous two. Fuckin' swear now on your mother's life, that you will *never* breathe a word to *anyone* of what happened here. Frank and Ted nodded their heads and swore they would never tell a soul.

"Good. Now we're goin t'get the fuck out of here, I suggest yous two lie low and wait till we're gone before doin' the same, d'you hear what I'm sayin?"

Frank and Ted nodded.

Alex walked over to Sean. "Come on, let's get the fuck outta here."

Without looking back they ran down the stairs to where Mickey was waiting. Frank and Ted were alone; they'd got the message. They were not to go anywhere until the gang had left, especially if they didn't want to bump into the older one who had killed the girl.

By the time Mickey, Alex and Sean reached the car; Brian was dancing round the flames waving his gun about like a madman. In the time they'd been gone, Brian had drunk the remaining half a bottle of whisky Sean had left on the back seat of the car.

Cautiously, Sean tapped Brian on the shoulder. "C'mon Brian, we need t'be gett'n ourselves away from here, someone's gonna phone for the bizzies for sure."

Brian's face was manic as shouted at him above the roar of the flames.

"Aye, you're fuckin' right n'all come on, its time we wasn't here."

As one they turned and ran across the marshland disappearing out of sight.

Although the flames and smoke could be seen from miles around, no one bothered to call the police. Cars were always being set on fire; it was nothing new to the people of Northern Ireland.

Frank and Ted cycled home that day as different boys than they'd been when they set out. Their childhood had ended, their youthful innocence tainted by the nightmare events they had witnessed. Almost home, they stopped and got off their bikes. They had not spoken, and now looked long and hard at each other.

Ted pulled a penknife from his pocket and slid the blade from its sheath.

"Let's make an oath and swear on our own blood that we'll never tell anyone what we saw."

They took turns to cut each other on the palm of their hands and squeezed them together wincing with the pain. They repeated the oath that they would never, tell a soul, about what they had seen and heard at the Keep that day. They would never go there again as long as they lived. For the next two days neither of them left the house.

The body of fourteen year-old prostitute and alcoholic, Sharon Byrne was never found because it was never reported missing.

Chapter 6

Canning Place
Friday 18 December 2004

It was late afternoon by the time Frank got back to his office on the 8th floor. He had managed to avoid being dragged into a probing conversation with DS Barry Ferguson who was on his way out on a job. DS Ferguson was the next senior CID officer in the team and he, above anyone else knew when Frank was keeping something to himself. No doubt the time would come when Barry would confront him. But not now.

On arrival at the main squad room chilled to the bone, he headed straight towards the biggest radiator. DC Mark Roberts gave him a look as he walked in. Frank returned it with his own look, the one that said, "Yes two sugars."

DC Mark Roberts was the junior member of the team; affectionately known as the Fledge, short for fledgling and the nickname for the latest recruit on the team. The previous Fledge, DC "Rob the Bob" Turner had handed the post over with the usual set of rules. The number one rule was to make sure the DI either had a brew or had at least been asked if he wanted one.

DC Roberts scuttled off to the kitchen in the far corner of the office to make the tea. Before Frank arrived at Canning Place, senior management had introduced a rule, which dictated that all officers should take their refreshments in the main canteen area in order to promote integration and good harmony between the troops. This was a rule that Frank had instantly disregarded, despite the risk of riling the DCI and the Chief Super. He forked out the cash for a complete set of brew kit including the kettle, enough tea and coffee to last the next three months, seven large mugs, one for every member of the team including the DCI, the Chief Super, and Janice Timms the secretary.

Bob Turner, the Fledge at the time, had been sent on the mission to buy the necessary items and told to be back within the hour, mission accomplished. The rest of the team knowing the views of management discussed the matter in Frank's absence, and it was agreed by all that they would keep quiet about it.

The first time the new ACC walked in to visit the department accompanied by the DCI and the Chief Super, the whole team were sat in the main office drinking tea.

DC Bob Turner was sat facing the door and was the first to spot them through the glass partition. He choked on a mouthful of tea when he saw who was about to enter the squad room, and was practically suffocating when he spoke.

"Err... guess who's just about to walk in?" He'd spluttered.

Frank had been expecting them having been briefed earlier by the DCI.

"Don't tell me it's the ..." DS Barry Ferguson cut him off.

"Fuck me Boss, it's the ACC with the DCI and the fuckin' Chief Super!"

The three senior officers entered the room to the sounds of shuffling in seats and nervous coughs. Instantly, the Fledge had stood up and asked the ACC.

"Would you like a brew Sir?"

To everyone's amazement the ACC had gratefully accepted, speaking in a strong Lancashire accent. "Aye I'll have a coffee thanks, not too much milk and two sugars, cheers."

Frank had looked at the Fledge and said, "Aren't you going to offer the DCI and the Super a brew?" The DCI and the Chief Super had looked at each other disapprovingly but with some reluctance accepted the offer. On tasting the coffee the ACC passed a comment.

"Bye eck that's better, not like that bloody awful stuff they're dishing up down the canteen." From that moment on, the subject of the MIT brew kit was never brought up by anyone in the department again.

Frank was still smiling to himself at this recollection when DC Roberts arrived with a steaming hot mug of tea.

Frank accepted it gratefully. "So Fledge, fill me in, where is everyone and what's the score with the drugs bust at that pub in town... the... er the er... whatsaname?"

"The Blue Parrott, Sir" DC Roberts replied.

Frank looked at him and frowned. "You still haven't got the hang of it have you son? Its Boss or Guv, got it? Sir is only for important visitors and members of the public to whom we treat with the same amount of respect. Got the picture?"

"Yes Boss" Said DC Roberts somewhat sheepishly. "Right err... Barry...I mean DS Ferguson's just nipped out on a job, something about the car jacking on Friday last week, I think he's gone to see the victim, see if she's up for giving a statement, says he'll be back in about an hour - ish."

Frank looked surprised.

"Is she out of hospital already? Fuck me they don't mess about at the Royal. Almost killed on Friday, admitted, and out in ...what's today? Tuesday, four days... and she's out already, I thought that was gonna be a week job at least."

"Yeah Barry's not too happy," said DC Roberts. "They never let him know at the hospital, apparently they only kept her in two days, she was out on the Sunday."

"Jesus, right, I'll have a word with the DCI, someone needs their arse kicked for this, its fuckin' sloppy, whoever hijacked the car could be in fuckin' Ibiza by now. What's Bob up to?"

"He's gone downstairs to see the uniform who nicked the dealer in the pub, said something about the possibility of arranging an identity line up for when the kid gets out of hospital. I've been chasing up the forensics on the shooting last night.

"Tell me about the ecstasy" said Frank in between gulping his tea.

"We're just waiting for the lab to get back to us to confirm what we got on the bust, we think it's the same ecstasy which has caused the other hospital cases. I'm off down the Royal now with a sample to show the kid who was last admitted, see if he recognises the brand mark."

"Do we know it's the same dealer?"

DC Roberts thought carefully before replying. "Pretty sure boss, this lad's the only one without an alibi for the time when the drugs were bought. We've got at least two witnesses putting him on the scene at the same time as the others. We're still confirming the alibi of one of the other known dealers, but all the others check out."

"An alibi? There's unusual," said Frank sarcastically, knowing full well the alibi was full of shit.

"Err...is there anything else I can help you with boss?"

Frank looked at the Fledge and smiled, maybe this kid was catching on after all.

"No... I'm in the office for the next hour or two if anyone needs me. Tell DS Ferguson to come and see me the moment he gets back."

"Will do boss, no probs."

Frank left the squad room with the back of his pants burning against his legs from the heat of the radiator, just as well because the chair in his office was fucking freezing.

The message light on his phone was flashing. One was from his ex wife, fussing and making sure he had not forgotten that he was supposed to be having Cram for the long weekend, and that he should have booked a days leave, plus the usual don't be late remarks, finished off with a hesitant and nervous goodbye. The second message was from the office secretary, it was Janice telling him that his wife had rang. *Talk about belt and braces.*

He stared out of the window through the rapidly fading daylight. In the distance he could just about see the coloured lights from the fairground in Chevasse Park. Beyond the park, the Liver Buildings were draped in huge banners announcing that in four years time Liverpool would be the *European Capital of Culture*.

He contemplated ringing Hilary. They had been married for nine years before she left him three years ago taking their son, Cram, who was now five years old. The job had always come first for reasons that Hilary would never understand and Frank could never successfully explain. She had been able to accept Frank putting his job before her; she'd half expected that before they got married. What Hilary could not accept was that Frank was able to put the job before their son.

The divorce was amicable and there had been no other parties involved, not until now anyway. Hilary was going away for a long weekend with her new partner. If there was an emergency Hilary's mother was always willing to have Cram at a moment's notice, which was just as well because that was often the way things panned out.

Frank picked up the phone and was about to dial the number he had retrieved from the answer phone when there was a knock at the door.

It was DS Barry Ferguson.

"Alright boss, the Fledge said you wanted a word."

Frank looked at the phone and thought for a second before answering.

"Yeh come in Barry, grab a seat," he said pointing to the small coffee table and three chairs in the corner of the office. Frank only spoke to his officers from behind his desk when they were in the shit. Barry relaxed, he knew from this unwritten rule that he was not in for a bollocking. Frank joined Barry at the coffee table. "So what's the score with the woman from the car jacking, the Fledge tells me she was out of hospital earlier than you expected."

"Yeh, I'm well pissed off, the contact at the hospital went sick and didn't think to let anyone know we wanted to speak to her as soon as poss. Turns out, she only went and discharged herself and now she's fucked off on holiday for a week!"

Frank could feel the frustration in Barry's voice. He was a bit like Frank in a way, impatient, always in a hurry wanting to get as much work done in as short a time as possible, *why?* So that he could get on with doing more work, it was like a fast moving treadmill impossible to get off.

"Okay leave it with me, trust me I'll sort it, it won't happen again. What's the score with the other car, any news on the make of the car that the hijackers used?"

Barry looked at his notes. "Yeh, a metallic blue Ford Mondeo, reported stolen two hours prior to the hijacking."

"Anything else?"

Barry was still reading his notes.

"Well it appears that she wasn't going to give up her Merc without a fight. By the sounds of it, and from what we have from two eyewitnesses, Mrs. Pearson steered the Merc into the side of the Mondeo, must have shit the jackers up pretty bad because they crashed the fuckin' Mondeo straight after and did a runner. Forensics have gone over the Mondeo for prints, DNA and the usual stuff. I was just about to give them a call when the Fledge belled me on my mobile saying you wanted a word."

Frank couldn't help laughing. "Sounds to me he was covering his arse as well as yours."

"The Fledge is okay," said Barry, leaning back in his chair folding his arms.

"He needs to get out of the office a bit more, specially in this weather, he could do with a bit of fresh air."

Frank smiled. "I'm okay with that, everyone being out of the office at the same time, just make sure everyone lets Janice know where they are, or use the location chart just in case the DCI wanders in and Janice isn't about."

"I'll see to it, anything else boss?" Barry was fishing and both he and Frank knew it.

"Nice try but not yet, I'll fill you in when the time is right. I'm shooting off in a bit, I've got Cram for the weekend and I'm off on Monday. Shit! Which reminds me I haven't put my leave in through Janice, do us a favour, have a word with her and get her to back date the form for me. Tell her there's a box of choccies in it for her and I'll see her on Tuesday."

"Err...boss, are you contactable – ish if anything crops up over the weekend?"

Frank stood up and was putting his coat on. "Yeah contactable – ish is about right."

Barry understood perfectly; he could contact him on his mobile but only in an emergency. He had another quick glance at his notes.

"Okay boss I'll brief the lads when they get back, see yer Tuesday, I'm off to have a word with forensics, after that I'll be having a word with Bob to see how he got on with the ID parade on the dealer from the ecstasy bust."

Frank nodded his approval to Barry as left the office. He knew the ship was in safe hands for the weekend. Barry would probably still be here at eight tonight before strolling down town with the lads for a pint before knocking off.

Frank had no intention of staying any longer. As he closed the door to leave the phone on his desk was ringing. *Hilary?* He didn't look back.

Chapter 7

Fifteen minutes later Frank was pulling up the driveway to his rented house on Grassendale Park just off the Aigburth Road, *which he later found out from Bob was pronounced Eggburth Road.* He had moved here following his divorce after Hilary had left him. He had just got enough time for a quick shower and change before he went to pick up Cram for the weekend. Aigburth Road led out of town towards what used to be known as Speke Airport but had recently been renamed as the "Liverpool John Lennon Airport."

Grassendale Park was in what could only be described as a *good* area to live in. For a start it was close to the River Mersey, handy for his long walks in the fresh air blowing across from the Irish Sea. If he fancied a jog or a game of golf Sefton Park and Allerton Park Golf course were five minutes away. Not that he had much time for playing golf these days.

On a good day it was only about fifteen minutes to the major motorway network linking up the M53 for Chester and the Wirral, the M56 for North Wales and Manchester or the M6 for Preston and London. But most importantly it was less than ten minutes drive into work and the town centre.

Inside the house he turned off the alarm system and glanced at the phone on the table in the hall. The flashing signal told him he had a message waiting, it could only be from Hilary, nobody from work had his home number. He pressed the messages button to listen but deleted the message as soon as he heard his ex wife's voice reminding him he was supposed to have Cram for the weekend.

The house was immaculately tidy as it was every Friday when he came home. His cleaner had blitzed the place as usual as she did for three hours every Friday and Monday. There was a strong smell of detergent and not a speck of dust to be seen. The washing machine had been emptied and the assortment of clothes he had put in it had been dried, sorted, ironed and put away.

He checked the fridge; fresh milk and his weekly list of essentials had been bought and put in their relevant places. All this for thirty-six quid a week, he had touched lucky with this woman; six quid an hour and she was worth her weight in gold.

He looked at the clock above the gleaming cooker door; it was ten to six, he had less than an hour before he had to pick up Cram. The phone rang again while he was in the shower; no doubt about it, Hilary was definitely keen to get away this weekend. He finished showering and got dressed into jeans, T-Shirt, jumper and slip on suede boots. He left the house before the phone rang again.

Driving in a in a North Easterly direction he headed towards Gateacre on the outskirts of Liverpool. Gateacre was so far on the outskirts of Liverpool in fact, that, people who lived here were affectionately called "woollybacks" or were known as "plastic scousers". Hilary who was originally from Childwall had said that this was as close as she wanted to be to Liverpool Town Centre and as far away as she wanted to be from her parents house in Childwall.

He was almost there when his mobile rang. He looked at the phone on the passenger seat and saw the caller display. He answered on the third ring and spoke before Hilary had a chance to berate him for not answering her calls.

"I'll be there in less than twenty minutes, no need to panic, you'll get your weekend away with your fancy feller, have you got Cram's ..." she hung up on him. Serves him right he thought. To say he was cutting it fine was an understatement. By the time he pulled up outside the house Hilary's new man was waiting outside with the BMW's engine running, Hilary and Cram were waiting in the hallway with the bags packed. Cram's face lit up as he saw Frank striding up the pathway to the front door. He was so excited he leapt off the top step at the doorway and into Frank's arms. Frank squeezed him tightly; as he closed his eyes he could feel the emotion and guilt rising within him.

Hilary had been standing there waiting with a look on her face like a bulldog stung by a wasp stared at the two of them. No matter what she thought of Frank and what she wanted to say to him, the sight of Cram wrapped in his fathers arms tore at her heart bringing a lump to her throat. She held back the tears. She couldn't say what she had wanted to say, so instead she closed the front door behind her and walked up to the two of them.

"Thank you" she said to Frank as she stood on tiptoe to plant a kiss on Cram's cheek, whispering into his ear.

"Don't forget Mummy loves you and be a good boy for Daddy". As she stepped away there was a strong scent of her perfume lingering nearby.

Frank could tell that Cram was nodding over his shoulder. He caught the glisten in her eye. "Don't worry and I'm sorry, have a good weekend" Hilary just nodded, turned and left before the tears welling up behind her eyelids gave away her feelings. Frank followed her perfume trail down the pathway and went towards his car. He loaded Cram's overnight bag with his bits and pieces into the boot then stood and watched as Hilary and her new man sped off into the night. Cram was already yawning as he climbed onto the back seat of the car.

"Hey come on now big man, no fallin asleep on me yet, least not before we've eaten. So what's it going to be then? McDonalds, KFC, or takeaway Pizza and a DVD or two?" Pizza and DVD's won hands down. He fastened his seatbelt, checked that Cram was strapped in and set off. He drove twenty minutes to a Pizza parlour and a DVD rental shop next door to each other less than five minutes drive from Franks house. Frank paid for the Pizzas and while they were being loaded into the huge brick oven to be cooked, he took Cram next door to help him select the DVD's.

Cram picked out Shrek Two and the latest Spiderman movie. He was sure Hilary wouldn't approve but what the heck, Cram would probably have fallen asleep on the couch before the end of Shrek 2 anyway. By the time they had selected and paid for the DVD's, next-door the pizzas were ready. Inside the car the aroma of the pepperoni pizzas made Frank's mouth water. This was the first time Cram was coming to stay with him for the weekend at the new house, he wasn't sure who was more excited.

Five minutes later they pulled up on the drive and unloaded the boot; Frank carried Cram's things, while Cram carried the pizzas and DVD's into the house. The first thing Cram wanted to do was explore the house and find the room he was going to sleep in. While Cram went exploring upstairs Frank unwrapped the Pizzas and put them on to plates in the oven to keep them warm. Twenty minutes later they were sat in the living room tucking into the pizzas. To Frank's surprise Cram finished off his pizza and, feeling quite at home helped himself to a yogurt and a glass of milk from the fridge. Frank meanwhile helped himself from a bottle of German Brandy pouring himself an Asbach and coke. Frank was not a heavy drinker. In fact he had a reputation for being a bit of a lightweight when it came to the team piss ups. No one dared accuse him of it though.

They settled down on the couch together to watch the Shrek 2 DVD. Cram was asleep within minutes of finishing his yogurt. The milk was left untouched on the glass coffee table. Frank carefully maneuvered himself out from under his sleeping son, slipped his arms underneath his body and carried him carefully up the stairs. He pushed the door to the large spare room open with his foot and then flicked the quilt back with his other foot. He lay Cram down on the bed and tucked him in. There was not a murmur or a peep out of him.

This would probably be the first time Cram had gone to bed for a while without getting changed into his pajamas and without brushing his teeth. *So what!* He kissed Cram on the cheek and whispered goodnight. He left the door open enough for the light from the upstairs landing to indicate the way out should Cram wake up in the night.

The last time Cram had stayed with him at his first flat he had slept right through but had wet the bed, something he had chosen not to mention to Hilary.

Back downstairs he ejected the DVD and turned the TV down so that he could listen for sounds from upstairs. Apart from the howling wind outside everything was quiet. Satisfied that Cram was fine, he poured himself another shot of Asbach and settled to watch television. As he unwound the effects of the Asbach kicked in. He began to think about the day's events and his meeting with Ted. He couldn't get the image of Ted's face out of his mind; he was disturbed by the worried look in his eyes when they had left the Blue Bar in the Albert Dock. Ted always appeared worried about something or at least concerned about someone, that was his nature, a caring person, he would have never have made it as a lawyer had he gone to university.

On a scale of one to ten for concerned looks, todays had been a ten. Frank hated that look, it haunted him. The last time he had seen a similar look on Ted's face they'd been kids growing up together in a troubled Northern Ireland. He hadn't slept for a week after seeing it then. *Maybe the Asbach would help this time.* He downed the rest of his drink in one and switched off the TV. In the hall he punched in the code for the alarm and went to bed. It was getting on for half past eleven and Hilary had not called him once. *She must be having a good time.*

He had only been asleep for an hour or so when he was woken up by the sound of faint crying noises. He went into Cram's bedroom to see if he was okay but was confused to see him still tucked up and fast asleep. Sometime between two and three am he was woken up again. He checked on Cram. There was no evidence of a restless tussle with the bedclothes or that Cram had been awake or crying.

It was only when he got back into bed the second time as his face sank into the pillow he felt the cold wet patch on his cheek. The realisation quickly dawned on him; it was his own tears soaking the pillow. It had been the sound of his own crying that woke him. Icy shivers rattled down his spine.

His thoughts again returned to Ted and the painful memories that had haunted their childhood. His vision blurred as his eyes filled up with tears rolling down his cheeks onto the pillow. It had been twenty-five years ago when his soul had become so troubled he had cried like this. His soul was troubled again now. The seeds of dormant memories from an event in his past long since buried with years of time had surfaced. Someone or something had poured water on them and they were flourishing once again.

If he was not careful they would grow and spread through his mind like a creeping vine until every waking thought was strangled by memories of the past.

The sun was just beginning to rise by the time he finally dropped off to sleep.

Chapter 8

Frank wasn't the only troubled soul struggling to sleep that Friday night. Once he had heard his mother say that if you looked up into the sky at night and saw a star directly above your head it was an angel who had been sent to look after you. They were there to look after your soul and keep you from harm.

Throughout his time as a police officer in Liverpool he had seen many people on the streets, sleeping rough in shop doorways and bus shelters. Drunks and wino's dossing under bridges with cardboard packed around them to shut out the night. Empty bottles of cheap wine, beer cans strewn all around them, evidence that they had probably drunk themselves into oblivion before turning in for the night, in some cases their last night.

Every time he came across one of these unfortunate souls he checked the sky above where they were sleeping, hoping that he would see a star. It disturbed him when there wasn't one. The stars looking down from the night skies above the City of Liverpool have no prejudice; they do not discriminate between old or young, good or bad. No matter what your creed or colour, how serious your crime, they stood guard and kept watch. Tonight they were watching over many troubled souls.

One man in particular was sat alone in the squalid, dimly lit living room of a rented two up two down bed-sit in Toxteth. He had chosen Toxteth as his base because despite being literally less than one and a half miles from Merseyside Police Headquarters, Toxteth was a perfect location.

People never stopped to ask questions, no matter what time of day or night you chose to be about. Toxteth had a reputation for being somewhat on the tough side and had been the flash point for the start of the infamous riots that tore the city apart for nine days in July 1981.

Sat alone in his room he stared at a list of seven names written in rough pencil on a piece of paper torn from a notebook. They were all women who lived in and around Liverpool. His bloodshot eyes stung with tears, stricken with grief he closed them and turned his head to the ceiling. The names on the list flashed boldly behind his eyelids.

Sharon Byrne R.I.P † Carrickfergus 1980
Elaine Topworth ✓ Redeemed November 2004
Sandra Pollock ✓ Redeemed December 2004
Angela Perriman
Margaret Smith
Allison Temple
Barbara Hunt

He opened his eyes and looked down from the ceiling to the piece of paper in his hands. He stared at the list until his eyes swelled with tears, blurring his vision, distorting the letters. The tears flowed down his cheeks again, dripping on to the piece of paper causing the letters to smudge. It wouldn't matter, he had re-written the list many times before, copied from memory carved inside his head. He'd crossed out the first name on the list adding the letters R.I.P and drawn a simple cross next to it.

Over time, after painstakingly discreet enquiries he'd eventually found out where every one of the remaining women lived. His extensive research into the lives of each of them complete, his mission had begun. The next two names on the list had a tick and a date indicating the day he had visited them. So far so good. Angela Perriman was the fourth name on the list and next in line. On Monday it would be her turn. Angela Perriman was about to receive a visit from the man who called himself, *The Redeemer.*

Chapter 9

Shortly after sunrise Frank was rudely woken by Cram pulling at his arm. "Dad I'm hungry, can we get up now and have breakfast?"

He looked at the fresh young face of his son, his deep blue eyes behind a fringe of blonde locks shining like mirrors reflecting sunlight. Frank tried to sound less tired than he felt. "Of course we can, let's get washed first. We'll need to change those clothes. Your mum will kill me if she finds out I let you sleep in them."

Cram pulled a face, giggling at the thought of his mum being angry with his dad. "She won't kill you you're a police man and anyway she won't know."

Frank climbed out of bed and gave him a wink, *that's my boy.* Twenty minutes later they were sat on breakfast stools in the kitchen eating cornflakes with ice-cold milk. Frank hadn't eaten cornflakes for breakfast since god knows how long ago, but this morning they tasted wonderful. A couple of rounds of toast and a coffee later Frank felt right as rain. He put his thoughts of last night away for the weekend.

"So, see if you can guess what we are going to do today." Frank had a special treat in store that he had not discussed with Hilary, not sure she would approve. Cram closed his eyes as if he was trying to think really hard.

"Errmm... we're going the funfair in the park near where you work."

"No not straight away, but we can go there later tonight if you'd like."

Cram could not think of anything else and looked disappointed. "Okay... but what are we going to do first?"

"Ahah not so easy, have another guess first."

"We're going to the big shops in town to see Santa in the grotto?"

Frank had been so set on his plans for the day he hadn't thought about any of his son's suggestions, but now that he had mentioned it, it wasn't a bad idea. Frank made a mental note to play this guessing game next time Cram came to stay.

"Nope not today but we can go there tomorrow."

Cram looked even more disappointed. The two things he thought they were going to do today weren't going to happen. Frank pulled a face to match Cram's.

"Now don't look like that, what we are going to do is much better."

Frank climbed off his stool and went to his coat hanging behind the kitchen door and took out an envelope from the pocket.

"Now close your eyes and put your hands out, no peeping. I'm going to put something in your hands." Cram sat with his eyes screwed tight shut.

"Okay I promise not to peep." Frank placed the envelope into his son's hands feeling as excited as a schoolboy. He crossed his fingers and hoped for the best.

"Okay now you can open your eyes," the anticipation was killing him.

Cram looked down at his hands confused. It was just an envelope. The suspense was too much for Frank.

"Well… open it and see what's inside."

Cram didn't need telling twice. He tore open the envelope and took out two pieces of red-white and silver card. His initial look of disappointment was instantly replaced by enlightenment followed by pure excitement when he realised what he had in his hands. The two pieces of card were tickets to see Liverpool v Newcastle at Anfield. He was so excited he nearly fell off the breakfast stool.

The game was kicking off at 12:30 because it was being shown on Sky TV.

"Aww… Dad are we really going to see Liverpool play I can't believe it wait till I tell my friends at school." Frank saw the delight on his sons face.

"Yep we are going to see Liverpool play and if we don't want to be late we're going to have to get our skates on, its ten-o-clock and the game kicks off in two and a half hours."

Frank knew there was plenty of time to get up to the ground, probably do the Museum tour and still have time to soak up the atmosphere before the game.

Between them they put the breakfast stuff away and got themselves ready. Frank made sure Cram had his warm coat and a pair of gloves, *sat in the main stand at Anfield in December the weather could be horrendous.*

Minutes later Cram was so excited he was waiting by the front door and couldn't wait to get going. Frank was pfaffing about looking for the car keys. After what seemed an age, Frank appeared with the keys. As they climbed into the car Frank looked in his rearview mirror and caught a glimpse of Cram's face, it was a picture to treasure. He put the car in gear and drove onto the Aigburth Road heading towards town. From there they would pass the Albert Dock, the Liver buildings, the Pier

Head ferry terminal and then skirt round the docks up on to Scotland Road in the direction of Anfield.

Frank knew this area like the back of his hand; he also knew where the safer places were to park without paying the rip off six pounds secure car-parking fee. He pulled into a small car park next to a plot of flats in Everton Valley and slid the car into one of the few spaces that wasn't covered in broken glass and debris. He hid the Merseyside Police Crime Stoppers window sticker in the glove compartment and they got out of the car. The young lads huddled on the corner trying to make a few bob on the backs of the football supporters were there and as usual quick off the mark.

"Mind yer car mate" Said the one with the bright red curly hair who, judging by the colour of his football shirt was an avid Everton supporter, *poor lad.*

Frank glanced towards them and gave them the nod of approval.

"Aye alright lads we'll see yer when we get back" he said accentuating the Liverpool accent. *It helped.* This brought the nod of confirmation from the lads; it was as good as a written form of contract. Frank knew that these lads would probably be tucked up inside their houses in the warm and back out again ten minutes before the game ended to collect their hard earned money. He also knew that if it came to it and some bigger lads came along to smash a window to steal the CD player, there wasn't a blind thing the younger ones could do to stop them. Still it was part of the ritual of going to the game.

In the annuals of Scouse humour there was a standing joke about two young lads asking a man if they could mind his car. The guy politely declines the offer saying he had a dog in the back that would look after the car.

"Puts fires out does it?" comes the reply. The guy dutifully pays up to have his car minded.

Frank and Cram began the one and a half mile up hill trek through the small housing estate that backed on to Walton Road before turning right into Walton Breck Road towards Anfield. The crowds were already making their way in their droves, decked out in hats and scarves, hands shoved deep into their pockets while talking about the results of the last game and the form of this player and that.

The pub crowds were spilling out on to the street with people gulping pints of beer like it was going out of fashion. Frank wondered where they put it all, *and where half of them got the money for it.* By now they could smell the burgers and hotdogs from the ensemble of street vendors.

The huge framework expanse that formed the back end of the Kop loomed in the distance. Frank glanced down at Cram who had thankfully declined the offer to hold his hand. There was an expression of uncertain anticipation on his face, making him look grown up.

Frank ruffled his hair and smiled at him. "Let's see if we can get you a hat and a scarf eh?" Cram looked quite proud as donned his hat and scarf, the look of uncertainty rapidly vanishing from his face.

"What do you fancy doing first? Get something to eat now and then into the museum tour for half an hour before we go in? Or do you want to wait until half time before we get something to eat?"

They chose the museum first and food at half time option. The highlight for both of them was standing on a preserved section of the old Kop when it had been standing room only watching a huge screen showing flaky pictures in black and white of Bill Shankly and memorable matches from the past showing legends such as Peter Thompson, Ian Callaghan, Emlyn Hughes and Sir Roger Hunt.

They came out of the museum and walked around the back of the Kop, now in full swing with the die hards chanting songs of old. The cacophony of noise coming from inside the Albert Pub was just as loud, you could almost feel the heat emanating through the back wall as they walked past it along the alleyway to the main stand.

It was ten past twelve by the time they had bought a programme and found their seats to the left of the directors' box towards the Anfield Road end of the ground. Frank wondered whether or not to try and somehow brief his son on some of the language that he was probably going to hear and then thought better of it. Best leave it and see if he mentions it.

The games against Newcastle historically produced lots of goals with this one being no exception. Liverpool won 3:1 via a Titus Bramble own goal and one each from Ian Mellor and Milan Baros. Patrik Kluivert scored a fluky goal for Newcastle. The Kop went home happy as did Frank and Cram. They had eaten hot dogs at half time but were both hungry again now. They drove into town and found a place to eat. It was dark by the time they left the restaurant and the rain was turning into sleet by the time they got home.

Cram was shattered from the day's excitement. After a quick wash and spin with the toothbrush Cram was tucked up in bed reading his Liverpool programme. He fell asleep within ten minutes dreaming of one day scoring the winning goal for Liverpool. Once he was asleep Frank left the bedroom door ajar and went down stairs.

He checked his messages to see if anyone had called while they had been out. There was only one message from Hilary asking if everything was okay. Frank looked at his watch and decided not to call her, he would give her a ring in the morning. He poured himself a large Asbach and Coke, set the Video to record Match of the Day and settled down to watch the highlights on TV. Half an hour later he was asleep on the couch. He woke up just in time to see Gary Lineker wishing everyone a good night and the closing montage of the day's goals going in. He had no idea what had caused him to wake so suddenly but one thing was for sure he was wide-awake now. No doubt he would be in for another restless night. He switched the TV off, locked up, set the alarm and went to bed. Two hours later he was still awake and staring at the ceiling.

Chapter 10

By the time Frank eventually dozed off the weather had already taken a turn for the worse. When he awoke he could hear what sounded like a mixture of sleet and hail stones thrashing against his bedroom window. Great, he thought, this isn't going to be a good day for traipsing round the shops in town or the fairground at Chevasse Park, but he didn't want to disappoint Cram. He would wait and see, things could change by the time they had breakfast.

He got up and went to check on Cram before going to the bathroom. The chill in the air on the landing told him that although the heating had been on, it had long since gone off. He really should have a look at the timer and change the settings for the weekend. Cram was still tucked up and fast asleep with the Liverpool programme lying on his pillow next to him. Frank left him to sleep and took a long shower, reflecting on his thoughts from the night before. He had no idea what he was going to do to help Ted and knew he had less than a week if Ted stuck to his side of the deal, giving it a week before contacting him.

He stared at his reflection in the mirror as he dried himself off. Not bad, the wrinkles around his eyes still looked like laughter lines and the faint showing of gray hair made him look distinguished as opposed to old. He was in the middle of shaving when he was startled at the sound of the house alarm going off.

"Shit, what the fu..." he uttered to himself and made a sprint for the stairs. He noticed the bedroom door to Cram's room wide open and the quilt was thrown back. He looked over the banister to the bottom of the stairs and saw the upturned face of his son in a stricken panic, about to burst into tears. "Da..ad"

He bounced down the stairs and punched in the code for the alarm.

The relief from the piercing shrill of the alarm was instant. He bent down and picked up Cram holding him close, he could feel his heart beating inside his chest. The distinct smell of his own flesh and blood creating an overpowering instinct to protect.

"I'm sorry dad I forgot about the alarm and I came down to ...."

"Don't you worry your little head about it big feller, its no problem at all, I should have thought about it and come down and switched it off before you got up. I won't forget next time that's for sure." Cram hugged him and kissed him on the cheek. Frank felt the lump rise in his throat.

"Now away upstairs and get yourself washed and dressed, if you need anything give me a shout." Frank watched as his son leapt up the stairs two at a time. Half an hour later they were eating breakfast and talking about what they were going to do for the rest of the day. The rain and sleet were easing off.

Frank drank coffee and sat reading the Sunday paper. The delivery boy hadn't pushed it fully through the letterbox so the half that had been sticking out was soaking wet. Thankfully the sport headlines were on the back page and were still readable. Cram lay on the couch watching the rest of the Shrek 2 video that he had missed from Friday. It was almost lunchtime by the time the sun had been out long enough to dry off the roads outside.

They wrapped up warm and made the trip into town. The shops were packed and it was no better outside. Christmas was coming and the usual last minute panic buyers were out in force. The walk from the NCP parking place in St Johns precinct to the central shopping area was a battle not made any easier with a five year old boy in tow. People were rushing everywhere, coming and going, buying everything in sight. The main pedestrian zone was packed with market traders and stallholders selling the usual Christmas tat.

"Cum on now! Get yer Chrizzy prezzies ere! Special offer, pack of Bic lighters ten for a fiver, Christmas wrapping paper twenty sheets the pound, triple A battries twenny four fer a fiver, cum on now last chance while stocks last." *Bollocks!* Frank knew full well stocks would be lasting through New Year into Easter and beyond.

At every corner and junction there were stall owners selling jumbo hotdogs pretending they were giant frankfurters from Germany. The sweet smell of candyfloss, toffee apples and heart shaped ginger bread draped in icing sugar drifted on the wind. Every now and then Frank spotted a few shifty looking characters selling "stuff" *unofficially*, usually dodgy looking Christmas tree lights from cardboard boxes. Frank felt as if every time he caught their eye, they returned his stare with a look that he swore was saying *"Awe come on copper I'm just tryin'ter make a few quid, you know t' feed the kids an that, I'm not doin any arm honest."*

Frank moved on hoping his face was not confirming that they had got it right in suspecting that he was a copper. By the time he and Cram had battled their way around the various department stores it was gone half past four and already pitch black outside. The winter chill stung their faces as they left the bright lights of St. Johns precinct. The wind was starting to whip up, sending the shoppers scurrying home laden with carrier bags.

Frank thought about walking back to the car and driving straight home without stopping at the fairground, but he didn't want to disappoint Cram, so instead he worked out the shortest way to Chevasse Park.

They turned right up behind the City Law Courts down into the Park. The sleet began to fall as the lights from the fairground came into view. The earlier rain from the morning and the multitude of people visiting the fair had turned the ground into a muddy quagmire. It was all they could do to stay on their feet, within minutes their shoes were caked in mud and their feet were wet. Frank paid for the two of them to go on the only ride that didn't have a massive queue.

As they reached the full height of the Ferris wheel for the second time the sleet was lashing down into their laps. Frank looked at Cram and could see by the look on his face that his heart wasn't really in it. A huge yawn confirmed it. They left the ride without a word. Frank looked down at his son, the poor lad looked shattered.

"Tell you what why don't we walk down to the main road, we'll grab a taxi back to the car park and get ourselves back home."

Cram clung to Frank's leg nodding his head in agreement. Frank reached down and picked him up not caring about the mud from his son's shoes. He balanced Cram on one arm, carried the shopping bags in the other and made his way precariously down the slope. They maneuvered their way out of the park through the throngs of people without falling over finally reaching the main road joining Wapping Street and the Strand.

At the corner of the Strand and James Street Frank hailed a black taxicab going in the opposite direction to where they wanted to go. The taxi squealed to a halt and made a U-turn that only black taxicabs can make, pulling up alongside them. The journey from James Street to the NCP car park at St Johns precinct would have taken them ten to fifteen minutes on foot. The taxi driver looked at them somewhat disapprovingly at the amount of mud on their shoes and even less favorably when Frank told the driver where they wanted to go. By taxi it would take only a few minutes but right now Frank would pay double just to get there.

The taxi driver set off at speed without even looking what was coming from behind. Even with the busy traffic they were at the entrance to the car park in less than five minutes. Frank leaned across to the partition and handed the driver a tenner without even asking what the charge was.

"Keep the change mate, Merry Christmas" The driver smiled his appreciation and looked at Cram sat beside Frank in the back of the taxi. Cram was already struggling to keep his eyes open.

"Cheers mate, he looks well knackered, an look at the state of is shoes, is mum'll go ape when she sees them." Frank looked at his son's shoes. *If only he knew.*

"Yes I suppose so, sorry about the mess."

"Aar don worry abourrit, probly won't be the last one tonight, see yer mate."

Frank and Cram left the taxi and made their way to the lift up to the third floor of the multi storey. He put everything in the boot and fastened Cram into the back seat.

"Thanks Dad, for a great day" Cram whispered sleepily into his ear.

Frank was choked. "No problem, any time." In the dark Cram could not see the glistening in Frank's eyes. They drove home in silence. By the time they got home

Cram was fast asleep. Frank took the bags from the boot and went into the house to switch off the alarm before returning to the car to get Cram. He managed to get him out of the car and into the house without waking him. Deciding it was too early for bed Frank removed his son's shoes and laid him on the couch in the living room then went upstairs to get a blanket.

He threw the blanket loosely over him and turned the heating up a few notches. After locking the front door he went back upstairs ignoring the flashing light on the telephone in the hall. He got out of his damp clothes and showered. The phone rang just as he got in. *Shit, that had better not wake Cram up.* He turned the water off and waited for the answer phone to kick in, it did but the caller hung up before the answer phone message had time to get to the *please leave your message after the tone* bit. It was obviously Hilary.

He quickly finished his shower, changed into fresh clothes and went downstairs. He checked the living room; Cram was still asleep. Back in the hall he stared at the phone for a second wondering whether he should just press the delete all messages button again. Instead he pressed the play messages button and sat on the bottom step of the stairs with the phone on his lap.

The branches of the old sycamore tree in the garden were groaning under their own weight as they swayed back and forth in the wind. The motion sensor security light picked up the movement and clicked on and off illuminating the hallway like lightning on a stormy night. The metallic voice of the answer phone spoke.

You have five new messages, said the electronic voice. Five new messages! *Hilary?* Who else would ring that many times? *First new message,* continued the voice. There was a click and a buzz and then silence. The first caller couldn't be bothered leaving a message. He pressed the delete button. *Second new message...* Same result. He continued until the fourth message.

"Frank its Hilary here, as if he wouldn't be able to tell, *where are you? I'm just ringing to let you know that Michael,* so that's his name, *has had a call from work. There is a bit of a panic, sounds like the company website has been hacked into and it crashed or something like that, any way he is going to have to go in tomorrow morning to help sort the problem out.... Which means that I will be home by about ten in the morning... so I just thought.... that if you ... wanted to bring Cram back home, I have got the day off anyway and I'll be there if you wanted to bring him back home... and... Oh... I'll ring you back later okay? Ring me on my mobile if you get this message."*

Hilary did not enjoy talking to machines any more than she enjoyed long conversations with him. The final message on the answer machine was another buzz click and silence type. Frank deleted all the messages as instructed by the electronic voice and then sat on the bottom step of the stairs deep in thought. The wind howled outside causing the flap on the letterbox to rattle and flip up and down with a clattering sound.

His first thought was Hooray for the internet, *well at least maybe now Hilary would see that it wasn't only him who sometimes had the need to put work before domestic family matters.* His next thoughts were not quite so simple. On the one hand he could take Cram back to Hilarys' first thing after ten o clock in the morning and then go straight to work. Or on the other he could ring Hilary and tell her that he and Cram had made plans so he would return him first thing on Tuesday morning as planned or at the earliest Monday night. The final thought was that maybe Hilary, Cram and he could spend the day together. He was pretty sure that Cram would go for that option if given the choice; he wasn't so sure about Hilary though.

He was still sat on the stairs when the phone rang again making him jump. It was Hilary. The conversation was short. The three options had been swiftly narrowed down to one. He would be going to work tomorrow. He looked up from the phone and saw Cram stood in the doorway rubbing his eyes. He'd heard most of the conversation and even in his state of semi-awakeness he had got the jist of what had been said.

In the hours that followed after the last phone call from Hilary Frank did his best to make as much of the time he had left with Cram. After he had been cleaned up and dressed into pyjamas they both had a light tea. It was far too late to be thinking about messing about with a Sunday dinner so Frank prepared one of his favorite snacks. He made cheese and tomato on toast and threw in some oven chips as an afterthought. Cram polished off the lot and still had room for some strawberry cheesecake Frank had discovered in the bottom of the freezer.

To his surprise Cram had taken the news that he was going back to his mum in the morning without much fuss. He was quite excited at the prospect of telling her all about his day at the football match. After tea they sat and did a jigsaw puzzle together that Cram had brought with him. They finished the puzzle and Cram said that Frank could keep it if he wanted to. How could he possibly refuse?

Shortly before ten o-clock Cram began to yawn again and was happy to go to bed. Cram picked out a story from a book he'd brought with him called *James and the Giant Peach* by Roald Dahl. Frank hadn't heard of the title or the author before. *Some father.* Cram was struggling to keep his eyes open and thankfully asleep by the time Frank had got to the bit where Aunt Sponge and Aunt Spiker were beating poor little James for no reason. Who *writes this stuff?* He sat on the edge of the bed looking at his son breathing deeply. The quilt was rising and falling in time with his breathing, his cheeks glowing from all the fresh air.

As he lay there fast asleep his lips were quivering, dreaming again no doubt that he had just scored the winning goal in yesterday's game. Frank's thoughts turned to his own mother and father. Had either of them ever sat like this and felt the way that he was feeling now? He wondered. Mother possibly, father definitely not. No matter where things led with Hilary and the new man in her life, Frank vowed he would never forget moments like this and make sure his son never came to any harm.

He leaned down and kissed his head and closed his eyes. The scent of shampoo in Cram's' hair still could not mask the childlike smell of his son.

"Good night and god bless, love you son" was all he managed to whisper. Cram, fast asleep let out a deep breath and his lips quivered almost mumbling, as if he was trying to reply in his sleep.

Frank switched off the bedside lamp and crept down the stairs. His heart was heavy and he was already regretting the decision to take Cram back in the morning.

He walked into the kitchen and set about making a half-hearted attempt at tidying up what was left from their tea. Putting most of the stuff in the dishwasher was about as much as he could manage. The cleaner would no doubt sort the rest out in the morning.

He poured himself an even larger than usual shot of Asbach and mixed it with a less than usual amount of coke. He promised himself if this did the trick he would go straight to bed as soon as his eyes started to close.

Sunday night television is not something that Frank would ordinarily stay up for. The choice of viewing left much to be desired, tonight was no exception.

Frank sat staring at the screen but not really seeing what was on it. He took a few large swallows of Asbach in the hope that it would start to kick in and he could go to bed. He lay on the couch and covered himself with the blanket his son had been wrapped up in earlier. He downed the rest of his drink in one go and decided to wait for a few minutes before making his mind up on whether he was going to pour himself another.

It was the sound of his own snoring that woke him up some time later. A glance at his watch told him it was a considerable time later in fact; four fucking hours later and his head ached like a bastard. He got off the couch, switched the television off and went to the kitchen to find something for his headache. He swallowed the tablets with half a pint of water and poured another half pint to take up to bed with him.

He set the alarm in the hall and checked on Cram before slipping into bed. He had been in bed an hour before he remembered he had meant to clean Cram's shoes, never mind they would just have to wait.

Chapter 11

Father Maloney had lain awake most of the night and at five o-clock, resigned to the fact that he could sleep no more, he finally got up for an early morning walk to try and clear his head. He got back from his walk feeling no better for it and a soaking wet pair of shoes was all he had got for his trouble. Sunday, and it had only been a few days since his meeting at the Albert Dock with Frank. A whole week of waiting was going to be an awful long time. When he got back from his walk he made himself a cup of tea and went into the sitting room for a five-minute nap before Mass.

Half an hour later he woke up in a cold sweat, his tea untouched was stone cold. He checked his watch and rushed to get changed, he had twenty minutes before Mass was due to start. The only thing he forgot to change were his shoes, now his feet were cold and his legs ached from standing more than usual. The sermon was almost at an end; feeling terrible he had kept it brief.

He stared at his congregation from the heights of the pulpit at the Holy Church of Trinity. Funny, how the weeks just before Christmas had an effect on the numbers who showed up for Sunday morning mass. For the first time in months there wasn't an empty seat to be had. He could tell from their faces that some of the regulars had had their noses put out of joint because the seats that they had sat in, week in week out, had been taken. He could almost hear the mental notes being made by the regulars, *must get here earlier next week!*

A fit of coughing from an elderly lady woke the old man sat next to her amongst the front rows. Father Maloney gave the old couple one of his most endearing smiles. His back ached, he was sure he was coming down with the flu. He summarized the sermon quickly.

"Thanks be to God. May the lord bless you and keep you, in the name of the Father, the Spirit and the Holy Ghost, Amen. We shall finish today's sermon with Hymn number 506".

The pipes of the church organ struck up with a rasping of bellows and the hollow clunking of wooden pedals. As the choir and congregation joined in, a faint resemblance of "The Lord is my Shepherd" echoed through the church.

Some of the characters amongst the congregation wouldn't look out of place in the *Giles* Christmas Cartoon Annual. One in particular was responsible for taking round the collection tray. As the wailing of the hymn trailed off he shuffled his way towards the largest group of *non-regulars* and quite deliberately dropped a £10.00 note into the collection tray knowing full well that the unsuspecting part timers would rummage through their wallets for at least a fiver instead of the usual handful of loose change.

At the end of the collection the old chap skillfully retrieved his tenner, replaced it with his usual pound coin and tipped Father Maloney the wink. The takings had more than doubled in the last few weeks.

Outside the early sleet and heavy rain had ceased and the following wind had blown all but a few of the darker clouds away. The sun made an appearance and was shining directly from the rear of the church outlining the huge oak wooden doors through the cracks as though an alien spaceship had landed directly outside.

As the congregation edged their way out from the rows of pews Father Maloney was already thinking of the Wedding ceremony due in at two-o-clock. He would have time for some lunch and maybe a snooze before then. By the time he entered the Sacristy most of the Choir had already disrobed and left, pushed for time before returning to sing at the wedding.

He left through the back door of the Sacristy down the steps and across the church grounds through the graveyard. The heavily weeded gravel path led him towards a black iron gate and out towards the Presbytery. The house was a sixteenth century building now almost entirely covered in ivy and surrounded by tall pine trees, with huge clusters of Rhododendrons making it completely hidden from the road.

He shared the accommodation with Father Timothy Francis and Andrew McClelland a curate who had not been with them long. Andrew had been suffering with ill health lately and was away on one of his many sabbaticals. Father Francis was visiting some of the sick or elderly parishioners who were unable to attend Mass.

Inside the house Father Maloney went immediately to the kitchen and prepared himself a light lunch of bread, cheese and the leftovers from a tin of sardines. Despite feeling tired and in need of a nap he made himself a strong coffee and made his way to the sitting room.

He settled into one of the three armchairs to read the newspaper that he'd picked up on his morning walk. The additional two armchairs had been bought to end the lengthy and rather childish debates between the three of them about whose turn was it to have the armchair. As he settled into his chair he made a mental note to change his socks and put on a dry pair of shoes. Ten minutes later with the unread paper sat on his lap, and his coffee untouched, he drifted off into a fitful sleep.

Almost an hour had gone by when he was woken with a start by the sound of Father Francis returning from visiting his sick parishioners. He touched his brow and not for the first time felt the cold beads of sweat on his forehead. *He was definitely coming down with something.*

"Good afternoon Ted, sorry if I disturbed you." Ted wasn't quite with it.

"Mmm, w'hat? Oh no, no you didn't, no problem, what time is it?" There was no answer; Father Francis was already off in the direction of the kitchen. He glanced up and squinted at the clock on the wall, it was a quarter past one. He looked at his cold mug of coffee on the small wooden table next to his armchair and decided against drinking it.

"I'd love to stay and chat", he shouted to Father Francis in the kitchen, " but I've got a wedding to attend to in forty minutes and I need to get changed."

As he climbed the stairs he heard the sound of Father Francis muttering something in the kitchen about ignoramuses with video cameras and flashing lights. He thought nothing of it. The sardines he'd eaten for lunch were coming back on him and he could tell that his breath stank. He took two aspirin tablets and brushed his teeth to remove the lingering taste of the sardines.

Ten minutes later he reached the iron gates, the tingling sensation of a blister on his big toe reminded him that he had not changed his shoes and socks. Never mind, who would know but him, he looked up to the sky and smiled to himself.

He arrived at the Sacristy and saw the mixed array of bicycles propped up in a tangled mess against the back wall. Oh well at least the choir were on time.

He climbed the steps and stepped through the door to the Sacristy where he was greeted by the noisy chatter of the choirboys hurrying to prepare themselves for the wedding. This was a scene he had observed hundreds of times before, and today was no different. Jackets, jumpers and a pile of the latest trend in fashionable training shoes were scattered all over the floor. He almost tripped over one of them as he greeted the boys.

"Sorry Father" said the boy nearest to him. He nodded in acknowledgment that he had heard him as he strode past and into the church. The rest of the boys went silent. Entering the church in a hurry he stooped to a half kneeling position, made the sign of the cross in front of the altar, then turned and walked down between the rows of wooden benches. He checked his watch; he had fifteen minutes before the choir would be taking their seats.

Mr. Jackson, the organ player was already in position and warming up the organ pipes with a tune he didn't recognise. Something between *Phantom of the Opera and Bohemian Rhapsody*. Groups of anxious and very nervy looking people were hovering at the back doors to the church, others had already ventured in and grabbed themselves a seat.

He skipped down the stairs to the lower level and smiled graciously at the guests who were thumbing their way through the list of songs chosen for the wedding. He recognised the two ushers representing the families from both sides of the happy couple. A good old-fashioned blend of Irish and Liverpudlian ancestry, what could *possibly* go wrong? *Thank God for rehearsals.* He greeted them with a firm handshake and an apologetic explanation for his lateness.

"Arr dat's no problem Father, everytings goin just foine," said one of the ushers.

"Is the groom here yet?" asked Father Maloney doubtfully.

"Eeerr... yerreel be ere in aminit, e's on is way now," replied the other usher.

"Is he okay?" Maloney enquired with some degree of suspicion in his voice.

" Yeh sound. No probs whatsoever, I was with im on 'is stag night last night and he was ome by aarf four"

"Really?" he answered trying his best to sound impressed with this amazing feat of conservatism. Judging by the overpowering smell of alcohol on both the men's breath, it was obvious that things were going more than *just, foine.*

"And the best man?" queried Maloney sounding concerned.

"Yerr e was ome by five an all"

Father Maloney gave them both a weak smile at the usher's last reply and decided he was better off not asking any more questions. He made his excuses and left to prepare himself. As he turned to leave, the 1000-watt light, mounted above a shoulder-held video camera temporarily blinded him and he almost clattered straight into the grinning, amateur cameraman.

"Eeer sorry bout dat Father, any chance of a wird fer the camra?"

With his eyes still blinded from the light, Maloney couldn't see who he was talking to.

"Sorry perhaps later after the ceremony", was all he managed to say as he rushed past towards the safety of the Sacristy.

"Any chance of usin yer power socket so's I can charge me batteries Father, Father?"

Something about ignoramuses that Father Francis had said back at the house came back to him.

Surprisingly, and much to Father Maloney's relief the rest of the afternoon went more or less without a hitch. The bride and groom remembered all their words, the best man looking rather more like the *worst man* remembered the rings, and everyone sang in tune. As usual the bride's mother wept profusely, the father of the bride could hardly speak, no one collapsed and the choir got paid. A job well done.

Father Maloney waved goodbye to the last of the stragglers making their way from the churchyard towards the waiting cars. He brushed confetti from the sleeves of his cassock and looked at the mess outside the back doors. Confetti, mixed with cigarette butts and discarded paper hankies were strewn all over the steps and across the yard. An open can of Carlsberg had been left half finished at the bottom of the steps and the single wooden waste bin was overflowing with what looked like several disposable nappies.

The overwhelming urge to grab a brush and start cleaning up the mess was outdone by an even stronger urge to get back to the house and take off his shoes and socks. The blister on his big toe felt as if he had got a piece of glass stuck inside his shoe. He left the church in the capable hands of two Eucharistic ministers who would oversee the cleanup operation and the security of the doors to the church.

On reaching the sanctuary of the house the warmth greeted him like a warm blanket enveloping him instantly. Judging by the smell wafting from the kitchen Father Francis had already got dinner prepared and was sat watching television in the sitting room. Father Maloney greeted him with a nod and asked what time he was expecting to eat.

"Oh when ever you're ready, it 'll only take a few minutes to lay out. Everything go all right?" he asked with one eyebrow cocked looking slightly skeptical.

"Oh Yes, everyone left happy as far as I could see. Jolly fine mess left behind outside though, we really should do something about that. Oh, and by the way you were right about the business with the video camera, the eejit with the camera almost blinded me with it, I almost knocked him over so I did, could've been a nasty accident. He even had the cheek to ask he if he could use a power socket to charge the batteries."

Father Francis gave him one of his *I told you so* looks and smiled to himself, but the matter of the mess left outside the church was getting him down.

"I agree, I propose we levy an additional cleanup charge on a no return deposit basis, and I think we should make a charge for the use of video equipment in the church. What do you think?"

Father Maloney was slightly uncomfortable with this choosing not to answer, shrugging his shoulders instead.

"I'm nipping up for a shower and change of clothes before dinner, about twenty minutes?" he said hopefully. Father Francis looked at the clock on the wall and then at him.

"Aye I suppose so, that'll just give me time to have a quick look at this" He leaned down to the floor at the side of his armchair and picked up a videocassette.

"What's that?" enquired Father Maloney.

"It's a video tape"

"Yes I can see that, but what of?"

"It's a tape of the Christening I performed last week for the latest addition to the young Pearson family. You remember, baby daughter Emily, good as gold she was. And I have to say the chap using the camera was quite discreet, very professional in fact." Father Maloney wasn't convinced.

"Ah well I suppose that's one good thing about the use of video, if the quality is any good it'll be somethin they can watch in years to come. Mind if I watch it with you after dinner instead?" Father Francis was only too happy to oblige.

"Of course not. It'll beat watching Antiques Road show. Go and get your shower, dinner will be on the table in twenty minutes."

Father Maloney hurried off remembering to take off his shoes before climbing the stairs. The relief from the pain was instant. The hot shower felt wonderful despite the stinging sensation as the soapy water washed over his blister. He dried himself off, dusted his toes with a sprinkle of talcum powder and got dressed in a cotton shirt, a pair of casual slacks and sandals.

By the time he got downstairs Father Francis had laid the table with cutlery, place mats, the usual condiments and a glass of white wine for each of them. There was even a small spoon at the head of the cutlery, which meant that Father Francis had taken the trouble to prepare a dessert. Not that he was a great chef, it just meant that he had probably bought something pre-packaged, more than likely some of the mini trifles he was so fond of.

They said grace and ate their meal in relative silence. The meal was over in half an hour and the shared task of cleaning up afterwards was completed before they both retired to the sitting room to watch the video. Taking the remains of their wine with them they settled down to watch the tape.

There was the usual pfaffing about with the remote to find the right channel, and then the initial distortion at the beginning of tape accompanied by a short snippet of the theme tune from *Coronation Street*. A thirty second section of footage from *The Bill* followed it. DCI Meadows was berating DC someone or other in his office. The images of the police officers distorted and then rolled upwards and off the screen.

Seconds later as whoever had been operating the camera attempted to zoom in; the somewhat blurred out of focus image of baby Emily lying in her cot appeared. The person operating the camera was giving a running commentary. Somebody else could be heard muttering in the background over the commentary with what sounded like *"Make sure its in focus"* followed by lots of shushing sounds from the camera operator. A pair of arms appeared out of nowhere and reached down into the cot. Lots of cooing, gurgling baby friendly type noises were being offered towards Emily. The amateur commentator continued giving his spiel.

"So ere we are on Emily's big day, the time now's just gone seven and Emily has just woken up, aaaand... she needs changing."

Father Francis looked towards the ceiling. Father Maloney saw the expression on his face confirming that they were both thinking the same. Father Francis frantically began to search for the fast forward button. After trying several different buttons and briefly causing the video player to start recording over the tape he managed to regain enough composure to hit the power off button and stop the tape.

Father Maloney was grinning like a Cheshire cat and it was all he could do not to break out into hysterics seeing the look of frustration and embarrassment on Father Francis's face.

"Do you mind if I have a go?" he enquired, diplomatically.

"Be my guest." replied Father Francis, " I'm going to make us some coffee, give us a few minutes and see if you can fast forward it to the ceremony, I don't think

I can handle more than that," he said scurrying off into the kitchen.

Father Maloney studiously cast his eye over all the different buttons on the remote and identified exactly what button did what before finally pressing the power on button for the video. He pressed the fast forward button without viewing the tape, letting it fast forward for a while and hit the play button.

Baby Emily was being carried to a car somewhere and strapped into a car seat. *Well at least it looks as if they are on the way to the church.* He pressed fast-forward again without stopping the tape. For the next few minutes the footage looked like an episode of the Benny Hill show with people rushing about everywhere and stopping suddenly to look into the camera. The next section of footage looked rather dark and blurred with strange images showing intermittently. He hit the play button to find out what was going on. From what he could make out the person doing the filming had inadvertently forgotten to switch the camera off. The next few minutes showed some close up footage of a pavement, someone's feet and the floor mats of the inside of a car before finally the inside the inside of the video camera storage bag.

He couldn't help chuckling to himself. *Britain's Funniest Home Video* programme would pay £250.00 for this without hesitation. What was it Father Francis had been saying about "discretion" and "very professional"?

He hit the fast-forward button again. The totally black screen now had a red circular light flashing in the top right hand corner, unless who ever it was operating the camera had brought spare batteries, this would be the end of the road for Emily's big day.

He watched with interest, completely fascinated as the camera was obviously being removed from its carrier bag. He hit play. Background conversation accompanied some footage from the inside of the car, the roof and the back of the drivers' head before a huge distorted image of a face appeared on the television screen. The operator had finally realised the camera had been left switched on to record. "Bollocks" accompanied by some other mild expletives could just about be heard in the background, followed with, "Wait don't get out of the ca...." The voice was cut off mid flow. The batteries had finally given up the ghost or the tape had run out.

The television screen went temporarily blank and then flashed into full picture again with shots of family and friends smiling and waving on their way into the churchyard. The batteries evidently had been replaced. Some fancy three hundred and sixty degree panoramic camera work followed and the picture went completely out of focus.

Distorted images of the car park, trees and the grounds surrounding the church whizzed quickly by. This guy was definitely not going to win any Oscars for best film producer. He stopped the tape and waited for Father Francis to return. Minutes later Father Francis arrived balancing two cups of coffee and plate of assorted biscuits on a tray.

"You managed to sort it then?" he asked feeling rather sheepish. Father Maloney maintained his diplomacy.

"Yes I think so, I have to say though if the rest of the film is as good as the bits I've seen so far the camera man won't be up for any awards."

They settled down to watch the rest of the tape. The amateur production was tiresome to watch and the thought of watching the Antiques Road show suddenly grew in appeal. The christening ceremony was at least shown with some clarity with baby Emily indeed behaving as good as gold just like Father Francis had said.

The final 'piece de resistance' on the video was some fancy fading shots from one person to another with a view of the car park in the background and people climbing into their cars, no doubt heading off to wet the babies head somewhere local.

The cars followed each other under the ivy covered stone archway at the end of the drive to the car park and turned left onto the main road, except for one that went in the opposite direction. Father Maloney thought that this was strange but thought no more of it. The video continued with more footage back at whichever pub they had all converged on to carry on celebrating in true style. Father Maloney switched off the tape, leant back in his chair and yawned, feeling suddenly very tired. He gave Father Francis a hand to tidy up in the kitchen and then made his excuses and wished him goodnight.

Hours later he was still wide awake. Something about the video was troubling him. When he finally did drop off, his dreams were occupied with one section of the video that replayed itself constantly in a loop. The cars leaving the car park after the christening ceremony were all turning left except for one. It was a small red Nissan Micra that had paused with its indicator blinking away, waiting for traffic to pass before it could pull out and turn right. The driver of another car behind it had impatiently beeped his horn.

The Micra stood out from the rest because it was the only car with a single occupant. The woman driving the car looked familiar and she was definitely in the church at the time of the christening ceremony. She had been caught briefly on camera. It looked as if she was leaving as the christening ceremony drew to a close.

There had been one brief second where she had turned her head and peered over her shoulder to see if anyone had noticed she was leaving. Almost as if she knew she had been caught on camera, she had quickly lowered her head as she turned towards the doors.

It was two-o-clock in the morning when the video loop playing inside his head came to an abrupt stop. When it did he woke suddenly and sat up in bed with a start. He felt cold and shivery, he rubbed his eyes and again he could feel the sweat running down his forehead. He climbed out of bed, put on his slippers and nightgown and crept quietly as possible downstairs. Making as little noise as he could he fumbled about in the semi darkness of the sitting room trying to find the tape cassette and the remote for the TV and video. With the sound turned down so as not to wake Father Francis he sat right in front of the TV to watch the tape.

A few rewinds and a couple of fast-forwards later he found the bit on the tape he was looking for. The noise from the ancient video player seemed so much louder at two-o-clock in the morning. He found a pen, tore off a strip of newspaper and made a note of the registration number of the car the woman was driving. He waited a moment before pressing the play button again hoping that he had not caused Father Francis to wake up.

Ten minutes later after watching it through twice, his own eyes confirmed what he suspected his dreams had been telling him for the past four hours. He was sure the woman driving the red Nissan with the registration mark KJ02 LFM, was the same woman he had taken the confession from five days ago. He went into the kitchen, turned the light on and poured himself a glass of water. If Father Francis came down, that would be his excuse; he was thirsty and needed a drink.

He looked at the calendar on the wall where he and Father Francis wrote their appointments. The appointments were written in two different coloured pens so as not to confuse them with each other. His were in black and Father Francis's were in red. On the calendar right there in front of him was the confirmation he needed. The christening ceremony Father Francis had written in red, and just below it was the word *Confession* in black.

He went back into the sitting room rewound the tape, ejected it and switched off the TV and video. He made his way slowly back upstairs, climbed into bed and lay there staring at the ceiling. The immediate question eating at him now, was could he wait a few more days before contacting Frank. He was still awake as the sun began to rise.

Chapter 12

The shrill sound of the alarm clock beeped away annoyingly for the second time. The rain driving against the bedroom window almost drowned it out. Frank lay awake staring at the ceiling, it was seven forty five Monday morning and he was going back to work. By eight thirty he was up, showered, shaved and changed.

He woke Cram and helped him get dressed into the clothes he'd arrived in on the Friday night. They sat in relative silence at the breakfast bar in the kitchen eating cornflakes and toast for breakfast. Half an hour later they were loading the car ready to leave the house.

As they pulled away from the drive the housekeeper appeared around the corner on her bike battling against forty mile an hour gusts and howling rain. *And I've got problems.* Frank gave her an embarrassed wave as she cycled past. She had her own key and he had entrusted her with the alarm code. He thought about the mess he had left the house in and made a mental note to drop something extra in her wages at the end of the week.

Most of the rush hour commuter traffic into town had dispersed, he made good progress up Aigburth Road and turned right onto Ullet Road before heading towards Sandown Park and Gateacre on the outskirts of Liverpool. He thought about taking a bit of a detour so they would arrive late. He didn't want to give Hilary the impression he was keen to get rid of Cram. The thought didn't last long; he was in no mood for a confrontation with Hilary.

They arrived at the approach road to the house just before ten. Frank pulled up outside the house and switched the engine off. He looked beside him towards Cram strapped into the front passenger seat clutching his Liverpool programme and a plastic Sainsburies shopping bag with his dirty shoes inside.

"Sorry about the shoes son," was all he managed to say with a lump in his throat visible from fifty feet. Cram did his best to raise a smile.

"It's okay dad...dad when will you come to see me again?"

Frank turned his face away lowered his head and pinched the bridge of his nose feeling like his heart had slowly moved up from his chest, bulging in the back of his throat.

"Soon son, soon. You can count on that." From the corner of his eye he could see Hilary hovering at the front door.

"Come on son your mums' waiting." They got out of the car and collected Cram's things from the boot. Cram stood on the pavement not sure whether to run and hug his mum or wait for his dad. Frank shouldered Cram's rucksack, walked to his son and peered down at his face. He held his arms out towards him and Cram reached up to meet him. They held on tight to each other for over a minute. Nothing was said, there was no need to explain, the love was there for all to see.

He carried Cram up the pathway towards the front door where Hilary was waiting and saw the emotion written across her face. She had shared the experience of their embrace. He lowered Cram onto the step and passed Hilary the rucksack.

"If it's okay with you I'll give you a ring tonight, I'm sorry about the shoes"

Hilary saw the plastic bag Cram was clutching and leaned over to inspect the contents. She looked disapprovingly at the shoes caked in a layer of dried mud and then smiled at Cram.

"Never mind we'll soon get those cleaned up. Did you have a good time?"

Cram clung on to her leg with one arm and looked up proudly showing off his Liverpool programme and nodded his head. Frank cut in.

"Er I'll explain later if that's okay."

Hilary smiled faintly. "You are welcome to come in for a while if you want."

He did want, but couldn't bring himself to say it.

"Thanks but I really need to get off, I'll call you later... oh and sorry your weekend was cut short." He leaned down, kissed Cram again and turned towards the car.

Unable to look back he struggled to hold back the tears. A minute later he pulled over into a lay by and sobbed, the image of Cram's face was breaking his heart.

Several minutes later having regained his composure he drove towards town, turning right off the Wapping Road opposite the Salthouse Dock and cruised towards the rear of Canning Place. A sign displaying the name, *Merseyside Police Headquarters* rose high above the perimeter fence letting the casual observer from out of town know that the old brown brick coloured building with its multitude of windows was not a block of flats. The restricted entry control gates obviously on the blink were wide open as Frank pulled up at the guardhouse.

The security guard inside the gatehouse looked up from his newspaper and waved in recognition at Franks' arrival. He pulled into his parking space at the back of the building at a quarter past eleven. Two uniformed officers greeted him with a respectful nod as he walked past them. The place looked busy and official. The lower car park was packed with a fleet of high-speed, high tech racing cars disguised as Vauxhall Astras. A row of Police motorcycles stood side by side in the far corner, their overheated engines clicking as they cooled down.

Using his swipe card he entered the building through the back door and stopped at reception to sign in. There was a constant flow of uniformed and plain-clothes officers coming in and out; the retired officer on the desk had his hands full.

In the lobby the dinging sound of a bell signalled the arrival of the lift. As the doors opened the *sandwich man* wheeled out a trolley with the left overs from his mornings delivery. Frank reached for his wallet sticking his foot inside the door while he selected his food. The man thanked him and apologised for the lack of choice.

On the eighth floor Frank walked into the deserted squad room heading straight for the kitchen. Janice, the office secretary was washing cups and cleaning up the mess left by the rest of the lads.

"Hi Janice" he said, announcing his arrival.

"Jeezus Frank, you shouldn't sneak up on me like that," she said jumping out of her skin.

"Sorry, force of habit, goes with the job, any messages?"

"Err... yes a couple. I've left them on your desk, you've also got some messages on your answer phone. Anyway what're you doing back? No one is expecting you until tomorrow."

"Oh you know the usual, bit of a long story. Did you get my choccies?"

"Yes thanks and you know you didn't need to bother. The rest of them are on Barry's desk, if you fancy one."

"That's the best offer I've had all day, you still watching your weight?"

"I won't dignify that remark with an answer!"

"Oops sorry, any chance of the kettle going on?"

"It's just boiled, what're you having?"

"Coffee's fine, can you bring it through?"

Janice sneaked a sideward glance at him. "What did your last slave die of?"

"Not doing as they were told," he winked.

"Yes okay go and get yourself sorted I'll bring it through in a minute, are you still off the sugar?" she smiled sarcastically.

"I won't dignify that remark with an answer!" he replied and headed towards his office. He stopped by the photocopy machine and glanced at the location chart to see where everyone was. The boys had still not quite got the hang of filling it in. The words "Out, back later" did not really tell him what he wanted to know.

He had practically finished his sandwiches while reading his emails before Janice brought the coffee through.

"There you go," she said, noticing that he had finished his sandwiches.

"Perhaps you might get to drink this one while it is still hot?"

"Yeh, Cheers Janice, maybe."

She left him to it. He read the handwritten messages Janice had left him, made notes in his diary and made some adjustments to the year planner on the wall behind him.

First Aid training and the new Diversity workshops were being touted throughout the headquarters. Every other email was a reminder to get yourself booked onto a course as soon as possible. There was a gentle reminder that the Chief Super was monitoring progress. So far none of Frank's team had attended either. Maybe he was going to have to get the ball rolling.

He reached for the phone to ring the force training officer and get himself booked in for a course and then thought better of it. He was distracted by the flashing light on the digital display indicating he had messages waiting. They probably all came on Friday after he left work. *Typical the minute you go off on a bit of leave, every man and his dog is after you.* He picked up the phone and pressed the recall button. The machine clicked into operation.

"Hi Frank, it's Daz. I'm at Mather Avenue. Any chance you can give us a bell, okay, cheers, speak to you later." Mather Avenue was the local Force Training School where all the Personal Safety training was done for Merseyside Police Officers. Danielle Vasquez, or Daz to her friends, was one of the Specialist Skills Trainers at the school and had been on the same Police Recruit intake as Frank.

Throughout the fifteen weeks training she and Frank had paired off together for the Personal Safety Training sessions becoming good friends. Half way through training the course gossip was, that they were having a bit of a fling after they'd been seen having a smooch during a drunken party. Danielle had got injured two weeks before their passing out parade and was back squadded. They were both totally gutted because they would not be passing out together. They had stayed in touch from time to time, although she had done most of the calling.

Frank scribbled on a Post it note and stuck it on his phone to remind him to ring her later. The next message was from the DCI.

"Hi Frank, sorry, forgot you were on leave, I'll call you on Tuesday, thanks bye".

He hated this type of message most of all because they gave no indication of what the caller had rang for in the first place. He punched the DCI's speed dial number and got the answer phone telling him to leave a message.

"Hello, boss, its Frank, just letting you know I got back early, you rang earlier, speak to you later, cheers." Frank hung up. *What did his boss want?* God that bugged him. *Guilty conscience?*

The rest of the messages were from various admin and clerical staff within the headquarters backing up emails about divisional meetings and the usual mundane stuff. He flicked through his diary and searched for Daz's telephone number at Mather Avenue. She answered on the second ring.

"Daz. Hi it's Frank. What can I do you for?"

"Frank, cheers for getting back to me. I spoke to Barry earlier and he told me you were on leave till Tuesday."

"Yeh I know, things went pear shaped with Hilary's long weekend, so I got to come into work earlier than expected."

"Everything okay?" She sounded concerned.

"Yeh, she's fine, her boyfriend got called back into work, something to do with the company website getting trashed by Internet hackers, he needed to go in and sort it."

"Right, how's Cram? Did you have a good weekend together?"

"Brilliant, we had a great time I took him to the match on Saturday, did you go?"

"Nah, I was working, saw the highlights on tele though, good result eh?"

"Yeh Cram was well chuffed. You okay?"

"Not bad, got knocked back again on my transfer request though, pissed off about that."

Daz had put her request in to transfer to MIT twice now and had been turned down a second time.

"Did they give you a reason?" enquired Frank.

"Sort of, but I don't believe it for a minute, some bullshit about a shortage of specialists and no one lined up to replace me, you know the usual crap."

"Anything I can do to help?"

"Well that's sort of why I was ringing… I wondered if there was any chance you could have a word like… maybe try and swing it."

"I'm on it Daz, consider it done. In fact I know someone here at the HQ who is fed up flying a desk and would jump at the chance to get on board at Mather Avenue."

Daz sounded optimistic. "Will they get released to do the specialist course?"

"Trust me, his gaffer owes me one, I'll give him a bell as soon as we're done. Give it until the end of the week and if you haven't heard anything give us bell."

"Okay, will do, can't wait! Listen I'll have to shoot off, I've got a class coming in a few minutes for a personal safety refresher course."

They hung up and Frank and made another note. He glanced towards his coffee and saw the skin forming on the surface. He drained the mug in one, couldn't have Janice on his case. His computer had timed out by the time he got back to it. He logged on to find he'd got another email since he'd last checked. It was from Daz.

"Cheers Frank you're a star. Thanks. Daz. x"

It was getting on for three o clock when the first of Frank's team showed his face. DC Roberts did a double take when he saw Frank sat at his desk, went straight into autopilot, knocked on the door and implemented rule number one. Frank looked up to see him outside the door.

"Yes Fledge?"

DC Roberts had obviously been out getting *some fresh air* as per recommendations from Barry. He stood in the doorway looking pretty wet.

"Hi Boss, wasn't expecting you back till tomorrow… er I'm makin a brew if yer fancy one?"

"Yep don't mind if I do thanks, coffee please." The Fledge turned to leave.

Frank put on one of his serious faces and called him back.

"Fledge?"

DC Roberts stopped halfway through the door. "Yes Boss?"

"An update would be nice," sounding more serious.

"Err…on what Boss?"

Frank almost lost it for a split second. "Like where the fuck is everyone would do for a start!"

The Fledge was taken aback. "Well …" he began to stutter.

Frank raised his hand to stop him. He needed to get a grip on his mood.

"Tell you what, go and get the brews sorted and you can fill me in then. Ask Janice if there's any bickies left."

"Right, Boss, back in a minute." DC Roberts left to sort out the brews feeling sorry for himself.

Frank sat back in his chair trying to work out what was eating him to make him snap at the Fledge like that. He was going to apologise to him when he returned. He closed his eyes and reflected on the time he'd spent with Cram and wondered where the relationship with Hilary and her new man Michael was going. A whole host of other work related topics filled his mind and pushed the domestic thoughts to one side.

Tomorrow was Tuesday and there were only three days before the deadline for his next meeting with Father

Maloney. He was still sat with his eyes closed when the DC Roberts returned with the coffee.

"Sorry about the wait Boss, I had to shoot down to the canteen to get the biscuits."

Frank was sorry already. "That's okay Fledge, stick it over there on the table in the corner. Where's your brew?"

"Its on me desk boss." DC Roberts looked at him slightly confused at the sudden change in demeanour.

"Go and get it then, we can't talk with your brew going cold on your desk"

DC Roberts shot off quickly returning with his brew and clutching a notepad in his other hand.

Frank apologised for having a go at him before he could launch into his update.

"Okay boss, no problem. Right, here's the score."

DC Roberts gave a comprehensive debrief on where everyone was and what they were up to. In a nutshell, the lads were all busy and the work was piling up. Frank thanked him, telling him to keep up the good work.

During the update Frank made notes, listing all the perfectly good reasons to approach the DCI with his request for additional support, and he had just the person in mind to bring in. DC Roberts left Frank's office feeling two foot taller. He was gone less than a minute when he rushed back in without knocking. He was holding a brown paper package.

"Boss, sorry I forgot. This was left at reception for you with a message saying that it had to be delivered to you personally." He left out the bit about *as soon as possible*.

Frank stared at the package. "What is it?"

DC Roberts shrugged his shoulders, "I've no idea Boss."

Frank had no idea either, but he was suspicious about unexpected brown paper parcels. At least this one had been here half a day and it hadn't taken the roof off the building yet.

"So who's it from?"

"Err... not sure Boss, I picked it up with the mail on the way in."

"Okay thanks, nip down to reception and check the signing in book for the post delivery, check who signed for it and get me their telephone number ASAP."

DC Roberts disappeared with the feeling that he was in the shit.

Frank felt the lightweight package in his hand. It didn't take a detective to tell what was inside it. He tore open the wrapping to reveal that he had guessed right. A post it note was stuck to the outer cardboard cover of a videocassette. The message was short and to the point.

Frank, sorry couldn't wait until Thursday. Please watch this and ring me as soon as you can. The message was signed off with, "Best Regards, Ted."

By the time DC Roberts returned from reception, Frank was sat in the incident room watching the tape. He went to find him after Janice had told him where he'd gone. On arrival at the incident room he saw that the blinds were drawn and the screen pulled over the window inside the door. The sign used for incident briefs and debriefs was hung inside the screen.

"Not to be disturbed"

This sign had an additional *unwritten* message that everyone in the department understood, when this sign was in the window it didn't just mean do not disturb, it meant do not disturb *under any circumstances whatsofucking ever.* DC Roberts chose to wait.

Inside the incident room Frank finished watching the tape. Although there was no other explanation with

Ted's note or on the video, he was smart enough to work out for himself what it was all about. He pulled his mobile out and dialed Ted's number. A rather quiet and frail sounding voice answered.

"The Presbytery, Father Francis speaking."

Frank felt slightly guilty about lying to Father Francis as he made up a load of old bullshit about being a parishioner, and what it was he needed to speak with Father Maloney about. A minute later the sound of Ted's voice crackled on the other end of the phone.

"Father Maloney speaking, how can I help?

"Ted its Frank, I've just watched the tape."

"Excuse me one moment would you please." There was a bit of a pause while Ted was obviously was trying to shoo Father Francis from the room. Ted's voice came back on the phone speaking quietly.

"Frank, thank you, it's good of you to call."

They spoke briefly before Frank agreed he would meet Ted at the Presbytery that evening. Frank retrieved the video and raised the blinds to the incident room.

To his surprise Barry was hanging about in the corridor with DC Roberts, both looking fidgety. The sound of Frank unlocking the door from inside made them even more nervous. Barry leaned towards DC Roberts.

"Fledge, how long did you say he's been in there again?" DC Roberts checked his watch. "At least thirty minutes."

Frank emerged and spoke before either of them could question him.

"Problem?"

Barry spoke up first.

"No Boss, we were just wondering if there was anything you needed a hand with? DC Roberts told me you were in here. I saw the sign was up and the blinds closed, just thought if something was up like… maybe we could help."

Frank thought about his answer before replying.

"Maybe I'm not sure…" he looked at his watch; it was only four o clock.

"Listen I'm knocking off, I wasn't supposed to be in today anyway. I'm off to a meeting tonight, something to do with this…" he said holding up the tape.

"I can't say any more than that for now, I'll explain later. Barry, if there's anything that can't wait until the morning after my meeting tonight I'll give you a bell on your mobile. Meanwhile if anybody wants me I'm unavailable until the morning."

DC Roberts was fidgeting with a piece of paper.

"Fledge, if that's the name of the person who signed for this," he waved the tape cassette, "leave it on my desk, it'll wait until the morning. I'll see you guys tomorrow."

DS Barry Ferguson shot a puzzled look at DC Roberts. "What the fuck was that all about?"

"I haven't got a *Scooby doo*," meaning he had no idea. "I know e's been acting a bit funny lately, he had a go at me earlier and then apologised two minutes later. Something's bugging him that's for sure." Barry was deep in thought. He knew Frank had something going on that he had so far chosen not to share with him.

"Right Fledge, get on the phone and call everyone in. Tell them I need everyone back here for a meeting as soon as possible. If the boss is going to a meeting tonight it's a dead cert he'll wanna do a *fill in* job first thing in the morning, if not sooner. DC Roberts disappeared to make the calls.

Chapter 13

By the time Frank left his office it was a quarter to five. He had just over two hours to kill before his meeting with Ted at the Presbytery. He left work and drove around town for the best part of an hour trying to make his mind up on whether to go home and have something to eat or stay in town. The road works were atrocious and he eventually found himself back on the Wapping Road having gone full circle around town. He made a last minute decision and swung hard left into a McDonalds literally five hundred metres from Canning Place.

As he approached the front door he studied the queue at the till and stopped in his tracks. DS Barry Ferguson together with DC's Roberts and Turner were in the queue. Barry had obviously called a meeting. He did an about turn and left the burger store without any food.

Two hundred metres up the road there was a guy selling food from a white trailer parked up at the side of the road. He pulled the car up at the back of the van, got out and ordered a double cheeseburger and coffee. He picked up a well-thumbed copy of the Liverpool Echo that was lying on the counter of the van and took it with him to the car. By the time he'd finished reading the print off the Echo, the coffee had almost melted the plastic cup. *The guy in the van must be using some kind of thermo-nuclear device to heat up the water.*

He looked at his watch, it was almost seven pm. Time to go. He pulled away in a hurry causing the remains of the coffee to tip out on to the passenger seat. The Echo soaked most of it up.

It was gone seven pm when he turned off Mount Pleasant and headed towards the Holy Church of Trinity. As he turned off the deserted side road on to the stony driveway to the Presbytery, he saw the huge old church looming eerily out of the darkness, towering above the trees surrounding it.

He maneuvered the car up the drive and heard the gravel pinging out from under the tyres. Every few feet, deep potholes filled with rainwater caused the car to roll and lurch from side to side like a circus car in a big top. Loud screeching sounds came from underneath the car as metal scraped against stone. Branches from the overgrown conifers and fir trees either side of the drive whipped and clung to the sides of the car like some crazy drive-in carwash. It was quite an achievement reaching the end of the drive with the exhaust still attached.

At the side of the Presbytery there was an area with enough room for three or four cars to be parked side by side. Leaning across to the glove compartment, he retrieved the videotape and tucked it into his inside coat pocket. He locked the car and made his way carefully around to the front, watching where he planted his feet, trying to avoid the deep puddles. A ferocious gust of wind blew through the trees and freezing drops of rain slipped from the branches to pelt him in the face.

Hanging from the heavy wooden archway that served as a porch to the front door there was single lamp. Frank half expected Dixon of *Dock Green* to turn up at any minute. The sickly yellow glow from the lamp was hindered by masses of cobwebs dripping from the rain. To the side of the porch there was ivy growing with roots as thick as lampposts strangling the front side of the house; its tendrils were creeping into the roof and virtually covered some of the windows. He shivered as he climbed the steps, then rang the bell and took a step back.

The heavy metal bolts clunked from inside as the solid oak door was pulled back to reveal Father Maloney dressed in casual clothes. Frank greeted him with a smile.

"Glad to see you are taking your personal security serious Father" he said sarcastically, as he climbed the final step and shook hands.

"Frank, good to see you, please come in." Frank stepped inside and looked around.

"Listen Ted, you know you should have one of those gadgets fitted which allows you to ask who's at the door before opening it, or at least a fisheye lens fitted so that you can see who it is." Father Maloney looked sheepish.

"I know, Father Francis is always going on about it."

"I could recommend someone for you if you'd like?"

"Yes I'm sure you could, now come on in and get your coat off." Ted took Franks' coat and hung it up on an ancient looking coat stand in the hall.

"Would you like a bite to eat? I've got some very nice home made vegetable soup in the kitchen if you'd like." Frank was still feeling stuffed from his meal earlier.

"No thanks Ted, I've eaten already, a cup of tea wouldn't go amiss though."

Frank surveyed the inside of the hallway like a burglar casing the joint. He had only been here once before, nothing much had changed. Next to the hat stand was a table on top of which was perched a shiny, black, old style telephone with the round dial in the middle and the holes in it with numbers showing through.

The floor was a magnificent display of polished granite in diamond shaped black and white tiles in a mosaic pattern. Either side of the hallway doors led off to a study and a room that looked like a prayer room cum quiet room. *Probably the church's equivalent of a police interview room.*

To the centre of the hall was a staircase made of solid yew wood, dividing left and right half way up leading to more stairs up to the next floor. An ornate banister with rails of ivory coloured twisted wood with small figurines decorated the stairway.

To the right of the stairs in the hallway another door led into the kitchen which looked as if it had received some degree of modernisation in the early seventies. Frank felt like he had stepped back in time, his face betrayed his thoughts as he turned towards Ted's grinning face.

"Tell you what Ted, Arthur Negus would have a field day in here you know."

The reference to the elderly expert from the Antiques Road show was not lost on Ted.

"Come on now Frank you need to get up to speed, things have moved on, its all David Dickinson and Bargain Hunt now don't'yer know?" he said laughing.

Ted ushered Frank into the sitting room and disappeared to make the tea.

Frank sat in one of the three armchairs and studied the room. The blackened wooden floorboards were almost completely covered with a huge vulgar looking rug with most of its tassels missing. Stained Oakwood cupboards filled the walls on two sides of the room with bookshelves fit to bursting with leather and cloth bound books emblazoned with gold leaf lettering.

The magnolia painted walls were so high it reminded Frank of an experience he'd had as a child inside the giant's house at a funfair in Southport. One wall was covered in photographs portraying the history of all the ministers who had served the parish. In the corner stood a nest of tables covered in cream coloured lace doilies and various small porcelain figures. An ugly looking vase containing some dead flowers occupied the single window ledge.

Either side of the vase there were three 8" x 10" picture frames with photographs of Father Maloney and the two other ministers currently residing at the house. There was a rattling of cups and saucers as Ted returned from the kitchen.

"Sorry about the wait. Here we are now Frank, a nice cup of tea." He plonked the tray with a jug of milk, a pot of tea and a plate of biscuits onto an oval shaped wooden coffee table in the centre of the room. Frank stifled a yawn.

"I have been admiring your rogues gallery, are those other two your co- conspirators?" Ted was taken back for a second, but laughed when he realised what Frank was referring to.

"Oh you mean those? Yes, that's Father Paul Francis on the left and the other one is our Curate, Andrew McClelland. He' not been well lately; he's off on an extended sabbatical in Scotland. I'm not sure when we will see him again. Father Francis is visiting one of our parishioners in hospital, seems to be an awful lot of illness around lately."

Ted poured two cups of tea from the china pot.

"So Frank how's the job treating you?" he asked obviously somewhat nervous about coming straight to the point.

"Oh, so so, you know how it is, the usual, too much to do, too little time, not enough manpower. Apart from that everything 's fine."

"And how's Hilary and the wee boy...err... Cram, that's his name, right?"

Frank wanted to tell Ted all about his weekend with Cram and the whole thing with Hilary and Michael but decided against it.

"Listen Ted, I did what you asked me to, I've watched the tape, and I think I know what you're going to ask me to do and I have to say right now bef...."

Ted raised his hand in an attempt to intervene before he could finish.

"Frank... Frank... Sshh...hang on a minute, just let me tell you what I think before you shut out my suggestion. Just give me a minute to explain."

Frank grabbed a handful of biscuits with his tea and sat back in the armchair to listen. It was going to be a long night.

***

Frank left Father Maloney at the Presbytery around eight thirty and went home via the Pizza Parlor on Aigburth Road. The coffee and biscuits had taken the edge off his appetite but he knew he would be hungry by ten o clock and he could never go to sleep on an empty stomach. When he got home he sat watching the television while he ate his pizza.

Although he sat and stared at the TV screen, his own thoughts were drowning out the sound, as if it had been muted. He was mentally preparing a list of things he needed to do.

The thoughts were lined up inside his head like racehorses waiting behind the starting line in the 1.30 at Aintree. He knew if he didn't write them all down before he went to bed he would be awake all night tossing and turning with the list of things galloping round inside his head. He got up and made himself a mug of tea grabbing a notebook and pen from the kitchen drawer while he waited for the kettle to boil.

When he finally started to write, his thoughts poured out over the paper in random order. He would sort the finishing order out later, for now he just need to get them out of his head. He had filled both sides of two sheets from the notebook and the kettle had boiled twice before he finally made his tea. He felt better already. Tomorrow he would get in early and brief the lads.

Chapter 14

Angela Perriman worked as an accountant in the pay section for Costco, the huge discount wholesale warehouse in Liverpool off Waterloo Road and Bath Street opposite Princes Half Tide Dock. Most of Angela's work colleagues at Costco described her as a bit of a "loner", and would say things like "She kept herself to herself most of the time, a quiet woman," and "she was a rather plain woman, looked a lot older than her twenty-nine years."

Angela worked the equivalent of five days a week with a half day on Friday and came in for a few hours on a Saturday afternoon to do the books. Tony Barker was her line manager and he was keeping a close eye on her. He had been monitoring her performance recently and had the impression that she was suffering from a bout severe depression. His suspicions were confirmed via the office grapevine when another member of staff found a half empty bottle of tablets in the ladies toilets.

The label on the bottle was printed with the name of the drug *Desipramine* and its brand name *Norpramine*, with dosage instructions underneath. The name Angela Perriman was typed on the label. The rumour round the office was now official. Gossip mongerers spread the news, *she's definitely a bit of a nutter, and no wonder she was always so fucking quiet. Doped up on Prozac, who wouldn't be?* All of this of course, only reinforced the other rumour, the one about the time that she had allegedly tried to commit suicide.

Angela had gone home on Friday looking tired and unhappy. Much to Tony's surprise she'd come in on the Saturday, but she didn't look well and there had been no discernible improvement in her demeanour. He was getting increasingly worried about her state of health. He didn't share in the office gossip about her. As far as he was concerned Angela was a good worker and a solid, reliable accountant. It was his responsibility to make sure he took the appropriate action as her line manager to make sure she was treated fairly and given as much help as she needed.

Following the weekend shortly after she'd arrived for work on Monday he talked to her and expressed his concerns for her well-being. He arranged a meeting for Tuesday at eleven am so that they could discuss her progress at work as part of a general welfare chat. She was very upset and had gone home early crying. On her way home she hadn't noticed the car following behind her.

For the past two months, without her ever realizing it, someone had been following her almost everywhere she went whether by car or on foot. Whenever she had been out walking around the shops in Liverpool city centre or around the area of Crosby Green in West Derby where she lived, a man had been following her, creeping behind her like a shadow. Everywhere she went he was behind her, watching and making notes of everything she did, gathering information until he was satisfied he could predict her every move. His philosophy was that all people without exception are creatures of habit rarely straying outside their comfort zone.

The Redeemer had followed the woman home from work many times before. Today she almost caught him by surprise by leaving work earlier than normal but he easily caught up with her as she drove off. After all he practically knew the route she took home as well as she did. He kept a good distance behind her along the West Derby Road, safe in the knowledge that she was going straight home.

She turned off the main road and then turned left towards her house. Certain she would not be going anywhere but home, he parked his car a few hundred metres round the corner from her house. He waited several minutes before walking past her house to confirm that the car was still on the drive and that lights were on in the house. He could see the blue coloured flickering of the television bouncing off the walls inside her living room, she was definitely home.

As soon as he satisfied himself that she was in for the night he walked back to his car and drove back to his flat in Toxteth to prepare himself. He knew the time was right, because tonight wouldn't be the first time he had been to her house. He'd done his homework. It never ceased to amaze him just how much you could find out about a person by simply plowing through the stuff people threw away. The information he'd been able to discover and record on this woman was infinite.

Many times over the last few months he had examined the contents of her wheelie bin and recorded his findings. He knew where she worked, how long she'd been there, how much she earned a month and how much money she had in her bank account. He had also discovered what she spent it on. He knew that she drank between three and five bottles of wine per week, one or two of which she would probably drink tonight, maybe because she was more depressed after returning to work after the weekend.

He knew which pub she went to, *alone more often than not*, how much it took to get her drunk and what her tipple was. He knew that that she snacked heavily on crisps and other quick fix comfort foods. He had found empty brown prescription bottles in her bin and used an Internet search engine to confirm that Norpramine was prescribed as an anti-depressant.

Over a period of weeks he had followed her round the supermarket where she shopped. Sometimes he made sure he was in the queue behind her as she emptied the contents of her shopping trolley onto the conveyor belt so was able to see what she bought and when she bought it. Other times he stood pretending to read the "For sale" notices on the boards opposite the tills, casually observing what she had in her trolley as she walked by. People are creatures of habit and this woman was no different, now he could practically recite from memory what would be in her shopping trolley from one week to the next. He'd found the shopping receipts in her rubbish to confirm it.

From his observations of her buying what she needed and from his forays into the contents of her bin, he had found out the most important piece of information, the time when her periods were expected. Using all of this information he was able to work out when she was likely to be the most fertile.

Earlier in the week he had re-checked the contents of her rubbish, confirming that he was right. By his calculations she was in the early stages of her ovulation cycle, this after all was the reason why, on this night he was going to visit her. Now *her time* had come and why in several hours from now he would be back at the house. Tonight he would be entering her comfort zone, the man calling himself *The Redeemer* was going to visit Angela Perriman.

Chapter 15

The torrential rain smashed off the pavements shattering like yellow diamonds under the streetlights. He was soaked, and now in the faint drizzle, steam rose through his clothes from the heat of his body. He was sure he had not been seen as he crept around the back, the rain had kept neighbors and dog walkers at home in front of the television. The bushes had not protected him from the rain as well as he'd hoped for.

Midnight, the lights in the house had gone out one by one, all except the bedside light she used for reading. His previous two missions had gone like clockwork. Tonight would be no different. He needed to be sure there were no signs of movement from within the house. He waited. Patience was the key to his success.

The odds were that she'd be fast asleep and wouldn't even notice the bedside light go out when he flipped the mains switch in the garage. On his way to the back of the house he'd checked out the side garage door confirming there had been no change since his last visit. Once the mains switch in the garage had been knocked off he would simply wait for a response.

He'd formulated the plan months ago knowing exactly what he would do in any situation. No response meant that she was fast asleep and he would be able to enter the house without wondering whether she was lying awake listening to his every move. Not that there would be much noise anyway. He was sure of that; many times he had practiced what he was about to do at his own home. The technique for opening the patio doors had worked every time.

Once he was inside the house the plan would unfold just like it had in his mind so many times before. For almost an hour he'd been huddled against the back wall of the house amongst the rhododendron bushes. It was time.

He moved slowly, methodically making his way round to the side of the house to the garage. The side door of the garage was never locked; it opened effortlessly without a sound. He took the tiny penlight from his pocket using the small beam of light to scan the concrete floor making sure there were no objects he could trip over on his way to the mains fuse box. He found a few old rags lying on a bench and used them to dry his hands, the last thing he needed was to be connected up to the national grid as he flipped the switch on the mains fuse box. Now was the time he'd waited for, the waiting was over, now became reality. His heart quickened with excitement at the thought.

He reached up to the fuse box on the wall, unscrewed the two plastic wing nuts and lifted the cover to reveal the switches. The switch to the right would cut off the whole of the electricity supply to the house. His heart thumped in his chest as his fingers took hold of the switch; there was a faint click as he pushed it upwards. Silence. He closed the door behind him and walked slowly round to the opposite side of the garage and waited behind the hedge. *Patience.*

The beauty of his plan was that it could be aborted without detection at any stage to be resumed at a later date if anything went wrong. He ticked off the possibilities in his mind. If she *had* been awake reading, she may have got up and tried to turn on the main bedroom light, at which point she would have discovered that there was a problem with the power supply.

She could have gone into the garage to check the fuse box. If she did come outside he could always take her down here, an action he had considered, but was not part of his plan. The success of his operation was dependent on entering the house undetected.

Taking her down here would be far too risky anyway, there would be a struggle, he could hurt her, she might escape, screams would alert the neighbours, it was out of the question. *Don't even think about it, deep breaths, patience.* If she came outside to investigate, he would remain hidden, waiting until she went back inside before making his escape. This way he could re-launch his plan in a few weeks time. He looked at his watch, it had been fifteen minutes since he'd turned off the power and there was no sign of her.

He crept out from behind the hedge and went to the front of the house to check the window of the bedroom where she slept. The light in her room had gone out and she hadn't even noticed. As he suspected she was probably in a deep wine induced sleep, making his job all the easier. The rain had stopped for the time being, but the distant rolls of thunder meant that it would probably return soon and could wake her. Time to move onto phase two of his plan.

He walked to the back of the house. The tools inside the canvas equipment bag he carried with him were made from a tough lightweight polyurethane material, especially designed not to damage or mark the UPVC framework surrounding the patio doors. Holding the penlight in his mouth he used the tools to lever the patio door upwards freeing it from its locking mechanism. His practice had paid off. It lifted without a sound. Once the door was raised up and in position he placed both hands onto the side support, leaned against the window just enough to ease the door inwards. He slid one hand through the gap he had created, took hold of the door handle and pushed it upwards. Now completely free the door slid it effortlessly to the right, opening just enough for him to be able to step through into the lounge. He entered the room and paused for breath, no need to rush, there was plenty of time.

He knew the burglar alarm was rarely set and never when she was in the house, especially at weekends. You would think that living alone; it would be completely opposite. Think about it, living alone, asleep, the alarm goes off, *what are you* going to do about it? Do you lie still and pray that whoever is in your house is just a burglar, a drug addict maybe, someone after a DVD player to sell just to pay for their next fix. *Or* do you investigate and confront whoever it is, *what would you do*? This lady, this creature of habit chooses not to set the alarm in the hope that the burglar will just leave with whatever they came for and leave her alone.

He waited to see if there were any sounds of movement coming from upstairs. All he could hear was the sound of a clock ticking from somewhere in the living room. He took out his penlight, picked up his bag and made his way from the lounge to the kitchen. A quick look round confirmed what he had thought earlier, one empty wine bottle sat on the kitchen work surface, several crisp packets lay on a plate next to the sink. The leftovers from the *meal for one* pack sat on a tray on the work surface next to the microwave. No sign of a wine glass anywhere and no sign of a dishwasher where she might have put the glass.

She had probably taken her glass up stairs with her, possibly with another bottle of wine; a quick glance inside the swing bin confirmed it.

The cork from a wine bottle nestled on top of the rubbish. The corkscrew was nowhere to be seen. Had she taken it upstairs with her to open the second bottle? *No, people don't do that.* He crept from the kitchen into the living room, shining his penlight on to the coffee table, there was the corkscrew with the second cork still entwined on it. This was going to be a piece of cake; she was probably blind drunk if not comatose. He would still have to use the chemicals he had brought with him to immobilize her completely, he could not have her waking up and interfering with his plan. He moved back into the kitchen.

He needed some space to spread out his equipment, the work surfaces were in a mess and he didn't want to risk any noise moving things around. He took a large tea towel from the radiator and placed it on the floor, kneeled down and undid the tassels on his bag, *no noisy zips or clicking buckles allowed here.* Piece by piece he took out what he needed and laid them in order on the tea towel. First he took out the small-insulated thermos flask, followed by the sterile plastic tubing. Then came the cloth flannelette and the brown glass bottle containing the chloroform. Next he carefully unscrewed the lid from the thermos flask. Inside the flask was the large plastic hypodermic syringe surrounded by the warm gel pack, which he had heated up earlier to exactly the right temperature.

Finally he had all that he needed in order to perform his task; he was ready to do what he had been waiting so patiently for. He placed all the items he needed with him inside his pockets making sure he kept both hands free. Nerves jangling, he sneaked silently from the kitchen into the hallway leading to the stairs. The stairs were covered in a thick layer of carpet deadening the sound of his footsteps as he slowly, methodically climbed the stairs. To avoid the nasty surprise of a floorboard creaking under his weight he used his hands to distribute some of his weight on to the banisters either side of the stairway, keeping his feet to the edges of each step. As he climbed the stairs he concentrated on keeping his breathing and heart rate under control, listening for the slightest sound as he went. He reached the top of the stairs and turned left onto the landing.

In front of him there were doors leading to other bedrooms and the bathroom. The one he wanted was partially open. Through the slight gap in the door he could see the faint glow of the street lighting outside. Just enough light filtered through the curtains enabling him to see inside the room. He could hear the deep sound of her breathing. She was fast asleep. Next to her on the bedside table with the pale light of the streetlamp reflecting off the glass was the other bottle of wine. Next to the bottle was a small brown prescription bottle. He looked to the bed where she lay, barely covered by the duvet, her chestnut shoulder length hair splaying across her pillow.

He knelt down and took the bottle containing the chloroform from his coat pocket and placed it with the flannelette cloth on the carpet in front of him. He laid the plastic hypodermic syringe containing his own carefully deposited semen next to it. He glanced quickly at his watch; it would all be over in the next twenty-five minutes. He was about to execute phase three of his plan and he knew that once this phase was initiated there was no going back; he would have to see it through to completion. He had considered the possibilities of the door creaking on its hinges, or noise from the door dragging along the carpet as he pushed it open, *although judging by the amount of dim light showing underneath the door, this was unlikely.*

If she woke up he would have to be quick. He carefully unscrewed the lid on the bottle of chloroform, held the flannelette over the end and tipped it up. The instant blast of chloroform almost caught him by surprise as the liquid soaked into the cloth.

Quickly replacing the lid on the bottle he picked up the syringe containing the semen and placed it between his lips. If she struggled he would need one hand free to restrain her while he held the cloth tightly against her mouth and nose. Gently without a sound, he pushed the door wider open. Like a cat stalking its prey one foot at a time he crept towards the bed, his hands held out in front of him ready to pounce if she moved. In the dim light filtering through the curtains, he could see she had drunk almost all of the wine in the bottle on her bedside table and the glass was empty. The book that she'd been reading lay next to her head on the bed. She had fallen asleep reading; drifted off into a sleep so deep she was almost unconscious. He was three feet away from her, still no sound, two feet and no movement; it was all going to plan.

Now standing over her he watched her chest rise and fall. He felt the warm draft and could smell the wine on her breath. She slept so peacefully she looked like an angel. The act of placing the cloth over her mouth and nose was swift and graceful; the chloroform had an instant affect. He had rehearsed this part so many times it was surreal, the free hand was not required, there was no struggle, she merely passed from her semi conscious wine induced stupor gently into complete unconsciousness. By his calculations he had less than ten minutes to do what he needed to do next. *Still don't need to rush this,* no need to be rough. He placed the cloth into his pocket and walked around to the end of the bed.

Her legs were exposed from her knees downwards. He gently lifted the duvet and slid it up towards her hips exposing her buttocks. There was no nightdress to get in the way; only a pair of loose fitting silk panties covered the areas that he now needed to access.

This could not have worked out better; he would not even have to remove her knickers for this part of the process. Her legs were sleek and bronzed, completely hairless. He gently eased them apart and was surprised at how loose and heavy they were. Like dead weights. He placed the legs into a position, which if she had been awake and upright would have given the appearance that she was squatting to take a pee. The vagina was completely exposed. With the thumb and forefinger of his left hand he gently parted the labia of her vagina and took the syringe from his mouth with his right hand.

The five-inch syringe was wet and moist from his saliva. The plunger was already depressed up to the point in which it came into contact with the semen. One quick push would see the silky milk coloured liquid containing his sperm shoot like an ejaculation on its way to the uterus. From then on it was down to nature to do what it did best. His sperm count was high so the chances of success were pretty good.

He slid the syringe carefully into the vagina, gently feeling for any resistance along the way, adjusting the angle and applying just enough pressure for the syringe to find its own way, no need to force it; *he did not want to hurt her.* Gradually the full length of the syringe had buried itself up to where his fingers held the plunger. He glanced up the bed towards her pillow; the faint light bouncing off her face showed no signs of discomfort.

He kept staring at her face as he pushed the plunger, still no movement, and no change in facial expression, although a deeper breath emitted from her nostrils causing them to flare slightly. He couldn't take his eyes off her face as he held the syringe in place with the plunger fully depressed; he counted the seconds in his head, 29, 30, 31…48, 49, 50. For two minutes he held the syringe in place allowing the semen enough time to begin its journey, carrying his sperm to the waiting fertile eggs.

Before he removed the syringe he looked at his watch again to confirm how long he had before the effects of the chloroform wore off. He had eight minutes to leave the room collect his equipment and make his way out of the house. He could do it in five; he had walked through this phase in his own house enough times he could do it with three minutes to spare.

He removed the syringe from her vagina and placed it into his pocket. Softly he drew her legs back together, repositioned the gusset of her panties to the original position and pulled the duvet back down over her legs, still keeping parts of them exposed. He didn't want her to get too warm so that she'd be tossing and turning for the rest of the night. If she got too hot she might even get up which wouldn't be good. The longer she lay still the more chance his sperm had of reaching its target, of nature taking its course.

He walked around the bed to the lamp and checked to see what type of switch it had, he was in luck, it was the silent slide type which you could make dimmer or brighter as opposed to the horrible *clicky* type which could be heard from downstairs when you switched it off. He slid the lever on the lamp to the off position and smiled. What would he have done if the switch had been the clicky type?

Easy, just unscrew the bulb half a turn, just enough so that it lifted from the contacts and would not come back on when he restored the power in the garage.

Why should he be bothered about restoring the power any way? *Why did he not just leave the power off?* Well there just may be a possibility that he might have to perform this operation again and he wanted the least amount of disturbance necessary. Besides why cause her the inconvenience of having to call someone in to sort the problem with her electricity supply out, *and of course he wouldn't want her to have the hassle of sorting out a defrosted freezer.*

He left the room pulling the door behind him so that it was just as it had been when he arrived. His eyes were well adjusted to the dim light by now and they focused on the bottle that he had left on the landing. He picked it up and just as carefully as he had climbed them, made his way down the stairs and into the kitchen.

He looked at his watch, still six and a half minutes to go. He picked up his bag from the kitchen floor, replaced the tea towel on the radiator, *slightly left of center*, remembering every detail, as it was when he came in. He had one final look around to make sure he had not missed anything, made his way back into the lounge and stepped out through the door onto the patio.

The air outside was cold against the beads of sweat on his forehead, cold enough for him to shiver now that his task was almost over. The door slid effortlessly back into its slots without a sound. He leaned against the bottom of the door and used his fingers to maneuver it back into position, the top slid backwards and with a gentle clunk it closed.

He picked up his bag and headed back towards the garage to restore the power. Inside he reached up to the fuse box and pushed the switch, then closed the lid turning the wing nuts to lock it into place. Seconds later he was out and away, as he left he turned to look at the front bedroom window. There were no lights coming on and no signs of movement inside the house.

The street for as far as he could see was clear; there was no traffic about at this time of the morning. As stealthily as he had arrived he left the Perriman house and walked the half-mile route back along Mill Lane to Queens Drive. He climbed into his car parked at the back of the Jolly Miller Pub where he had left it. It would take him roughly half an hour to get to his flat in Toxteth, time for a quick scrub down, a bite to eat and off to bed for some sleep.

He would be back several times over the next few days to check up on things, he would continue to follow her and watch where she went. He would be interested to see if and when she went to see her doctor at the Ellergreen Medical Centre on Carr Lane. He knew when she was next due to have her periods, a simple visit to the site and an inspection of the contents of her bin would confirm whether or not his mission had been successful. In the meantime he also needed to prepare himself for tonight. The fifth woman on his list was Margaret Smith. Tonight would be her turn for redemption. *The Redeemer*'s mission was gathering momentum.

Chapter 16

It had been a sleepless night, Frank's mind wouldn't switch off; the Grand National had been waiting to start. Twice throughout the night he had cursed the angry wind blowing off the Mersey, which only seemed to infuriate it even more. The wind made him uneasy, his bed was a mess. Tuesday morning saw the return of the rain well before his alarm clock went off. He gave up on sleep and trudged wearily into the bathroom.

He looked at his reflection in the mirror; it wasn't pretty, the horses had left their marks. He let out a yawn and rubbed his eyes feeling more tired than when he had gone to bed. The usual ablutions didn't do much to help.

After a quick breakfast he scanned through the list of the things he had written down from the night before and added a few more thoughts that had raced around his head in the night. He threw the breakfast plates in the sink and left for work.

As he approached the junction of Ullet Road and Park Road in Toxteth, the seven o-clock news came on the radio; it was still pitch black outside. Torrential rain mixed with sleet and snow blasted his car from every angle forming small drifts of slush to pile up either side of the windscreen. The traffic was in chaos, at the rate he was going it was going to take him an hour at least to get into work. Headlights from oncoming cars highlighted the exhaust fumes from traffic all around him. The rain magnified and distorted by the sickly yellow glow of the streetlights made the exhaust fumes appear to dance above flames.

Even with the wipers on double speed Frank could hardly see anything through the windscreen. The heater on full blast was drowning out the voice of someone on the Merseyside Breakfast Show trying to tell him what he already knew; traffic moving into the city centre was slow.

As he crawled along Park Place and St James Place he saw the traffic backed up all the way from Canning Place and Wapping to the corner of Upper Parliament Street.

"Bollocks to this" he swore and instead of turning left he gradually inched his way out into the traffic, forcing a path over the cross roads into Great George Street inciting the wrath of several other motorists as he did so.

"Yeah same to you to mate." The other driver he had cut up on the main road was making hand signals that were definitely not in the learner drivers' handbook. He edged his way into Great George Street and turned left along St James Street. From here he made better progress passing in between a myriad of small industrial units and backstreet warehouses. Transit vans and flatbed trucks were parked in every side street with the hazard lights flashing. Men, supposed to be loading or unloading the vans were sheltered in doorways drinking scalding hot coffee from polystyrene cups and smoking roll ups. He could see the Police HQ in the distance at the end of Park Lane and Paradise Street. He looked at his watch, a quarter to eight.

" Three quarters of a fucking hour to do what normally takes less than twenty minutes?" He pulled in through the back gates of the HQ and nodded to the security guard without winding his window down.

As he filled in the staff register at reception he scanned the list of names of people who had already signed in. The usual suspects were on the list, but what struck him most was that everyone of his team were already in. DS Barry Ferguson was on the ball as usual, he knew something was up and the adhoc meeting at McDonalds last night confirmed what Frank was thinking, *they knew something was brewing.*

As he walked into the main office there was a burst of activity with everyone moving about like he had walked into a film set where the director had just shouted *"and action."* Phones were suddenly being picked up, computer screens were being studied intently and large bundles of files and papers shuffled about from overflowing in trays.

The only person who made eye contact was Barry. Frank held up his hand indicating with two fingers a message that his DS would understand. Barry looked towards DC Mark Roberts and coughed.

"Fledge get us two coffees willyer mate, bring them through to the boss's office soon as you like."

"Sarge." The Fledge dutifully complied, disappearing in the direction of the kitchen. Frank looked towards DC Bob Turner.

"Bob do us a favour mate?"

Bob was up; ready and eager like a red setter.

"Yes Boss?"

"Nip into the incident room and drag one of them portable TV combos into my office."

"Bob on Boss, no probs,"

Frank turned and disappeared into his office with Barry close behind. Seconds later Bob was banging on the door with his foot, slightly out of breath, gripping the TV combo with both hands.

"Cheers Bob" Barry took the TV off him and was plugging it in as he left.

Bob left the office and headed straight for the kitchen where Mark was making the brews.

"So what do you reckon then, what's the Boss got so wound up about?"

DC Mark Roberts was stirring milk and sugar into the coffee as he spoke.

"Haven't got a Scooby do mate, but one things for sure, we are gonna find out real rapid. If it's a big job and needs all of us on it we are gonna need some help. I'm strapped as it is."

"Yeh me too", Bob agreed, "what we gonna do?"

Mark shrugged his shoulders. "I spoke to Barry about it last night, he reckons the Boss's got it in hand, some bird from Mather Avenue, Danielle Vasquez. Do you know her?"

"Daz? Yeah I know her; she took me through my probationer's course at Bruche Police Training Centre. She's all right, a good egg. She'll do well here an its about time you lost your L plates."

"Cheers mate, get the door for us will you."

The Fledge placed the mugs of coffee onto a tray and disappeared in the direction of Frank's office. As he approached the door flew open and Barry let him in.

"Cheers Fledge, just stick them on the table in the corner mate."

Frank watched as the Fledge precariously lowered the steaming hot cups onto the table.

"Cheers Fledge, do us a favour will you mate, you and Bob, don't go disappearing off anywhere in the next hour or two."

"No problem Boss, I think Barry's already..." Barry shot him a look.

"Err that's all for now Fledge, shut the door on yer way out, cheers."

"Sorry Sarge... I err..."

"Door Fledge" The Fledge sloped off and shut the door.

Frank smiled at Barry as he sat down opposite him.

" You keeping these lads on a tight reign Barry?"

Barry smiled back, picked up his coffee and downed a third of it in one gulp.

"You know the score Boss, cruel to be kind and all that."

"Okay, let's get down to business. It doesn't take the brains of an archbishop to suss out I've been pondering over something the past few days."

Barry leaned forward, elbows resting on his knees.

"You could say that. I've been wondering when you would get around to filling me in. What, with last night and you locking yourself in the incident room, the Fledge was bricking it! I've had the lads prepped for nearly a week."

"Yeah I know, I saw them all in McDonalds last night." Frank looked at Barry, waiting for his reaction.

Barry looked at him, *how the fuck did he know we were in McDonalds last night?*

"Its okay Barry I wasn't keeping tabs or anything like that, I just had one or two things to do before going home and stopped by McDonalds to grab a bite to eat, saw you all in there and decided not to spoil the party."

Barry shook his head and sat back in his chair. Frank laughed aloud.

"Pure coincidence Barry, nothing else I can assure you, anyway like I said, down to business."

Frank opened his briefcase and pulled out the notes he'd made last night. He laid them out on the table and placed the videocassette from Ted next to them.

"Before I continue," said Frank, "everything we talk about for the moment is officially, unofficial." Barry knew what this meant. If this was a case of some sort, for the time being anyway, it did not exist. Preliminary enquiries, a bit of digging, nothing recorded on official forms, everything kept low key. No talk outside the department, the rest of the lads in the team would be tasked but not given the full reasons why. Even the DCI would be kept out of the picture until it became a need to know basis.

"Right Boss, got the picture, where do we start?" For the best part of two hours Frank briefed Barry on the situation and discussed his plans. Frank gave a running commentary while they watched the video, filling in the blanks. As soon as the video was finished they drew up a tasking list prioritising the actions for the rest of the team. No one interrupted them or left the building. Just as Barry got up to leave, the phone rang. Frank answered it after the first ring indicating to Barry with his hand to wait.

"Hello, DI Carroll speaking." It was the DCI. Two minutes later Frank put the phone down. Barry had picked up on the conversation whilst pretending not to listen.

"That was the DCI, he wants me to attend a case conference in his office in half an hour. The Chief Supers gonna be there. Might be a good time for me to plug the case for getting in the extra bod I've been after, what do you think?"

Barry agreed. "No time like the present eh Boss. What do want me to tell the lads?"

"Same as before, no one leaves the building without me knowing about it. Get everyone in the incident room for about two-ish." Barry left the office to brief the team. Frank looked at his watch, it was already a quarter past eleven, he had fifteen minutes to get his case notes together and prepare himself before the case conference.

By the time Frank reached the DCI's office the Chief Super was already sat in the corner of the office drinking tea. Frank knocked on the door and entered.

"Morning Sir, Boss."

The DCI motioned towards the tea and biscuits Janice had brought in earlier. Frank helped himself while the DCI filled him in.

"Chief Inspector Munroe sends her apologies, says she's tied up in court all day. She asked if she could meet up with you tomorrow morning so's you can bring her up to speed."

Frank opened his diary and made a note to ring her first thing in the morning.

"She also told me to tell you not to rely on getting the usual amount of support from uniformed division this week, half her staff are down with the dreaded lurgy. They are absolutely strapped."

Frank looked towards the Chief Super who promptly looked down into his teacup as if he had not heard what had been said. Frank grabbed the moment.

"Well that is something I was hoping to talk to you about today Boss, I've got a proposal I would like to make," he said raising his voice slightly.

The Chief Super looked up from his tea.

"Maybe that is something we can discuss later, after we have got the case conference over, is that all right with you Andy?" The DCI looked towards Frank looking for confirmation that this was acceptable.

"That okay with you Frank?" Frank nodded his head at Andy and spoke deliberately in the Chief Super's direction.

"Fine Sir, Yes no problem, shouldn't take more than five or ten minutes, I really just need the nod to go ahead that's all." Frank knew that by the time the case conference was over the Chief Super would be itching to get away and there was a good chance he would give the nod just to get away. He made a mental note to drag the case conference out as long as possible without kicking the arse out of it.

After an hour and a half the case conference was drawing to a close. It was almost lunchtime. The Chief Super was sat fiddling with his hat and looking like he was about to make a break for it. Frank seized the opportunity.

"If you like sir I can ask Janice to get some sandwiches brought up and a fresh pot of tea." The Chief Super smiled appreciatively but looked uncomfortable.

"No, thank you Frank, that won't be necessary, I'll get myself something from the canteen on the way back to my office." The DCI deliberately kept quiet, he was looking at something interesting in the bottom of his teacup. Frank took his cue.

"Well Sir this is what I'd like to propose."

Four minutes later the Chief Super left the DCI's office pausing only to nod his farewell. "Andy", he said to the DCI and shook hands with Frank as he left.

DCI Andy Williams could hardly contain himself.

"Well done Frank, excellent job, couldn't have hijacked him better myself. You get what you wanted?"

Frank smiled at his boss. "Sure did Boss, thanks for setting it up, all that about Chief Inspector Munroe and half her staff down with the lurgy swung it I reckon" The DCI's face went a touch pink around the cheeks and cracked with a sheepish looking smile.

"Oh that? That was a load of old bollocks Frank. One thing you can count on for certain, the only thing the Chief Super hates more than me getting on his back about staffing, is Joanne Munroe getting her oar in as well."

Frank stood up and they shook hands, he had to take his hat off to him; he hadn't got to the rank of DCI without some skullduggery along the way.

Something Frank's father used to say came back to him, *Son,* he used to say, *Old age and treachery will always overcome youth and skill.* A lesson Frank never forgot.

"I guess not eh? Well thanks anyway." Frank gathered his notes and turned to leave.

The DCI reached for his phone as Frank left.

"Anytime Frank, keep up the good work." Frank left the office and went to ring Daz with the good news.

Shortly after Frank had left for the DCI's office DS Barry Ferguson had called the team together in the incident room. Bob was the first to speak.

"Come on then Barry fill us in, what's the big *hush hush* about?"

Barry looked at the faces of Mark and Bob and recognised the look of anticipation. Barry was lot older than both of them; they looked to him as a kind of father figure, with total respect for his age and experience.

At just under six foot tall, his thick bushy hair was an even colour gray all round with 70's style sideboards to match. His face had a ruddy complexion and looked as worn as his clothes.

"Okay! Okay! Hold yer horses will yer, all in good time." He paused for effect, milking the moment, eyes like pools of crystal blue water from a background of gray stone.

"The boss says he'll brief you *thisavvo* in the incident room. Be there for two pm."

Chapter 17

Tony Barker was sat behind his desk in his office at Costco staring at the phone almost willing it to ring. Angela Perriman his accounts officer had not turned up for work and subsequently missed the appointment for her welfare and progress meeting. He had just left a fourth message on her answer phone at home. Her works mobile sat on his desk in front of him with a flat battery. A quiet woman she may be, a bit on the sad side possibly, but unreliable she definitely was not.

The fact that she had not rang in sick or returned any of his calls worried him. He picked up the phone and dialed the speed dial number for personnel.

"Hi Sally its Tony here, could you do us a favour, dig out Angela Perriman's home address for me and bring it through as soon as you can...yes, two minutes that's fine, cheers bye." He was contemplating ringing Angela's home number again when there was a knock on the door. Sally walked in carrying a photocopied printout of Angela's home address.

"Thanks" he said as she left.

He knew the area of Tuebrook and West Derby well enough to picture how long it would take him to get there. Lunchtime would be as good a time as any to make the three or four mile journey over to her house. He waited for an hour for her to return his calls before leaving for the car park. It took him fifteen minutes to drive across the top of town and onto the West Derby Road. The Liverpool A to Z lay on the passenger seat next to him. He'd scribbled some rough directions on the back of the photocopied printout with her address on it before leaving the office.

The remains of his pre packed sandwich and a half empty styrofoam cup of coffee sat amongst the sheets of paper. The A5049 led him straight to Queens Drive where he turned right and then swung a left past the school and into Mill Lane. According to his map Crosby Green was somewhere on the left.

Two minutes later he pulled up outside her house. The rain was lashing down again and he was reluctant to leave the warmth of the car. He sat and finished what was left of his sandwiches, drank his lukewarm coffee and lit a cigarette. Through the rain spattered passenger door window he surveyed the house. It was a well maintained neat little property with mature shrubs and bushes all around the house.

From what he could see, the downstairs blinds were all closed and the upstairs curtains were drawn. Her car was parked on the drive. It was quite conceivable that if she was ill and she had been to the doctors she would not have received his calls, *she could be ill in bed with the volume turned down on her phone,* he thought. He finished his cigarette and pulled his mobile phone from his coat pocket. He punched in the number from the photocopied printout. Four rings, five, six. The BT standard answer phone message cut in and he hung up.

He stared at the house again; the rain on the windows distorted his view. *Were there any lights on?* He pressed the button on the door to his right and the passenger door window slid down with a drone; rain sucked its way in drenching the A to Z in seconds. He knew he had no choice; he would have to get out now that he was here. He left the car unlocked and made a dash for the front door. He pressed the doorbell and let it ring for a good few seconds before releasing it. If she was awake she must have heard it, if she wasn't it should have woken her up.

He waited doing his best to get as close to the door as possible and shelter from the rain. No answer. He rang again. No response. He banged the heavy doorknocker several times while peering through the letterbox. No sign of any activity. He thought about calling her through the letterbox and decided against it. He turned from the door, folded his coat collar up against the rain and headed round the back of the house.

He passed by the back door to the garage and took a cursory glance before moving round the back of the house. Through the kitchen window he could see that she had been home and not cleared up from the night before, but nothing struck him as totally out of the ordinary.

The view from the back patio doors into the dining room showed nothing unusual either. He stood there for several moments wondering what to do. *Maybe the neighbours know where she is?* With this possibility in mind he returned to the front of the house. Just as he emerged from between the garage and the side of the house the neighbours to the left were getting into their car at the top of the drive.

"Excuse me," he said, waving his arms to attract their attention. An elderly man got out of the car and confronted him.

"Err what're you doing if you don't mind me asking?"

Tony spoke in a hurry trying to put the old man at ease.

"Oh Yes sorry, sorry I must have startled you, sorry about that. I'm Tony Barker and I work at Costco with Angela, I was just wondering if you might have seen her, its just that she did not turn up for work this morning and I am a bit worried about her, do you know where she is?"

The old man still looked at him suspiciously.

"So that's her name is it? Well I never knew that. She's a strange one that one, doesn't say hello or good morning, nothing. My wife and I have given up trying to establish neighbourly relations with her, five years she's lived there and we've not spoke the whole time." Tony repeated his question.

"Have you seen her today?" "Or yesterday?" he added.

"No I'm afraid we haven't, sorry, any way have to go, can't stand here in this bloody weather."

The old man sat himself back in the car and waited a while before reversing off the end of the drive. As he got there he wound his window down.

"The wife says phone the police if your worried, they'll be here in a minute they're only up the road."

"Yes, yes thanks I might do just that. Thanks, bye." The car pulled away slowly.

Tony took one last look at the house and got back into his car. The clock on the dash showed it was almost two-o-clock. *Shit! I never thought I'd be out this long.*

He pulled his mobile out and dialed the office number. He spoke to Sally and gave her some story about his car playing up in the bad weather. He told her he would be unavoidably delayed and possibly not back until the morning. She hung up convinced he was having an affair with Ms Perriman and went off to spread the rumour. He started the engine and headed off in the direction of Tuebrook Police Station on West Derby Road. He had no idea what he was going to say to them.

Chapter 18

On the roof of Merseyside Police HQ there is an array of satellite dishes antennas and aerials to such a degree that you could be forgiven for mistaking the building for one of NASA's space launch centres. The equipment on the roof enabled Merseyside Police to digitally send and receive audio and video images to any law enforcement establishment in the world. With the technology available to them, they could tune in to any radio frequency available, cut in on CB radio, Pirate radio stations or any other illegal broadcasters.

Footage from CCTV cameras anywhere in the city could be relayed, viewed and recorded instantly without the need to collect tapes. All of this technology fed straight into the MIT incident room. There were enough telephones and computer systems to accommodate up to a hundred and sixty officers all working at once.

In full swing during the Toxteth riots in 1981 the noise inside the room had been so loud all the officers working the phones had to be fitted with headphone sets so they could hear what was being said to them. The room had been set up like a modern day war planning office. Maps and charts covered every inch of wall space.

Huge tables had been brought in and pushed together to provide a platform for the huge area maps of the city, and Toxteth in particular. There were a series of telescopic sliding screens driven by electronic motors, which at the push of a button would slide across the room dividing it into four separate briefing areas. The push of another button brought down blackout screens covering the windows on two sides of the room. On one of the walls there was a bank of fifteen television screens all connected to the remote video link network.

When they were all on it was like walking into a showroom window of Dixons or Currys. Dry wipe boards, flip charts, smart boards, and Perspex see through screens lined the full length of the room. In the centre of the room there were four ceiling mounted projectors that could be rotated in any direction onto drop down video screens.

During the Toxteth riots, senior officers from Cheshire, Greater Manchester, Lancashire, North Wales, Cumbria and South Yorkshire had been brought in to personally monitor the developments in case similar incidents broke out within their own force area. Nobody expected Brixton in London to be the next to follow suit. Officers from the MET were flown into Speke Airport and were brought to the HQ by helicopter within six hours of the riots kicking off in London.

Such was the capability of the modern day police force. Since 1981 the incident room had been left pretty much the same. A lot of equipment that had been brought in to help deal with the Toxteth riots had remained at the HQ.

DS Barry Ferguson, DC's Mark Roberts and Bob Turner were sat in the far corner of the incident room. Mark had prepped the TV and video for the briefing at two o clock. They were sat round a table with blank notepads, pens and pencils. At ten past two Frank walked into the incident room carrying a handful of files and his briefcase. He walked to the head of the table and as usual chose not to sit. He pulled a handful of notes and the video from the briefcase along with the tasking list he and Barry had drawn up earlier.

Everyone sat up ready to give him their undivided attention, pens and paper at the ready.

"Okay, sorry to have kept you waiting. Before I get started, I would just like to say that the matter we are about to discuss could be something or nothing, I'm hoping it will turn out to be nothing but you never know. But for now I want this kept very low key. Also, before we go any further let's get one thing absolutely clear, the information I am about to share with you is sensitive to say the least. If we handle this wrong a very good friend of mine will be in deep shit. Additionally the department will suffer, with yours truly out on his arse and you lot looking through the Situations Vacant section of the Echo in the not too distant future. Do I make myself clear?"

The team unanimously nodded, giving their assurance the message was understood. For something that could turn out to be *something or nothing,* as their boss had put it, he was being extremely cagey.

"Everything I am about to tell you is as far as you are concerned is strictly unofficial and will remain so unless I say different. This is to be kept between us; no one outside this room gets to hear a dicky bird. For now I am only prepared to give you the bare bones. The less you know for the moment is for your own protection, plus the less you know the less you have got to forget if the shit hits the fan."

He paused to let his words sink in. There was a shuffling of seats while everyone made themselves more comfortable.

"The only thing I am prepared to say at this moment in time is that the subject of this enquiry, is a woman, she is a potential witness to what may turn out to be a serious crime. The problem being that the crime has not as yet been *officially* identified. There was a confused look from everyone. Frank raised his hands.

"Yes I know, I know what you're thinking, but trust me, you'll know as soon as I know. At the end of this briefing Barry and I will hand out the tasks we've allocated to each of you."

Frank continued giving the team a *bare bones* briefing on the background of what was required. If they needed to know more he would decide on what and when they would be told. When he was finished he loaded the videotape into a wall-mounted player. They took notes only when he told them to. When the video finished he paused to see if he had missed anything before he continued.

"Tasking then, Barry will oversee everything and help out where needed. Mark, I want a PNC check on the vehicle seen on the video, a Red Nissan Micra index number KJ02 LFM. I want to know who the woman on the video is. She was driving the vehicle so I'm guessing she is the owner.

I want to know where she lives, where she works, who her friends are and anything else you can find out about her, the usual stuff, shops, hairdressers, GP's surgery, library, the full kit and caboodle, anything you can get."

Barry elbowed Mark who was frantically writing notes like his life depended on it. "Don't panic Fledge I've got a copy already scripted." he whispered.

Frank continued. "Bob," Bob prepared to write. "I want two copies of this video made and the original secured in the back safe for now. I also need a couple of still photographs of the woman taken from the video, get me the best image possible, enhanced blown up, the full monty." Bob just nodded and kept writing.

"Okay Barry, this next bit, I want you to get started on pronto, As soon as you've got a name and address for this woman I want a surveillance team on her to fill in the blanks as previously mentioned. Once we have her movements a friend of mine will approach her and hopefully persuade her to give an official statement. If we get that then we can progress. No statement, no progress, therefore no case and its the end of the matter as far as I'm concerned. As I said before, something or nothing."

At the end of the briefing Frank could see that his team were itching to ask questions. "Okay that's it for now. Questions? DC Bob Turner was the first to ask.

"Boss, this very good friend of yours, it wouldn't be anything to do with the visit you had the other day, you know the guy from the church, Father Maloney?

Frank knew the team had considered this and he had to give them an answer.

"Correct, okay that's it, no more questions. You have got until two pm tomorrow to crack on with what you're being asked to do; we'll meet back here for an update. Thanks for your time"

He gathered his papers and left. The team stayed behind to discuss their plans. Back in his office he gathered his thoughts. It had only been a few days since his weekend with Cram and already the job was beginning to create distance between him and those memories. He swore that as soon as this was over he was going to make more effort to keep in touch.

Chapter 19

Barry was sat at his desk ploughing through paperwork trying to complete the RIPA authorisations for the surveillance team Frank had requested. It was taking forever and he was losing the will to live when the phone rang.

"Good afternoon, Merseyside Police, DS Ferguson."

"This is inspector Phil Taylor from West Derby Police Station, is that you Barry?"

Barry recognised the voice on the other end.

"Yes Phil, what can I do you for?"

"I've been trying to contact DI Carroll but only got his voice mailbox. Janice tells me he is in a meeting, not to be disturbed, any idea what he's up to?"

Barry detected the level of concern in Phil's voice.

"Yes, he's on a case conference, can I help?"

"Yes, tell Frank we've had a drop in at the station, a guy by the name of a... Mr. Tony Barker. He wanted to report that a female colleague of his had not turned up for work, a Miss Angela Perriman. He's her line manager. He sounded genuinely worried about her, some concern over her mental state. He tried to reach her by phone all morning but got no answer. He went round to her house to check on her, her car was on the drive, curtains closed, all doors and windows locked. He spoke to her neighbours but got no joy."

Barry was scribbling notes as he spoke.

"Right okay I've got all that, anything else..."

"Well...because Mr. Barker seemed genuinely concerned for Miss Perriman, I sent two officers round to the address. They had a look around the property and radioed in to confirm what Mr. Barker had said, they believed there was reason for concern. I authorised them to force an entry to the property to investigate further.

Turns out that Mr. Barker was right to be concerned. Angela Perriman was found dead upstairs in her bedroom. At first they suspected it was suicide..."

Barry dropped his pen. "Whoa...hang on a minute Phil, okay Phil, sorry about that, right I'm with you now, carry on, you say it was suicide?"

Phil continued.

"Yeah, according to my officers, there was sufficient evidence to tag it as suicide, they found alcohol, tablets and stuff on the bedside table. I just spoke to them a few minutes ago; one of them is a trained paramedic, worked for Mersey Regional Ambulance before she joined the job. Something about the woman's pallor and facial expression was not quite right. She thinks there could have been foul play, my officers are still at the scene as we speak."

There was another pause. Barry frantically scribbled more notes.

"Anyway, I just wanted to run it by Frank and see what he thought. What do you reckon?"

Barry looked at his notes.

"Right Phil, tell your officers to remain where they are and not to touch anything, stay by the phone, either myself or Frank will ring you in the next five or ten minutes, give us your number."

He wrote Phil's number down at the top of his notes and hung up. Barry checked his watch; it was a quarter to five. He peered in through the window to Frank's office; he still wasn't back. There was no sign of Mark or Bob either so he tried the incident room.

As he approached the foyer adjacent to the incident room he could see the door was open. Frank was stood just inside the door talking to Bob.

Bob saw Barry approaching and indicated with a nod in his direction.

"Boss, Barry to see you."

Frank turned towards Barry and knew from his face instantly, something was up.

"Boss, I need to talk to you, something's just come in from Phil Taylor over at West Derby Lane." He pointed to his notes.

"Okay, I'm just about done here let's go to my office. Bob, crack on mate we'll be back as soon as we're done."

Back in the office Barry briefed Frank on what he had been told by Inspector Taylor. Five minutes later Frank dialed the number at the top of Barry's notes. It answered with the sound of Phil Taylor's voice.

"Inspector Taylor, West Derby Lane Police Station."

Frank kept it brief.

"Phil, Its Frank Carroll, sorry you had trouble reaching me mate. Right I've been briefed. Tell your officers I'll be there in half an hour." They hung up. He looked at Barry and read his thoughts.

"Fancy a trip over to West Derby?"

"Don't mind if I do."

"Okay, give me five minutes to bring Mark and Bob up to speed and we'll be off."

Ten minutes later they were ploughing their way through traffic along Lime Street heading towards West Derby Road. They arrived at the address Phil had given them in twenty-five minutes without the need for the blues and twos. Already it was pitch black outside and raining heavily. They got out of the car and walked up the pathway to the front door, as they approached it opened revealing the two uniformed officers. Frank introduced himself and Barry.

"Sir, Sarge" The male officer said as Frank and Barry stepped inside. They shook hands. Frank spoke first.

"Okay, just run by me what we've got here." The male officer explained what they had found and the female officer told them her suspicions. Frank and Barry were putting on latex rubber gloves while they listened.

"Anybody informed the next of kin?" enquired Frank. The male officer spoke first.

"I don't think so sir, would you like me to..." Frank interrupted before he could finish.

"Tell you what, get on the blower to Inspector Taylor back at the station, and ask him to get in touch with the guy who... what's his name again?"

The male officer pulled out his pocket notebook.

"A Mr. Barker, sir. Mr. Tony Barker, he's her... was her line manager." Frank detected the note of embarrassment.

"Well ask Inspector Taylor to get Mr. Barker to pull the deceased's personnel record, I need a name and address of the next of kin pronto. Oh and ask him to fix up a time when we can come and interview Mr. Barker as well, preferably tomorrow around lunch time-ish."

The two officers nodded and got on with it. Fully briefed Frank and Barry climbed the stairs to the landing and approached the bedroom where the dead woman had been found. Before entering Barry had a quick glance around the room surveying the scene taking in every detail before stepping inside.

Satisfied it was okay to enter Frank moved across to the bedside and looked down at the woman. The duvet appeared to have been kicked or pushed to the bottom of the bed. The woman was scantily dressed in a vest and knickers. Her dark brown eyes were wide open. Looking into them made him uncomfortable. Someone had once told him, *the eyes are the windows to the soul*. If this was the case he was looking right into hers and he couldn't see a thing.

Her skin had taken on a pale gray colour. The look on her face and the way the lines around her eyes were creased displayed a sort of sadness, perhaps *mixed with fear*. Her mouth was fixed half open in a sort of "O" shape as if she had been about to say something and stopped. The lips and the tips of her nostrils had a strange blueness to them.

"What do you reckon to this Barry?"

Barry leaned over to see what Frank was looking at. Frank took out a small torch from inside his coat and shone it inside the mouth. The tongue had not fallen back into the throat to block the airway. He was no expert pathologist but from his limited experience there appeared to be no distinguishing signs of violence or evidence of a struggle. He looked at the bedside table and saw the empty wine bottle next to the small brown plastic bottle of tablets. He crouched down for a closer look and shone his torch on the bottle. Without touching anything he read the label.

"Anti depressant medication, bottle still looks half full." He wondered if Barry was thinking along the same lines as he was.

"You'd think if you were going to commit suicide by overdosing on tablets and alcohol you would go the whole hog and take all the tablets wouldn't you?" said Barry.

"Yep that's just what I was thinking." He shone the torch back to the dead woman's face.

"And here look at this." Barry leaned closer.

"Look around here" Frank said, pointing to the area around the mouth and nose.

"See that sort of pinkish discoloration on the skin around the chin and above the lip?"

"Looks like some kind of rash or something," said Barry.

They both thought it strange that there appeared to be evidence of suffocation or asphyxiation judging by the blueness around the nose and lips and the pale gray complexion, and yet there was a two to three inch area with the discolored reddish tinge to it.

"Okay I've seen enough lets go back downstairs, you brief the two officers, I need to make a phone call."

Barry went downstairs to speak to the officers. At the top of the landing Frank paused, pulled out his mobile phone and dialed the number for MIT. Back at the office Bob picked up the phone.

"Yes Boss?"

Frank issued his instructions.

"Bob, I need you to get onto the coroners office right away. I need the duty pathologist to come to the following address, pronto." Frank waited while Bob made note.

"I also need a forensics team and SOCO down here soon as you like, got that?"

"Yes Boss I'm on it, anything else?"

"No that's it for now, after the Boys in white have done the business I may need to call another meeting, I'll let you know." He rang off.

On the way downstairs he could see Barry talking with the two officers. They turned round as he approached the bottom of the stairs and the female officer spoke to him.

"Sir, we got in touch with Mr. Barker, he didn't need to pull her personnel record, he knows for a fact that there is no next of kin listed. From what we can gather talking to Mr. Barker, Ms Perriman was an only child. To the best of his knowledge, her parents were divorced a long time ago and haven't been in touch since. There is however a number listed as an emergency contact, we rang the number and got a name and address of an elderly lady, lives out near Halewood in Garston."

"Who is she?" asked Frank. The male officer chipped in eager to help.

"Not exactly sure sir, she sounded quite frail on the phone and we didn't want to alarm her any more than we already had." Frank glanced towards Barry.

"Any chance you could rustle up some support? Maybe get a car round there, someone with a sympathetic ear." He turned back to the uniformed officers.

"See if you can get some background on Ms Perriman. You did well to call this one in; your suspicions would appear to be valid. Well done, both of you."

"Thank you sir", they said in unison. The female officer continued.

"We're due to finish our shift in half an hour but if you don't mind sir we'd like to hang around and assist if we can."

Frank understood exactly where they were coming from. They were both keen and eager to see this job pan out in full so that they could learn from it for the future.

"I'm sure if I give your Inspector Taylor a ring, he'll be happy to square away the overtime."

Forty minutes later the duty pathologist arrived from the Coroners Office on Old Hall Street with the SOCO in tow. Within the hour the pathologist confirmed what Frank already knew, exact cause of death unknown but there was sufficient reason to believe it was a suspicious death.

"Can't be certain about the time of death, but she's been dead at least 12 hours."

They would need to get the body back to the morgue where the Coroner would perform a full post mortem. Frank would have the initial findings of the autopsy by the morning. The SOCO took photographs of the body with close ups of the face and then took more shots of the inside of the bedroom and the bottle of tablets next to the wine bottle. On Frank's instructions he also photographed all the remaining rooms in the house from every angle. A plain white van arrived from Old Hall Street to collect the body just before ten pm.

The forensics team got to work collecting and bagging evidence from the scene. Additional uniformed support turned up from West Derby station. By ten thirty pm the area was cordoned off with the official blue and white tape, "*Police Line Do Not Cross*" Neighbours from most of the nearby houses were peering from behind the curtains to see what was going on.

Within half an hour considering the pouring rain and the time of night an unusual amount of people were out walking their dogs. All they got was a nod from a uniformed officer stood outside the front door and politely told to move on. Frank and Barry had done all they could do for the time being. They drove back to the MIT office in relative silence.

They walked into the main office to find Bob and Mark still there. Frank and Barry brought them up to speed and agreed they would pick it up again in the morning. Frank eventually got home at half past midnight.

Chapter 20

At 32-years old Margaret Smith was a childless divorcee. She worked part time as a bar maid at the Stanley pub on the corner of Robson Street and Walton Breck Road in Anfield. With only a part time job and no husband to support her, she supplemented her income by small time dealing in soft drugs. Her other sideline in prostitution helped pay the bills.

Her husband had spent time inside at HMP Liverpool and promptly done a disappearing act following his release. She hadn't seen sight nor sound of him in the last three years. The mid-terraced house on Venmore Street where she lived was situated in Anfield almost opposite the Kop end of Liverpool's stadium just off the Walton Breck Road.

The Redeemer had visited this area many times before performing his reconnaissance with almost military-style precision. He knew who the neighbours were on both sides of Margaret's house and who lived opposite. He knew when they were at home, where they went and at what time they would be back. The kids in the street gave up the information freely. There was an uncanny amount of trust in an area that could be perceived as a *dog eat dog* place to live.

Of those houses still occupied, to say most of them were in a bad state of repair was putting it mildly. Those that weren't, were either boarded up completely, or had been bought up by entrepreneurial landlords renting them out to the student population of Liverpool.

The whole area on either side of the Walton Breck road was a maze of back streets and back alleys running parallel to each row of houses. Bits of broken glass were crudely cemented into the tops of walls and anywhere kids or burglars could climb over.

The bins in the back alleys were overflowing, mostly with the remains of chippy takeaways plastered with curry sauce. Piles of burst open black bin sacks were strewn about at the end of the alleyways and behind walls. Next to them old bike frames, car tyres, clapped out washing machines, fridges and smashed up televisions were left to rust. Rubbish was everywhere. Recycling was not high up on the list of priorities for the people who lived here.

Along the Walton Breck Road over a distance of less than a mile there were a number of shops and amenities. Newsagents mostly, Asian owned and occupied. They sold just about anything and everything you might need. They were open almost twenty four seven. The serving areas and the tills where the eagle-eyed staff stood were raised up beyond the height of small children and protected by what looked like bulletproof glass.

Every fifty or sixty metres or so there was either a pub or a Chinese owned Fish and Chip shop. On match days these were packed full, the queues would be twenty feet long. A couple of tanning studios doubling up as hairdresser's salons and a chemists shop ran down one side of the road. An off licence, a betting shop and a corner café ran down the other. Everything was either right on your doorstep or within a five-minute walk. Judging by the amount of time the men spent in the pubs any income they received either from the government or from working may as well have been paid out in beer tokens instead of cash.

Despite the apparent hard-up appearance of the area, people on the streets, especially the teenage girls, all wore clothes that were the latest trend in fashion, carrying the most sophisticated mobile phones and pushing the newest baby buggy on the market.

When *The Redeemer* first walked along Venmore Street past the house belonging to Margaret Smith he was saddened by its appearance. The house she lived in was no different to the rest. From the pavement outside there was a five-foot by two-foot area of cracked flagstones surrounded by a concrete wall heavily painted in dark green. The gate was missing. The flagstones were barely visible due to the multitude of weeds, nettles and thistles that had somehow managed to find a foothold in what soil there was in between the cracks. Empty cigarette packets and plastic bags nestled among the weeds with the discarded beer cans and plastic milk bottles.

A naked plastic doll with no head was wedged into the steel grill of the rusty remains of a shopping trolley. Downstairs there was a bold concrete bay window frame painted in the same dark green with single glazed sash windows. Through the window between the badly hung heavy looking drape curtains it was easy to see the basic threadbare settee, some wooden furniture and the drabness of the woodchip wallpaper. A nicotine stained table lamp burnt almost constantly in the corner.

The front door looked as though it had been kicked in or forced open several times. Upstairs both bay windows had been smashed at some time. One was boarded up from the inside, the other was held together with mastic tape and layers of black polythene. At the back of the house the gate to the yard hung off its hinges serving no purpose whatsoever. The yard itself was identical to the flagstones at the front only bigger. The back door leading into the kitchen had previously contained a glass window and a cat flap, both were boarded up.

On his previous visits both during the day and night the back kitchen door was not only unlocked, but also ajar. Other than her small portable television Margaret Smith did not keep anything worth stealing in the house. If the television went missing she knew where to find it. It would be in the pawnshop or the kids next door had nicked it for their bedroom.

To the left of the kitchen door a coalbunker overflowing with bin sacks and other household rubbish looked as if it had recently been set on fire. Sheets of metal grilling used in bakeries had been used with some success to protect the windows from kids throwing stones.

Sometimes at night from the street looking through the bay window he had seen Margaret curled up asleep on the couch. Several cans of stellar and the remains of a takeaway were lying next to her. He had gone round the back unobserved, entered the house and after checking she was sound asleep gone upstairs to survey the layout of the two bedrooms and bathroom area. He was in the house for half an hour without her ever knowing. Now he had all the information he needed, his planning was over. Tonight Margaret Smith was going to be Redeemed.

Chapter 21

Tired from her busy lunchtime shift at the Stanley Pub, Margaret Smith was on her way home for a few hours sleep before going back to do the night shift. Heavy thunderclouds darkened the sky and the rain was in for the day. The wind ripped right through her flimsy anorak causing it to fill out behind her like a parachute. The broken zip was stuck halfway up the front so she was trying to keep her hood in place with one hand and grip the broken zip together with the other. The plastic bag she was carrying in the hand holding the zip contained five cans of Stellar; it was swinging in front of her hindering her progress.

Doing her best to protect herself from the wind and rain she walked as fast as she could with her head down. She did not see the man sloping along behind her as she hurried on her way. She carried straight on past the enticing smells wafting through the doors of the kebab shop and the chippies along the way, doing her best to resist the temptation to pile in and spend what money she had left on a takeaway. She would have just enough for chips, peas and curry sauce later.

The landlord of the Stanley paid her *cash in hand* on a daily basis so that she could not blow the lot in one go. This was an act borne partly out of kindness and partly cunning strategy; this way meant that she would always turn up for work. *Dog eat dog.*

She turned the corner into Venmore Street and walked immediately into the back alley. *The Redeemer* paused on the corner knowing it would take less than three minutes before she arrived at her back door, let herself in and draw the curtains in the front room. He saw the light go on and then fade as she pulled the curtains to. He looked at his cheap plastic Casio watch and pressed a button that made the tiny light come on. It was five-o-clock. He backtracked and crossed over the road to the café on the corner of Lake Street where he could still get an all day breakfast for one pound ninety five.

The Redeemer had no fear of showing his face in any of the shops, pubs or chip shops in this area. Do it often enough and you become known as a regular, someone who spends money, making a contribution to the local economy. It was strangers who became conspicuous and would be the first ones to spring to mind should the police or any one else come sniffing around asking questions.

He entered the café and walked up to the counter, nodded and smiled politely at the plump lady in a flowery patterned pinafore who was serving behind the raised counter.

"All day breakfast is it?" She said, barely looking up from wiping down the counter and pouring cups of tea.

"Fifty Nine!" Hollered the woman stood next to her. He confirmed his order and found a seat. An old guy with long greasy gray hair dressed in a full-length duffel coat shuffled up to the counter to collect his plate of scouse stew for ninety-nine pence. This was his one solid-ish meal of the day. He stuck his tongue out through a set of teeth that looked like a row of bombed shithouses, licking his lips behind nicotine stained moustache and beard. He paid for the stew, waited for his penny change then shuffled back to his place spilling half the stew on the way as he stooped to pick up his bread roll off the slimy floor.

"Sixty two!" Bellowed one of the women from behind the counter.

His all day breakfast was ready. He collected it and sat back down. By the time he'd eaten it, the cafe was almost closing. The old guy in the duffel coat would be asleep in a doorway next to the Salisbury pub in less than an hour. *The Redeemer* left the warmth of the café and headed along Walton Breck Road in the direction of Sleepers Hill where he had parked the car. Sleepers hill was almost opposite the Stanley and from here he had been able to watch the woman leave the pub. He needed to get home and carry out the final act of preparation for his work later tonight.

***

Shortly after Margaret Smith left for work that evening, The Redeemer crept unseen along the dark alleyway behind the row of houses that formed Venmore Street. He approached from the opposite end of the alleyway checking behind him that he was not being followed. The back gate from the alley way was wide open; he entered the yard unobserved, heart beginning to pound. The unlocked back door opened easily and he stepped inside the kitchen. The smell in the kitchen was a mixture of stale cigarette smoke, burnt toast, cheap detergent and even cheaper perfume. The sink was stacked full of dirty pots and plates. Used tea bags sat in a pile on the draining board.

In the semi darkness he was able to make out a pile of clothes next to the cupboard under the stairs. Next to them was a plastic bin sack full of empty lager cans and polystyrene trays reeking of rotten food from leftover takeaways. The whole lot was covered with a ton of cigarette ash and fag ends. She was evidently not house proud. He decided the best place to sit and wait for her was the single back bedroom overlooking the back yard. This room was used as a junk room, to the right of the window between the piles of boxes full of magazines and newspapers, there was a single armchair covered in a heavily stained green felt. The chair was virtually concealed by a large metal-framed clothes rack full of hangars with jackets and other garments. From there he could keep a watch out for her returning from the pub.

An hour before Frank arrived home on Tuesday night; Margaret Smith was staggering along Walton Breck Road. She was blind drunk with the wind gusting at her full in the face. She'd finished her shift at the Stanley and stayed for a few hours overtime. This in itself was not unusual, but then she'd stopped behind for a lock in which had finished earlier than expected due to a fight breaking out and the arrival of the Police.

She'd been chatting up a potential punter in the bar at around ten thirty-pm. The fight had broken out when the punters wife turned up and demanded that he should get his *fuckin' arse home right now.* First there had been the usual pushing and shoving, a few pints got spilled and minutes later all hell broke loose. Margaret had slipped out of the Stanley unnoticed amongst the mayhem. The bitter freezing cold air outside the pub had hit her hard but did nothing to sober her up. She was in no fit state to get a takeaway on her way home tonight.

She was almost bent over double with her chin on her chest and her hands thrust deep in the pockets of her anorak trying to protect herself from the icy wind.

Her eyes focused as best they could on the pavement in front of her as she made her way home.

Staggering and trying to keep her balance she took two steps forward, one to the left and one step backwards, doing her best to remain on the pavement. She reached the corner of Vienna Street and Walton Breck Road and leaned against the wall to catch her breath before turning into Venmore Street and into the alley that led to the back of her house. Waiting for her inside *The Redeemer* strained his ears to hear above the howling wind outside. She was later than he'd expected.

Margaret reached the back door to her house and let herself in. She stood in the hallway wheezing from her exertions against the wind outside. From the room upstairs *The Redeemer* heard the rasping sound. His pulse rate began to increase; he could feel the thumping of his heart inside his chest. He took slow deep breaths to compose himself and listened for sounds of her movements. He heard the sounds of her kicking off her rain soaked shoes as she struggled with the zip on her anorak.

The next sounds were unexpected; the footfalls were heavy and laboured, she was coming straight up the stairs. She paused halfway holding on to the stair rail to steady her self. He remained absolutely still as she passed the back bedroom and into the bathroom. It sounded like she was using the toilet. Moments later after flushing the toilet she staggered past the doorway to the back bedroom. She had removed her wet trousers and socks and left them in a heap in the bathroom. In bare feet and knickers she staggered further along the landing and almost fell down the stairs. She was drunk; *this would make things easier for him.*

He waited and listened for further movement. He heard her closing the living room curtains and the sound of the television going on downstairs. After half an hour the only sounds he'd heard was the background noise of the television and the sound of cans of lager being opened. For the last ten minutes he had heard nothing. He waited. A few minutes later he heard the sounds he had been waiting for, the deep heavy nasal sounds of her snoring. She was fast asleep on the couch. He was prepared for this. His plans included the possibilities that she would go straight to bed or fall asleep on the couch. Either way he would still be able to perform his task.

Silently he negotiated his way through the junk in the bedroom and onto the landing, pausing to listen for sounds of movement downstairs. There was only the sound of the television and her snoring, louder now than before. At the bottom of the stairs he crouched down in the hallway and undid his rucksack.

The door to the room where she lay was slightly ajar. Peering through the two-inch gap he could see her semi naked body flopped on top of the couch. She had used several cushions to cover her top half in an attempt to keep warm. Her head was propped up with another cushion on the arm of the chair; her mouth was half open as she snored.

He opened the rucksack and took out the bottle of chloroform wrapped in soft flannel cloth and laid it on the floor. Next he took out the flask containing the plastic syringe and removed the warm gel pack he had used to maintain the correct temperature. He could see his sperm inside the syringe glistening in the soft light shining into the hall from the living room. He was ready.

He slowly pushed the living room door open an inch at a time pausing to see if there was any sign of movement. Gradually the door was open wide enough for him to get through unhindered.

He picked up his equipment and crept through the door taking a quick glance towards the curtains to make sure they were fully drawn before going any further. The television being on was a distraction but he dare not switch it off in case the alteration in noise level woke her. He had to act now. With the syringe between his teeth he unscrewed the lid from the bottle of chloroform being careful not to let the smell catch him like it did last time. He held the cloth to the neck of the bottle, took one glance towards the sleeping woman and tipped the bottle up soaking the cloth.

The next few minutes were almost a blur; it was a strange feeling he couldn't quite make out. It was almost as if he was watching someone else doing what he himself was doing. He placed the cloth over her mouth and nose; there was no struggle just a slight relaxing of the body as she inhaled the fumes. The rest of the procedure went exactly as planned. He left her on the couch exactly as he had found her. He left the room and pulled the door to behind him, he noticed she'd stopped snoring but thought no more of it.

In the hall way he checked his watch, it was a quarter past one, job done, all over in less than an hour since she had got home. He packed away the items he had used into his rucksack, fastened it up and slung it over his shoulder. As he headed towards the back kitchen door he was already thinking about his next appointment in two days time. He would have time to carry out his observations on the last two women on his list as well as this one before then.

He approached the back kitchen door, reached for the door handle and took hold of it. He was in the process of pulling open the door when all of a sudden; to his complete horror the door was pushed towards him from the outside. The door flew open with a loud bang and caught him on the forehead causing him to step back temporarily stunned. The door flying open had taken him totally by surprise, the searing pain from the impact of the door made him stand still for a second holding his head and blinking with the shock.

Through his hands he looked towards the open doorway. Slumped in a heap on the step he could see there was the shape of a man slowly picking himself up from the floor. Before he could figure out what was going on the man stood up and stared at him full in the face. The punter who had been chatted up by Margaret in the Stanley earlier spoke with a drunken slur.

"Who the fuckin' ell are you?"

In blind panic he charged towards the man and rammed him backwards through the kitchen door. The punter toppled backwards catching his heels on the lip of the step as he did so. *The Redeemer* stood and watched as the punter frantically waved his arms in the air trying to propel himself back up.

It was no use. There was a sickening hollow thud as the sound of the punter's head cracked and split open, fracturing the skull on the concrete floor in the yard. There was a violent twitching and convulsing as the brain cut off its connection to the rest of his body. His arms jerked in spasms like an angry frustrated puppet, then they froze temporarily before collapsing by his sides. There was no further movement. The man lay there. A dark coloured liquid seeped from his head like a snake leaving its hole, gradually spreading in a pool mixing with the rain.

The Redeemer stared in disbelief at what had just happened. He touched his head where the door had hit him, there was blood. It was all going terribly wrong.

What seemed like minutes went by while he gathered himself together and tried to decide on what to do. *What was he going to do?* He quickly weighed up his options. He could just leave without doing anything else. *But the dead man's body would be found first thing in the morning which would bring the police around in swarms and he did not really want that if it could be avoided.*

He walked back to the hallway and peered through the gap in the living room door. Amazingly she had not even moved from the couch, she was still fast asleep. He went back to the kitchen to where the pile of clothes were and rooted through them until he found two large towels. He took them outside and closed the back kitchen door. He checked to see that no one was about in the alleyway and looked up at the windows of the two houses either side. No lights had come on, there were no neighbours looking out of the windows to see what had caused the commotion outside.

He went back to the body in the yard and stared down at the man's face. The dark lifeless eyes stared back up at him. He was definitely dead. *Who the hell was he?* There had been no sign of a boyfriend on the scene during all of his surveillance on the woman. He knelt beside the body and reached inside the man's trouser pockets, he found nothing but a stained handkerchief and a bus ticket. He felt inside the jacket pockets and pulled out an old black leather wallet and a set of keys. In the dim light he could just about make out there was a credit card, some loose change and a photograph of the man and another woman inside it.

Reasons for which, he had no idea he stuffed the keys and wallet into his own coat pocket. He stood over the body and placed one of the towels under the head so that it would soak up most of the blood. Then he went over to the coalbunker in the corner of the yard and started removing the bin bags and boxes full of decaying rubbish. The smell coming from inside the coalbunker grew steadily worse the deeper he got. By the time he had emptied most of the rubbish out of the bunker the stench was almost unbearable.

No doubt it was going to get worse in the days to come, he thought. Leaving the first towel in place on the floor he wrapped the second towel around the dead man's head and lifted the body off the floor. He staggered under the incredible weight and had to pause holding the body against the wall before he could summon enough strength to lift it up and over into the bunker.

The body fell awkwardly through the three-foot square hole on top of the bunker, folding at the waist with the head catching on the rough edges of the hole as it fell in. The body landed with a thumping sound on top of the remaining mush inside the bunker. He went back to where he had picked up the body and did his best using the towel to mop up the rest of the blood. Satisfied he had got most of it he threw the towel into the bunker.

He then carefully took all the bags and boxes of rubbish in the same order he had taken them out and placed them back inside the bunker. Despite the freezing cold, by the time he had finished he was drenched in sweat and he was covered in filth from the rubbish in the bunker. He looked at his watch, it had taken him over half an hour.

Dog tired he stood for a moment surveying the back yard trying to imagine what it would look like in the morning when the woman who lived here stepped into it. He made sure that there were no bits of rubbish lying around that were not there previously. Hopefully she wouldn't notice anything wrong.

The rain was falling again and with any luck would wash away any traces of the dead man's blood by the morning. All his planning for these missions had prepared him for most eventualities but it had definitely not prepared him for this. He picked up his rucksack from the corner of the yard and wearily made his way through the gate and back along the alley. He couldn't wait to get home. He would dump the wallet and keys somewhere later.

Chapter 22

Frank walked into the MIT office at dead on half past seven Wednesday morning. As usual Barry, Mark and Bob were there before him.

"Morning Boss, not sleeping too well?"

Frank sat in a chair in the corner of the office rubbing his eyes.

"No, now that you come to mention it, and neither have you three looking at your faces, you look like how I feel."

"That's my fault," chirped Bob, "we went for a curry and had a few beers instead of going straight home last night."

"Thanks for that, I thought it smelt a bit oriental in here. Anyway moving swiftly on, you just about done here Barry? I want to get down to the Coroners Office ASAP."

Barry drained the rest of the coffee from the mug on his desk.

"Yep, I'm done, I'll get me coat."

They left together in Frank's car. The journey from Canning place to the Coroners Office on Old Hall Street took less than ten minutes. The Coroners Office was situated inside a building constructed in the early 20th Century known as the *Cotton Exchange*.

They parked opposite in one of the pay and display bays and crossed the road to the front entrance. Frank never ceased to be impressed by the atmosphere created by this building. At the entrance inside was a massive foyer that looked positively regal in its appearance. The light brown marble floors were highly polished and shone like deep clear pools covered in glass. Tall marble pillars reached majestically up to the ornately arched daffodil yellow ceilings where huge decorative dome shaped glass light fittings hung.

The lighting was sympathetic and created and atmosphere that spoke of respect and peace and serenity. Around the perimeter walls chairs with soft brown cloth upholstery were situated for people to sit while waiting with grieving families and relatives. There were wooden beech coloured doors leading discreetly off to quiet areas for privacy and consultation.

The large oval shaped reception desk to the rear centre of the foyer was split into sections by huge pillars. It looked orderly and graceful in its appearance, it gave you a feeling of trust and piety.

The few staff present were dressed uniformly in smart dark blue suits, they were always unhurried and relaxed in appearance. The overall impression they gave was one of competence and professionalism mixed with understanding and empathy. When you walked in you respected the function of this building and you paid due respect to those that came here.

Frank and Barry walked up to the reception desk and discreetly showed their identification badges. The female receptionist calmly nodded her recognition and asked them politely to take a seat while she informed the coroner they were here. They took their seats and waited in silence. Frank sat forward with his elbows on his knees and let his eyes wander around the room.

Even at this time of the morning there were people sat in corners anxiously waiting for news of loved ones or nervously preparing themselves to identify the bodies of those that had died. Death had no opening or closing times.

A few minutes later the receptionist answered the call signified by the small flashing light at her desk and then indicated that the coroner was ready to see them. She took them from the foyer and escorted them along a wide corridor to the left that led to the mortuary. She left them with a respectful nod at the point where the sign said, *"Authorised Staff Only"* and turned back towards the reception area.

They entered the first corridor, which split into three more long corridors with doors leading off each one to separate rooms. Frank recognised the coroners' assistant who came to meet them.

"Good morning John, thanks for this, hope we haven't caused you too many headaches."

John smiled graciously.

"None at all Sir, the coroner will see you now, if you'd like to come this way." He led them off through a side door to the left and through two large swing doors into the autopsy suite. In the centre of the room underneath giant arc lamps stood a large stainless steel table on a block of brown marble. Laid on top of it was the covered body of Angela Perriman. A *Diener* was hosing down the floor surrounding the table.

Waiting for them was the coroner and with him, Professor Harkins the pathologist who had attended the scene at the Perriman house the previous evening. The coroner was washing his hands at a sink in the corner, Harkins was still dressed in his pale blue coloured scrub suit, wearing gloves, shoe covers and a plastic see through face mask. They had obviously been busy, probably up until late in the night and very early this morning.

Barry stood near the entrance, eyes transfixed on the table in the centre of the room, notebook in hand. Frank waited for the coroner to finish washing his hands before speaking. When he spoke he addressed the coroner as Sir. It never did any harm to stay in favour with these people. Another lesson he'd learnt from his father.

"Son" his father would say, I'd rather call a Lance Corporal Sir than call a Colonel a you know what." His father would never actually use the awful *C* word.

"So Sir, can you give us the cause of death, are we right in believing it to be suspicious?"

The coroner as usual, gave the standard answer.

"Well Inspector I'm afraid it's still a bit too early to say for definite, something's *not* quite right that's for sure. We've taken skin and tissue samples from inside the mouth, the whole of the respiratory tract, lungs and stomach. We've taken a biopsy of the liver and collected adipose tissue samples for analysis. Everything has been sent to the toxicology lab, we'll need to wait until this afternoon for the initial results."

Frank remained hopeful. "So what have you got that you *can* tell us?"

The coroner approached the table where the body lay and threw back the sheet just enough to reveal the face.

"Well I can tell you what it certainly is not, the rest is supposition until we get the lab results back." Frank pulled out his pocket notebook and prepared to scribble some notes. The coroner continued in a tone sounding routinely non-committal.

"Okay, firstly time of death. Judging from the time the body was found and the condition it was in when it arrived here, early stages of rigor mortis and core body temperature would indicate that she has been dead at least ten to fifteen hours. That would put the time of death at approximately sometime between one am and four am." Both Frank and Barry made a note of the time.

" Secondly cause of death. Traces of alcohol found in her blood and stomach match that as found in the wine bottle by her bedside. Neither the percentage of alcohol by volume or the amount consumed was significant enough to cause her death."

The coroner folded his arms with one hand on his chin as if deep in thought.

Harkins coughed and drew Frank's attention.

"However we do concur that this maybe a contributing factor." He said looking towards the coroner. The coroner unfolded his arms and leaned forward against the marble block.

"Yes, agreed. The tablets found by her bedside were fairly strong anti depressants either from the group known as SSRIs, Selective Serotonin Re-uptake Inhibitors to be more specific; or from the Tricyclics group, typically Amitriptyline or Norpramine. In other words Prozac or Elavil to you and me."

Frank looked up from his notebook.

"Any idea how many she had taken?"

The coroner looked thoughtful.

"I would say no more than what is the prescribed dosage, certainly not enough to kill her even combined with the alcohol. I think the lab results will prove that I am correct in my assumptions."

From the far side of the room Barry suddenly became more interested in the conversation.

"So not a suicide then, you're suggesting we can rule that out?" he asked.

"I'm not suggesting anything, I'm merely stating facts as I see them." said the coroner.

"You both agreed that the alcohol could have been a contributing factor, do you believe the same to be true with the anti depressant tablets?" Frank queried.

The coroner moved to the side of the table.

"There is a strong likelihood that this is the case...but there is a third element to this that fascinates me. Look here at this reddish discoloration around the mouth and nose, do you see that?"

Frank and Barry leaned across and saw what they had seen the previous night. It looked like mild nappy rash as seen on a baby's bottom.

"That is what I am concerned with. Your female police colleague at the scene did well to spot this and pick up on it. These marks have been caused by an abrasive substance, or a chemical irritant of some kind, probably acid or ammonia based which has caused mild burning of the skin tissue surrounding the mouth and nose."

"Any idea what it is?" asked Frank looking back and forward between coroner and pathologist. Harkins chipped in again.

"Think back in time, Victorian London, Whitechapel late 1800's and one very infamous serial killer." Frank thought quickly but Barry beat him to it.

"Jack the Ripper! Surely your not suggesting we've got a..." The coroner cut him off unceremoniously.

"Nooo... certainly not. But if you think back to what the Ripper would have used back then to subdue his victims and I think you'll find our substance."

"Which is?" enquired Frank.

Barry answered the question before anyone else.

"Chloroform? Are you saying this is what killed her?"

The coroner was once again uncommittal.

"No I am saying that Trichloromethane or Chloroform as it is commonly known caused the burns around her mouth and nose. However with Chloroform being a respiratory suppressant and that together with the presence of alcohol and the anti depressant medication, it is a strong possibility. An additional side effect of some anti depressant medications particularly with the Tricyclics is a slowing down of the heart rate and a drop in blood pressure." Barry was writing as fast as he could while Frank continued to listen.

"All of this added together would lead to lack of oxygen to the brain causing it to shut down. I suspect and hopefully the lab results will confirm it, that the cause of death was pulmonary cardio and respiratory arrest brought on by asphyxiation. So… there you have it Inspector"

Frank suddenly had a hundred or more questions running through his mind.

"So what, exactly, is Chloroform? What's it used for?"

The coroner was looking at his watch. Harkins took his opportunity to impress.

"In answer to your first question Inspector, Chloroform is a colourless liquid, forty times sweeter than sugar. It was used in the mid 1800's as a surgical anesthetic; it was given to Queen Victoria during the birth of her eighth child. It was also found in cough syrups and liniments, that sort of thing. However its use was discontinued due to its many side effects. The main one being that there was a possibility of paralysis of the respiratory system, which in turn led to heart failure and death."

The pathologist was on a roll now like a runaway University lecturer, there was no stopping him. Frank cut in anyway.

"Err... excuse me, sorry to interrupt, but can you tell me what's it used for now?"

The coroner was visibly impressed with what Harkins had just come up with and not to be outdone quickly stepped in and picked up where he'd left off.

"Well... to the best of my knowledge refined Chloroform is now more commonly used in the chemical and pharmaceutical industry as a solvent used in the extraction of organic compounds, the purification of penicillin and such like."

It was 2:1 to the coroner but he was the only one keeping score. Frank hit them with more questions while they were feeling talkative.

"And why would someone use it to subdue her? Is there any sign of sexual activity?"

The coroner and Harkins glanced towards each other. Harkins stepped aside and allowed the coroner to continue. The coroner pulled the sheet back over to cover up the face then moved round to the far end of the table. Barry took several steps backwards not sure that he was going to want to see what was coming next.

"I was wondering when you were going to come around to that," the coroner said, glancing at Harkins as if he had just won a bet.

"This is a bit of a mystery." He threw back the sheet to reveal the legs and lower torso up to the naval.

"Tell me what do you see here?" Frank and Barry stared at the most obvious point in question and then up and down both legs looking for something that they were supposed to be able to see. After several seconds Barry had had enough.

"I can't see anything!"

"Neither can I.?" added Frank.

"Exactly, there is nothing to see, nothing whatsoever, well externally anyway."

"Meaning?" asked Barry.

"There are absolutely none of the typical signs of sexual activity, specifically rape. No evidence of bruising or swelling, no chafing, no redness or pressure marks anywhere to be seen. If there *had* been any violent sexual activity we would have seen or found something that would have given us a clue."

"However there did appear to be some kind of discharge, which had dried up around the area of the vagina. This in itself is not unusual. There is often a releasing of normal bodily fluids following death. Further inspection of the area surrounding the vagina and an internal examination revealed that there *were* traces of semen inside her."

Barry looked visibly shaken by what he'd just heard. Frank had stopped scribbling ages ago; he now stood and stared in disbelief at what he was hearing.

"So what you're saying is, that there is evidence of sexual activity but not necessarily rape? That this woman has maybe had consensual sex with someone, and this someone used Chloroform on her?" Frank was exasperated.

"This is crazy, none of it fits. There was no evidence at the scene to suggest that anyone else other than the deceased had been in the bedroom. All the doors and windows were locked from the inside, our officers had to force an entry to gain access into the premises."

The coroner just shrugged his shoulders.

"You are right Inspector it doesn't make any sense. That's why you're the detective; it's your job to figure out the puzzle, my job is just to give you the pieces to put together. We'll have more to give you by this afternoon once we get our results back from the lab, but in the meantime I think you have got enough to be going on with don't you." Frank nodded and thanked them both.

The coroner promised to fax over the preliminary report later that afternoon.

Frank and Barry left the autopsy suite and headed back towards the entrance. They acknowledged to the reception staff that they were done and left the building. The cold air outside hit them. Frank pulled up his collar.

"I didn't know you were some kind of *Ripper* buff?" he said.

Barry shrugged his shoulders and smiled.

"One of my all time favourite mystery stories, the unexplained crime, who was Jack the Ripper?"

They crossed the road and returned to the car to find that the meter had expired and a fixed penalty sticker giving notice of a £40.00 fine for illegal parking had been stuck on the windscreen. Frank tore it off and shoved it in his pocket.

"I've got a feeling this is going to be one *shit* day," said Frank. Neither he nor Barry knew it, but it was about to get a whole lot shittier.

Chapter 23

Frank steered the car through the narrow streets turning right onto Tithebarn Street and out into heavy commuter traffic opposite the Liver Buildings. Barry was on his mobile talking to Tony Barker at the Costco warehouse. He was expecting them. They continued along past Princes Dock and onto Bath Street before turning right into Paisley Street. The huge white painted building that housed the Costco discount warehouse stuck out like a sore thumb. It was the newest building in the area and was in stark contrast to the red brick buildings surrounding the old docklands area.

They left the car in one of the bays at the back and made their way to the front entrance. Tony Barker had arranged for someone to meet them at the door and bring them to his office. The fresh faced young lad looked suitably impressed when Frank and Barry flashed their ID badges. Minutes later they were in Mr. Barkers' office drinking tea and exchanging pleasantries. It was good to break the ice before asking the sixty four thousand dollar question.

Mr. Barker had no idea, but until the possibility of another suspect emerged, Frank had no option but to put him down as the number one suspect. Ten or fifteen minutes went by while he asked the routine questions and made notes in his pocket notebook. As soon as he had gleaned all the necessary background surrounding Angela Perriman and her history of depression, he was ready.

"So, Mr. Barker thank you for your assistance in this matter, I would like to assure you that we really appreciate your co-operation.

I'm sure you will appreciate that this is just routine, but do you mind if I ask you where you were between say… midnight last night and say four-o-clock this morning?" To his surprise Mr. Barker didn't bat an eyelid.

"Certainly not Inspector, only too happy to oblige. I was at home with my wife. We watched television until around a quarter to eleven and then we went to bed. My eldest son called us around nine thirty and I spoke to him for about half an hour."

A solid enough alibi, thought Frank.

"Just to keep everything above board we will need a statement from you so that we have everything on record right from the start of this investigation. Oh and we'll need a supplementary statement from your wife and son, this is for your own protection, you understand?" Mr. Barker looked slightly less comfortable with the idea of his wife and son having to make a statement but made no objections.

"You could either come to the office at Canning Place or we could send someone along to take your statement here or at your home, which do prefer?"

Mr. Barker chose the last option saying that he would arrange for his wife and son to be present at the same time.

"I'll send someone to see you at a time convenient to yourself. I'd also like to get a statement from the two members of staff who had the most contact with the deceased as well if you don't mind. Thank you once again and if we need anything else we'll be in touch."

They left the office and went back to the car park. Once inside the car Frank turned towards Barry. "Well, what do you think?"

"I think that you're *barking* up the wrong tree if you excuse the pun. Mr. Barker has shown genuine concern for his member of staff throughout and has displayed a certain public spiritedness, which is to be both commended and encouraged. That's what I think."

Frank nodded. "I couldn't agree more, he isn't who we are looking for, but you know how it is, standard procedure and all that. Let's get back to the office; I need to make some calls.

Chapter 24

In the house next door to Margaret Smiths' in Venmore Street the two little girls were home from school. Together they had walked the half-mile distance from Breckfield Road Primary School in Vienna Street sharing a bag of chips. To any one who didn't know them Hayley and Rebecca looked like a pair of little angels and as if butter wouldn't melt in their mouths. In fact it was the exact opposite.

Although they were only aged nine and eleven, they were streetwise and sharp as knives when it came to looking after themselves. They had needed to be from an early age; both from different fathers Rebecca the eldest one had been given the key to the front door when she was just eight years old. With their mother working shifts and all hours god sent, the age of the proverbial *latchkey kid* was getting younger all the time.

Their mother would not be home before eleven pm that night and she had left them both a note with money for them to get their tea from the chippy. For less than two pounds they could get a sausage dinner each and sweets from the corner shop on their way home.

They had got changed out of their wet school clothes, put them on hangars and hung them up to dry as soon as they got home. They only had two sets of clean school uniform and today was only Wednesday, they would need the same uniform again tomorrow. Once changed they sat at the table in the kitchen and helped each other do their homework.

Tough kids and streetwise they may be, but one lesson their mother had taught them was, that if they didn't want to finish up working their arses off in a dead end job like hers they needed to do well at school. This was a lesson that hadn't been wasted on either of them. No matter what time their mother got home, one of the first things she would do is check their homework. They actually took pride in presenting their homework to the highest standard possible.

Satisfied that they had finished their homework to their usual high standard they left their workbooks on the kitchen table for their mother to see when she got home. Now they were sat in the tidy but scarcely furnished living room and wanted to watch a pirate video of *Honey I Shrunk the Kids Two,* one of the latest kids movies doing the circuit. They had saved enough money between them to buy it from the money their mother had been leaving them for their tea. It wasn't just sweets they were buying from the corner shop.

There was only one problem; the ancient video player was on its last legs and had chewed up the last video they had tried to play. They had tried to prise it out using a kitchen knife but had so far been unsuccessful. They knew what they would need to do if they wanted to watch the video. They had done it before and so far not been discovered, or at least that's what they thought. If they were quick they could be in and out with the portable video-combi from next door.

They would have time to watch the movie, go and get their tea and put the TV back before either their mother or Mrs. Smith next door got home. They had often thought about staying in Mrs. Smith's house and watching the video there so they did not have to lug the TV round to their house. It just didn't seem right somehow sat in someone else's house and using their electricity. This way nobody knew and everybody was happy.

They left via the back door through their back yard and into the alleyway. Even though it was dark they were careful not to let anyone see them or what they were up to. They entered the yard to Mrs. Smith's house and as bold as brass opened the back kitchen door. What neither of them had noticed until right now was that instead of the house being in total darkness, there was a light on in the living room and from the hallway just inside the kitchen they could hear the faint sound of the television.

Confused but not put off from what they were about to do they crept quietly to the living room door. Maybe Mrs. Smith had been home at lunchtime and had gone back to work forgetting to switch off the light and the TV? Rebecca slowly pushed the door open just enough for them to see into the living room. The TV caught their attention first, some cookery programme with celebrity chefs and Ainsley Harriet talking about red tomatoes and green peppers.

They stepped into the living room and looked towards the couch. To their surprise Mrs. Smith was lying on the couch. They froze on the spot. On the floor next to her were several empty cans of lager. Maybe she was drunk and had not gone back to work after all? She was completely still and lying in a position that looked uncomfortable, not one that you would normally lie in unless you were *very* drunk.

One leg was still on the couch, the other hung down towards the floor. One of her arms was straight out behind her head and the other was hanging down with the fingers resting on the floor. The head was bent at the neck at an unusual angle balanced right on the edge of the couch. Some of the long died black hair had fallen partially over her face; the rest was touching the floor. The mouth was lolling wide open. They could hear no sound of breathing. The two of them stood transfixed at what they saw, neither of them wanting to go in any further to investigate.

"Do you think she might be...you know what?" whispered Hayley.

"Sshh don't say that." Rebecca replied.

Curiosity was getting the better of them both but neither of them could quite muster up the courage to go over to the body. Suddenly without warning Hayley spoke up, quietly at first.

"Mrs. Smith its Hayley and Rebecca from next door, are you okay?" No response. Louder now.

"Mrs. Smith? MRS. SMITH?" Nothing.

"She would have heard that," said Rebecca. The pair of them were still icily cool. They had both seen dead bodies before. They had been to the funeral of both of their grandparents and seen them laid out in the front room of the house before the burial. It was nothing new. Rebecca took Hayley by the hand and together they approached the body on the couch. Rebecca held out her hand from a respectable distance and laid her fingers on the woman's cheek. She snatched her hand back as if she'd been burnt by a hot stove.

The skin was cold and lifeless; the sensation caused Rebecca to squeeze Hayley's hand involuntarily making her jump with fright. Their previous coolness swiftly vanished and they turned and ran for all they were worth. It wasn't until they got out of the house and into the alleyway they started screaming.

Chapter 25

Back at Merseyside Police Headquarters Frank had been sat in his office for an hour tying up loose ends, prioritising who was going to do what and when. Barry was checking upon the progress made by Mark and Bob. In the last hour he had also pulled in a few favours, alerting outlying stations throughout Merseyside that he may be calling upon them for support officers to help work the case. There was never usually any shortage of volunteers willing to spend some time working with the Major Incident Team.

In his office Frank was ticking off a checklist. Uniformed officers had been dispatched to carry out a door-to-door operation, officers were knocking on doors of all the houses in the vicinity of the Perriman house at Crosby Green, potential witnesses were being identified, interviews were underway and statements, being taken.

Frank looked up from his list, as there was a knock at the door. The door opened to reveal a face of someone he knew very well and one he was very happy to see.

Danielle Vasquez was beaming all over her face as she greeted him.

"Boss." was all she managed to say before they shook hands. Frank gripped her hand and yanked her towards him. There was a short embrace as they slapped each other hard between the shoulder blades. The bonding that had occurred between them back in training was as strong as ever. It did not go unnoticed by Barry who was standing hovering in the doorway.

"Err Boss, if you've got a minute?"

"Certainly Barry, no problem. One thing though before we get started, make sure Daz here is brought up to speed on her duties as soon as possible."

"What, on the case Boss?"

"No…on her new appointment as the *Official Fledge*, I'm sure Mark will take great pleasure filling her in." Daz was grinning all over her face.

"Its already sorted Boss, Mark wasted no time. Coffee, no sugar right?"

Frank knew she was going to fit in just fine.

"Cheers Daz, we'll speak later yeah."

"Thanks Boss." She disappeared to make the brews.

Frank motioned for Barry to follow him into his office. Barry wasted no time in bringing him up to date on the progress from Mark and Bob.

"Right Boss, the owner of the vehicle, the red Nissan Micra is a Miss Sandra Pollock. She lives by herself at an address in Wellington Avenue just off the Smithdown Road near Wavertree. The PNC check brought up nothing whatsoever. The car isn't registered in her name.

We checked through DVLA and got the last known keeper. An elderly chap by the name of Mr. Tomlinson lives over by Sandown Park way, he sold the vehicle to her six months ago, he's got a valid bill of sale and it all looks legit. He gave us a mobile phone number for Miss Pollock; we checked the mobile phone company records and came up with the address. For some unknown reason Miss Pollock has chosen not to register the car in her own name, it's not taxed either."

Frank didn't show any sign of reaction to the fact that the vehicle wasn't licensed to Sandra Pollock.

"Any body been round to check the address out?"

"Yes Boss, Bob was round there first thing this morning. The car was parked outside her house in Wellington Avenue; the tax disk in the window is six months out of date. At eight thirty this morning Bob followed her as she left her house.

She drove the car to her place of work. It's a Florists' just off Penny Lane about five minutes drive from where she lives. She's got a set of keys for the place but doesn't own the business. She opened up the shop at about a quarter to nine."

Frank was impressed, the boys had been busy, he looked at his watch.

"Good work, what's the latest update at the florist's."

Barry was scanning his notes.

"Well according to Bob, she left on foot and went to a café on Penny lane for half an hour at twelve thirty pm. She was back in the shop just after one pm."

"Okay so what's the situation now?"

"Bob is still at the Florists shop, Mark is in the incident room. They've got all the photos and video stuff you asked for. Mark and I have got as much of the information you asked for on this woman as we can get without speaking to her directly. Most of it's here." he pointed to the buff coloured file on the table.

Barry passed Frank the file with all the documents in pertaining to Miss Pollock. Frank again was impressed.

"Good work Barry, excellent. Leave this with me. I need to make some calls."

In the meantime get on the phone to Bob and tell him to stay with her wherever she goes after work. Oh and tell him I might be dropping by with a visitor, depends on whether he is available at short notice, if not it'll have to be tomorrow."

Barry closed his notebook and prepared to leave just as Daz appeared with Frank's coffee. Frank looked up.

"Cheers Daz, just put it on the desk."

Barry noted the absence of the word *Fledge*.

"Right Boss. There are some loose ends Mark has asked me to give him a hand with, and I need to catch up on with the business surrounding the dodgy ecstasy tablets and the car jacking from last week. Okay if Mark and I crack on with that?"

"Yep no problem, let me know if you need anything. Barry will give you a bell if there are any developments."

Barry and Daz left the office together. No sooner than they'd walked out the door, Frank picked up the phone and rang Ted. There was no answer. He sat there tapping his fingers.

"Come on, come on." He muttered impatiently. Now that things were happening he wanted as ever things to move even quicker. The answer service cut in and he was just about to hang up when the voice of Father Maloney interrupted the tape.

"Good afternoon, the Presbytery, Church of the Holy Trinity, Father Maloney speaking."

Frank came straight to the point.

"Ted its Frank here, look I have done some digging. We need to meet, are you free now?"

Five minutes later Frank tipped the wink to Barry in the incident room and told him to let Bob know the visit to Miss Pollock was on. He left to pick up Father Maloney.

Chapter 26

The 999 call came in to the Liverpool central emergency services at 16:05 pm Wednesday afternoon and was routed to the Walton Lane Police Station at 16:10 pm. The desk Sergeant at Walton Lane Police Station recorded the details and hung up. He looked at what he had written and then dialed the number of the caller that he'd been given by the emergency services. He spoke with the caller for a few minutes and took some more details.

At 16:20 pm the desk sergeant dispatched a car and two uniformed officers to the address at Venmore Street in Anfield. On arrival the elderly man who had made the call was waiting by his front door. Stood next to him were the two girls Hayley and Rebecca.

The presence of a police car in and around Anfield was nothing new. It didn't stop the kids in the street from gathering round to have a *nosy* and see what was going on. The officers removed their hats and introduced themselves.

"Mr. Oliver I'm PC Mick Harton, this is PC Dave Warren, we're from Walton Lane Police station. We understand you made a 999 call concerning a neighbour of yours," he looked at his pocket notebook, "err... a Mrs. Smith is that correct?"

Mr. Oliver confirmed that he'd made the call and invited the officers into his house. The police officers followed him inside the house with the two girls. Once sat inside the old man offered them tea and biscuits which he'd already prepared. PC's Harton and Warren gratefully accepted.

While he went to fetch the tea the two officers scanned the house. The old man was obviously very proud of his home; it was the exception to the rule, immaculately clean, tidy and tastefully decorated. The two girls sat in silence the whole time.

PC Harton, the older of the two officers spoke first.

"So tell me which one of you is Hayley and which one is Rebecca?"

"I'm Rebecca," said the taller of the two proudly pointing to herself, "and she's Hayley my sister, she's nine and I'm eleven."

Tea and biscuits were brought in on a trolley and they all sat in the living room together. The old man just looked on and smiled at the apparent calmness shown by the girls. Outside the window in front of the house a bunch of kids were jumping up and down to see if they could get a better view of what was going on.

"Should I draw the curtains officer? It's just the kids outside you see, getting a bit nosy like."

One of the officers stood up, he moved towards the window and shot them a stare that made them scatter up the street.

"I think that's sorted them for now, no need to draw the curtains Mr. Oliver."

The old man busied himself with the tea and biscuits.

"Okay," said the older officer, "in a few minutes myself and PC Warren are going to go into Mrs. Smith's house to have a look at what you've seen, we need to ask you some questions. Before that though, I want to tell you that what you both did was very brave and that neither of you are in any trouble for being in Mrs. Smith's house. Do you understand that?"

They both nodded.

"Now I'd like you to tell me briefly, what happened from the time you got home, what you did and if you could remember the rough time that would be helpful."

The two girls went on to give a shortened account of their afternoon since they'd arrived home from school, with each of them contributing as much as the other. They were nervous around the subject of them being home unsupervised and worried that their mother might get into trouble. They gave their mothers mobile phone number to the officers so that the officers could arrange for someone to contact her and let her know what had happened.

PC Warren left the room and was speaking to someone on his radio in the hall. Rebecca and Hayley could hear him giving them their mother's mobile number. When he returned they confessed to their habit of *borrowing* Mrs. Smith's TV without her permission. The officers just smiled as they took notes.

When they were finished they asked the girls to stay with Mr. Oliver while they went next door. The old man saw them as far as the back door and left them to it. When he returned the girls were eating biscuits and watching TV. The kids outside were back in front of the window. He pulled the curtains closed and sat down.

In the yard next door the officers put on gloves and let themselves in through the back door. They were careful not to touch anything on their way through the kitchen and into the hall. Before they even reached the door to the living room the smell they'd come to recognise only too well was there, emanating through the gap in the door. Slowly they pushed the door to the living room open and there in front of them on the couch was the woman.

Just as Rebecca and Hayley had described right down to the positions of each limb and the hair hanging over the face to the floor. They had both seen plenty of dead bodies before and this one was definitely dead, but one of them still had to do the obligatory pulse check and visual observation for signs of life before reporting in what they had found.

They scanned the room for any clues as to what might have happened. There was no evidence of a struggle and nothing to suggest a suicide. That left only death by natural causes or possible accidental drug and alcohol overdose. PC Mick Harton pulled out his mobile phone and called his desk sergeant back at the station.

While he was relaying the details over the phone PC Dave Warren took a closer look at the body mainly out of curiosity. He noticed that the eyes were not fully closed which spooked him a little bit. There was also a strange smell that he couldn't put his finger on. Then he noticed the speckled rash around the mouth, lips and nose of the dead woman. PC Harton was still on the phone.

"Ere Mick come and have a butchers at this."

Mick looked over towards the body.

"Scuse me a sec Sarge, Dave has spotted something."

He crouched over the body with the phone pinned to his ear. Dave pointed out the rash to Mick and shrugged his shoulders.

"What do you reckon?"

Mick spoke into the phone.

"Yes hello Sarge, there also seems to be some kind of unusual looking rash, a discolouration of some kind around the face particularly the mouth and nose. Yeah that's right, a reddish colour looks a bit like a,…a burn or something like that."

There was a pause before Mick spoke again.

" What? Right okay Sarge will do." He hung up.

Dave looked at his colleague puzzled.

"What did he say?"

Mick looked just as puzzled.

"He said that we've to treat this as we would for a murder scene, we've got to seal off the front area of the house and the back alley way, then he wants us to wait outside and make sure no one else gets near the house until someone from MIT gets here."

They left the house through the back door, walked around the front to their car and got out the blue and white crime scene tape. The number of kids on the street doubled as soon as the word got round that something was going on. The buzz spread quickly. The word was that Hayley and Rebecca had been arrested and the "*bizzies*" were sealing off the area.

Back at Walton Lane Police station the desk Sergeant was re-reading the information displayed on the computer screen in front of him. The latest Merseyside police software package "MERCEDES", Merseyside Crime Elevation Data Entry System was not more than a few weeks old. A lot of the *old school* officers had scorned the idea that it would have any effect on crime overall, and that it was just some more red tape that would slow things down, preventing coppers from doing any real work.

The desk Sergeant wasn't *old school* and right now he was impressed.

He'd entered the details given to him over the phone by PC Mick Harton and nothing had come up at first. As soon as he added the details of the reddish coloured rash that PC Warren had spotted, the screen changed automatically to another page. It was flagged up with details matching another event of a similar description.

The flashing message at the bottom of the page told him that this had to be passed over immediately to MIT at Merseyside Police HQ. He picked up the phone and called his inspector who was sat in his office upstairs.

"Sir something's come up on MERCEDES. Two of our lads are at the scene now, MIT need to be informed straight away."

The Inspector was down at the desk beside his Sergeant in less than a minute. He verified the details as accurate and picked up the phone in the back office. He got straight through to the MERCEDES central control unit who routed him through to the officer who had entered the details on the system from the flagged case.

"MIT, Detective Sergeant Ferguson speaking."

"Sergeant this is Inspector Tony Blackwell from Walton Lane Police Station."

Barry grabbed his notebook and a pen.

"Yes sir, how can I help?"

The Inspector relayed what he'd been told by his desk sergeant.

"Two of my officers are in attendance at a job in a house on Venmore Street over in Anfield. The emergency services routed a call through to us from a member of the public who lives in next door. The officers are still on site and have investigated the matter. They just rang with their findings and we've entered the details into MERCEDES.

It's come up flagged up as an MIT case. Your name is shown as the point of contact. Any of this making sense to you?"

Barry Smiled at the comment, the underlying skepticism was not hard to detect. As soon as the

Inspector had mentioned the name MERCEDES he was already logging onto the system while he listened.

"Perfect sense sir, can you give me the case reference number it was flagged up with?"

There was a pause while the Inspector got the details off the desk sergeant.

"Right here it is, the number is, BFMIT 00099 / 04."

"Thanks sir, just give me a second." Barry keyed the number in and reached the screen with the list of cases logged on to the system by him. As he scrolled down through the list he was pretty sure he knew which case it would refer to. He was right, he had only just put it on the day before. The screen with the drop down menus was now in front of him and he stared at it.

One particular drop down menu was highlighted and flashing on and off in red. He clicked on the menu heading and below that a number of words dropped into view. The words *red rash, discolouration, burns and asphyxiation* were amongst them. The first words *"red rash"* were also flashing. Barry spoke into the phone wedged between his ear and his shoulder.

"Hello sir, this was only put on the system yesterday. Detective Inspector Frank Carroll is the SIO on the case."

Barry waited for a reaction. The Inspector sounded nervous when he spoke.

"Right, so what happens now?"

"Well sir, the DI is out on a matter directly related to this case as we speak. In actual fact his present location is not far from Anfield. I will inform the DI on your behalf. The DI and myself will be at the scene in less than half an hour."

"So what do *we* do in the meantime?" The Inspector clearly was not happy.

"Nothing sir, just inform your officers that MIT are on their way. I only need to make one more call and a full SOCO with forensics support team will be on route by the time the DI and myself arrive."

Barry waited for an answer and got only silence.

"Hello sir?"

"Yes okay Sergeant, thanks for that. What about updating MERCEDES?"

"No need to, your entry will automatically be updated as we update the case. You will be able to log on and view the progress as and when you need to. Is there anything else I can help you with Sir?.. Hello Sir?" The Inspector had hung up.

Back at Walton Lane the *old school* Inspector was booking himself a crash course on MERCEDES with his desk Sergeant.

Barry put the call through to his boss's mobile and got him first ring.

Frank was sat in his car fifty metres up the street from the florist shop in Penny Lane. He'd picked Ted up on his way and dropped him off at the shop. Ted was inside talking with Sandra Pollock.

"Boss, its Barry. I've just had a call from an Inspector Blackwell at Walton Lane. MERCEDES has flagged up something to do with the Angela Perriman case. A 999 call from a member of the public was put through to them from an address in Venmore Street over in Anfield.

They've got officers at the scene now. It's the *red rash* connection that caused it to be flagged up." Frank sat up in his seat.

"Right, I am outside the florist shop. I'll brief Bob here and bring him up to speed. Give us the address and I'll meet you there in … say thirty minutes?"

"Okay Boss, see you there." Barry hung up. Franks mobile rang again immediately. He looked at the display and recognised the number. It was the DCI back at Canning Place. Frank tossed the mobile on the front seat unanswered, got out of the car and walked over to where Bob was sat in his car reading the Echo. Frank tapped on the window on the passenger side, opened the door and climbed in beside him.

"Right Bob, I've just had a call from Barry back at the office. Something's come up and I need to shoot off. I want you to wait here until Father Maloney comes out. When he does get him back to Canning Place and stay there with him. I'll need a full brief when I get back, anything important I need to know call me on my mobile."

Bob acknowledged he understood what he was to do.

"Right Bob, I need to get to Venmore Street in Anfield, which is the quickest way from here?" Bob was like a human SATNAV system when it came to giving directions around Liverpool. He thought for a minute.

"Okay Boss, it's probably not the shortest route but with the traffic at this time of day it's more than likely to be the quickest. Do a right at the end of Penny lane and go left at the next junction onto Queens Drive. Stay on that until you get to the fourth major crossroads after the Queens Drive flyover. Do a left along Townsend Lane and keep going until you hit the first big crossroads, turn right there into Oakfield Road and that will bring you right outside Anfield stadium. Venmore Street is on the left just opposite."

Frank had started losing the will to live after the second set of instructions, but as ever was impressed. He winked at the young DC.

"Cheers Bob, I knew there was a good reason for letting you get on the team, see you later."

He got back in his car and drove off towards Queens Drive. Bob as usual was *Bob on;* the build up to the rush hour traffic hadn't reached Queens Drive. In minutes he was on Stoneycroft passing Broadgreen Hospital close to West Derby and Crosby Green where he had been the previous night. Five minutes later he could see the football stadium looming up on his right.

He had a quick flashback to the game he had been to see against Newcastle with Cram. He never did find out what Hilary had thought about him taking Cram to the game, or the dirty shoes in the plastic shopping bag. He made up his mind he would ring her tonight and speak to Cram before he went to bed.

He slowed down as he drove alongside the stadium and pulled up at the end of Venmore Street. He saw the red and white police car parked on the right a third of the way up. Behind it was Barry's car. One of the uniformed officers from Walton Lane was stood with his arms folded on the front step of the house, blue and white police tape was flapping in the wind. He pulled up behind Barry's car and got out. The officer on the doorstep came to meet him.

"Hello Sir, I'm PC Mick Harton from Walton Lane, are you by any chance DI Carroll from MIT?"

Frank flashed his ID badge.

"Thank you Sir, DS Ferguson is next door with the two kids and Mr. Oliver."

As they spoke two plain white vans turned up. SOCO and a forensic support team had arrived.

"Okay thanks Mick, I'm going straight inside for a shufty at what we've got, tell DS Ferguson I'm here and to join me inside ASAP. In the meantime I want you to move your car and block off the entrance to this street. I want the rest of it cordoned off about fifty metres further up. No one gets in or out unless they live here. Is the alleyway at the back secured and cordoned off?"

"No Sir, not the alleyway just the back door, PC Warren is there making sure no one gets near."

"Good, as soon as you've given DS Ferguson the nod that I'm here get on the blower to your nick and tell them I want at least another four uniformed officers here pronto. Come back to me if there's any problem with that."

Frank left the officer to get on with it and went inside the house. What a difference between this house and the one in Crosby Green. Same City, less than ten miles away and yet it could well have been on another planet so vast was the difference. It was dark and dingy inside. The walls had at some time been papered with a wood chip wallpaper and been painted over so many times the bumps from the woodchip were barely visible.

Judging by the dark yellow almost brown colour of the paint the last coat had been applied sometime in the late sixties. The skirting boards and the banister leading up the stairs were covered with the same layer of paint.

In a crumpled heap at the foot of the stairs was a green coloured anorak. There was no shade over the light fitting, which had also been entombed with the same paint as the banister and walls. In the hallway various smells hit him straight away. There was the musty smell of old carpets and damp walls.

Stale cigarette smoke and a faint smell of take away food blended with disinfectant was emanating from the direction of the kitchen. But lurking behind all the smells was the one you never forget, the smell of death. Not very strong, but it was here. According to what he'd been told so far, the body was discovered late this afternoon. Even with his limited knowledge he estimated the body had been here since at least last night.

He pulled a pair of latex gloves from his jacket pocket and put them on before entering the living room. On the couch exactly as she had been when the kids next door had found her was Margaret Smith. Frank leaned over the body; the sweet sickly odour of death was stronger here. The skin had a chalky look about it and had turned a dusty gray in stark contrast to the died black hair. He could see the unmistakable markings around the mouth and nose; they were almost identical to the ones he had seen at the Perriman house last night.

Who ever had been here and done this had more than likely been at the address in Crosby Green less than twenty-four hours ago. He heard the sound of voices coming from the direction of the front door. DS Ferguson was asking the SOCO to give him five minutes with the DI before they got to work. Already gloved up Barry tapped on the door to the living room and entered.

"What do you reckon then Boss?" Frank confirmed what Barry had already worked out for himself. He had seen the photographs from the Perriman woman that had been emailed across to MIT ahead of the Post Mortem report.

"I'm absolutely certain this is identical to the one we've got already. I heard you've got us five minutes before the cleanup team gets to work. Come on let's do a walk and talk."

They made some quick notes then left the living room and went upstairs pausing at each room to try and picture for themselves what had happened here. They stood on the landing and stared into the small back bedroom that served as a junk room.

From where they stood, through the half drawn curtains of the window they could see the top of the wall surrounding the back yard and the alleyway. Beyond that they could see the old gray slate roofs of houses in the next street. Windows previously smashed and now boarded up appeared like dried up scabs on old wounds. It was dark outside already and not much else to see.

Frank stepped into the room and surveyed the junk. An old upright hoover stood alongside several battered cardboard boxes full of bric-a-brac, old board games, tired looking teddy bears and worn out shoes. A pair of stereo speakers with the fronts missing and what was left of a 1960's record player was stacked on top of a pile of folded linen and an old rug.

Several more boxes containing old newspapers and magazines were stacked in a corner. One of the boxes was split and piles of magazines were spread all over the floor. Obscuring some of the view from the doorway was a metal clothes rack. The chrome bar was straining at the centre with the weight of clothes on hangars.

The clothes looked as if they spanned a fashion period from the late fifties to the mid seventies and had ground to a halt almost as if the person had stopped buying clothes at that point.

Beyond the clothes rack against the wall there was a large wooden framed chair that looked totally out of place. It was upholstered in a tatty green felt held in place with round-headed brass studs several of which were missing. The seat was threadbare and some of the lining had been exposed. The high back of the seat had a darkened greasy patch where many years of unwashed hair had taken its toll.

Something about the position of the chair struck Frank as odd. It was side on to the window with the backrest practically hidden from view by one side of the curtains.

"Anything strike you about that chair?" asked Frank. Barry had been thinking along the same lines.

"What I find strange Boss, is the fact that in a room full of junk with hardly an inch of floor space to be seen, the chair isn't covered in anything or been used to stack more junk on top of it."

Frank agreed.

"When we're done, I want SOCO to give that chair the full *Monty*. If someone's been sitting in that chair in the last twenty four hours I want to know who it was, when it was, how long for, when they last went for a shit and what they ate for breakfast. Come on let's move on, this place is starting to give me the fuckin' eebie jeebies."

They did a swift scan through the rest of the rooms making notes of anything that struck them as unusual. In the bathroom every inch of conceivable space was covered in plastic tubes and pots containing all manner of face creams, hair products, dental paste and deodorants. There was a hair dryer lying in the sink plugged in to an extension cable coming from the hall. Orange and blue BIC razors lay all around the bathtub and the plug was blocked with a congealed mess of soap scum and what looked like pubic hair.

The window ledge and shelves were covered in dust and strands of hair. Brown stains left behind from unattended cigarettes were everywhere. They made a note of the shoes, socks and the trousers left in the centre of the badly fitted carpet on the bathroom floor.

"Come on Barry this place is fucking minging lets check the rest and get out of here."

In the main bedroom the picture was similar to the bathroom. The bed looked as if it hadn't been made since new. Overflowing ashtrays, discarded make up products, packets of unused condoms and a pile of unread junk mail littered the dresser. Tucked into the corner of the wooden frame was a small yellowing picture of David Cassidy. The mirror was cracked in several places and held together with the same tape that was holding the bedroom windows together.

Next to the wardrobe in the corner of the room there were two black plastic bin sacks filled with empty beer cans, fag ends and polystyrene take away trays. The curtains were practically glued together with nicotine. Frank couldn't help get the feeling that maybe this woman was better off out of it.   Downstairs they surveyed the kitchen. The same sad messages resounded from every corner.

They stepped outside into the yard, flashed their ID badges and introduced themselves to PC Warren. Frank looked at the ashen coloured face of the young constable before him.

"You don't look too well son, you feeling all right?"

The officer looked embarrassed.

"Yes Sir I'm okay thank you, just got a bit queasy with the whiff coming from those bin bags in the corner, I'd keep up wind of them if I were you."

Barry went and stood next to the coalbunker.

"Fuckin'ell Boss, this hasn't been emptied for at least a year judging by the smell, its absolutely fuckin' heaving."

Frank didn't need to go any closer to it; he had picked up the smell of rotten decay as soon as he had entered the yard.

"Yeh I know it's a real Health and Safety nightmare. I want the phone number of the local council authority when I get back. I've a good mind to drag them here and make them fuckin' empty it themselves."

Frank walked backwards to the gate at the entrance to the yard and tried to imagine what had happened at this house. He looked up at the window of the back bedroom and shivered.

"Come on I've seen enough, go and let the forensic boys in and let them do their job, I'll brief the SOCO."

Minutes later the place was crawling with figures in crinkly white suits and face masks. Frank was issuing instructions faster than they could keep up with. The pathologist was in the living room inspecting the body.

Frank recognised him, it was Harkins, the same guy he had met at the coroners' office.

"So what do you think Doc, we got the same MO here or not?"

The professor turned towards Frank and nodded.

"Hello Inspector, yes I would say so, looking at the markings here, and particularly *here*," he used a small penlight to highlight the areas he was referring to, "this is identical to what we saw last night. In my estimation this woman was probably seriously intoxicated before the Chloroform was used to subdue her. Not that she would have needed subduing." He pointed to the empty lager cans. Frank could see there were at least nine empty cans lying about on the floor.

"We can't say for certain that she drank all of them last night, we'll have to wait for the post mortem report."

The professor was kneeling next to the couch.

"One other thing inspector, take a look at this."

He pointed to a tattered looking black leather handbag. The zip on the opening of the bag was wide open and he was using a plastic rod to shift the contents of the bag.

The bag was full of the paraphernalia associated with womens' handbags. Tubes of lipstick, make up compacts, hairbrush, bunches of keys with luminous green rubbery toy key fobs, half empty Bic lighters, cigarette packets and a purse made up the contents. Nestled amongst all of this at the bottom of the bag was a blue and gray coloured tube with an opening for a mouthpiece.

"See that?" He pointed out the inhaler at the bottom of the bag.

"This woman was an Asthmatic or at least that's what the inhaler would indicate, whether she used it frequently or not is another matter. I would guess that the combination of alcohol plus any other substances yet to be identified and the use of Chloroform would have triggered severe respiratory distress. If she was asleep on her front, positional asphyxiation probably played a part. She's been dead at least twelve to fifteen hours. Time of death I would say sometime between midnight and two-am this morning. If you need more than that ring me at around ten o clock tonight, I'll have a bit more for you then. The rest will have to wait until tomorrow."

Frank thanked him and went to find Barry. He was outside the front door talking to PC Harton. Two more police cars had arrived from Walton Lane with five additional uniformed officers. Frank tapped Barry on the shoulder and indicated he wanted a word in private. They went to Frank's car and got inside.

"Okay Barry here's the score. You know that case we were working on that I said was unofficial?"

"The one involving your colleague...Father Maloney?"

"Yeh my colleague...Ted alright, Father Ted Maloney is his name, I've known him since I was born. Any way that case has just gone ultra fuckin' official from this moment on. The Sandra Pollock case, the job we attended last night and now this. They are all linked. This is now a full-scale murder enquiry and we're going to throw the fuckin' works at it. There's a fuckin' nutter out there and I want the bastard locked up by the end of the week at the latest."

Barry could feel his adrenaline levels rising with every word his boss said. From now on they would be working round the clock and adrenaline was going to be permanently on the menu.

"Right Boss, I know you've got a plan, you always have, so let's hear it."

Frank looked at him and smiled.

"No flies on you eh Barry? Okay here it is. I am going straight back to the office and get things moving from there. I've got a shed load of calls to make first. I need you to stay here for a while and make sure everything is boxed off properly. Leave SOCO and forensics to get on with it inside the house. As soon as they're done and the body is off to the morgue I want this place properly secured. See if we can get a locksmith out here I want new locks front and back, no one other than ourselves is to get any where near this house for at least forty eight hours. Get hold of the uniforms from Walton Lane. I want a full sweep of this street and the back alley. When they've done that get them on a door-to-door asking questions. Who knew this woman? When was she last seen and by who? Where did she go last night? You know the score. Stay in contact, if anything comes up let me know first. I'll see you back at HQ when you're done."

Frank paused trying to think if there was anything he had missed. Barry jotted some notes down in his pocket notebook.

"What time are we meeting for the briefing?"

Frank looked at his watch; it was almost six o'clock.

"I'll brief you all together once I've made the calls to get everyone I need. I'll bring our lads up to speed first. I also need to find out from Bob what happened with Sandra Pollock at the Florists'. Unless you hear different, say eight pm tonight in the incident room.

"Okay see you later." Barry opened the door and climbed out of the car.

He was about to close the door and leave when Frank called him back.

"Oh and Barry!"

"What?"

"See if you can get on the phone to the council and make some enquiries about that rubbish in the back. I want it fuckin' shifted like yesterday, make sure there's at least one of our lads there and someone from forensics with them when it happens."

"Okay Boss, I'll get it sorted."

As Frank drove off, in his rear view mirror he saw Barry gesticulating and issuing instructions to the uniformed officers from Walton Lane. Not paying attention he almost crashed into the council street sweeper as it trundled past the end of the street.

Frank reached for his mobile phone on the passenger seat and didn't see the driver of the council truck flipping two fingers up at him. There were five missed calls on his phone; one was from Bob back at the office. The other four of them were from his DCI.

Chapter 27

Pete Harris and Terry Jones were in their makeshift office at The Liverpool Herald & Tribune. As struggling freelance journalists their mission since they'd left University was to get full time posts with one of the big national newspapers. Now, on a months trial, with the promise of permanent positions if they, "done the fuckin' busines" as Tom Scallion, the editor had bluntly put it to them, they were desperate for a break. Pete was pacing the floor struggling to put together a story for the evening edition when the phone rang. Terry picked the phone up and punched the speaker button.

"Herald and Tribune, news desk?"

"Terry its Jimmy at the council, let me speak to Pete."

"I can hear you Jimmy, what's up mate?" shouted Pete from the other side of the room.

"Pete, I just got a call from one of the lads doing the road sweeper run over in Anfield. Something's goin on, the coppers are all over the place. They wouldn't' let him up the street. The road was still blocked off half an hour later when he went past."

"What's happened?" queried Terry.

"Not sure, the driver said he saw some kids and asked them the same question."

"And?" asked Pete impatiently.

"The kids said something about the coppers arriving and two girls had been arrested for murder."

"Where about in Anfield?" Terry cut in, notepad at the ready.

"Venmore Street, right outside the Kop."

"Fuckinell Jimmy, cheers mate, we're on our way, speak to yer later."

Jimmy hung up. Terry grabbed his camera bag and followed Pete who was already on his way out the door. A new trail of rubber was burnt into the road as they left the car park.

By the time they arrived it was getting dark. Pete brought the car to a crawl as they neared the entrance to Venmore Street. As they cruised past they saw the police car still blocking the street.

"We've got no chance of getting up there, let's park up the road and walk back," said Terry. They did a u-turn and left the car three streets away. As they walked back Terry was fiddling with his camera settings trying to keep up with Pete. At the corner of Venmore Street they stopped to see what was going on.

Sure that they had been clocked by the police officer inside the car blocking the street they kept walking to the next street and turned right. They were going to have to go to the end, turn right and come back down Venmore Street from the opposite end. As they entered the street they saw a group of young kids sat on a wall. Pete walked up to them.

"All right lads, what's goin on?" he asked hopefully.

"Dunno," said one of them with a shrug of his shoulders.

"What's the bizzies doing blocking off the street?" asked Terry, thinking they would respond to his use of slang.

"Go an ask them yerself," said another kid. Pete glanced at Terry.

"Come on we're getting nowhere here."

They walked further along the street and stopped to speak to some more kids sat on bikes about thirty feet away from the blue and white scene of crime tape.

Pete tried feeding £1.00 coins to them as if they were slot machines and got nothing in return. A £5.00 note from Terry finally got them the names of the two kids who found the body and the old man who'd made the 999 call. Another fiver got them the house numbers.

Armed with this information they doubled back to the café on the corner of Lake Street for a bacon sandwich and a coffee. Pete used his mobile phone and rang directory enquiries. Five minutes later he had the numbers for both the old man and the mother of the two kids. When he tried to interview Mr. Oliver over the phone the old guy was having none of it and threatened to call the police when Pete offered him money. The mother of the two kids was a lot more accommodating and quite happy to negotiate a price over the phone for information.

Pete and Terry agreed with her on a price of £1,000.00 with the possibility of more to come if they got themselves a major story. Thirty minutes later they met her in the bar of the Salisbury pub half way down Walton Breck Road to do the deal.

Once she'd told them everything she had been able to get out of Rebecca and Hayley, Pete handed her a cheque for the money. Things were looking up, they knew they were on to something but not quite sure of the full extent of what exactly, it was they were on to.

They were about to leave the Salisbury and head back to the office on James Street when things got even better. Terry's mobile rang. It was the contact from the City Council with the tip off about the rubbish collection scheduled for the next morning at the address on Venmore Street. Hardly believing their luck they took a chance and went back to see if they could get a closer look at the alley at the back of the house.

From the corner they could see the uniformed police officers behind the tape outside the house. Deciding not to risk fronting it out with them they walked up the next street directly behind Venmore Street. Three houses up into Vienna Street they calculated that they were exactly opposite the back of the alley adjacent to the house in Venmore Street.

As bold as brass Pete knocked on the front door hoping to speak to the owner of the house. They struck lucky, the owner wasn't available but the bunch of students who lived there were happy to do business. After a short conversation over money Pete and Terry were invited inside and allowed to go upstairs to have a look from the back at what sort of vantage point they would have. It was perfect. From the window in the bathroom they had full view over the walls of the alleyway and right into the backyard of the house on Venmore Street.

Even in the dark they could see the tape flapping in the wind and the faint outline of another uniformed officer outside the back gate to the yard. They practically fell over themselves as they went back downstairs to speak with the students. It had been a struggle to keep a straight face as they agreed the price of £100.00 for each student. Had the students known it they would have probably gone to at least double that amount. Still it was another cheque for £400.00. With the £1000,00 already paid out they had practically blown a whole months worth of slush money. It was a gamble, but they had the feeling it was going to be worth it.

The students told them they would all be at tutorials in the morning so they handed over a key to the front door with the alarm code for the house. Pete and Terry promised they would drop the key through the letterbox as soon as they were done. They shook hands on the deal and left for their car parked up the street.

On the way back to the office they called in to pick up kebabs and coffee. While Terry waited to pay for the food Pete disappeared. He was back ten minutes later with a smile on his face and holding a duplicate key from the one given to him by the students at Vienna Street. They got back to the newsroom at the offices of the Herald & Tribune around 9.30 pm. It was going to be a busy night.

Chapter 28

On his way back to Canning Place Frank made several calls on his mobile. DC Bob Turner was first on the list.

"Yes, Boss?"

"Bob, guess what? The person who performed the job Barry and I were at last night has been busy. I've just left the pathologist at the scene of another one. He's positive it's the same MO. I'm on my way back to Canning Place now to call everyone in. I need the incident room jacking up with everything as per MIT Scale 1 procedure, if you haven't already done it get everyone available on it now. I want it ready for briefing and orders at eight pm tonight."

"Okay …err…boss there's something you need to know…"

"Yeh, I'll sort it later, what's the score with Father Maloney and Sandra Pollock?"

"Its all good news Boss. After you left, she shut up shop and came back here with Father Maloney and myself. She's signed all the consent forms and given us a full statement, it makes interesting reading."

Frank couldn't believe his luck.

"Where are they both now?"

"They needed to get off Boss, we gave them a lift home about an hour ago."

Frank thought about this and couldn't make his mind up whether this was a good thing or not.

"Bob, in Sandra Pollock's statement, other than the main point in question, any mention of anything else unusual, you know like medical complaints of any sort?" Frank waited not expecting anything.

"What, like a skin rash you mean? Yeh, it says here she had some kind of rash on her face a few weeks ago. Even went to the chemist and bought some cream for it. Didn't do much good by all accounts, seems to have cleared up by itself."

Frank was stunned by this news. He had just got his first witness to whatever crime it was that was being committed by this nutter. More importantly she was still alive to tell the tale.

"Okay Bob, thanks, you've done a great job. Crack on with what you need to do, I'll see you shortly."

Bob wasn't quite finished

"Boss?"

Frank jumped the lights onto Scotland Road.

"What?"

"I think you should know the DCI has been taken ill, an ambulance was called to his home by his wife about an hour ago. He'd gone home not feeling too good. He's been taken to hospital. Mark and Daz went to see him. They rang me fifteen minutes ago. The doctor they spoke to reckons the boss has had a stroke; apparently his blood pressure has been through the roof for yonks. He didn't look well when he was up here earlier looking for you."

Frank felt both guilty and saddened at the news. He had known for some time his boss wasn't well but it wasn't something they often discussed.

"Okay Ian, sorry to hear about the boss and thanks for letting me know, I'll be back there in about twenty minutes."

Frank hung up and floored the accelerator.

By the time he got back to Canning Place the incident room was buzzing with activity. There were a lot of faces he hadn't seen before, people who had been drafted in and others from within Canning Place. They all turned towards him as he entered, expecting him to say something. He wasn't going to let them down.

"Okay everybody, just a quick word if I can."

The hustle and bustle came to a rapid halt.

"I just wanted to say quickly before the briefing tonight that your help is much appreciated, I'd like to see you all in the incident room at eight pm. There will be a full update and briefing at that point. Anything else you need in the meantime I'm sure DS Ferguson and the rest of my team will be only too happy to help. Thanks, I'll see you all shortly."

Frank glanced towards Bob and Mark.

"Bring everything you've got on Sandra Pollock to my office. Daz let me know the minute DS Ferguson gets back."

Bob, Mark and Daz nodded, acknowledging the fact that they knew that their DI had just confirmed in front of everybody exactly who was running this show. Bob collected everything he had on his desk and followed his boss to the office.

"Here's everything we've got so far Boss." Bob placed a bundle of files and papers on the desk. Everything Frank had asked for was there. Amongst the documentation were photographs of Sandra Pollock, bank statements, social security reports, copies of utility bills, electoral voters registration documents, PNC printouts and vehicle documentation from DVLC. Sandra Pollock had no idea most of this had been acquired. The other three documents she had given with full consent and knowledge of what she was doing.

The first document was a consent form with her signature saying that she agreed to undergo a supervised pregnancy test and that she had given her permission to take DNA samples not only from her but also from the unborn baby inside her womb. The second document was a signed consent form allowing her medical records to be accessed. Bob had been quick off the mark and sent Daz over to her GP to collect the information they needed. The final, somewhat lengthy document was the statement taken from Sandra Pollock.

"Okay Bob, thanks for this, you've done a top job mate, give us half an hour and then get back in here with Mark and Daz." Bob left the office. Frank sat and read through the statement. When he finished reading it, he read through it again and jotted some bullet points down on his notepad. There was no doubt about it; his talk with Ted had worked. He and Ted had sat down at the Presbytery and talked about how he should approach Sandra Pollock at the Florist's shop.

Together they had gone through exactly what Ted should say to Sandra Pollock like a barrister preparing a client for court. The right buzz words to use, words to show empathy, understanding, to trigger realisation and ultimately co-operation. The statement had been prepared the same way; it was a complete chronological account of what had happened to Sandra Pollock.

At this moment in time all Frank knew was, that she was pregnant, but she was sticking to her story that she has no boyfriend and had not had intercourse with anybody. Her medical report confirmed what was in her statement. Sandra Pollock had been raped at the age of twelve. Now she lived alone, she has no boyfriend and hadn't had sexual intercourse with anyone since the rape. For all intents and purposes she was still a virgin.

Frank leaned back in his chair and tipped his head up towards the ceiling, yawning and rubbing his eyes. He sat deep in thought for a moment with his eyes closed and hands clasped behind his neck. When he opened his eyes again he found himself staring at the wavy patterned ceiling of his office.

He yawned again and his eyes began to water causing the pattern on the ceiling to become a total blur. He found himself blinking rapidly to try and clear his eyes when something very weird happened. The ceiling gradually faded until it disappeared altogether. In its place was what looked like an old movie screen.

Strange, blurred and distorted images in black and white danced across the screen in fast forward mode. The images gathered speed, too fast to recognise anything. His eyes continued to blink and yet the watery effect was still there, *was he crying?*

The screen flickered, lights flashed; black and white images on a film zoomed in and out of focus appearing to get larger then smaller. There was a sudden acceleration in the film speed and like magic the black and white images changed into colour and came into focus before his eyes.

He could see kids playing on cobblestone streets and row after row of dirty brown terraced houses. Groups of girls were playing hopscotch and others with ropes singing skipping songs *"Rosy Apple Lemon and a Pear"* Boys on bikes were chasing each other up and down the street. Mothers in headscarves and flower patterned pinafores wearing knee-length socks and slippers stood in huddles smoking cigarettes watching the children play. The film started accelerating again.

He saw pictures of his own face looking up and crying and then a blown up image of his knee with a plaster on it. He caught a glimpse of his dad mending his bicycle at the front of the house. He saw smoke drifting into a dull gray sky from chimney tops and smoke stacks from factories in the background. He could see a huge black and gray gasworks cylinder with railings and a ladder; there were sounds of steam trains shunting by behind it.

The picture went out of focus for a second. When it refocused he could see an image of huge green gates at the sloped concrete entrance to an outdoor market. He heard a child's voice counting down from ten and shouting, *Coming ready or not!*

The film moved on to a park with old metal railings around it surrounding a concrete area with swings and a round-a-bout in the middle. Gangs of kids all sat cross-legged on the grass eating penny lollipops, watching a Punch and Judy show clapping and cheering. The film speeded up again with images moving so fast he couldn't tell what they were.

When it slowed down again he swore he could smell chlorine from the swimming baths, he heard an ambulance and saw hospital images, and worried faces with handkerchiefs. The picture faded to the sound of a school bell ringing and a thousand children's voices were cheering. Then there was …blue…bright blue…the sky was bright blue and the sun shone high in the sky, the wind whistled in his ears and made his eyes water so that tears streamed off his face. The bike was freewheeling down the hill; it felt like a hundred miles an hour.

The Belfast Lough on the right glistened like a sea of gold under the rays of the sun. The gauze bushes were in full bloom to the left, millions of bright yellow flowers blurred past looking like they were on fire. His feet felt wet, there was mud on his shoes, and he could taste lemonade and smell the aroma of malted bread.

Greystone walls surrounded him, they were cold and damp, and he felt afraid. He could hear someone laughing and another person screaming. There was a loud bang and the screaming stopped. Now *he was crying!*

There was the sound of an angry voice and shouting. Someone was next to him; it was his best friend Ted. They were clung together, their faces turned away from what they might see, they were crying. A splashing noise coming from deep below them. Out of the dark a voice spoke to them.

"Okay sonny boy, and you wee man, just fuckin' listen to me now."

He could smell stale cigarettes and whisky and he heard himself talking.

"Yer not goin t'kill us are yez?"

The voice with the whisky and nicotine tainted breath spoke back.

"No fucker is gonna kill no fucker, d'yez here me all right?"

There was a loud ringing noise in the background. The screen went blank and everything went dark. Frank opened his eyes; he was back in his office staring at the ceiling. On his desk the phone was ringing. He stared at it as if it was still part of what he had just been experiencing. When he answered it he spoke cautiously. The voice on the other end brought him sharply back to the real world.

"Frank its Chief Superintendent Bright here, I take it you've heard the news about Andy?"

Half an hour had passed. Frank felt as if he had been asleep for hours.

"Er... Yes Sir DC Turner informed me about an hour ago. DC's Roberts and Vasquez went to see him. Doctors say he's had a stroke, he's critical but stable."

"That's right, I just spoke to the consultant on the phone, he's being kept in for at least a week. After that he'll be off to the convalescence and rehab center at Harrogate. Could be six months before he's back, if he comes back at all. You know he's got less than twelve months to run before he's due his pension?"

Frank was wide-awake now. He was in no hurry to see the back of his boss.

"Yes Sir I was aware of that, but we're not quite ready to organise his retirement do just yet."

"Well I appreciate that Frank but that's the reason I'm calling you. Until further notice you are acting DCI in his place, I'd like a nomination from you of who you'd recommend or would like to fill your shoes when the time comes. I don't need an answer right now but in a day or two if you don't mind, give it some thought would you?"

Frank had already given this some thought on numerous occasions. He knew exactly who he wanted as his DI, but Barry Ferguson had always said he wasn't interested in the job. He was going to discuss it again with Barry and give him first refusal.

"Yes Sir I'll do that and get back to you as soon as I can."

"Good, get Janice to complete the necessary paperwork and get it to me for signature. Now I hear you've been extremely busy in the last twenty-four hours. Its half past seven, the car park is still half full and your place was buzzing when I popped over earlier. What time's your briefing? I want to be there."

Frank looked at his watch and couldn't believe that nearly an hour had gone by since Bob had left the office and the freaky film show on the ceiling started.

"I'm just waiting for DS Ferguson to get back sir, but I've told everyone to be in the incident room for eight pm."

Chief Superintendent Bright confirmed that he would be there and hung up.

Frank replaced the receiver and looked at the pile of paperwork on his desk. It was going to be a long night. He stood up stretched and checked his watch again, he had less than half an hour to change his suit and get his act together before the briefing.

He gathered all of his notes and headed for the changing room where he kept a spare set of clothes. As he walked towards the door he felt something cold around the area of his crotch. He looked down and couldn't believe his eyes. There was a darkened patch around the front of his trousers. He felt it with his hand and withdrew it straight away.

His mind raced back to the film he had seen earlier. He thought back to the only time something had scared him so bad he had wet himself. He remembered what it was. It had been the sound of the voice in the Keep back home in Ireland all those years ago that had caused him to piss in his pants. Now he had done it again. Twenty-four years since he had first heard that horrible voice, someone or something had caused him to do it again. One thing in his mind was certain, whoever it was, the bastard was going to fucking pay for it.

Chapter 29

The Redeemer was back at his flat in Toxteth staring at the list of names in front of him. He had not touched a drop of alcohol for almost two years but on his way back to the flat he called in to an all night convenience store and bought two six-packs of lager and a bottle of whisky. He hadn't eaten and he'd been drinking solidly for the last five hours. Half the booze he'd bought was gone.

His head ached and he felt tired and ill. Since the unexpected outcome of his last visit when things had gone horribly wrong he hadn't slept. Every time he closed his eyes in an attempt to sleep, he was disturbed by the haunting images of what he'd had to do to get rid of the body after his encounter with the man at Margaret Smiths house. He knew it wouldn't be long before someone complained about the smell coming from the coalbunker in the back yard.

When they did the police would be all over the place looking for the murderer. He had to lie low for a while. His mission would have to be put on hold until the dust had settled and it was safe to carry on. Murder had not been part of his plan when he first set out on this mission. He looked again at the list of names, each one indelibly stamped in his brain; he could never forget them no matter how much he drank. Painful memories flooded back to him.

He remembered the first time he'd seen the list of names. He'd reluctantly agreed to visit his Father who, according to the doctor he had spoken to had literally days, if not hours to live. They'd long since abandoned each other and there'd been no love lost between them.

His father was in the ward for the terminally ill at The Royal Liverpool Hospital. The news that his father was in hospital had come as no surprise. After a period of over twenty years of drug abuse and prolific unprotected casual sex his father had been diagnosed as HIV positive five years ago. Poetic justice some might say.

He had thought long and hard on whether he should bother visiting him at all. If he did, it would be in the knowledge that this would be the closing of an unsavory chapter in his life, because he knew this would be the last time he saw his father alive.

As a direct result of his lifestyle, justifiably he lay on a bed and was dying from Aids related illnesses, pneumonia and septicaemia to mention a few. His immune system had given up completely and something as simple as a cold could kill him. The doctors had said it was just a matter of which virus got to him first.

The Redeemer closed his tear filled eyes and the vision of his father lying on the hospital bed was there with him in the room. He remembered how he had approached the bed and watched his father stirring in a drug-induced sleep. He seemed to be tormented by something that kept him hanging on.

He sat next to the bed and reached for the jug of water on the table by his father's bedside. There, sat next to an empty glass was a gold locket shaped like a heart. A tiny diamond glistened in the light from the bedside table. Under the locket was a folded piece of paper, the paper on which his father had scribbled the list of names. He picked it up not knowing what it was. As he sat reading through the names his father opened his eyes and was looking at him as he stared at the piece of paper.

When he heard it, his fathers voice surprised him, for someone so close to death it was remarkably clear and audible.

"Daniel, t'anks for coming t'see me…" he said. There was a pause for breath before he was able to continue.

"I wanted to talk to you about something… I want to make a confession. Something which I can't leave without sayin… and you're the only one I can talk to."

He looked down at his father; the use of his name surprised him. In all the years he'd known him he had never heard his father talk like that and he couldn't remember the last time he'd called him by his first name. He thought about whether he wanted to listen or not, and then he considered how would it be not knowing for the rest of his life what it was that his father had wanted to say to him on his deathbed.

The knowledge that he was about to die persuaded him. So he'd listened. First he'd been surprised. His surprise gradually turned into amazement followed by sheer disbelief. Yet amongst all these emotions somehow there had also been an element of understanding. As he'd continued to talk, his father spoke about things he had never told him before. It had all come flooding out, the whole story of his father's wretched life and how he'd grown up into a life of crime.

He told him of his escape from Ireland. How he still had a nagging feeling that the law was still hunting him. He had talked about his first time in prison, about how and why he'd turned to drugs. Finally from his father he'd learned who his real mother was. It had all been too much to take in and he began to feel pangs of guilt and regret, wishing they could start all over again, maybe, just maybe things could have been different. Then had come the ultimate deathbed confession and the revelation of the facts behind the women's names on the list. Sadness turned to hatred.

Chapter 30

Frank got showered and changed; putting on a single-breasted charcoal grey suit, light grey shirt and black and white striped tie. He had ten minutes to scan through his notes and get his head sorted before the briefing. At five minutes to eight he emerged from the locker room just in time to see Barry heading towards the incident room.

"Barry, I need a quick word before we go in for the briefing."

Barry was in a mind of his own and took a second to react.

"Sorry Boss, I was miles away there for a moment, its been a hectic few hours back at Venmore Street. The press has got wind of the story and a couple of photographers turned up about ten minutes before I was about to leave."

"Shit! Still I suppose we should have been prepared for that. I'm surprised we haven't heard from them before now. We'll need to brief the PLO's to prepare a bog standard statement. Never mind, you can bring me up to speed on what happened later, right now I need to tell you something."

Barry had an idea what he was about to say.

"Boss, if it's about the DCI, I know what's going on. Daz gave me a bell as soon as she got the word from the hospital." Frank didn't sound surprised.

"Yeh I thought you would, but that's as maybe, listen what you don't know is that the Chief Super rang me about half an hour ago, I've been made acting DCI and its looking like it could be permanent if Andy takes early retirement.

The Supers' asked me to nominate someone to take over as DI and I want to give him your name, or at least give you the chance to turn it down before anyone else gets a shot."

Barry looked flabbergasted.

"Okay Boss, thanks I appreciate the vote of confidence, I'll give it some thought."

Barry had given this possibility all the thought he was going to give it in the car on the way back to Canning Place and had already made his mind up. The rank of Detective Sergeant was high enough up to get some respect and low enough to avoid all the extra shit that came with the rank of Inspector. He looked at Frank and swore he was reading his thoughts.

Frank had his suspicions, but he was keeping them to himself.

"Alright then let's get on with the briefing."

As they neared the door to the incident room they could hear the sound of voices buzzing in anticipation inside. Frank pushed the door open, placed his hand on Barry's shoulder and ushered him inside ahead of himself.

As the door opened the noise levels died instantaneously. Waiting inside, sat around the huge expanse of tables, was the team of officers from all over Merseyside who had been called in to assist with the operation. Sat amongst them were members of PITO, the Police Information Technology Organisation, here to help out with the complex database and spreadsheet requirements.

Merseyside Traffic Officers and representatives from Merseyside British Transport Police were sat next to colleagues from Mersey Regional Ambulance Brigade. Two senior officers from the Prison Service had been called in as liaison support and other officers from the Community Support team were there. To the right of them were two Press Liaison Officers and a photographer.

As Frank and Barry entered there was a shuffling of seats and gathering of papers, sounds of pens being readied and nervous coughs, the whole setting gave an air of a performance about to begin. Barry took a seat in the front row with Mark, Bob and Daz. The Chief Super was sat out at the front.

Frank glanced around the room and recognised the faces of officers who had helped out on previous operations. He placed his files alongside his notes on a small table just in front of the huge Perspex screens arranged in a half circle against the wall. Photographs with names written underneath had been stuck in a large oval shape across the screens. In the center there was a blank piece of white card with no name on it.

Stuck to another screen was a large-scale map of Merseyside, next to it was a blown up version covered in pins and arrows drawn with coloured markers. To the left of all this was a drop down ceiling mounted screen with the video projector loaded ready to roll. Briefing packs had been handed out to everyone in the room and they were all ready to go the moment Frank gave the green light.

The full might of Merseyside's police machine was about to be unleashed on this case. Frank looked down for the last time at his notes, cleared his throat and looked up.

"Ladies, Gents, before I begin with introductions and briefing there are a few things I would like to say. Firstly good evening, welcome to you all, and thank you for your help and support with this operation. Secondly, I would like to inform those of you that don't know of the news received earlier this evening."

If a pin had been dropped, everybody would have heard it.

"At approximately 18:45 hrs, sadly my boss, DCI Andy Williams was rushed into the Royal Liverpool Hospital suffering from a stroke. He's since been transferred to the Cardio Thoracic Centre and is reported to be critical but stable. I am sure you will all join my colleagues and I, in wishing him well and our hope that he has a speedy recovery."

There was a respectful sound of thumping of tables mixed with a loud voicing of "here, here's" from everyone in the room.

When the noise had died down Frank began again.

"Thank you…okay next up introductions. I am Detective Inspector Frank Carroll acting up temporarily as DCI and I am the SIO in charge of this case."

Frank looked to his side.

"To my right here for those of you that don't know, is Chief Superintendent Norman Bright." The Chief Super took his cue and nodded in appreciation for the introduction.

"The rest of my team here in front of you I think most of you know, for those that don't we've got DS Barry Ferguson, along with DC's Mark Roberts, Bob Turner, and our latest addition to the team acting DC Danielle Vasquez. Once the briefing is over these officers will be pulling you together into teams for tasking."

There was a brief buzz of chatter around the room as the collective group assembled in the room witnessed a professional at work.

Chief Superintendent Bright was looking suitably impressed and was busy writing notes on his pad.

Danielle Vasquez sat back in admiration watching Frank perform the role he did so naturally. She'd known from the time they first met, back in training he was going places. As she watched him, she thought about the time she'd made a pass at him during a drunken party in the accommodation block back at Bruche, or at least she thought she had. Frank had not even noticed the fact that she had *actually flirted with him.*

Years later they'd met again at a Divisional Christmas Dinner at a posh hotel in town. Many of them, including her had booked rooms for an overnight stay. Frank had not bothered, saying he would probably leave early and get a taxi home. As it was he got absolutely blind drunk and they had even danced together during the night. She kept it discreet and professional but she had dropped at least two strong hints that if he wanted to, he could doss down for the night on the sofa in her room.

It had been almost a year since his split with Hilary and there seemed to be no one else on the scene so she had thought, *fuck it* why not? She had fancied him for longer than she could remember but had decided to bide her time after the split.

Had he taken her up on her offer, she simply would have developed things from there. Shortly after one am in the morning with the hotel party still in full swing he had made some lame excuse about not feeling too well and wanted to nip outside for some fresh air. That was the last she had seen of him.

She looked at him now as he was about to deliver one of the most important briefings he had given so far and wondered if he'd known about the way she'd felt about him. If she was ever in his thoughts, he was doing a very good job of not showing it.

The sound of Frank's voice brought her back to the briefing.

"Right! Let's get on with it. If you'd turn to the first page in your briefing packs please. Feel free to ask questions at any time, although if they can be held to the end there will be ample time to go through them then. As you can see from the inside of your packs, the name of this operation is *Operation Round Up*. My aim is to kill two birds with one stone here. We are going to finally draw a line under *Operation Recall* while at the same time apprehending whoever is responsible for the crimes we are currently investigating."

Operation Recall was an initiative that had been launched over twelve months ago and was aimed at investigating unsolved rape cases throughout Merseyside. It had been high up on the political agenda at the time but had been overtaken by the "Safer Streets" campaign.

There were murmurings around the room showing a general consensus that everyone would be glad to see the back of Operation Recall. Frank continued.

"If I can draw your attention to the information we have so far and the photographs behind me. A crime is being committed by a person *or* persons unknown, for the time being, until we have evidence to the contrary we are working on the assumption that this is one person, a male."

He pointed to the blank piece of card in the centre of the photographs.

"This is the person we need to identify and arrest as soon as possible. We have a number of victims, all female, including the latest discovered at 16:30 hrs this afternoon. This amounts to three so far that we know of."

He drew everyone's attention to the remaining pictures and pointed out the locations on the map where each of the victims had been discovered.

"The latest two victims have died as a result of actions carried out by our so far unidentified perp. Now I am pretty certain that our perpetrator whoever it is that is committing these crimes has not intended for the victims to die as a result of their actions. Never the less there have been two deaths so far that we know of, accidental maybe, but the fact is they would probably still be alive if this crime hadn't been committed." He paused and allowed this to sink in.

"So let's look at the crime. Intelligence gathered so far by SOCO at each of the locations, and from the pathologist's reports would indicate that the perpetrator is using a chemical, which we believe to be liquid Chloroform to subdue the victims prior to some kind of sexual ritual or act. The Chloroform acts as a respiratory suppressant. Further evidence suggests that Chloroform has been administered prior to each act by using a cloth of some description soaked in the liquid and placed over the mouth and nose of the victim. Both the coroner and pathologist concur that Chloroform is the chemical used in each case. You can see from the rash or burn marks around the face here, and here."

Frank used a telescopic rod to point at the blown up close ups of the mouth and nose regions of the last two victims.

"The cause of death in each of the last two victims was asphyxiation, triggered by the combination of Chloroform and the presence of excessive amounts of alcohol and in one case anti depressant medication by the name of Amitriptyline, common name Elavil."

Notes were being furiously scribbled. The Chief Super continued to be impressed.

"I think it is important to add that there is no evidence that a rape has occurred, at least not in the form that we know it."

More rumblings from the audience. People sat up in their chairs and looked at each other with puzzled expressions. Frank waited for the noise to settle.

"Although there is evidence that a sexual act has been committed there is no evidence or indication that there was physical contact in the traditional sense. It is a bit of a mystery, but traces of semen have been found to be present in the vagina of each of the deceased victims and yet the perpetrator has left no other signs of having had intercourse with these women."

Frank could see by the looks on their faces everyone in the room was trying to work it out in their head.

"The coroners report following each post mortem highlights the fact there are no signs of bruising or other markings that would indicate that a sexual act in the true sense of the word has been committed."

Whispers echoed around the room as officers leaned their heads to one another.

"Further evidence which confirms the crime probably has a sexual motive is that the first of our known victims is pregnant as a result. We have obtained DNA samples from the sperm found inside the last two victims. I fully expect that the DNA from the unborn fetus of the pregnant woman will prove to be a match with our perpetrator.

We expect to get confirmation of this from the results of the DNA test by first thing tomorrow morning."

A hand went up at the back of the room with a question.

Frank pointed in the direction of the raised hand.

"Yes, you have a question?" Practically everyone in the room turned to look at who was asking the question. The officer introduced herself.

"Yes Sir, WPC Dawn Adams from Woolton Station."

"Are you saying Sir, that whoever did this is somehow artificially inseminating the women he is choosing as his victims?"

Frank knew it was only a matter of time before someone else would come to the same conclusion he'd reached himself.

"It would appear so WPC Adams, I can't personally think of any other way there can be semen present and yet no evidence that actual intercourse has taken place. I believe that there is an intention to artificially inseminate these women to get them pregnant, but don't ask me why."

WPC Adams had just asked the question that everyone else in the room wanted to ask. More hands went up. Frank batted off most of them with answers and asked for others to be saved until the briefing had ended.

"So picking up on WPC Adams' comment there that the perpetrator is *choosing* his victims, it would be reasonable to assume that each of these women have something in common, a certain criteria which is being applied in the selection process. There has to be a logical explanation as to why these women were chosen. The perpetrator is obviously following a pattern of some kind.

If we are going to catch this person we need to find out what these criteria are and identify the pattern."

There were nods of agreement from all around the room and mini discussions breaking out amongst the groups. Frank took the opportunity to quickly scan his notes before he called for everyone's attention.

"There are a number of questions for which we need answers to. For example, how many more are there going to be? Who's next? When? How long have we got before the perpetrator strikes again?"

Frank could tell already that his audience was itching to get started on this. There was a healthy mix of competitiveness and rivalry amongst them all, but most of all a sense of duty to the people of Merseyside to put a stop to this as soon as possible.

"One other thing we need to take into consideration is the fact that if the perpetrator is aware by now that the last two victims have died as a result of their actions, they may well go to ground and possibly not surface again. In my opinion it will depend on what the motive is for committing these acts, so I'd like everyone to give some thought to this."

Heads went down as more notes were taken.

"I will be open to any ideas and suggestions on how we are going to catch this person, if any of you have a brilliant plan I want to hear it. In the mean time here is the method I propose to kick us off with so please pay attention."

Everyone in the room sat up.

"Working under the guidance of my team at the front here and myself, this is what I want. Working in teams we are going to pull up everything we've already got in place from Operation Recall. We are going to go through every rape case on record over the last ten years, both alleged and proved.

From PITO I want a database constructing with all the relevant information, from this, I want two printouts. On one, I want the names and last known addresses of every person, alive or dead, who has been accused of, and or convicted of rape. I want this information cross-referenced with the sex offenders' register. Of those convicted I want to know who is still in prison and who isn't."

The officers from PITO looked visibly excited and were obviously up for the challenge. This was something that for them, pressed all the right buttons. Frank wasn't quite finished.

"From those who have been released I need to know how long they were locked up, when they came out and where they are now. Check the records and make a note of every single one we have with fingerprints and DNA on file. Without exception I want prints and DNA samples from all those of who we *haven't* got."

By now everyone in the room was writing furiously.

"Moving on. The second printout I want, needs to show the names and last knowns of every single victim, I want all the details, whether the case went to court or not and whether there was a conviction from those that did. I want a cross reference done, matching DNA types of every known offender with each of the victims.

Finally from all of this, when the list is complete I want to know the whereabouts' of every known and suspected rapist over the last ten days. *Anyone* who doesn't have a solid alibi for the days and times in question I want brought in for questioning"

Looking around the room the only thing Frank could see was the tops of everyone's heads as notes were being written. For the first time during the briefing he sat down. He leaned towards Barry and whispered.

"Have I missed anything?" Barry looked up from his own notes.

"Not a thing Boss, absolutely fucking spot on so far."

DC Bob Turner chipped in with a "Bob on Boss," for good measure.

Frank collected his papers together then sat and waited for everyone to stop writing. When they all eventually finished their notes and sat up their faces told a picture, the enormity of what they were being asked to do had stunned them.

For the next hour Frank continued with his briefing. By the time he had covered the administration, risks, communication and safety elements of his briefing it was just gone half past ten. The refreshments of coffee, tea and biscuits had long since run out.

The Chief Super satisfied that his new, albeit acting DCI had everything wrapped up, made his excuses and left. The first thing he did on leaving the incident room was call up the duty officer and ordered her to get someone to open up the canteen and have enough pizza and chips prepared for sixty people.

"But sir I'm not sure there will be enough…"

"I don't care, order it in if you have to, use the GPC card and my name as the authorising officer." He hung up. If his team were going to work through the night he could not expect them to do it on tea and biscuits.

He got the message up to Frank in the incident room that the food would be there for everyone as soon as they were done. By the time they were all finished with questions and the teams had been appointed with tasking lists, it had gone midnight.

Finishing off, Frank thanked everyone again for their attention and their patience, reminding them that the clock was ticking. The briefing room disbursed quickly as everyone headed to the canteen.

Frank tapped Barry on the shoulder as he was leaving.

"Barry, if you want to discuss anything with me I'll be in my office for the next half hour or so. After that I'm off home for some kip, I'll be back at about six-ish. Enjoy your pizza." Barry nodded and headed off in the direction of the canteen.

Frank got to his office and sat down. The light on his phone told him he had messages waiting. No time like the present he thought, he listened to each one and scribbled some notes before deleting them. It was half past midnight and he was about to go home. He needed some time on his own to gather his thoughts and prepare himself for the task ahead of him. He could do with a walk by the river to clear his head.

Just as he was gathering his papers together and preparing to leave there was a knock at the door. It was Barry carrying a tray with a plateful of pizza and chips and two Styrofoam cups of coffee on it.

"Come in Barry, grab a seat mate."

"Cheers Boss. Thought you might be hungry, there's enough pizza downstairs to sink a fucking battle ship."

Frank looked at the food suddenly feeling very hungry.

He took the tray of food from Barry and immediately tipped the coffee from the Styrofoam cup into a dirty mug that had been sat on his desk for at least two days.

"Thanks Barry, if I wasn't going to have trouble sleeping tonight this should do the trick. You want some?"

Barry smiled as his boss sat back in his chair put his feet up on the desk and got stuck in to a large slice of the pizza.

"No thanks Boss I'm stuffed."

"So let me guess what you're here for. You've come to tell me your taking the job, right?"

"No, not exactly Boss, I really wanted to run a few things by you before you shot off and maybe you could let me know what you think in the morning."

Frank couldn't help feeling disappointed by the answer he got, but then he should have known better from Barry. He never mixed business with pleasure, he was a professional.

"Okay fire away, lets hear what you've got."

Barry pulled out his notebook and fired away.

"Firstly Boss, the rubbish at the back of the house in Venmore Street. After you left I made some phone calls and got through to someone at Liverpool City Council. They weren't happy at first but I told them that if they didn't arrange to shift it, I would arrange to shift it myself and personally deliver it to their offices to see how they like living in that state."

Frank laughed at this, not because it was funny, but because he knew Barry would do it. Those who knew Barry the closest knew him as the *quiet hard* man.

He never made a threat that he wasn't prepared to carry out. A memory came to him in a flash. Not long after he had first met Barry, they'd all been out on the town celebrating the fact that Bob had passed his promotion exams to Sergeant at the third time of asking, and they'd had a few. A bit of a kafuffle broke out between two groups of teenagers arguing about who was next in the queue at a taxi rank.

A punch was thrown and a young teenager had got knocked to the floor. Barry stepped forward and intervened before it got out of hand. Several youths from one group confronted him and looked to threaten him. Barry stood his ground and said something that Frank would never forget.

"Okay lads, lets just stop for a second here, I'd like to make a suggestion. I can see from looking at you all that you're probably in your late teens, Yeh? Full of the joys of spring, bursting with enthusiasm and energy. Would that be a fair assumption to make?"

The group had just stood looking at him not really sure where he was going with this. A particularly gobby one stepped to the front and spoke up.

"Yeah worr ovit mate?"

Barry spoke to him directly.

"Well the problem here is that all of you combined have got far too much energy for me to deal with, I mean if we started fighting it would all be over very quick and it wouldn't be much fun. So what I'd like to propose is that if you wouldn't mind lining up and waiting your turn while I deal with you one at a time."

Barry had pointed to the gobby one.

"We'll start with you first, if the rest of you could just be patient enough to wait your turn I'll be with you as quick as I can."

Barry had removed his coat and was staring at the young lad who looked absolutely petrified. Within minutes the group had dispersed and walked off in another direction with mutterings from a safe distance of "Yeah worrever mate" and "Think yer somthin special don't'yer." That had been the end of the matter.

Barry had been staring at his boss during Frank's brief period of reminiscence and had to ask why he was smiling.

"What's so funny Boss?"

"Just the thought of you tipping up outside Liverpool City Council offices with a truck full of rubbish. So what happened with the council?"

"Well they contacted someone at the Refuse Collection and Waste disposal center and rang me back. There will be someone there at eight tomorrow morning to arrange for the removal of the rubbish and do a bit of a clean up at the site. I am going to meet them there with one of the forensics boys who was there today. I've arranged to pick him up at seven and get there early."

Frank added something to his notes on his desk.

"Okay, I'll be back here by seven, give me a bell if there are any problems. What else is on your mind?"

"Well Boss I have run a few checks on this Chloroform stuff, you know things like where you can get it from, how much does it cost, that sort of stuff."

Frank rolled his eyes preparing to make more notes.

"So what have you come up with?"

"Well you'll be surprised Boss, just how much you can find out on the Internet."

Frank was never surprised at just how much Barry could find out from anywhere. He was like a bloodhound. If he smelled blood, he never stopped chasing it until he caught up with it. Right now, judging by the amount of paperwork Barry had brought in with him, Frank guessed he was on to something.

"Go on" he said, stifling a yawn.

"There are companies advertised on the Internet who are selling this stuff. I've printed off a list of all the UK based companies and made a few enquiries. There are some of them who produce it and sell it on for industrial use. Anything from production of flurocarbon-22, used as a refrigerant, or as a solvent in photography and dry cleaning agents.

It is even used in dental procedures and other medical practices. I contacted one of them and found out that you can buy a 100ml bottle of 99.9% pure laboratory strength Chloroform for £14.95. You don't even need to open an account or say what you need it for. Can you fucking believe that?"

Frank knew where Barry was going with this and was suddenly wide-awake.

"Let me guess, you are running a check with every company who supplies it to see if any of it has been sold to someone in the Liverpool area, when it was bought and by who, am I right?"

"Spot On Boss, I'm expecting to hear from them before lunchtime tomorrow."

Frank picked up his mug and swallowed the rest of his cold coffee in one gulp before he spoke.

"Anything else?"

"Yes Boss, one more thing. I've got a theory on motive for why this guy is doing this."

Frank picked up his pen and turned to a new page in his notebook.

"Which is?"

"Well, this guy's intention no matter how sick his methods might sound, is to get these women pregnant right?"

Frank nodded while Barry continued with his theory.

"I believe he is trying to get them pregnant in order to give them some kind of gift, something that either they can't have or haven't got. Almost as if he's doing them some kind of favour. In my opinion this guy is under some kind of delusion that he is doing a good thing."

Frank pondered this for a second and then asked the question.

"So where've you got this idea from, what's drawn you to this theory?"

Barry knew Frank needed more for him to be convinced.

"I've looked at the files we have so far on each of the women." Barry answered. "The things they have all got in common that we know of."

He held up his hand as he ticked off the list.

"One, they are all single women, two they all live alone, three they are lonely and don't appear to be in any kind of relationship."

"Your point is?"

"My point is Boss, why are they alone? This Sandra Pollock woman, does she strike you as the type of woman who would not attract a partner?"

Frank thought about it.

"No she's young and fairly good looking, independent, reasonable job, I can't think of any reason why she would want to live alone."

"Exactly, that's what I thought, and then I got to thinking what do we know about Sandra Pollock that we don't know about Angela Perriman or Margaret Smith?"

Frank's mind was running through a checklist like a computer searching for a file. It only took a second to come up with a result. When it arrived it came with a bang.

"Sandra Pollock was raped at the age of twelve! Fuck me that's it, that's why she lives alone and is not involved in any kind of relationship!"

Barry looked at his boss as all the pennies dropped at once. It was amazing the way their minds worked once they were primed.

Frank pursued the theory.

"Not only that Barry, I think this guy knows it as well, for all we know he could have been the man who raped Sandra Pollock. I bet if we get hold of the past medical records for these last two women there will be something there in the history that gives an indication of a trauma, something like a rape for instance. This is incredible, absolutely fucking unbelievable!"

Barry knew his boss well enough to see he was convinced.

"So you think we should give it a shot then?"

Frank stood up and leaned forward over his desk.

"Barry you are a fucking genius mate, do you know that? If any of this comes up trumps and we catch this bastard as a result I'd like you to be the arresting officer.

In fact, I absolutely fucking insist on it. Oh and while I'm at *fucking* insisting on things, consider yourself promoted to Detective Inspector with immediate effect. I'm not taking no for an answer."

Barry looked as if he was about to object and Frank cut him off before he had chance to speak.

"No arguments Barry, it's a done deal as far as I am concerned, if you're not happy about it, fill out a grievance form and get someone to sign it. I'll see you in the morning when you get back with the forensics from Venmore Street. I'll run your theories by the team in the morning, don't worry I'll make sure you get the credit." Frank stood up and held out his hand. Barry shook it and left the office.

Chapter 31

At six-am they felt like they looked. Pete was sat on a couch picking the remains of a kebab from his teeth with a plastic fork. With his bleached blonde hair and chunks of brown roots showing through he looked more like Johnny Rotten from the Sex Pistols than contemporary chic. Terry hadn't shaved for two days and was sat on a swivel chair at a desk running his fingers through the stubble on his chin. His balding head of hair was greasy and the skin on his face and neck was full of craters left by acne.

He looked again at what they had so far, a few photographs taken from distance in bad light of a street full of kids and the odd police officer bimbling about. It was hardly groundbreaking material. He turned and spoke to the tired looking journalist sat on the couch behind him.

"Pete, we got Jack Shit worth the print never mind a front page job. Unless we get some juicy pictures this morning we are gonna need a lot more info. We need to get our arses back over there pronto and get ourselves set up before the bods from the council turn up with their dust pan and brush."

The journalist had a look on his face that said that he agreed but it was contradicted by the rest of his body language. At only twenty five he was already massively overweight and had high blood pressure to match. He rubbed his eyes and spoke at the same time.

"Yeh, Yeh, whatever, I just need some anaesthetic!"

The photographer looked puzzled.

"What for?"

"So's I can have the operation to get this fuckin' couch off me back!"

"Okay, so I'll get the double espressos in on our way there. Come on shift your arse, it's your story not mine."

The journalist got off the couch, stood up, let out a massive yawn and stretched, the exertion causing an equally massive fart. The photographer headed for the door.

Forty-five minutes later they parked the car at the disused petrol station half way up Walton Breck Road and walked round into Vienna Street. They got to the house where the students lived and let themselves in. The alarm had not been set. Two of the students had obviously decided to sack off the tutorials and were still in bed. They never even came to see who had let themselves in.

By half past seven Pete and Terry were settling down in the bathroom getting themselves ready for action. At ten minutes to eight there was movement in the alleyway. A man in a plain suit accompanied by another man dressed in a white protective over suit approached the officer stood outside the recently repaired gate to the yard. Both men were wearing gloves. Terry held the camera up to the gap through the small window, fired off half a dozen shots and sat on the edge of the bath to view the pictures through the LCD screen on the digital camera.

Pete stuck his head back up to the window. The uniformed officer fished in his pocket for a key to the padlock, opened the gate and let the two men into the yard. Another key was produced and the kitchen door was opened.

The two men went inside and the officer returned to the alleyway. Fifteen minutes later the boys from the council turned up in a miniature version of a rubbish disposal truck. They reversed it along the alley way up to the back gate of the yard. The driver and another man got out and started talking to the officer. On cue the two officers emerged from the kitchen to meet them.

Terry caught it all on camera while Pete was scribbling something on a pad. So far so good. The bathroom door opened and one of the students came in with his eyes glued shut with sleep dressed in only a pair of boxer shorts. Pete and Terry did their best to ignore him as he walked up to the toilet, flipped up the lid and urinated for about ten minutes farting intermittently; his eyes remained shut the whole time.

Terry swore the student was still asleep and had not even noticed they were there. The student left them alone and they refocused on what was happening in the yard. The boys from the council were removing black plastic bags of rubbish from the top of the coalbunker. The other two men were inspecting the contents, removing things they saw fit to remove and lining them up outside the back door.

The man in the white suit took photographs while the other officer sealed some of the items into clear plastic evidence bags. Once the bin bags had been checked the boys from the council slung them into the back of the truck parked in the alleyway. Some cardboard boxes that had got soaking wet in the rain, split as they were lifted out spilling rubbish all over the floor. The whole process looked slow and laborious and by the looks on the faces from the boys from the council a complete pain in the arse.

Terry and Pete continued to observe the officers at work. They removed a few more bags and were slowly getting deeper into the coalbunker. One of the council workers was kneeling on top of the bunker, using a pole with a hook on the end of it to retrieve the rest of the rubbish bags. He fished something out on the end of the pole. Through the lens of Terry's camera it looked like a bath towel. The camera clicked away. The man reached inside the bunker again and fished out another towel.

The other two men were paying lots of attention to the towels; which were photographed and bagged up. Terry was getting all of it on film. Pete scribbled more notes, getting his thoughts on paper in the heat of the moment. What happened next took both of them by surprise.

The guy on top of the coalbunker stopped what he was doing and was staring at something inside the coalbunker. Suddenly he leapt off the coalbunker and bent over next to the kitchen door. Terry zoomed in with the camera sensing that something was about to happen. The guy who'd leapt off the coalbunker was being sick in the corner of the yard. Terry fired off more shots.

Pete squeezed his head alongside Terry's camera to get a look at what was going on. There seemed to be a discussion taking place between the two men from the police. The man in the white suit climbed on top of the coalbunker and peered inside the hole. He raised his head and indicated to the other officer to pass him the camera. The flash on the camera went off at least six or seven times before he handed it back again.

There was another discussion and the officer in the plain suit was talking on his mobile. The officer in the alleyway had stepped into the yard to find out what the commotion was. There was further discussion amongst them and more phone calls being made. Ten minutes went by and nothing happened.

The two guys from the council were stood in the alleyway having a smoke, everyone else waited in the yard. Thirty minutes had elapsed and still nothing was happening. Pete and Terry were wondering what the fuck was going on when one of the officers got a call on his mobile. A minute later the two guys from the council were told to unload all the bags off the back of their truck and move it out of the alleyway.

Five minutes later two police cars and a plain white van turned up in front of the house. Uniformed police officers collected the bags that had been removed from the rubbish truck and took them to the white van. Two more men in white protective suits turned up, one of them climbed on top of the coalbunker carrying a torch and leaned inside. Seconds later he emerged issuing instructions.

Four of the men in the yard began heaving at the pebble dashed stone slab that formed the top of the coalbunker. It didn't move. Two more joined in throwing their combined weight behind it. There was a grating of concrete against concrete, grinding as the six by four foot slab slid to the side a few inches at a time. Slowly they pushed it far enough to one side, until finally, it tipped up and fell off the edge. It crashed to the floor with a hollow thud and broke into several pieces.

The man in the white suit and two of the uniformed officers climbed back into the bunker. Terry was snapping away the whole time. He knew that any moment now he could be taking pictures that would be worth a damn sight more than what they had paid to get them.

The backdoor to the kitchen opened and two more men emerged carrying a stretcher covered in black plastic sheets. They held the stretcher up next to the lip of the coalbunker. Terry had his finger poised on the button of his camera, Pete stood next to him with his fingers crossed staring in disbelief.

The heads of the three men who had crouched down inside the bunker slowly appeared; it looked like they were struggling with something heavy. Then their shoulders emerged and finally, cradled in their arms, the body of a dead man. The money shot.

Terry zoomed the camera in focusing on the body. Bang, he got the shot. He zoomed right in on the head, more shots. Pete and Terry saw the bloodied face of the dead man through the LCD screen. The powerful zoom picked up the eyes, which were wide open. Maggots were wriggling and squirming through the dead man's hair, more were trying to avoid the light and escape back inside their meal via the nose and mouth.

Terry was feeling sick, revolted, he turned his head away. Quickly he gathered himself together and zoomed out slightly to get the full scene in shot. He pressed the button and held it down for several seconds. The officers inside the bunker carefully maneuvered the body onto the stretcher. The officers holding the stretcher carried it towards the kitchen door and lowered it to the ground.

Terry fired off the last few shots before the body was covered up and removed from the scene. He looked at Pete who was looking a shade whiter than normal.

"You okay, Pete?"

"Yeh, I think so, come on lets get the fuck out of here, if we're lucky we might be able to get a few shots from the end of the street before they all pull out."

They left the house forgetting to put the key through the letterbox on their way out. As they stepped out of Vienna Street they could already see that the end of Venmore Street was blocked off by a police car with its blue light flashing.

There was no point in going any further; they needed to get back to their editor with what they'd got. They did an about turn and walked back to the disused petrol station where they'd left the car.

Chapter 32

Frank breezed into the incident room at a quarter to eight Thursday morning and was surprised to see everyone already there. He had only had about four and a half hours sleep but surprisingly he'd slept like a log and was feeling refreshed.

"Good morning ladies, gents."

One of the officers poured some coffee from an urn on a table in the corner and brought it over holding out his hand.

"Cheers sir, oh and congratulations on your promotion by the way."

Frank recognised him as one of the officers from Walton Lane station he'd seen at Venmore Street the day before. Frank shook his outstretched hand realizing that this was the first time anyone had mentioned his promotion.

"Thanks," he said, "Pity it couldn't have been under better circumstances." He sat down and drank his coffee familiarizing himself with everyone in the room.

"Right let's get down to business." He gave a brief update on the previous days events before picking up where he left off with Barry from last night. He outlined the theories he and Barry had discussed by everyone, and then asked them to come up with alternative scenarios in case they needed a plan B.

"So I'd like everyone to try and keep an open m..." He felt his mobile vibrating inside his jacket.

"Excuse me a sec..."

He looked at the display. It was Barry.

"Excuse me ladies, gents, I'll be back shortly." He left them pondering over theories and strategies. Outside the room he hit the call button.

"Barry what's up?"

"Boss I'm at the yard in Venmore Street, you'll never believe what we've found in the coal bunker..."

Frank returned to a babble of noise inside the incident room ten minutes later and made the announcement. There was instant quiet.

"Okay everyone listen up, there have been further developments at Venmore Street. Another body has been discovered. A man this time, found about ten minutes ago buried beneath a pile of rubbish in the coalbunker in the backyard of the house. We'll have more information by lunchtime today. So whatever theories or motives you've come up with I'd like you to figure this latest development into the equation. I'll be in my office if you need me."

As he left the babble struck up like an orchestra. On his way to the office he bumped into Mark, Bob and Daz returning from a meeting. Before they had chance to speak he brought them up to speed on the news from Barry. From the looks on their faces he got the distinct impression that they already knew.

"Okay so tell me what happened, Barry rang you lot as well?"

Bob spoke up first.

"Err... not exactly Boss."

"What do you mean not exactly?"

Bob looked at the others then answered.

"Well Boss, there's two PLO's downstairs. It looks like the shits' hit the fan."

Frank had no idea what he was on about.

"Well come on Bob lets have it, what the fucks going on?"

"Well apparently Boss, one of the PLO's... guy called John, he took a call about ten minutes ago from someone at the Liverpool Herald & Tribune. He gave them the bog standard statement they'd prepared."

Frank was still none the wiser.

"And?"

"Well it seems that they weren't happy with the statement. When John told them that's all they were getting, they came up with their own version of events. It took him a bit by surprise when he found out how much they seemed to know already."

"And what do they know?"

"Well it's not so much as what they *know*; it's what they've *got* by the sounds of it. A journalist and one of their photographers were at Venmore Street this morning following a tip off. They've got everything on film and they've sent two pictures by email to the MIT inbox to prove it."

Frank was beginning to get the jist.

"So what have they said?"

"That they are going to publish their own version of the story, with colour pictures, the full ish, if they don't get an exclusive."

Frank looked towards Barry's desk to see if his computer terminal was on. It wasn't.

"Okay guys, nothing we can do about that, should've expected it I guess. I'd love to know who tipped them off. I'm going to check out the pictures in the mailbox. If you see Barry before me, tell him there's no need to panic, but I'd like to see you all in my office as soon as he gets back."

They all nodded and got about their business, surprised and relieved at how well their boss had taken the news.

Frank closed the office door and sat behind his desk.

"Fucking bollocks. Fucking wanker."

His hands clenched into fists as he banged the table causing a coffee mug to bounce up and fall onto the floor. He logged onto his terminal and opened up the inbox.

"For fucks sake..." he muttered to himself through clenched teeth.

The pictures were there all right, along with a short note.

"I'll fucking sort him." He picked up his diary and searched for a phone number for the editor of the Herald & Tribune.

Grading wankers into categories was a favorite pastime of Frank's. Every day, everywhere he went, he met them. Young kids smoking dope, driving round in boy racer cars, music bouncing off the inside of black tinted windows so loud you could feel the vibrations from the pavement.

Every now and again some doped up spotty faced git would lean out of the window and gob a mouthful of green phlegm out of the window. Either that, or jettison the remains of a half eaten burger with a half gallon plastic bucket of coke out the window on to the street. God, how he fucking hated that.

The other wankers he hated even more were the ones at airports.

The pig ignorant ones who, no matter how many times they were reminded, would still not switch off their fucking mobile phones, texting or talking to someone as if their life depended on it. They would be talking to someone equally stupid with that *look at me everyone aren't I important* tone of voice, talking about the latest developments in their extremely busy but *pointless fucking* lives.

Then there were the others. Frank could recite the announcement from memory…

Good afternoon ladies and gentlemen this is a message for all passengers flying with British Airways on flight number AB8150 to Majorca. This flight is now ready for boarding. To enable us to get everyone on board as quickly as possible could all passengers with tickets for seat numbers 30 to 60 please come to the front with their passports open and their boarding cards at the ready. Thank you.

Immediately all those twats who hadn't taken a blind bit of notice of the announcement because they were too busy *texting*, rush to the front only to be told by some hardnosed stewardess, "If you wouldn't mind stepping to one side Sir while we board all those *with* seat numbers 30 to 60". *You stupid useless fucking arsehole!*

Frank usually walked past them staring directly into their faces, only just resisting the urge to say, "She's right you know, you are a stupid useless fucking arsehole"

These were usually the same ones who despite the sign saying, *Please Fasten Seatbelts* were always first to undo their seatbelts before the plane finished taxi-ing to a halt. Then they stand up, fighting to be first to get their stuff out of the overhead lockers and eventually finish up whining like fuck when they have to remain standing up for more than ten minutes. Wankers all of them…

There was someone at the Liverpool Herald & Tribune who fitted all of the above. He thought that all life revolved around him, that he was the biggest mover and shaker in town. Frank knew as long as you played him right, letting him believe that, you could get what you want.

A bit of bullshit went a long way, and some kowtowing to his ego got you a damn sight further. The trick was to let him think that you were ever so grateful and that you would be forever in his debt.

Right now Frank was in no mood for bullshit, he just wanted the editor of the Herald & Tribune to slow things up with the two cowboys who had taken the photographs. He found the number and punched it into his phone. A youngish sounding woman answered.

"Liverpool Herald & Tribune, Samantha speaking, how can I help?"

Frank got straight to the point.

"I'd like to speak to the editor please."

"May I ask who is speaking please?" Samantha continued politely.

Frank obliged. "Yes tell him its Detective Chief Inspector Frank Carroll from Merseyside Police."

There was a slight pause while Samantha regained her composure.

"Certainly Chief Inspector, one moment please."

There was a second or two of silence while she put him through. When Frank heard the laboured breathing he knew who it was. It was the slightly asthmatic voice of Tom Scallion.

"Fraa...ank! I hear you've been promoted, congratulations, what can I do for you?" Frank spoke calmly wanting to keep things absolutely under control. *Condescending bastard!*

"Morning Tom, I hear your lads have been busy. They've got themselves quite a scoop by the sounds of it." Scallion knew exactly what Frank was referring to.

"Well that's what I pay them for Frank, they are just doing their job, if they weren't I would be disappointed.

Same as you would be if your lads weren't pulling their weight. I guess you'll want to meet somewhere to discuss the terms for the exclusive. Shall we say the usual place in about…lets see, what time is it, say forty five minutes?"

Frank looked at his watch.

"Yeah that's fine Tom I'll see you there at ten thirty, I've got your mobile number if I'm going to be late, shouldn't be more than ten or fifteen minutes though. Your lads aren't the only ones who are busy you know."

Scallion laughed heartily.

"I know Frank, I know, see you then, and tell DS Ferguson there's no need to panic this isn't going anywhere yet."

"I already did Tom, see you in forty five." He hung up. *Wanker.*

He looked at the list of people he needed to call and those who he wanted to see before the briefing he'd arranged for five pm that afternoon. Hilary and Cram were moving down the list getting closer to the bottom as the list grew.

Father Maloney was at the top. He was just about to give him a call when there was a knock at the door signaling the arrival of Barry and the rest of the team.

Barry and Mark sat on chairs in the corner of the room, Bob and Daz had brought their own. Frank spoke to no one in particular.

"Okay one thing at a time. The press, I'm off any minute to meet the editor of the Tribune and square things up with him. Barry, have you seen the photo's?"

Barry handed over a loose-leaf file.

"Yes boss, these are the hard copies."

Frank looked at the two full colour pictures to see what Scallion and his boys from the Tribune were going to barter with. No doubt about it they were in the driving seat.

"No problem, leave these with me and I'll sort it. If any of our PLO's come looking for me, I'm unavailable for the rest of the day on a strictly need to know basis. In the meantime, Mark, Bob and Daz get your heads round this lot."

He handed Mark a pile of notes he had taken from his meeting with Barry the night before.

"I want everyone up to speed on this and as much done as possible with the information before the meeting tonight. Any problems speak to Barry and he'll fill in the gaps, he's done a lot of work on this already so I'll want answers before the meeting. After I've finished with the guys at the Tribune I'm going straight to Angela Perriman's house in Crosby Green. Daz, get on the phone to the nick at West Derby Lane and tell them to make sure someone is there to meet us with a key so we can get in."

She nodded. "Err…us…as in we Boss?"

"Yes Daz, we. I want you, Mark and Bob to meet me there; we are going to do the full walk and talk, up and down, inside and outside.

Someone got in there and I fucking well want to know how, so make sure you have got your Inspector Clouseau kits with you. I'll ring you as soon as I'm done at the Tribune. Mark, get hold of the forensics report and anything you've got from SOCO including photographs, make copies for everyone and bring them with you. Barry, you hang on here and crack on with things until we get back from the Perriman house."

Frank pulled his mobile out of his inside jacket pocket and checked the charge level, it was on one bar. He'd have to charge it in the car on the way to meet Scallion.

"Right that's me done, get cracking you lot we've got shedloads to cover before tonight."

Outside in the car park Frank dodged the rain and sprinted to his car, plugged his mobile into the charger from the cigarette lighter and drove off. Ten minutes later he was pulling up into Hope Street and driving past the Liverpool Institute of Performing Arts. LIPA as it was known, was set up by Sir Paul McCartney and officially opened by the Queen in 1996. Big crowds had turned up to see Liverpool's favourite son shaking hands with the queen. Frank had overseen the security operation. He'd seen neither of them since.

Just off Hope Street there was a bistro cum wine bar on Falkner Street. He parked right outside in one of the parking bays and went inside. As he pushed open the door, the rush of noise hit him; there was the usual ten decibels of loud raucous chatter and people laughing like hyenas.

On the plus side it was noisy enough to avoid the possibility of anyone overhearing your conversation. The place was over half full with the usual combination of businessmen and women in suits plying clients with wine, and Arty student types eating pasta and drinking beer in posh glasses. Amongst them there were the usual amount of *professional* bistro goers reading the papers, smoking and drinking late` and cappuccino.

In the far right corner up one level sat a man with a *Bobby Charlton* haircut wearing a suit and a smile. Frank caught his eye and gave him the Peter Kay hand signal for, *did he want a drink.* The Editor of the Liverpool Herald & Tribune held up his half empty glass of diet coke and gave him the thumbs up. With not much change from a tenner Frank bought a straight coffee, a large diet coke and took them to the table.

Scallion greeted him with a glassy eyed smile showing badly stained teeth. Probably from drinking too much coke and smoking large cigars. Frank put the drinks on the table and held out his hand. Scallion gave him one of those dead fish handshakes, cold, wet and limp. He sat down and discreetly wiped his hand on the upholstery underneath the table.

Scallion recovered a half smoked cigar from the ashtray and proceeded to re-ignite it. The end glowed like red hot molten lava from a volcano reflecting in some tacky bling on a chubby wrist and fingers. Amidst clouds of billowing blue smoke and pap pap sounds as wet lips puffed on the cigar, Scallion spoke.

"So Frank, or should I call you Detective Chief Inspector now, what have you got to offer me?"

What besides a punch in the fucking mouth!

"Well Tom, you know how it is, naturally we want to nurture our good relationship with the press and of course keep the tax paying public informed of how good a job we are doing with their hard earned cash." *Where the fuck did that bullshit come from?*

"But at the same time we want to make sure anything we release is to our advantage and so that we don't jeopardise our chances of catching the person responsible."

Scallion launched a plume of cigar smoke from his mouth that hung in the air like the fallout from a neutron bomb.

"Really Frank, with answers like that you are wasting your time being a detective, have you ever thought about politics? I can see why you have been promoted. Please give my regards to your predecessor by the way; I hear he took a nasty turn for the worse." Frank made a humongous effort to stop his thoughts appearing on his face. *Cheeky bastard, I'll fucking turn you for the worse if you come out with another crack like that.*

"Certainly Tom, kind of you to say so, I'm sure Andy will be back soon, I'll pass on your good wishes."

Scallion thought he could detect a note of sarcasm in Frank's voice but wasn't sure. Frank was fucking absolutely *sure* there was. Scallion continued talking between huge puffs on his rapidly diminishing cigar.

"According to my assistant liaison officer who spoke to your press officer at Canning Place, they got the usual short shrift, "*Yes we have no tomatoes today*" sort of spiel. Yet I'm sure you'll agree from the photographs we've sent you, and believe you me, you haven't seen the half of it, there is something very big and very very serious going on. We have our duty to do as well you know Frank, the tax paying public as you so nicely put it, have a right to know what is going on in their city, wouldn't you agree?"

No I fucking wouldn't.

"Yes of course Tom, but you must also agree that the most important thing is for us to catch this person and put them away." He said this with as much conviction as he could muster, almost as if he believed it. But it was no good, Frank saw from the look on Scallions face he was going nowhere with this particular tack.

"Look Tom, I know you're keen to put this out before the nationals get involved so let me make you a promise. Give me until midnight tomorrow just so that we can follow up some important new lines of enquiry. If we catch this person any time between now and then you get the first call and a full exclusive account of our operation. If we don't catch them we'll still come to you with everything we've got up to now. I can't say fairer than that, what do you say…do we have a deal?"

Scallion took a final puff on his cigar, extinguished what was left of it, downed the rest of his diet coke in one go and let out a smoke filled burp as he plonked the glass down on to the table.

"That's more like it Frank, now that's what I call a good deal. My boys'll go nowhere with the photo's until I say so. You've got until midnight tomorrow."

There was no handshake as Frank left the table. Scallion was ordering another diet coke and blitzing his way through the specials menu as Frank stepped outside into the rain. He got into the car, picked up his mobile phone still plugged in to the charger and rang the office.

"Daz, it's Frank. Meet me at the Perriman house in half an hour."

Chapter 33

It was almost mid-day by the time Frank got to the Perriman house. The clock on his deal with Scallion was ticking. He had roughly thirty-six hours to catch who ever it was that was doing this before he would have to lay out what he'd got in front of Scallion.

As he pulled up in front of the house there was a police car with two officers in it from West Derby Lane. Mark, Bob and Daz were parked up behind them. They all bailed out as he pulled up behind their car.

"Bob, get one of the guys in uniform to check out all the cars parked up this street, anything at all looks like press I want them moved on. I've had enough of that lot for one day. Who's got the key?"

Daz pulled a set of keys from her pocket.

"Here you go Boss, front and back door, garage, side door and patio door."

"Right here's the plan. We need to figure out where and how this person got inside the house. Mark, Bob I want you two to work together, what one of you doesn't see the other might. Put yourselves in the position of the person we are looking for and think, how you would get in? I want every door and window checked inside and out, make comparisons with what you see and what's written in the forensic reports or the photos from SOCO. We're looking for marks, dents, or scratches, anything which might point towards forced entry."

Mark dished out the reports from forensics.

"Also before you go, be careful where you are treading; check the ground in front of you in and outside the house before you go over it. Remember it was probably dark when he got in. Make notes of everything, whether you think it's important or not. Take your time. Any questions?" They had none.

"Daz I want you to come with me, we'll bounce a few thoughts around and see what we come up with. Okay get to it, we've got about two hours, three at tops."

She followed Frank through the front door. Once they got inside she spoke up.

"Fran...err Boss...are you sure Mark and Bob are okay with this, I mean with them sent off on their own like and me getting the cushy number. I wouldn't want them thinking there was any favouritism here." Frank looked at her and smiled.

"Cushy number! Favouritism! You must be fucking joking Daz; they are well off out of it. It's you who drew the short straw." Frank could see by the look on her face that she wasn't quite getting it.

"You're not getting chaperoned here, this is your first chance to prove to me you are going to make it as a detective. You're on probation for twelve months don't forget."

Her face took on a distinctly worried look as Frank headed off down the hall towards the kitchen. She might have been slightly less worried if she could have seen the grin on Frank's face.

For the next hour and a half they walked and talked trying to envisage what had happened less than two days ago. They discussed theories and possibilities, making notes as they went along. They bumped into Mark and

Bob from time to time, sharing information and going back to revisit their theories. Frank showed her the bedroom where the suspected murder had taken place. She spotted something straight away.

"Boss, look at the alarm clock on the bedside table."

The bright red LCD display on the digital radio alarm clock was flashing on and off. Frank couldn't believe he hadn't noticed it on the night he was here and there was no mention of it in the SOCO's report.

"Get downstairs and check anything that might have an LCD display, video recorder anything." A minute later she was back in the bedroom.

"The video recorder's display is flashing on and off, so's the clock on the oven in the kitchen."

Frank was deep in thought.

"Daz, you go away on your holidays, you get back and see the display flashing on your alarm clock, what's the first thing that comes into your head?" She had already asked herself the same question on her way back up the upstairs.

"There must have been a power cut Boss."

"That's right; he turned the power off at the mains. We need to find the fuse box."

They went downstairs to look for it, as they reached the hallway there was a shout from Bob outside.

"Boss! Daz! Come and have a look at this!"

Outside, Mark was kneeling down by the patio doors with Bob leaning over him. Frank knelt down beside him.

"What's up?"

Mark pointed to the white UPVC windowsill running parallel to the patio doors. There was an almost indiscernible mark of some description running square to the window towards the ledge. Mark ran his fingers along the sill.

"Feel this Boss, it's indented as if it's been subject to pressure of some kind, possibly forced with a jemmy?"

Frank ran his fingers along the mark.

"Okay, so do you think this is where he forced the patio doors and let himself in?"

"Not *think* Boss, we know this is where he got in," said Bob, "look at the laminate flooring in the dining room." Frank looked inside. There was nothing to see. No mud, nothing.

"I can't see jack shit."

"Stand up Boss and look at the floor from this angle."

Frank stood and looked. He could see what Bob and Mark had spotted. There was a set of footprints made by rubber-soled shoes with a very distinctive pattern. In any other light, from any other angle, the prints would never have been seen. He had the feeling that he'd seen the markings somewhere before but couldn't put his finger on it.

The footprints were going in two directions, both to and from the kitchen, which, one would assume, meant that who ever it was that had been here had come and gone via the same route.

Daz, remembering that she was still out to prove herself made a suggestion.

"Boss a while back I heard something about a string of burglaries round Kensington way. Turns out the person doing the burglaries was an ex double-glazing window and door fitter. Who else would know their way around the security on these doors? Why don't we get one of the double glazing companies on the blower and see if we can get someone out here to show us how it was done."

Frank gave it some thought and decided it was worth a shot.

"Good idea, do it. See if you can get them here in less than an hour. Otherwise one of you will have to stay here until they arrive and watch them do it."

Daz went inside the house looking for a Yellow Pages directory. Frank looked at Mark and Bob who were looking quite pleased with themselves.

"Good work lads." Bob was grinning like a Cheshire cat.

"What's up Bob?"

"It gets better Boss, have a shufty at this."

Bob opened up the folder with the photographs in it from SOCO. Frank looked at the particular pictures he was referring to. There were shots of the same footprint taken at the front of the house in between the bushes and shrubs. More pictures taken alongside the garage. Frank guessed that was why he'd thought the prints were familiar. He turned the pictures over to look for the comments from SOCO forgetting that they were photocopies.

"Shit, never mind. Mark as soon as we get back dig out the originals and see what the SOCO has said about them, make of shoe, materials, size, that sort of stuff."

Frank took Mark and Bob with him inside the house to look for the fuse box explaining on the way what he and Daz had deduced from the electrical appliances. In the hall he could hear Daz on the phone using her gentle powers of persuasion to sweet talk some double-glazing geezer into coming round.

"LOOK MATE! Just get your fuckin' arse round here now, or I'll have someone come round and give every one of your vehicle documents the official once over!"

Frank chuckled to himself as he walked round to the garage. She hadn't changed a bit.

There was no sign of the fuse box in the house.

"It's probably outside in the garage Boss, that's where mine is." Suggested Bob.

They left Daz giving details of the address to the subtly berated person on the end of the phone. Outside in the garage they found the fuse box. While everyone else was looking up at the box on the wall Frank was staring at the floor.

It was made of concrete and covered in dust. Smack bang in front of the workbench just in line with the fuse box was another set of footprints matching the ones they'd already seen on the laminate inside the house. Anyone not specifically looking for them would never have seen them in a million years.

They all turned and looked as Daz appeared in the doorway of the garage.

"Guy says he'll be here in' bout twenty minutes Boss. I told him to bring his housebreaking gear with him."

Frank looked back at the floor.

"What did he say to that?"

"He said that he had no idea what I was talking about."

"But he knew someone who did right."

"Several."

"Good make sure we get a fucking card off him when he gets here."

They all laughed together, the boss was on a roll. Back inside the house they helped themselves to water from the tap in the kitchen and put together what they had got into some sort of order. A picture was definitely forming. Maybe Frank would get to keep his end of the deal with Scallion after all.

The noisy exhaust of a white and rust coloured transit van was heard pulling up at the front of the house. There was a knock at the front door and one of the uniforms came to tell them that there was someone to see the DCI.

Frank went to the front door to meet them. The two men were dressed in T-shirts, with filthy white coveralls and steel toe capped boots. Frank introduced himself and took them round the back to the patio doors. He told them what was going on and explained what he wanted them to do without going into great detail.

Mark had already pulled the patio door shut and locked it with the key from the bunch Daz had given him. The older one of the two guys pulled two pieces of equipment from an oily looking canvas bag full of tools. Less than two minutes later the patio doors were standing wide open. There had been almost no sound whatsoever and the guy had not even broken into a sweat. Bob was impressed.

"Fuck me mate, absolutely fucking bob on. Do this for a living do yer?"

Frank gave him a look that said *Leave it Bob!* Bob shrugged his shoulders and left it.

The driver of the van pointed to the locking mechanism on the inside edge of the patio door.

"If you look closely at this piece here, and that bit there you can tell this door has been lifted out of its seating position. These are normally dead tight but look how slack they are."

They all watched as he took hold of one of whatever the fuck they were and waggled it for effect.

"See that, it's been forced to make it go like that."

Frank looked at him. The guy was obviously an expert.

"How old would you say these doors were." he asked.

The guy did one of those… sharp intakes of breath noises as if it were a difficult question and needed some thought.

"Couldn't say for deffo, probably at least fifteen years old, but I know they don't make them like these any more for exactly the reason you've just seen. The security systems shite."

Frank wondered if that was a technical term but decided not to ask.

"Okay fellers that's it, thanks for your help it's very much appreciated. Next time you're near Canning Place do drop in for a coffee."

The sarcasm went straight over their heads. They left in the van making sure their seat belts were fastened and they indicated before pulling out.

Frank looked at his watch and decided they had got enough to be going on with; they needed to get back to the office. It was starting to get dark already, there was less than three hours before the meeting and he still needed to catch up with what Barry had dug up for him on the Chloroform. They left in convoy for Canning Place.

Chapter 34

Back at the flat in Toxteth The Redeemer had waited, anxiously pacing his room half expecting a knock at the door. Police! Open up! We know you're in there. It never came. Twice when he heard footsteps in the hallway outside he'd broken out into a cold sweat, his heart practically beating a hole in his chest with fear. He listened to all the Radio Merseyside news bulletins but heard nothing of the intruder he'd killed at the house on Venmore Street. There was no way he was going to spend another day like that.

After a sleepless night he left his flat in Toxteth at six am with no intention of returning until after dark. If the police were on to him they would have his flat under surveillance sooner or later. He knew a thing or two about surveillance and he would use his own self-taught counter surveillance tactics to check it was safe before going back. After leaving the flat he called in to the newsagents opposite the junction on Park Road and Northumberland Street.

Armed with all the local papers he made his way down to Brunswick dock. Overlooking the Mersey on one side and the dock harbour on the other, there was an old warehouse full of small commercial industrial units. Most of them had gone out of business but the cafeteria on the first floor at the end of the building still thrived. It wasn't flashy; in fact it was exactly the opposite. But then he didn't need flashy.

He climbed the rusty spiral stairway to the first floor and walked along the dimly lit corridor towards the café. As he approached the swing doors the smell of fried bacon and sausages mixed with cigarette smoke was lingering in the air.

Inside there was an assortment of people, smart looking businessmen in suits, delivery people from the Royal Mail and Parcel Force sharing tables with a range of men and women of all ages from the remaining offices inside the warehouse. Nobody paid any attention to him as he walked in. Here you could be inconspicuous. He ordered a full English from the counter and sat in the corner with his newspapers. There wasn't a single article about his activities in any of them.

Surely by now the press must have got hold of something. He was either very lucky or the police were extremely clever, covering up what they had found. Maybe they hadn't found anything. While he waited for his food he evaluated his position. This was hardly the outcome he'd expected when he started on his mission.

He should have felt elated; relieved of the burden he had inherited from his father. With his debt paid he would have been able to get back to some kind of normality. Right now, his mission was incomplete. Until it was he would still feel obligated to see it through. He had come too far to give up on it now. A man had died at his hands, a terrible price to pay for the redemption of another. He felt as if he owed it to the man who died at the address in Venmore Street to continue.

The problem now was that his schedule was out of synchrony, the two names left on his list would have to be re-shuffled. For one of them their redemption would come sooner than expected, the other would have to wait. He thought about this for a moment. Maybe this was to his advantage. Not only would he still be able to complete his mission, now there would be an element of randomness that would provide a safety net preventing him from being captured by the police.

The early morning rush of people in the café started to thin out; sad looking people were reluctantly making their way back to work. He cautiously looked at the list of names on the piece of paper he was holding under the table. He folded the piece of paper up, put it into his pocket, and pulled a small pocket diary out of his coat. He flicked through it until he found the correct dates and pencilled in the times for his last two appointments. The sound of plates clattering on to a counter interrupted his thoughts.

"Number twenty four, full English?"

He put the diary away, stood up and went to collect his food from the counter. The red-faced woman behind the counter looked tired and overworked.

"Help yerself to milk and sugar mate." He put the tannin-stained mug of tea onto the tray with his breakfast and moved over to the till to pay.

"That's £1.75 please," the woman said to him in a busy no nonsense fashion.

"Thanks," he said avoiding direct eye contact. He paid her the right money and took his food to the table. Three rashers of bacon, two sausages, fried egg, beans, tomato, two rounds of toast and a steaming hot mug of tea for £1.75. He still couldn't believe how they managed it.

He finished his breakfast and drank two more mugs of tea while he finished reading the print off the papers. Almost two hours later he looked at his watch, ten thirty, it was time to go. He left the newspapers behind for the rest of the day's customers to read before they would be thrown in the bin shortly before closing at six pm that night. He left the building and walked headlong into an icy blast of salty rain soaked wind whipping up off the Mersey.

Chapter 35

Frank called a meeting in his office as soon as he got back from the Perriman house. Present were his team and the two press officers. The press officers were there at the insistence of the Chief Super, following a bit of a whinge by the senior press liaison officer. Waiting outside to present their results of the database enquiries were the two officers from PITO, each carrying half the Brazilian rain forest in paperwork.

Frank felt they had accomplished quite a lot in the time so far and he let everyone know it. He summarized what they had put together at the Perriman address. Pieces of the jigsaw were falling into place. All it needed now was for someone to recognise the picture.

"Right that's me done, Barry, I believe you've got some news for us."

Barry handed everyone a copy of what he'd got.

"Okay, let's start with the Chloroform enquiries first. I've conducted a search of every UK Company that supplies this stuff. I've spoken to them and faxed over a DPA (23a) with details of what we want. They were pretty wilco all things considered. Every company faxed us back with a copy of their customer database showing all sales to clients in the UK and specifically those based in the Merseyside area over the last twelve months.

I took a bit of a risk, but in view of the time restraints I contacted most of them by phone. They all had business accounts with these suppliers and the business addresses all check out. Following the enquiries I've filtered out all the ones that are legit. That left us with only two other addresses in the Merseyside area. We've got both addresses under surveillance as we speak. If you look at page three in the folder it shows the name, address and method of payment for each transaction. The one we are particularly interested in is the second one, a Mr. Andrew Pollitt, which we believe could be a fictitious name."

Everyone had their heads buried in the file as he continued.

"Trouble is, the delivery address is a PO Box number at the main post office distribution centre on Copperas Hill near Lime Street station. I called the distribution centre and got an address for the owner of the PO Box number. We sent someone round to check it out; it's a block of flats just outside town."

Frank could feel his pulse quickening as Barry continued. He jumped in with a question.

"Sorry to interrupt, I don't suppose there are any CCTV cameras operating at the PO Box collection office?" Barry shook his head.

"Plenty of CCTV cameras Boss, but none of them in operation. They are waiting for the whole system to be upgraded."

Frank looked disgusted.

"How fucking typical is that? No wonder stuff goes missing all over the place...what's the score at the bank... sorry I didn't mean to jump ahead, crack on Barry."

"Well, as I said the address which is in a block of flats not far from here is under surveillance, so far there have been no signs of anyone going in or out. We've spoken with the landlord. Turns out he's not exactly doing things by the book when declaring the revenue from the rent he receives on the flats. Not surprisingly, he's only too willing to co-operate. If there's no movement by ten o clock tonight we're going in to the place with his full blessing."

Frank listened while signing off the paperwork for the surveillance team.

Barry continued with his brief.

"Going back to the method of payment and the electronic bank transfer, as it happens the address used for the bank payment matches the flat address we got from the post office. We're pretty sure this is our man Boss, false name or not. Once we pick him up tonight and get a DNA sample, we'll match it with the types we got from Sandra Pollock and the other victims, its job sorted."

Mark and Bob nodded their agreement. All through Barry's briefing, Daz sat staring in awe at the way things were panning out as a result of the combined efforts to solve this puzzle. Right now there wasn't anywhere else in the world she would rather be. *Except, maybe being first in the queue when they came to raid the flat.*

Frank saw the look on her face and knew what she was thinking. *Not if I get there first you won't.*

"Good work everyone. Bob let the boys from PITO in I'm dying to see what they've come up with."

Bob stood and opened the door to let them in. An hour later the PITO team left the office. Frank was impressed. They had come up with everything he asked for and more. He'd wondered why so many people were waiting downstairs inside the lobby. Now he knew. They were potential suspects who'd been brought in to be interviewed and give statements while voluntarily donating tissue samples for DNA profiles.

They were happy to co-operate, anything to be eliminated from the police enquiries. The process had been in full swing since early-o-clock that morning. In less than twelve hours the remains of *Operation Recall* had been mopped up and put to bed.

The prison records had been given one of the biggest kicks up the arse since Ronnie Biggs got put away the first time. People still locked up had been spoken to; those that had been let out were visited. The sex offenders' register had some new names added to the list as a result of discoveries made during the operation.

Officers from the whole of Merseyside had crawled all over every name on the database, tracked them down and personally escorted them from their homes and places of work. Some came willingly, others had complained.

"But I haven't done anything. Don't let my wife hear you. I could lose my job."

All the usual whinges. One chap in particular was met getting off a plane at John Lennon Airport on his return from a two-day business trip abroad. He offered no resistance, freely giving up the £250.000 worth of drugs he had smuggled in from Turkey, before the officers even had a chance to explain why they were there. That had to go down as a result in Frank's book; in fact he was seriously considering re-naming his operation from Round Up, to Operation Clean up.

The DNA samples from Sandra Pollock's unborn baby matched the profiles on the samples from the semen found inside the vaginas of the female victims. Slowly, painstakingly one by one the suspects were whittled down to a number you could count up to in one breath. It still wasn't small enough but the final few candidates would emerge once the rest had assisted the police with their enquiries.

With any luck when they picked up this guy tonight at the flat there would be a pair of rubber soled boots lying in the hallway matching the description of the prints found at the Perriman house. All the evidence was coming together like nails in a coffin. The more nails you had the less chance there was of the lid coming off.

Frank was going to make absolutely sure there was no chance of the lid coming off on this one. In fact, if he had anything to do with it, when they knocked on this guy's door later tonight his DNA would be processed at the same time as he was being read his rights. This was going to be a done deal and Tom Scallion could go and fuck himself for his exclusive. He would have to come crawling on his hands and knees if he wanted it, pictures or no fucking pictures.

Chapter 36

The briefing at five pm went like clockwork thanks largely to the input from Barry. Frank thanked everyone and congratulated them on their efforts. Some officers worked twenty-four hours without rest until all the information had been pulled together. There was the usual amount of back slapping and funny handshakes going on round the room. By the time the briefing had ended there was a feeling of euphoria creeping in amongst the whole team involved in the operation. It made Frank nervous.

Any number of things could go wrong with so many variations on the possible outcome. He couldn't get something he'd heard, called *The Beetle factor* out of his head. A scarab beetle flying through the air makes a dodgy landing and finishes up upside down spinning round on its back with its legs waving in the air ten to the dozen. The scenarios and possible outcomes of its predicament were many. It could finish up lying there upside down long enough until it became exhausted and died or it could get lucky and manage to flip itself over.

A few hungry looking ants circling like vultures could develop into hundreds until there were enough of them to smother it completely and carry it away to their nest. The hungry blackbird sitting and singing away merrily in the bushes nearby might spot it and with one peck of its beak lay open its insides before flying away when it found it didn't like the taste. *The ants would have an easier job to do then.* If it was really lucky a freak gust of wind might catch it and lift it high enough for it to take flight. Or then…possibly…just maybe…the person, who was watching it go through its tormented frustration at not being able to right itself, might come and gently turn it over or lift it to safety.

"Boss…Boss?" Barry was stood in front of him. Frank had watched his lips moving but not heard any sound.

"Sorry Barry, I was fuckin miles awa…never mind, what's up mate?"

"I wondered if you wanted to go straight into the brief for the raid tonight?"

Frank checked the time. Six thirty-pm.

"Any news from the guys doing the obbo at the flat?"

"No further developments Boss. No sign of anyone coming or going. The guys either done a runner or he's topped himself in the flat.

Funny how the beetle never considered that option, thought Frank. He didn't know it yet but there was still one more option that nobody could have imagined, the one where the beetle magically turns back time so that the dodgy landing never occurred in the first place.

"I'm fucking starving. I haven't eaten since breakfast. Is the canteen still open?"

"Daz is on to it Boss, she should be on her way up here with a box full of scoff any minute now."

"Genius, pure fucking genius. Come on let's go to my office."

They shut the door and sat in the corner of the office.

"Its been a good day so far," said Frank, "apart from the meeting with that tosser from the Tribune, God how he makes my skin crawl."

Frank could still smell the cigar smoke on his jacket.

Barry tipped his head back and struggled to stifle a massive yawn, pulling a face like a *ripped welly,* as Bob would say.

"Aaagghhhggummm...fuck me I'm tired, I'll be glad when we tag this guy tonight, I'll be able to get me head down and have some decent kip for a change."

Frank knew the feeling.

"We'll have a few beers later, wrap things up until the morning. I might even have a lie in." he joked.

A figure appeared at the door struggling with something. It was Daz carrying a boxful of wrapped portions of chicken and chips. Bob was close behind her with a tray of steaming hot mugs of coffee. Frank took one of the mugs and piled into the box before Daz had chance to put it down.

"Cheers guys, grab yourselves a seat. Any ketchup Daz?"

Daz left the others to dive into the box of food and then like a magician pulled half a bottle of Heinz tomato ketchup from inside her coat. Frank could tell she was clearly enjoying her new work environment and not looking the least bit tired. Radiant even, some might say. Strange, how she's never mentioned a boyfriend? He would have to make sure he dispelled any possible rumours from starting that she might be batting for the other side.

"That's another tick in the box Daz, keep going and we'll have you signed off by the end of the week. Where's Mark?" he asked.

Bob stood up and pointed through the window.

"He's going for the golden blanket award Boss." Frank stood up to see what Bob was pointing at. Mark had taken his shoes off and was at his desk with his feet up beside the computer monitor. He was practically horizontal in his chair with his head tipped back and mouth wide open.

Frank knew this was a particular skill that Mark had shown on many previous occasions; he could sleep on a clothesline. In ten minutes he would be wide awake and ready to take on the world.

"I'll go and drop a chip in his mouth," joked Daz.

"You first aid trained?" enquired Bob.

Frank almost choked while he was trying to swallow and laugh at the same time. The banter was on the up and the best bit was still to come.

There was a polite knock on the door and the Chief Super stepped into the room. He raised his hand in a sort of *please carry on*; don't let me interrupt you from your food type of gesture. None of Frank's team looked like they had any intention of being interrupted.

"Gentlemen, I just wanted to say thanks for all your fine work yesterday and today, and to wish you good luck with the job tonight. I'm having dinner with the deputy commissioner this evening so I won't be around to welcome you back. I take it you'll be having a beer or two later tonight so here's my contribution."

He took out his wallet and pulled out two twenty-pound notes and dropped them onto Frank's desk. Frank started thinking about the beetle spinning on its back again. He grabbed one of the serviettes on his desk and wiped the chip fat and ketchup from his mouth and hands.

"Well that's very generous of you sir, if its okay with you I'll put it into a kitty for now and we'll all chip in. We can have a bit of a blow when this is all over and

DCI Williams is out of hospital...if that's alright with you sir?"

The Chief Super looked slightly put out but didn't say so.

"Yes, yes absolutely, totally agree, good idea Frank, anyway must dash."

On his way out he turned to the others in the room.

"Good luck lads."

Frank took the twenty-pound notes and put them in his desk drawer. A unanimous "Cheers sir." followed him out as the Chief Super left the office. As they left Mark walked in looking right as rain.

"Cheers guys, why didn't someone tell me the scoff had arrived?"

Daz had covered her bases.

"We did, yours is in the microwave in the kitchen, probably just needs a minute to heat it up." Bob looked towards Frank.

"No flies on her eh Boss? She might just get on here."

"Nope but you can certainly see where they've been." Frank winked at her.

"Go and get your scoff Mark. Now that we're all awake I want to get on with the script for tonight."

Mark disappeared towards the kitchen. For the next hour Frank and his team relaxed, finishing off the remains of the chicken and chips and drinking coffee while they talked through the logistics for the raid on the flat. Not that it needed much talking about.

At ten-pm tonight Frank and Barry would meet the officer in charge of the surveillance operation and the landlord prior to entry. They would knock on the door and Barry would be given the privilege of carrying out the arrest when the person opened the door. If no one opened up, the landlord would be ordered to open the door and they would search the flat.

Swabs would be taken from any items that might provide a DNA sample, toothbrushes, toilet rims, and hairs from pillows. The evidence would be collected then they would simply leave the building. The place would be kept under surveillance until such time as the person was back on the plot, at which time they would be arrested. All they had to do now was sit tight and wait for an update from the surveillance team. They waited.

By nine pm there was still no change in the report from the surveillance officers at the flat. By nine-fifteen pm Frank and his team were assembled in the car park. Two unmarked police cars and an unmarked police van were lined up in the car park ready to go. There was a small contingent of officers from the Tactical Aid Group (TAG) fully booted and suited in full body armour and helmets. Several of them carried weapons ranging from plastic bullet launchers to hand pistols. Two forensics officers were also on board.

The TAG officers climbed into the van with the guys from forensics, Frank and his team wearing protective stab jackets under their coats climbed into the two cars. They pulled out with half an hour to go before the cut off time. The convoy was less than five minutes away from the location when there was a buzz of static and the radio of the lead car burst into life.

"All stations this is Alpha 1, Standby, Standby; Standby, the subject is on the plot."

It was the voice of the OIC at the location on the radio announcing that there was activity at the scene.

"Alpha 1, this is Alpha 2, I have eyeball over, repeat I have eyeball."

After a long period of inactivity at the location, the excitement and energy levels were suddenly elevated.

Frank could feel his own adrenaline levels rising with them.

"All stations this is Alpha 3, I have eyeball, the subject is IN, IN, IN!

A second later Frank's mobile phone vibrated in his hand.

"DCI Carroll?"

"Sir, it's Sergeant Harrington here, the subject has just arrived onto the plot, we have confirmation from inside that he has entered the flat."

Frank was ecstatic.

"Good news Sergeant, thanks. I estimate we will be with you in about five minutes. Keep me posted."

Frank looked behind him and smiled at Barry in the back seat.

"Looks like we're on Barry."

Barry nodded quietly, deep in thought, staring out of the car window into the night.

The van and the two cars pulled up in the glass-strewn car park around the back of the block of flats. They weren't expecting trouble but it was best to be safe. The drivers remained with the vehicles and everyone else got out. Frank's team along with the officers from TAG moved into their pre-designated positions.

Frank and Barry made their way to the front entrance of the flat with two other armed officers leading the way. The plan was that they would climb the two flights of stairs, knock on the door and wait for an answer. The worse case scenario was that as soon as the subject heard the knock at the door and realizing it was the police, he would pick up a loaded shotgun and fire both barrels straight through the door. Frank and Barry were counting on them opening the door.

If there was any sign of trouble or aggressive resistance the armed officers would capture and detain the subject before securing the area. As soon as the situation was under control, Barry was going to do the honours and read him his rights. If the subject refused to open the door it would be forced and they would take him inside.

They reached the landing on the second floor. Frank and Barry took their places four feet either side of the doorway. The first officer took his position closer to the door. The second armed officer remained partially hidden on the stairs with his pistol aimed straight at the door. A third officer was at the entry door to the flats. The first officer glanced at his watch and then at Frank.

"Ready when you are sir?" Frank gave him the nod. The second officer on the stairs gave the thumbs up to the third officer at the foot of the stairwell.

Radio static. "All stations Standby."

The first officer raised his hand to knock on the door. What happened next took everyone by surprise. Before the officer had a chance to knock, the door opened wide to reveal a very surprised and startled man with his coat on ready to leave the flat.

It was hard to tell who was more surprised, the man in the flat or the officer in the doorway. The man in the flat spoke first in a heavy scouse accent.

"FUCK ME … Jeezus you scared the fuckin' life out of me, what the fu…"

The officer responded quickly and cut him off with calm but firm instructions. He took a step backwards, arms thrust out palms facing downwards before speaking.

"Okay sir! Keep absolutely still. Stay calm. Do not make any sudden movements. Keep your hands in front of you where I can see them."

The man did as he was told.

"Thank you sir, now just step slowly out of the doorway and turn to face the wall."

The officer indicated where he wanted the man to stand. As the man stepped out of the doorway he saw the second armed officer on the stairs, then turned and saw Frank and Barry either side of the doorway. Any thoughts he may have had of physical resistance immediately vanished from his head.

The officer removed a set of handcuffs from his belt and instructed him to place his hands behind his back with the palms facing outwards. The man placed his hands behind his back. As he did so he turned his head to speak.

"Scuse me officer, but can you tell me what the fu..." The officer was on him in a flash and the cuffs were applied in a second. The officer indicated to Barry that it was safe to approach. Barry stepped behind the man and took hold of his arm with a firm grip.

"Andrew Pollitt, I am arresting you on suspicion of murder. You do not have to say anything, but it may harm your defence if you fail to mention when questioned anything that you later rely on in court. Anything you do say may be given in evidence. Do you understand?"

The man did not understand and began to protest.

"Who the Fuckin'ell is Andrew Pollitt, I've never eerd of him, and what's with the fuckin' lone ranger pointing the fuckin' gun at me, come ed officer you've got the wrong man ere, I've been at me mum's all day. I was only goin out t'get some fags from the offy before it shut."

He began to struggle. Barry applied just enough pressure through the elbow for the cuffs to bite on the wrists.

"Aaagghhh...Oww that fuckin' hurts what're yer doin that for...."

"Stop struggling and calm down, everything'll be explained to you in full when we get you down to the station."

The man stopped struggling and Barry relaxed the pressure on the elbow.

"Okay that's better, now keep calm we just need to ask you some questions down at the station, you can say your bit then, okay?" The man knew there was no point in offering any more physical resistance. It didn't shut him up though.

"Yerr okay, worrever, but just you fuckin' wait till me brief ere's about this, e'll ave me back home in an hour."

Barry escorted the man down the stairs, the verbal protests continued. A door cracked open on the first floor, an elderly lady was peering through the gap to see what was going on. The man glowered at her,

"Get back inside you yer fuckin' nosy bitch!"

Barry re-applied the pressure to the elbow, "Calm down and stop swearing!"

"Alright, alright, enuff with the fuckin' torture already willyer?"

Barry eased the pressure.

They got outside without further incident.

The van and the cars had been brought around to the front entrance of the flats. Uniformed officers remained behind with the two officers from forensics. Frank spoke to them as they went in.

"I want that place turned over till you find something. Get the DNA fast tracked, I want the results on my desk by eight o clock tomorrow morning."

Barry eased the man onto the back seat of the front car and climbed in beside him. Frank climbed into the front seat. Everyone else boarded the van and headed back to Canning Place.

Half an hour later the subject was sat under escort in an interview room smoking a cigarette and drinking coffee while he waited for his brief to arrive. Frank had sent Mark, Bob and Daz home to get some sleep. He and Barry were sat in the office drinking coffee waiting for the arrival of the subject's brief, itching to get in and interview him. Frank did not let on to Barry that he was sure they had got the wrong man. Little did he know, Barry was thinking exactly the same thing.

Chapter 37

The duty brief arrived to consult with her client at around eleven pm. She spent fifteen minutes getting the low down from Frank and Barry before going to see him. When she arrived at the interview room the suspect was already half way through a packet of cigarettes and going hyper from the amount of coffee he had drunk while waiting. The uniformed officer who had been left inside the interview room to keep an eye on him left feeling as if he had just smoked half of them himself.

The brief stood with the door open for five minutes before venturing inside.

"Mr. Pollitt my name is…" She got no further.

"Me names not fuckin' Pollitt its Grainger, Paul Michael Grainger an I've got form t'fuckin' prove it. Just get Inspecter fuckin' Morse an is mate out there to put me details in an y's'll find me picture an everythin."

The brief recovered well. "Well Mr. Grainger if you'll just allow me to introduce myself and we'll see what we've got here shall we?"

Half an hour later she was back inside Frank's office asking for her client to be released. In the time they had been waiting Frank had ran a PNC to check the name Paul Michael Grainger on the system. The claim to have previous form made by the person they'd arrested was indeed true. Burglary, shop lifting and car theft nestling amongst several drunk and disorderly charges was there on record. The last charge of drunk and disorderly was over eighteen months ago; it would appear that Mr. Grainger was keeping his nose clean for a change.

They had his fingerprints and DNA profiles already at their disposal. They would not need to wait until morning for DNA results. Fingerprints taken from the flat and from the man they had in custody would be compared to the ones they had on his record, it would be a short interview. Frank was already thinking about plan B before he spoke to Barry.

"See if you can get on the phone to the forensics boys at the flat; tell them I want a decent set of prints over here ASAP. It's just a formality but I want to do it any way. I'll see you downstairs in …say ten minutes?"

Barry was already dialing the contact number he had been given by the senior forensics officer at the scene.

"Okay Boss, see you downstairs in a bit."

Frank left him to it, nodded to the brief on the way out and they both left for the interview room. Five minutes later Barry joined them outside the interview room. All three of them entered the room and went through the formalities for the benefit of the tape machine, formal introductions and a reminder that the subject was still under caution.

Frank was being as diplomatic as he could be in order to pacify the man they had arrested, and convince the brief that they had been completely above board in their procedures.

"Mr. Grainger firstly I would like to thank you for your co-operation and willingness to assist us with our enquiries. Also I would like to apologise on behalf of my officers and Merseyside Police for any inconvenience we may have caused you. I trust that since your arrival here you've been looked after and have no complaints about your treatment."

Grainger sat back in his chair and smiled.

"Yerr I ave got one complaint, these Silk Cut fags you got me are crap. I've strained me fuckin' neck suckin on them."

Frank glanced at the brief, who was also smiling and decided it was probably best not to acknowledge the joke.

"Mr. Grainger, I think you appreciate the seriousness of the crimes that we are investigating here and that we had reasonable grounds to suspect you were the perpetrator. As a result of our enquiries we had sufficient evidence to allow us to carry out this arrest. We are…"

"Such as?" Grainger interrupted.

Frank gave him the standard spiel.

"Unfortunately as this is an ongoing investigation I am not at liberty to divulge that information to you, but suffice it to say we wouldn't have arrested you without reasonable evidence. Any way we've checked out your previous' as you suggested.

We do have records that would appear to corroborate the fact that you are who you say you are and not Mr. Andrew Pollitt as we suspected. The fact is Mr. Grainger; we suspected that the name of the person we are looking for might well be fictitious so it came as no surprise to us when you told us that you were not Mr. Pollitt."

The brief coughed to attract Frank's attention making a deliberate act of looking at her watch but not saying anything. Frank got the message and pushed on.

"So Mr. Grainger what we are proposing to do is just to ask you a few questions, some routine stuff for the record and then all being well we should be able to have you on your way. Half an hour tops. Does that sound okay with you?"

Grainger looked towards his brief for advice. She nodded her approval.

"Yeah okay let's gerron with it," said Grainger.

Barry took the lead with the questions.

"Mr. Grainger I'd like you to take your time and think about your answers before you say anything, okay?"

Grainger nodded, it was fine.

"Firstly then, Mr. Grainger please tell me, how long have you lived at your current address?"

Despite Barry's words of advice Grainger was quick to answer, short and to the point.

"Just over six months, check it out with the landlord."

Barry had already asked Bob to check Grainger's tenancy agreement with the landlord and knew he was telling the truth. The previous tenant had moved out and hadn't left a forwarding address. The name the landlord had on his books didn't match any of the names they had under investigation. The trail had gone cold.

"Okay thanks for that. Now I 'd like you to tell me where you where between seven pm and midnight on Sunday, Monday and Tuesday of this week."

Grainger looked pissed off already.

"I thought you said I wasn't the suspect fer this?"

Frank answered him.

"You're not, we just want to completely eliminate you from our enquiries and to do that we just need to record your whereabouts on the nights in question. It's routine stuff and it has to be done before we can move on."

Grainger looked to his brief again who was doing her best to stifle a yawn. She whispered something in Grainger's ear that made him sit up. The rest of Grainger's answers came without interruption or distraction on his part.

Forty minutes later after the prints had been checked and two out of three of Grainger's alibis had been verified,

Grainger was collecting his belongings from the custody officer. Frank thanked the brief for her assistance but before he let her go he was dying to know what she had said to Grainger during the interview to get him to cooperate as swiftly as he had done.

He asked the question. The brief smiled.

"I told him if you wanted to you could keep him in custody until midnight tomorrow night while you completed your enquiries if he didn't cooperate."

Frank shook her hand as she left. At half past twelve Frank and Barry were back in the office.

"I'm not drinking anymore coffee." said Frank.

Barry yawned.

"Nah me neither. In fact I'm going home if that's all right with you Boss. I'm absolutely bolloxed."

Frank knew how he felt.

"Yeah come on, there's nothing more we can do tonight. Let's call it a day, we'll look at everything we've got in the morning and re-assess the situation."

They stood up and made for the door. On his way out Frank pulled out his mobile and rang Bob at home. It answered on the first ring.

"You still awake then?" enquired Frank.

"Certainly am Boss. What's the score with the suspect?"

"Bad news I'm afraid, we had to let him go. Barry and I are just leaving the office, we'll see you about nine-ish in the morning. Do us a favour and hold the fort until we get in. Bring everything we've got so far to the incident room. Be ready for about nine thirty we need to regroup and think again."

"Okay Boss, see you then." They hung up.

Frank was home by twenty past one and asleep by half past.

Chapter 38

At the time Frank and his team were carrying out the arrest at the flat in Toxteth, The Redeemer was in Everton Valley outside the flat where Barbara Hunt lived. Allison Temple was going to receive her redemption roughly a week later. The decision to reverse the order of the last two women had not been easy. The overriding factor swaying his decision was his desire not to get caught. Even more so now he'd killed the unexpected visitor at Margaret Smith's house.

It was going to take at least two more days before he could be sure the timing was right. He had checked and rechecked the research that he had prepared on the two women. According to his calculations he had two days to wait before his window of opportunity would open up, from then he would have fifteen days to complete his mission. Mapping out the menstruation cycles of so many different women had not been easy.

Before he could continue he needed to confirm that his calculations for the cycles for Barbara Hunt and Allison Temple were accurate. He also needed to re-establish that their movement patterns hadn't altered.

Earlier that evening he'd followed Barbara Hunt from where she worked as a sales assistant at a trendy clothes boutique in town. She had, as expected gone to a local wine bar on Mathew Street where she went with two friends after work. Her lifestyle pattern was always the same. She would have two glasses of white wine, maybe a baguette, or salted nuts with nibbles.

She left the boutique at a quarter to six and was in the wine bar with her friends by five to six. When he saw her leaving the boutique he felt strange. It was almost as if he knew her well enough to say hello to her, like meeting an old friend. He was convinced throughout his surveillance she'd never even noticed him.

Especially this time of the year, it was virtually pitch black by four-o-clock. Apart from that, it was usually pouring down with rain and most people were hidden underneath umbrellas, too busy shielding their eyes from the rain to notice people following them.

From where he stood opposite the wine bar he watched as Barbara and her friends walked inside and took their seats next to the window. From his position across the road he watched her until seven twenty five-pm. Any time now she would be getting up to leave. A *creature of habit.* She would look at her watch; take the last drag of her cigarette and then down the rest of her wine in one swallow. Her bus would be leaving in five minutes.

He walked towards the bus stop within a few hundred yards of the wine bar and waited out of sight until she joined the queue. He hovered outside a shop until a few more people fell in behind her then joined the queue to get on the same bus. The first time he'd done this he stayed on the bus when she got off. He just needed to confirm which stop she got off at.

On several previous occasions over a period of time he had waited in the vicinity of the stop where she got off and followed her to find out how long it took to get to her flat in Everton Valley. Less than five minutes after she got off the bus she was fumbling inside her handbag for the keys to her flat.

It had been easy to find out which flat she lived in. He'd stood outside in the dark and watched through the frosted windows following her outline as she made her way up the stairway to her floor. Next all he had to do was wait and observe which lights went on in the flats either side of the hallway as she went in. A few times he got there before her and went inside the flats waiting on the landing above the floor where she lived.

As soon as she arrived and closed the door to her flat, he went up to it and listened for her movements. Once inside she would either turn the telly on, or put on music. Sometimes he'd heard the bath or the shower running. It was all fairly straightforward.

The communal rubbish disposal had caused a few problems but through persistence he had collected enough information to calculate when she was having her periods. He'd followed her every day for a week to find out when and where she did her shopping. Once a week she would catch a bus that passed a KwikSave on route to town. Depending on whether it was raining or not, or on how many bags she had to carry she either caught the same bus coming back from town or jumped into a taxi.

He simply waited until she arrived home with the shopping, hiding in the large smelly room where the huge communal skips were kept for the rubbish. Within minutes she'd unpacked her shopping and he heard the rustling sound of crumpled plastic KwikSave bags slipping their way down the waste disposal chute. He'd caught the bags before they landed in the skip and took them home with him. Once home, he'd find the receipt with the items she had bought.

From regularly checking the receipts he knew whether she had bought tampons. They usually turned up listed amongst the buy one get one free offers. Once he'd confirmed what he needed to know he'd been able to work out his window of opportunity give or take two to three days.

Earlier tonight he had been back to check that she was still at the same address. Even more importantly to see that she was still following the same routine. She most certainly was, and by his calculations he would only have to wait a few days before he'd be able to complete this part of his mission. Tomorrow he would complete the final surveillance on Allison Temple.

Chapter 39

Thursday morning at half past seven Father Maloney was sat in the kitchen at the Presbytery eating breakfast. It had been several days since he'd heard from Frank despite having left at least five messages on his answer phone. He hadn't slept very well and was worried that he'd still not heard any news.

He finished his breakfast and was thinking about going to Canning Place to see him when the phone rang. He looked at the clock on the wall above the phone table before answering.

"Ted its Frank, sorry I've not been in touch, I got your messages, I've been meaning to ring..."

"Frank, don't worry about it, thanks anyway. You're up early, where are you?"

"I'm at Canning Place, we've been busy."

"I was wondering how you were getting on, I've been listening on the radio for news and reading all the newspapers. Sandra Pollock has been to see me again; we've been discussing how she feels about the baby. It's difficult for her being Catholic and all. She's been asking a lot of questions most of which I couldn't answer. She also asked me how you are getting on with the case, I couldn't answer her I'm afraid. I told her I would come and see you if that's all right?"

Frank thought *he* had problems, he couldn't begin to think about the decisions Sandra Pollock needed to make about whether she should keep the baby or not. Poor old Ted was stuck in the middle, God on one side and a whole world of shit on the other. He was definitely going to make more of an effort to stay in touch with him.

"Listen Ted, it's probably not a good idea for you to come here today. I can't say too much but suffice it to say we had a suspect in custody last night, turns out we got the wrong man. We had to let him go so we are back to square one. I'm going to be tied up until at least lunch time but if you're free this afternoon I could come to see you."

There was silence at the other end of the line. "Ted are you still there?"

"Yes, I'm still here Frank, I was just thinking what I needed to do this afternoon. I've got a few things I need to arrange but it should be fine. If I'm not at the presbytery I'll be at the church, just come and find me, if that's okay with you?"

Frank was going to make damn sure it was. "Yeah no problem, I'll see you around two-ish."

Ted sounded relieved when he hung up. Frank picked his notes up off the desk and headed for the incident room. He'd been in since seven and downloaded his thoughts onto paper for half an hour before finally ringing Ted. The rest of MIT were in before him. Barry had rung Mark, Bob and Daz giving them the script for the morning. The incident room was already prepared when Frank walked in.

"Morning Boss." They said collectively.

"Morning Guys and thanks, you know it's appreciated."

For the next two hours they bounced ideas and theories off each other. At a quarter to ten there was a knock at the door. Daz got up to open it; it was Janice with a tray full of mugs of steaming hot coffee and a packet of Jammy Dodgers.

"Here you go Sir, lady, gentlemen."

Frank looked up at her. It was the first time she had addressed him as *Sir* in all the time he'd known her.

"Cheers Janice you're a star, and lets drop the Sir bullshit if that's alright with you. It makes me nervous."

Janice smiled at him. "Why Frank I never had you down for the nervous type. Oh and before I forget there was a call for you a few minutes ago, something about a MERCEDES report. It was reported late last night."

Frank shot a glance towards Barry and was about to ask him to go and pull it off the system. Too late, Daz almost knocked the tray of coffee out of Janice's hands on her way out the door.

Janice recovered doing an amazing balancing trick like a juggler in a circus act eventually managing to place the tray on the table with hardly a drop spilt. She left them in silence while they waited for Daz to return with the report. She was back before the coffee had time to cool with a printout of the report.

"Boss, it looks like we might have something here."

Although the original report had been made late last night it hadn't set any alarm bells off until the officer at the station had updated his report this morning. Ian spent the next few minutes briefing them on the contents of the report.

A woman had walked in to the Police Station on Stanley Road at ten-pm last night claiming she was being stalked. According to the report, in her statement she said that she thought it had been going on for months. She was going to report it when all of a sudden it stopped.

But now it had started again and she was sure it was the same man. She had given a good description.

The indicators that had caused it to be flagged up on MERCEDES were that she was single, aged thirty to forty years old and lived alone. Her name was Barbara Hunt.

Half an hour later Frank and Barry were sat in the office pouring over a copy of the statement that had been faxed over from Stanley Road police station. Bob and Daz were dispatched to the address at Candia Towers in Everton Valley to interview Barbara Hunt. Mark was putting together an identi-kit picture from the description she'd given.

Frank organized the clearance for twenty-four hour surveillance on the address at Candia Towers. He'd also arranged a team of covert surveillance officers equipped with hidden cameras to follow Barbara Hunt everywhere she went for at least the next forty-eight hours. If she had been tagged as the next target surely sometime sooner or later they were going to find the man matching the description she had given them.

A team of plain clothed officers forming part of an arrest squad would be ready to take him as soon as he was identified. Frank's thoughts were running wild. *She might be the next target but she wasn't going to be the next victim.* Not if he could help it. After the disappointment of last night he hadn't been sure where the next break would come from or what leads they were going to follow up.

He was miles away when the phone on his desk rang. It was Janice.

"Sir I have got Inspector Blackwell from Walton Lane station on the phone he'd like to talk to you."

Frank asked her to put him straight through. "Frank its Tony Blackwell here from Walton Lane, I've got some news for you concerning the body found in the coal bunker at the address in Anfield."

Frank reached for his pen and notebook and punched the speakerphone button so that Barry could listen in. "Fire away Tony."

"Okay, you know there was nothing found on the deceased to identify him right?"

"That's correct, I also know you've done a complete check of every station in Merseyside for a missing persons report and nothing's come up, correct?"

"Yes, but we have just had a woman come in to the station this morning to report her husband missing. Her name is Mrs. Doreen Tanner. Turns out that she and her husband had had a bit of a row on the night he went missing."

Frank was hunting in his drawer for a new notepad. "Just give us a sec there would you Tony, …okay thanks… go ahead, you said that they'd been rowing on the night he disappeared?"

"Right, according to Mrs. Tanner he left the house at some time around six pm and he wasn't home by ten thirty so she went to look for him. She found him in the Stanley Pub on Walton Breck Road chatting up a woman at the bar."

Frank took a stab in the dark. "Wouldn't happen to have been Margaret Smith would it?"

"Absolutely, Margaret Smith no less. There was a bit of a set to by all accounts, some pushing and shoving, the usual stuff until someone smashed a bottle and the landlord called the police. Four of our officers were dispatched to the scene to deal with it and by the time they arrived all hell had broken loose with half the people in the pub involved. We've got three of them before the magistrates this morning. In a statement from one of them, it says that Mrs. Tanner's husband, Norman

Tanner knew Margaret Smith and the duty gossip is, that he'd had a bit of a fling with her before. Mrs. Tanner says she can't find his wallet or his keys to the house and thinks he must have had them on him when he left the house."

Frank considered what had just been said. "Well I suppose that explains one or two of our mysteries, although I hardly think that robbery was the motive for our perpetrator to kill Mr. Tanner. My bet is that Tanner had gone round to Margaret's house after hours to see if he could pick up where he had left off in the pub."

Frank was staring at Barry who was nodding his head in agreement.

"Our perpetrator was disturbed or interrupted during the act, Tanner got in the way and would have been able to identify our killer. So he was killed, possibly unintentionally."

Frank drew a line under his scribble and thanked the Inspector for the call. He hung up and looked at Barry who was still making his own notes. "Any views Barry?"

Barry looked up. "Well Boss, the second forensics inspection discovered traces of blood and hair from a stain in the yard about six feet from the back door. The coroner who did the PM on the body we found in the bunker reckons cause of death was a sharp blow to the back of the head. Trauma to the neck area indicates that what ever caused it was heavy. Maybe it was the weight of his own body? If they had got into a fight and he fell backwards onto his head. It all adds up."

Frank was inclined to agree. "Sounds reasonable, although it doesn't explain why he took the wallet. There were two blood types and three lots of DNA found on the towels found in the coalbunker, one being Mrs. Smith's, so that would back up the fight theory." Frank checked his watch. He had ten minutes to get to the presbytery.

"Right I'm off to visit Father Maloney, I promised him I would be there by two. You can get me on my mobile, let me know as soon as Bob and Daz get back, I want to know as soon as we hear anything from the surveillance team." Frank picked his coat off the back of the chair and stood to leave. Barry looked as if he wanted to say something but didn't.

"You okay Barry?"

"Yeah fine Boss, my heads a bit shedded but I'm okay. I'm going to plough through the DNA profiles we've got so far, see if there is anything we've missed."

Frank left him to it. Minutes later he pulled out of the car park at the back of Canning Place. He didn't see the blue Renault 307 parked across the street at the entrance to Park Lane. His attention was only drawn to it by the blast of a car horn when the driver pulled out, cutting up another car as he tried to avoid getting stuck at the lights. The car pulled out on to Wapping and was still behind him as he turned left up hill onto Parliament Street.

Frank's instincts told him that Scallion had his boys following him, the same bastards who got the pictures at Venmore Street no doubt. If it was them, there was no way he was going to lead them up the driveway to the church, Father Maloney had to be kept out of this at all costs.

Seeing them still behind him he drove up and down Upper Parliament Street a few times until they either realized he was onto them or they got pissed off with it. After the fourth trip up and down Parliament Street the blue Renault turned off down Great George Street and disappeared. He did a U-turn before he got sucked in with the main traffic going back into town.

It was almost a quarter past two in the afternoon by the time he approached the driveway leading up to the presbytery. The sun, which had made a rare and brief appearance throughout the morning, was already sinking in the ever-darkening sky getting ready to disappear altogether. Long shadows from the fir trees loomed, plunging him into almost total darkness as he steered the car up the drive. Climbing out of the car he felt the chill closing in for the night.

He rang the bell three times without an answer, and then remembered what Ted had told him about being in the church if he wasn't at the house. As he turned to leave, the door opened. Father Francis was stood at the door.

"Sorry about that. I was reading upstairs and must have dozed off. Can I help you?"

Frank pulled out his ID and introduced himself. "DCI Frank Carroll, I'm a friend of Te... Father Maloney's, he's expecting me?"

"Oh that's right he is. He told me you were coming Frank. Never mentioned the DCI bit though. Still I don't suppose it does any harm to have friends in high places though eh?"

Frank smiled; *they don't come any higher than yours mate!*

"Ted's over at the church but you can come in and wait for him if you'd like?"

"No thanks Father, if it's all the same to you I'll go and see him at the church, I'm on a bit of a tight schedule." He said goodbye and set off down the gravel path towards the church.

He walked through the wrought iron gates and stared across the courtyard. The sun had almost disappeared behind the church blackening the outline against the sky. It was built out of huge blocks of sandstone in various shades, interwoven with intricately shaped mustard coloured stone to form a classic "T" shape.

A welsh slate roof arched towards a steeple at either end. To the right was the Sacristy flanked either side by two cylindrical towers with conical shaped roofs reminding him of a castle he had seen in a fairy tale book a long time ago. The stained glass windows were practically obscured by metal grills put there to protect them from vandals throwing stones at them.

He climbed the worn stone stairs to the main entrance and saw that the door was slightly ajar. He slipped through the gap feeling a bit uncomfortable. He had that naughty child like feeling you get when you are doing something you shouldn't be and someone is watching you. Inside the church it was even darker than outside and looked to be empty. He blinked a few times closing his eyes trying to refocus in the dim light.

When he opened his eyes he saw the rows of shiny wooden pews on either side of the narrow aisle way. Hymnbooks and tired looking prayer mats were scattered intermittently along each pew. The rows of pews fell away in front, reaching their way along the aisle to the steps leading to the benches where the choir sat. On the left the tall gold coloured pipes of the organ rose majestically towards the domed ceiling. A huge intricately carved wooden eagle sat perched on top of the magnificent white marble and granite pulpit. He felt humble, almost childlike.

As he walked further along the aisle towards the pulpit, a candle flickered above the altar; in front of it was the figure of Father Maloney. Standing as still as a statue, wearing a long plain black cassock, arms in front of him and hands clasped deep in prayer.

Frank couldn't believe that he hadn't seen him as soon as he had walked in. He all of a sudden felt very guilty for being here unannounced. He thought about sneaking out and making another somewhat noisier entrance so as to alert Father Maloney of his presence. He decided against it and instead sat in the nearest pew to him. Surprisingly there was not a creak or a groan from the ancient wooden bench.

He was half hoping something would give away his presence without scaring Father Maloney half to death. The voice of conscience rose inside his head and spoke to him. *Maybe you should do some praying while you are here?*

Another voice answered. *Don't be such a hypocrite; it's not like a supermarket where you can just pick up a little forgiveness while you're here. You have to be a signed up member!* It was the voice of reason.

After the troubles at home in Northern Ireland, Frank never had a membership card as far as he was concerned. He knelt on the purple felt covered prayer mat and closed his eyes. He opened his eyes a moment later and looked towards the altar where Father Maloney had stood. At first he thought that Father Maloney had disappeared but when his eyes refocused he could see that he was now kneeling at the foot of the altar. The flowing folds of his cassock fell around his legs revealing the bottom of the legs on his trousers and the soles of his shoes.

They were a light orange colour with a very distinctive pattern. Frank closed his eyes again. It was as if he had been staring at the sun too long before closing his eyes. But instead of seeing the round image of the sun flashing behind his eyelids the only thing he could see was an image. It was the pattern on the soles of Father Maloney's shoes. He'd seen the pattern somewhere before and tried to remember where. Slowly it came to him, the pattern was identical to the prints that he'd found at the Perriman house. Now he didn't want to open his eyes in case he saw the pattern again.

He tried opening them, nothing. It was as if someone had just nipped over and super glued them together. He willed them open at last. When they opened Frank almost jumped out of his skin. Father Maloney was stood right in front of him.

"Frank! What's up? You look as if you have seen a ghost." Frank was feeling too weak to stand up. "I think I just might have", he replied.

Chapter 40

The Redeemer parked the car in the cul-de-sac just off the hill in Torr Street. From here he had a clear view of the flat in Candia Towers where he would be able to keep a look out for Barbara Hunt without being seen. Another car slowed down on Netherfield Road and indicated to turn right into the cul-de-sac. The car drove up the hill, did a three-point turn and parked two cars behind him. Before the occupants got out he slid off the seat into the foot well jamming himself up against the pedals.

The two occupants walked past casting shadows across his car, he was sure he hadn't been seen. He left it a few seconds before slowly raising himself out of the foot well and back on to the seat. Still keeping his head low he peered above the dashboard to see where they were going. There were two of them, a woman dressed in smart slacks and matching jacket, the man dressed in casuals and an overcoat crossed the road onto the car park at the front of Candia Towers.

He watched as one of them pulled a piece of paper from his jacket, they were both looking at it. Seconds later they entered the front door to the flats and began to climb the stairs. They were police, had to be. *What were they doing here?* Was this just pure coincidence, a routine visit? *No, he was sure they were up to something.*

Whatever it was, they didn't want anyone to see their car pulling up in front of the flats. Were they just being discreet, or were they being careful?

Either way he didn't want to be here when they came out. He would move the car into the next road up into Devonshire Place and wait for them to come out. When they did he was going to follow them and find out where they went.

Five minutes later he was parked up in Devonshire Place with the back of the car facing towards Candia Towers. He adjusted his rear view mirror to give him a clear view of the car park in front of the flats. He switched on the radio and tuned in to radio Merseyside to listen out for the news. He still hadn't seen anything in the newspapers. He settled back in his seat and waited. Just over an hour later the two men emerged from the flats and headed towards their car.

He waited until they had crossed the road and disappeared into Torr Street before he turned the ignition and started his car. He quickly turned the car around just in time to see them pass along the road in front of him heading towards the junction of Netherfield and Kirkdale Road. He followed keeping two cars between his and theirs along Scotland Road towards town.

At the end of Scotland Road as they approached the John Moores University buildings the car indicators flashed to turn right leading towards the Albert Dock and the Tourist attractions.

If he was right they would turn left along the front of the Liver Buildings and onto the Strand. Conveniently, this was practically the route he would have taken to get to his flat in Toxteth. As the traffic flowed along the Strand he kept in the right hand lane just far enough behind them to see the car indicating to turn left into

Canning Place. They were police and they were on to something.

This was going to seriously jeopardise his chances of performing the act of Redemption on the last two women on the list. He was going to have to re-think his strategy. Before he could complete the mission there was something he had to collect. It was unfortunate that he would have to miss out the last two links along the way.

Maybe it was time to become invisible. He got back to the flat and packed his things, it was time to disappear for a while.

Chapter 41

It took Frank a second to regain his composure after being confronted by Father Maloney inside the church. He was about to speak when his mobile phone went gone off. "Ted, excuse me one minute?" He took the call outside.

"Barry?"

"Boss, just letting you know, Mark and Daz met with Barbara Hunt at her flat. She's scared but I think they assured her it'd be okay. She's on her way back to work; the surveillance teams are all in position."

"Cheers Barry, where's Mark now?"

"He's here with me, do you need a word?"

"Not now I'll speak later."

"You okay Boss?"

"Yeah fine, give me an hour, I'll speak then." They hung up.

Frank pocketed his phone and turned to see Ted a good distance away discreetly attending to some flowers at a graveside. One half of his brain was trying to absorb the information from Barry; the other half was battling with the image of the pattern on the soles of the shoes Ted was wearing.

Maybe it was just coincidence that River Island or whoever sold this type of shoe had also sold a pair to

Ted as well as the killer. He walked over towards the gravestone.

"Sorry about that Ted, should've switched it off before going inside the church."

Ted was smiling. "Don't be worrying yourself about that Frank; you'd be the first if you did. It can be a nightmare on some Sunday mornings; honestly the kids nearly all have them these days. One of the choirboys had one that went off during a wedding last week. And the little blighter whoever it was still hasn't owned up to it."

"You want me to do a trace on all their mobile phone records?" said Frank smiling.

"Nooo, I don't think it needs to come to that Frank. I'm pretty sure it won't happen again."

Ted slapped Frank on the back and steered him up the pathway towards the Presbytery. "Come on, let's be getting ourselves inside for a coffee, you look as if you could use one." They headed off towards the house. As they stepped inside the hallway, the smell of fresh filter coffee wafted through from the direction of the kitchen.

"Looks like Father Francis has got the good stuff out. You're honoured Frank; only special guests get this treatment. I don't suppose you happened to mention you were from the police by any chance did you?"

Before Frank could answer, Father Francis shouted from the kitchen.

"Detective Chief Inspector Carroll, glad you could find the time to stop. Care to come and join us for coffee?" Frank looked at Ted and shrugged his shoulders.

Father Francis walked into the hall waving his hand towards the direction of the sitting room. "Come on through to the sitting room Mr. Carroll, or would you prefer I called you Frank. I'll bring the coffee right through, I've got some delicious fig rolls that go really well with the coffee."

Ted looked embarrassed at his colleagues' slightly over the top behaviour. Frank helped him out. "Frank's just fine Father, no need for the DCI bit or the Mr. Carroll if that's okay with you."

"As you wish Frank." Father Francis disappeared in the direction of the kitchen.

Ted and Frank made themselves comfortable in the sitting room; Ted sat with his legs crossed in one of the armchairs. Frank sat opposite unable to keep his eyes off the sole of Ted's shoes. They were actually more of a boot than a shoe, made of tough looking tan-hide leather with orange molded rubber soles. A brand name of some description sat high up on the outside of the ankle. Frank was still trying to avoid staring at them when Father Francis walked in with the coffee.

"Here we go Frank, thought you'd like a mug."

Ted rolled his eyes. Frank helped himself to a fig roll and picked up his coffee. Father Francis was looking at a trail of dirt leading from the hall into the sitting room.

"I see you've been doing a bit of gardening this morning Ted, speaking of which..." he paused looking at Ted's feet.

"Ted, you haven't got those awful boots on again have you, honestly, really you know they carry muck everywhere. You know Andrew won't be best pleased when he finds out you have been wearing his new boots for the gardening."

There was an unpleasant spluttering and coughing sound as Frank almost choked on the coffee and fig roll. He was struggling to keep the mush of coffee and figs inside his mouth and pulled a handkerchief from his pocket to wipe his mouth.

"Are you okay Frank", asked Ted, looking concerned.

"Yes... I think so... coffee's just a bit hotter and stronger than I'm used to. The stuff we have in our office is like gnats pi... well let's just say by the time I get around to drinking it its usually stone cold. This is very nice though Father, thank you very much." Frank was frantically trying to phrase the next two questions in his head without making it blatantly obvious what he was thinking.

Ted bought him some time. "Francis don't be making such a fuss, I'll get the vacuum hoover out later, and anyway, Andrew won't mind, he's got the other pair he took to Scotland with him for his long walks. Lets just say I'm breaking these ones in for when he gets back."

Frank took a chance and casually threw his first question to Father Francis.

"So, how is er...Andrew? Ted tells me he hasn't been well lately." Frank pretended he wasn't really all that interested and helped himself to another fig roll.

Father Francis sat with both hands clasped around his mug of coffee giving the question some thought.

"Well to be honest we don't really hear from him very much, if at all. And we can't contact him either, that's the whole point of a sabbatical. He's supposed to be left totally undisturbed. Cut off, far from the madding crowd so to speak. We know he goes walking a lot and often stays in different places when he is away from the Abbey."

Franks' mind was now working on an exit plan to get himself out of the Presbytery as quick as possible. He needed one more piece of information first.

"An Abbey in Scotland, that sound's very nice, just the place to get away from everything. Our staff get to go to a convalescence home in Harrogate if we're really lucky."

He paused. He was doing well so far; neither Ted nor Father Francis had raised an eyebrow at his sudden line of questioning. He went for the money question doing his best to sound like a tourist in a holiday shop. "What's the name of the Abbey? It sounds really nice, I might drop by for a look if I ever get the chance to visit Scotland."

Father Francis obliged. "It's the St Thomas of Assisi Abbey just outside Perth. Some famous authors have stayed there to complete their novels you know. In fact I'm sure if you really wanted to visit, Ted could pull a few strings for you and arrange accommodation at the Abbey."

Ted looked uncomfortable. "Now then Father don't go promising the Inspector something that I can't possibly guarantee, besides he's far too busy to be swanning off to Scotland. Aren't you Frank?"

Frank put his empty mug on the coffee table.

"Would you like some more Frank? There's plenty in the jug in the kitchen. It won't take a moment."

Frank made a deliberate act of looking at his watch as if he was seriously considering the offer of another coffee.

"No really, thank you Father I need to get going if you don't mind. I've some meetings to attend later this afternoon." He stood up and pulled out his mobile phone pretending that he was checking for messages, while racking his brain trying to remember which buttons he needed to press for the video function.

The display light came on unexpectedly. "You know, I have still not quite got the hang of this new fangled technology, I keep deleting my messages before I've read them. Not good for someone in my position."

Ted creased up with laughter at the sheepish look on Father Francis's face.

Frank walked towards the bay window with the pretense that he was looking outside to see if the rain had stopped. He turned his back to the window with his mobile phone discreetly held at his side and pushed the button on his phone, hoping to god the flash didn't go off. With any luck it was pointing directly at the photographs on the window ledge.

Five minutes later he was at the front door shaking hands with Father Francis and saying his goodbyes. Ted walked him to the car. The earlier rain had frozen over the windscreen and all the other windows were beginning to ice up.

"Ted, I'll give you a call in the morning if that's all right. I didn't really want to say any thing about the case in front of Father Francis."

Ted understood perfectly, he looked forward to his call. Before he left they shook hands and embraced each other like brothers. Despite his apparent calmness Frank could tell deep inside, Ted was hurting from the strain of everything. Maybe that's what he was praying about at the altar in the church.

Frank was struggling to forgive himself for his thoughts when he had first seen the pattern on the soles of the shoes Ted was wearing. How could he have possibly ever allowed the thought to enter his head? It was all he could do to stem the tears he felt welling up inside him. He said goodbye and climbed inside the freezing cold car. With the heater on full and the fan turned up to maximum he drove off, doing his best to avoid the potholes.

As soon as he got a reasonable distance on to the road leading away from the drive he pulled over and reached for his phone. Barry answered on the second ring.

"Yes Boss?"

"Barry I'll be back at the office shortly, meantime do us a favour would you. See if you can get an address and phone number for the local nick in Perth, Scotland. I want the name of the DCI in charge of the gaff and I want to talk to him as soon as I get back."

There was a pause at the other end. Frank knew Barry would be scribbling notes. "Right, got that Boss, anything else?"

"Yes, get hold of some maps of Scotland. The larger the scale the better. Find an Abbey by the name of St. Thomas of Assisi, its somewhere just outside Perth. I also want a list of bed and breakfast places, guest houses and small hotels within a forty mile radius of the Abbey."

Frank pictured Barry on the other end of the phone waving frantically to Bob or Mark to get ready. Barry's voice had a note of sarcasm when he spoke.

"You planning on going on a walking holiday Boss?"

"Not if I can avoid it Barry, I'll explain everything when I get back, see you in half an hour. There's a few things I need to do."

He hung up and scrolled through the phone book on his phone until he found the number he was after. He hit the call button. He recognised the female voice with the posh scouse accent.

"Hello Samantha, this is DCI Frank Carroll here. I want to speak to Tom Scallion now!"

There was a clicking sound in his ear as he was being transferred. Tom Scallion's wheezing voice came on the line. "Yes Frank, what can I do for you?"

"Tom, the twelve o clock midnight deal we spoke about for the exclusive is off. You had your boys following me today, blue Renault 307? You must be paying them far too much. Anyway it was out of order. I'm not a happy bunny, so you can wait until I'm good and ready." He knew what was coming next.

"Well in that case Frank we'll just have to go ahead with what we've got so far. It'll be in the evening edition tomorrow."

"Fine go ahead, but as we speak two of my officers are talking to three of the major tabloids with the intention of giving them the complete works for tomorrow mornings papers. It'll be old news by the time yours comes out. If you want your exclusive I need you to co-operate. I need another twenty four hours."

There was a short silence at the other end before he got an answer. Tom Scallion was willing to co-operate.

"Oh and one more thing Tom, if I find out your boys are pulling any more stunts like they tried today you forfeit the deal. I'll call you tomorrow." He hung up.

The next call he made would be slightly trickier. He hit the speed dial number for Chief Superintendent Bright. The chief Super was notorious for not answering his phone to outside mobile calls. Frank had got Janice to sneak into the Chief Super's office and update his caller ID display. Surprisingly he answered straight away.

"Sir, its DCI Carroll here." The Chief Super didn't sound in the least bit surprised.

"Yes Frank, what can I do for you?" *Good answer boss, just wait till you hear this.*

"Sir, I need authorisation for the exclusive use of a helicopter for the next forty eight hours."

Chief Superintendent Bright was not very good with fastballs and stalled for time before making a decision.

"I take it that this *is* something to do with the current investigation?"

"Yes Sir it is. I believe I have got positive identification of the suspect and a major lead that will lead to his arrest. This is the breakthrough we've been waiting for. Trouble is I need some assistance from our colleagues in Scotland. If I'm right we should have everything done and dusted by this time tomorrow." Frank sounded more confident than he felt.

"Okay Frank, I'll have Janice prepare the paperwork, see you when you get back. Good luck."

Frank thanked him and hung up. He crossed his fingers and pressed the video play button on his mobile. After a short clip showing his feet and the legs of the coffee table inside the sitting room at the Presbytery, the light dimmed and then refocused in the light from the bay window. The face that stared back at him from the small LCD display was that of Curate Andrew McClelland.

Chapter 42

Barry pressed the end call button on his mobile and stared at it for a few seconds. It was Bob who spoke first.

"Well, come on Barry don't keep us all in suspenders, what's the Boss up to?" Barry looked at him smiling at the use of the word suspenders instead of suspense.

"I've got no idea, but I've got a feeling we might be planning a trip up north. The Boss 'll be here in half an hour." Barry dispatched everyone in accordance with the instructions he'd received. He added a few of his own while he was at it.

"Daz, I want you to check up on train times out of Lime Street to the nearest station to Perth in Scotland, while your at it check with Liverpool and Manchester Airports for flight times in the next twelve to eighteen hours." Daz was on the phone in less than a minute talking to someone at British Rail. The rest of the team was just as quick.

Maps appeared within minutes, Internet searches were being done to find tourist information on bed and breakfast or guesthouses around Perth. Printers buzzed into action spouting off reams of lists with addresses and telephone numbers. Barry sat in Frank's office and made several calls to Tayside Police, starting with the force Headquarters on West Bell Street in Dundee, the Central Division for Perth and Kinross in Scotland.

It took him less than five minutes to get hold of a number for the DCI at the Western Division of Tayside Police.

He checked his watch, it was almost six pm. He hoped he would still be able to reach someone. He dialed the number he had been given. He was expecting someone with a gruff sounding Scottish accent to answer, so was quite surprised to hear a pleasant sounding female voice answer with no trace of an accent.

"Tayside Police, Serious Crime Office DS Jayne McCulloch speaking, how can I help?"

"Jayne, my name is DS Barry Ferguson, I'm ringing from the Major Incident Team at Merseyside Police Headquarters in Liverpool. I was expecting someone sounding a bit different. You took me by surprise for a moment there."

"Oh that's okay, I'm Scottish from my mother's side of the family, but I was born in Suffolk, anyway enough about that, what can we do for you?"

Barry filled her in on most of the details but kept out the sensitive bits that he knew Frank wouldn't want mentioned. She told him she would get hold of DCI McAllistair straight away and get him to stand by for the call from Frank.

By the time Frank walked back into the office the team were just about done and looking pleased with themselves. They looked like eager sheep dogs waiting to chase after another stick and, just like sheep dogs they were not getting tired of it.

They gathered in Frank's office to listen to what he had to say. Ten minutes later Janice knocked on the door and walked in.

"Sir the authorizations for the helicopter? The Chief Super has already signed it, I just need your signature here, and at the bottom on page three." Frank picked up a pen and scribbled his signature where she'd indicated. When he'd finished, she said, "Thank you, I just need to know from when exactly will you be requiring it?"

Frank pondered the question. "It could possibly be tonight, but more than likely first thing in the morning. Give us half an hour and I'll let you know for definite, I need to make a call first."

Janice left the office with the paperwork still on Frank's desk. Barry's face was a picture. "I take it your not slumming it then?"

"No *we* are not. I've got a hunch, which, if proved right means we'll be doing a fair bit of traveling in the next forty-eight hours. I think I know who we are looking for."

He pulled his mobile phone out of his jacket pocket and switched it on. They all watched as he fiddled with the buttons. He played the video and paused it on the image he was looking for. He turned the phone round and showed the image on the display to everyone in the room.

"If I'm not mistaken, I believe this is the man we're after."

The image was of a man matching the description given by Barbara Hunt in her statement, a man in his late thirties, square jaw, rugged complexion with blue or gray coloured eyes. The most distinguishing features were the eyebrows, thick bushy and black, and medium length black hair thinning slightly on top.

Frank filled them in on the details. "This man is Andrew McClelland which, actually might not be his real name. Either way I think he is passing himself off as a member of the Roman Catholic clergy. I also think that he is using the sanctuary of the church to hide his true identity and his whereabouts". If he knows we're on to him he may well have gone to ground and I suspect he is probably hiding at the Francis of Assisi Abbey in Scotland"

The team couldn't help looking impressed at Frank's discovery; they leaned forward to get a good look at the image. Mark was the closest and was itching to get his hands on it.

"Mark you're the whiz kid with this kind of stuff. I want you to work out how to download this video footage off my phone and on to a computer. I need a quality image blown up and digitally enhanced or whatever you call it. I want hard copies for everyone involved in the investigation and an electronic version ready to be emailed to whoever needs it. Get cracking."

Mark took the phone off him and examined it. "I'll need the instruction manual and the leads for this Boss."

Frank was looking sheepish. "I think I threw them out with the box. I only kept the charger. Find someone else in the building who's got the same phone. Failing that send someone round to that mobile phone place in town and buy another lead."

Mark did not need telling twice. He sent an email to everyone in the building. Five minutes later his phone rang. He went to collect the lead from downstairs. Barry handed his notes over to Frank with the phone number for DCI McAllistair.

"Okay guys give me a minute will you I need to speak to this guy in private." They all left the room. Bob and Daz sat in the main office and discussed who would get to go for a ride in the helicopter. Barry went to check how Mark was getting on with the mobile phone.

Frank picked up the phone and dialed the Perth number. Someone sounding remarkably like Inspector

Taggart answered. "Tayside Police, Western Division Serious Crime Office, this is DCI Angus McAllistair speaking."

"Angus, this is DCI Frank Carroll here from Merseyside Police. I believe one of my officers has spoken to your DS McCulloch earlier?"

"Och that's right Frank, glad to be of help, what ken we do for ye?"

Frank liked this guy already. "Well it's a bit of a long story but I'll try and give you the shortened version. Half an hour later they were still talking. Frank was doing his best to answer a barrage of questions from DCI McAllistair.

"Yes, that's right absolute discretion. The three most important things are, firstly to protect the source from where the information came from. Secondly, it's crucial we find DNA material from the room that our suspect was staying in at the Abbey. We'll pick up the tab for fastracking the sample. Lastly, if we don't catch him at the Abbey we're going to need a lot of help in finding out where he's gone. We'll need to check the airports, flights, passenger manifests, train schedules, credit card booking lines, ferry ports, the full shebang."

Frank paused for an answer. The DCI spoke. "Erm… just give us a wee minute there would ye Frank."

On the other end of the phone Frank could hear the DCI barking out instructions. His gruff voice came back on the phone. "Right Frank, my guys will be up to speed on this in a wee mo. How long's it going'te take fer you and the boys t'get up here?"

Frank considered this for a second. He had no idea how long it took to fly to Scotland in a helicopter. "I'll get back to you on that, give me ten minutes and I'll ring you back."

Five minutes later he was back on the phone to Dundee.

"Angus, its Frank. Okay it'll take about an hour and a half for the flight but we need about an hour this end to wrap things up before we leave. DC Mark Roberts should have emailed you about five minutes ago, did you receive the pictures?"

"Ay, Frank that we did alright. Some of my people are circulating it as we speak. I've got half a dozen officers on their way to Dundee and Edinburgh airports and I've been in touch with immigration at both of them. They're checking incoming passenger lists scheduled for the next twenty-four hours, and all outgoing flights that have left over the same time period. There should be a surveillance team in position at the Abbey in less than an hour from now; I'm just waiting for a call from them. In fact I thought that was them calling when you rang. We'll meet you at the helipad in Dundee. It'll take no more than half an hour for us to drive to Perth; the Abbey is about five minutes north of there. Is there anything else we can be doing tae help in the meantime?"

"No, thanks, sounds like you've got everything just about covered. I'll ring you just before we leave."

After he put the phone down he checked his list of things he had to do before they left. Everything was ticked bar toothpaste and brush. He left the office and went to find Janice. On the way he found Barry at his desk sifting through a mountain of crime reports and DNA profiles from operation Round Up.

"Everything's set at the other end, grab your overnight bag we're going to Scotland in an hour."

Barry looked up pulling a face. He had his bloodhound head on. Frank had seen it before and knew what it meant. "You've found something haven't you?"

Barry looked back down to the reports spread out on his desk. "I'm not sure Boss. I've seen something, but I can't quite work out what exactly. It's been bugging me for a while."

Frank asked him the obvious. "Do you need to spend more time on it?"

The expression on Barry's face told him that he did.

"Okay, you stay behind and finish what your up to, you're better off here if you're on to something. I'll take Bob and Daz with me. Mark can keep you company back here. I'll let you break the news to them; I'm off to let Janice know we're going tonight.

***

At seven-pm, Frank, Bob and Daz were waiting outside for the Sikorsky T311 that was going to fly them to Dundee. The car park had been completely emptied to provide a landing pad. They heard it before they could see it and looked up to the sky.

Out of the darkness came the glaring lights accompanied by the *whop-whop-whopping* sound of the rotor blades from the police helicopter. The down draft from the blades forced the icy wind right at them blasting spray from puddles of freezing rainwater. The noise from the engine was deafening and the smell of aviation exhaust fumes fouled the crisp air.

Immediately on landing the side door sprung open and an officer dressed in dark blue flight coveralls and helmet waved at them to come forward. They lowered their heads and made a dash for the door. The officer held out an arm and pulled them on board. They took their seats and strapped themselves in. The flight officer passed headsets and earphones to everyone indicating which way round they should be put on. As soon as they were ready he spoke to them over the chopper's radio intercom. They all put their thumbs up to indicate they could hear him as instructed. The earphones crackled and the pilot's voice buzzed over the intercom.

"Welcome aboard, lady, gents, just waiting confirmation for permission to take off. I expect to be airborne and on our way in five."

Ten minutes later the lights over Liverpool had disappeared as they flew in a North Easterly direction towards the Yorkshire Dales. Bob looked out of the window and could see the M62 joining Manchester to Leeds. It was a solid line of traffic in both directions.

He tapped Daz on the shoulder. "Sod that for a lark, imagine having to do that every day." She nodded as if she'd heard every word he said.

The lights below disappeared and the dark gloomy landscape of the Pennines and the Yorkshire Moors reached up towards them. A few minutes later the flight officer looked behind him to check they were all okay. Each of them had brought a small kit bag with overnight essentials and vacuum-packed sandwiches from the vending machine on the first floor at Canning Place. All three were fast asleep.

Chapter 43

The Redeemer opened his eyes, startled at the sound of the flight attendant making an announcement over the speaker.

"Ladies and Gentlemen we shall shortly begin our approach to Edinburgh International. We would ask that you now return to your seats and keep your seatbelts fastened until we have landed and the aircraft has come to a halt. We hope you enjoyed your flight and would like to thank you for flying with Easy Jet and on behalf of the crew I wish you a "safe" onward journey."

The Redeemer rubbed his eyes clearing away the sleep sticking to his eyelids. His hand fell to the gold crucifix hanging from his neck, *onward* journey he would definitely have, whether it would be safe or not was out of his hands. The plane taxied to a halt and the fasten seatbelts sign went out. He undid his belt and stepped into the aisle.

Someone bumped into him from the next seat and turned angrily towards him. The woman was about to give him a mouthful when she saw the flowing black cassock and the crucifix. "Oh I'm sorry Father I didn't mean to…"

He raised a hand. "Don't worry about it, no harm done." He collected his holdall from the overhead locker and joined the line of passengers queuing to get off the plane. On his way out the flight attendants nodded respectfully as they said their goodbyes.

He had no luggage to reclaim so once inside the airport and through the arrivals area he headed straight for the exit. He wasn't taking any chances, lingering around the airport was the last thing he was going to do. If the police were doing their job properly the airports would soon be on the lookout for him, if they weren't already.

Outside the icy cold Scottish air hit him full in the face causing him to catch his breath. He looked up to the cloudless sky and saw the stars hurrying the sun along to set. He was already shivering; it was going to be a cold night.

He climbed into one of the waiting taxis. The taxi driver looked at him in the rear view mirror. "Where to Father?"

"Take me to The Bridge of Earn just outside Perth if you wouldn't mind."

The taxi driver didn't mind, this would probably be the best fare he would pick up that day. "Certainly Father, it'll be about £35.00 if that's okay with you?

The rapidly sinking sun had almost disappeared as the taxi sped off around the outskirts of the City of Edinburgh. By the time the taxi joined the M90 in the direction of Perth the light was beginning to fade completely. *The Redeemer* sat back in the taxi and gathered his thoughts. He would get out at The Bridge of Earn and walk the half-mile along the path across the fields to the Southern side of the Abbey.

If there was anyone waiting for him or watching the front entrance on the Northern side he wouldn't be seen. He would also be able to stop and observe from the trees at the back of the Abbey how many lights were on. This would give him an indication of how many residents were home. Thirty minutes later the driver turned and spoke to him, slowing as they approached The Bridge of Earn.

"Where exactly would you like to be dropped off Father?"

"Here will do just fine," he gave the taxi driver two twenty-pound notes.

"Keep the change."

He climbed out and reached back inside to get his holdall, then paused.

"I know this might sound a bit strange, but do you think you could wait for me here? I may need a lift to Fife. I'll give you another forty pounds now and if I am not back in exactly one hour you may go and keep the forty pounds."

The driver looked puzzled at the request then glanced at his watch. What the heck, forty pounds for an hours' sleep. "Okay Father I'll wait until half past five, but if you are not here I'll have to go."

He handed over the forty pounds and thanked him for his patience. The driver turned the car around and parked in a lay by on the opposite side of the road. He sat and watched as the strange man of the cloth strode off into the darkness across the fields with only the light of a rising moon to light his way.

Mine is not to reason why, he thought.

The Redeemer had walked this path many times before and it was only a matter of minutes before he could see the slate tiles, shiny and wet reflecting the pale moonlight from the roof tops above the Abbey. Cautiously he made his way around through the undergrowth at the rear of the Abbey.

He paused catching his breath, hidden amongst the trees at the back of the Abbey; the building was almost in total darkness. Only the lights from the kitchen and small living room area were on. Through the darkness he saw the faint trail of wood smoke as it spiraled from the main chimney into the starlit sky.

He kept to the bushes edging his way around to the East side of the Abbey to get a clear view of the car park. There were only two cars parked up alongside the minibus used by the housekeeper. It was still too risky to go in by the front entrance so he made his way back to the rear of the Abbey. He left the holdall behind a tree and precariously made his way down the scree slope, trying to focus on the ground floor window of his room.

Almost there he lost his footing as a boulder shifted under his weight. He lost his balance and threw his arms out in front of him to break the fall. He hit the ground and winced as the sharp chunks of slate slashed the palms of his hands. His heart pounding, he got to his knees and paused, waiting to see if anyone had heard him.

There was only the sound of the wind whipping round the Abbey and curling its way through the trees further up the slope. His ankle hurt and was already swelling up, he stood up and tried a few steps. Limping he reached the wall below the window of his room and leant against it for support.

The accommodation at the Abbey was comfortable but sparse with a bedroom, sitting room and a small room with a toilet and washbasin. Showers and baths were part of a communal arrangement along the hall. The old-fashioned sash window frames had been painted over so many times they were almost impossible to open from inside or out, even when unlocked.

When he first arrived at the Abbey he'd spent hours scraping away the paint from the sliding mechanisms so he could open them quickly should he need to escape. He looked up to the window of the small room where the toilet and washbasin were situated, reached up to the ledge and pushed.

The window slid open a few inches but he wasn't tall enough to open it any further. He dragged three large rocks up against the wall balancing them on top of each other. With the extra height he pushed again, there was a screeching sound as the window slid open giving him just enough room to get his head and shoulders through. He gripped the ledge and jumped, pulling himself up until he was balanced half way through the window. He pressed his hands against the ledge and straightened his arms using his back and shoulders to force the window higher. It shot up and stopped with a bang.

He had two choices, wait and see if anyone came to investigate what the noise was or go for it. If he was lucky he could get in and out before anyone came to see what was going on. He slid over the edge into the room until his hands reached the floor. Using his arms to take his weight he scrambled his legs down the wall behind him until they reached the floor.

Exhausted he stood up and paused to catch his breath, listening for a key being turned in the door by the housekeeper. The only noise he could hear was the sound of his heart thumping its way out of his chest. He quickly rinsed his hands in the sink washing away the blood and grit from his hands. Using a towel on a hook next to the washbasin he dried them and wiped away the sweat from his face and neck.

Feeling a lot better he pushed the door open and went into the sitting room. He looked towards the gap under the door leading to the hallway outside checking for a light. Satisfied that there was no one coming to investigate he walked across to the open doorway into his bedroom. The curtains were open just as he had left them. He had left only the bare essentials behind to give the impression that the room was still occupied. On the bedside table was his alarm clock with glow-in-the-dark hour and minute hands. A half full plastic water bottle and a handful of loose change sat on top of a book on the other bedside table. A pair of shoes stuck out from under the bed and a woolen pullover hung across a chair in the corner.

He went to the bedside table with the alarm clock on it and slid the drawer open. Except for a pen and a blank notepad it was empty. He removed the drawer and turned it upside down. Sellotaped to the underside of the drawer was a gold chain, hanging from it was a locket shaped like a heart. He tore it off the back of the drawer and held it in his hand. The small single diamond in the centre of the heart twinkled in the light of the moon shining through his bedroom window.

He remembered the first time he had seen the locket in his father's hand. A flood of memories swept over him and his eyes filled with tears. He choked them back wiping his eyes with the sleeve of his cassock and thought about the task ahead of him. The glow-in-the dark hands on the alarm clock told him it was time to go.

He had less than half an hour to get back to the taxi. He stuffed the locket into his trouser pocket and replaced the drawer into its slot. On his way out he took the plastic water bottle from the bedside table and filled it with water from the tap in the bathroom. He climbed feet first out of the window and lowered himself down before dropping to the ground narrowly avoiding the rocks below.

Scrambling up the slope he reached the tree where he had left his holdall, grabbed it, put the water bottle inside and set off in the direction of the path across the fields. As he approached the road at the edge of the fields he could see the taxi parked in the lay by with its engine running.

He crossed the road and looked through the window, the driver was asleep. He tapped on the window causing the driver to wake with a bit of a start. The electric window slid open to reveal a tired looking face.

"Blimey Father, gave me a bit of a fright there…what's happened to you?"

"Took a bit of a tumble, no bones broken though." He opened the door and climbed in hauling his holdall onto the seat beside him. "Thank you for waiting."

The driver turned the heater down a click. He turned towards him and asked where he wanted to go.

"Fife railway station please if it's no trouble."

The driver pulled away looking at his watch. Another five minutes and he would have been on his way home. He switched off the dispatch office radio. They didn't need to know where he was; he was in his own time now.

"Aye that's no trouble at all Father, no trouble at all."

The Redeemer closed his eyes and was fast asleep in minutes.

Chapter 44

Back at Canning Place Barry was at his desk studying DNA profiles, scrutinizing statements and wading through crime reports produced by forensics officers on every rape case linked to Operation Round Up. It was 9pm and he had been hard at it since Frank left for Dundee with Bob and Daz.

Not convinced of the point of it, Mark had been helping him sort the DNA paperwork from each case into three separate piles. One for those suspected of rape, those proved with a conviction, and another for unsolved cases. It was a laborious pain in the arse and Barry suspected if Frank's theory was right it might turn out to be a pointless exercise. Still it was better than sitting twiddling their thumbs waiting for news from Dundee.

He kept two piles to himself and gave Mark the other with instructions to sift through the DNA profiles selecting the top four closest matches in the pile. An hour and a half later they pooled their results together placing each profile in descending order according to how close the match was to the DNA profile they had got from the semen found inside the victims.

The two of them rechecked the records on file for each offender and compared notes. The two closest matches had already been eliminated from further investigation. The suspect whose DNA was at the top of their list had to be discounted because he'd been interviewed already. His alibi was bomb proof. The person in question was a transsexual and had undergone a sex change; he was still in hospital recovering from the operation to remove his manhood when they'd interviewed him.

The second on the list had been excluded from further scrutiny because initial enquiries had discovered that the person had died twelve months ago. The suspects third and fourth on the list were still in prison so that ruled them out. After lengthy discussion Barry agreed with Mark that the remaining eight matches were so far out, the probability of any of them being linked to the man they were looking for was nil.

Barry made the command decision to draw a line under their research and sent Mark home to get some sleep. If everything went according to plan in Scotland neither of them would be needed anymore tonight. Mark didn't need telling twice. After he'd gone Barry sat at his desk staring at the final list of DNA profiles they had put together.

Something was still nagging at him, the second name on the list for some reason was screaming out at him. He drew a circle in red pen around the name and put a question mark against it. He leaned back in his chair and yawned until his jaw hurt. Whatever was bugging him would have to wait until the morning, he needed some sleep. The name he had circled was Brian Thomas McBride.

Chapter 45

The Sikorsky T311 landed on the Helipad at Dundee International just after eight thirty-pm. Frank, Bob and Daz had slept most of the way. Now, wide-awake each of them shook hands with the flight officer and exited the helicopter. The crew had been briefed to park the helicopter inside one of the hangars, get some rest and await further instructions.

It had been fairly cool inside the helicopter but compared to the temperature outside it had been positively balmy. On the helipad the temperature was minus eight degrees and sinking. DCI Angus McAllistair and DS Jayne McCulloch were waiting with two unmarked police cars to meet them.

The exhaust fumes from both cars were lit up by the floodlights from the helicopter and gave the impression they were standing in thick fog. As they ran across the icy tarmac to the waiting cars, Bob and Daz were doing their best to stay on their feet.

Frank shook DCI McAllistair's hand as he introduced himself. It was like shaking hands with the bough of an oak tree. He was the size of a Canadian grizzly bear on steroids and twice as ugly. His head was completely shaven, a jet-black goatee beard and moustache protruded from black stubble on his face. As Bob was to inform Mark and Barry later, he looked *well ard*.

"Angus, I'm DCI Frank Carroll and this is..." he turned to see Bob and Daz still negotiating their way across the ice.

"Och don't tell me, let me guess, Torvil and fuckin' Dean nae doot. C'mon Frank we'ken dae the introductions later its fuckin' freez'n oot here."

Frank wasn't going to argue with him. McAllistair ushered Frank into the front car and climbed in the back seat next to him.

DS McCulloch was left to look after Bob and Daz in the second car. Bob took one look at her and had no complaints at being split up from the boss. The cars pulled off in succession and headed for the exit to the airfield. McAllistair wasted no time in bringing Frank up to speed.

"Right-oh Frank here's the story so far. What wud'ye want t'e hear furrst, the bad news or the really fuckin' bad news?"

Frank was still trying to get his head round the DCI's incredibly strong accent. "Don't suppose it's worth asking if there's any good news is there?"

"Aye there's some but wait tillye fuckin' hear this."

McAllistair relayed to Frank what had happened since they had last spoken. It wasn't good. "Okay here we go, first off, the search of the passenger flight manifests for Glasgow, Edinburrrgh and Dundee turned up a result. Andrew McClelland did board a flight fae Manchester tae Dundee." Frank looked hopeful.

"The only trouble was that the flight was at two-pm this after fuckin' noon. The barstard had already cleared passport control and was way oot'e there affore they mob fae Tayside had arrived." Frank had the feeling that McAllistair was even more disappointed than he was.

"That's no the fuckin' end o' it. By the time my boys tippy toed up t'e they fuckin' Abbey, the guys been in an fuckin' oot'e there like the fuckin' man fae fuckin' Milktray."

Frank couldn't help but smile, the tough Glaswegian DCI just might have the edge over Bob when it came to the funnies, Merseyside humour or not, this guy would take some beating. He asked about the good news.

"Och aye that' bit, well wait tillye fuckin' hear this." Frank couldn't wait.

"It turns oot that oour guy McClelland must have cut hissel climin through the doonstairs windae tae the room at the back of the Abbey and left enough DNA material behind'te sink the fuckin' Queen Mary."

Frank didn't know whether to laugh or cry. "Do you mind if we can go back for a look around?" he asked.

"Och aye nae bother, we're on oour way there noo. I had a feelin ye'd still want'e get in there for a shufty roond. We'll be there in aboot forty minutes right enough."

Frank made a mental note to bring a Glaswegian phrasebook with him if he ever came to Scotland again. The rest of the journey passed in relative silence. Back in the second car Bob and Daz had been given the cleaned up version of events by DS McCulloch.

It was a quarter past nine at night by the time the two cars pulled up into the car park in front of the Abbey. Frank climbed out of the car and was taken aback with the sheer beauty of the sight before him. A heavy frost had settled outside all around the Abbey and it looked just like a scene from a Christmas greeting card.

The grass verge around the car park was covered in a glistening white dusting of ice. The trees up the slope to the side of the Abbey reminded him of a scene from the *Lion The Witch and The Wardrobe*. He could feel the tiny hairs inside his nostrils freezing as he breathed in through his nose. The smell of wood smoke hung heavy in the air. The sky looked as if every star in the universe had gathered in one place, it was immaculate.

It was the day before Christmas Eve and if it had been under different circumstances, right now, he couldn't think of any place he would rather be. He thought of Cram. He would love to see this; this was how Christmas should be.

"You quite finished takin in the view Frank coz a'm fuckin' bustin fer a pish."

DCI McAllistair led the way to the huge arched oak wooden door, his heavy footsteps crunching across the gravel as he went. He rang the bell and waited. He was about to lift the heavy knocker and give it a good thump when the housekeeper Mrs. McCreedy opened the door. "Evenin Ma'am. A'am DCI McAllistair and this is DCI Frank Carroll fae Liverpool. I spoke tae ye on the phone earlier. Mind if I use the lavvy."

He stepped through the door, pushed past her and disappeared inside looking for the toilet. Once inside the lobby Frank was left to introduce his team along with DS McCulloch. The two drivers followed them in and took a seat in the lobby.

Bob and Daz had polished off their sandwiches in the car on the way to the Abbey but they gratefully accepted the housekeeper's offer of "some lovely hot tea and a piece of chocolate cake." She ushered them all into the separate dining room and asked them to take a seat while she went off to fetch the tea and cake.

On his way back from the toilet McAllistair nipped down the corridor on the ground floor to the accommodation. He unlocked the door using the key that had been given to him by one of his officers who had secured the room earlier. He went inside to check that no one had been in to tidy up before their arrival. Satisfied that nothing had been touched he locked the door behind him and left. McAllistair arrived back just as Mrs. McCreedy was returning with the tea and cake.

He declined Mrs. McCreedy's offer of chocolate cake on the grounds that he was keeping an eye on his waistline but gratefully accepted the tea.

"Aye a nice cup o tea would'nae go amiss, three sugars if ye don't mind." No one said anything.

Frank had polished off his piece of cake and drunk his tea before anyone else. McAllistair could see he was itching to get into the room.

"Any chance we could get to see the room?" asked Frank.

"Och aye here ye go, fill yer boots." McAllistair took the key out of his pocket and handed it to Frank. "Its room number eleven on the left doon the corridor through the lobby. Jayne and I wull wait fer ye here."

Frank nodded to Bob and Daz and the three of them left McCulloch and McAllistair alone together.

They reached the door to room number eleven, unlocked it and went inside not really sure what to expect. Daz switched the light on inside the sitting room. Apart from a pair of shoes under the bed and a sweater on a chair, there was nothing to indicate that anyone was staying here; it was the same in the bathroom. Bob went to the window in the bathroom where the forensics team from Tayside had found the blood. Traces of it were still there. With a bit of a struggle he pushed up the sash window and looked outside to the floor below. He saw the pile of rocks that McClelland had stood on to climb in through the window. This must have been a man on a mission. *If only he knew.* He closed the window grateful to get away from the freezing cold air blowing through the gap.

In the bedroom Daz and Frank were looking through cupboards and drawers.

"Found anything?" he asked.

"Nope, and I don't reckon there is anything to find either. It's almost as if someone lived here but didn't *really* live here" said Daz.

Frank agreed. "You're right, he didn't really live here. He just wanted to create the impression that he was. Gave him the perfect Alibi, a sabbatical in Scotland, almost non contactable, a sanctuary, no one would have thought of it."

Bob looked thoughtful for a moment and then, acting purely on instinct walked over to the chest of drawers with the luminous clock on top of it. He picked up the clock and turned it around in his hands. It reminded him of a similar clock he'd had himself when he was a child. He put the clock down and pulled open the drawer.

"I've looked in there, its empty," said Daz. Bob took no notice and pulled the drawer completely out of its housing and flipped it over. Stuck underneath in the centre were the remains of several strips of sellotape. He looked closer at the clear plastic tape. There was something stuck to one piece of tape.

"Fuck me look at this." Frank and Daz came to his side and leaned over to see what he was looking at. Sticking to the back of one piece of sellotape were a few gold flakes and a small round metal link with a tiny clasp, the kind you would find on a ladies necklace or bracelet. The metal link looked old and tarnished with age.

Someone had pulled off whatever it was that had been taped in place leaving behind the gold flake paint with the link and worn clasp.

"So come on then Sherlock," said Daz, "what was it that made you look underneath the drawer?"

Bob smiled. "Oh that? That's easy. I used to do the same thing to hide me fags from our kid when I was goin out. It was the clock that made me think of it, I used to ave one almost the same on me bedside table."

Frank stared at Bob who was looking quite pleased with himself.

"Well done Bob I'm glad we brought you along for the ride, worth the petrol money alone. Any thing else you want to have a look at while you're on a roll?"

Bob grinned. "I wouldn't mind avin a closer look at that DS McCulloch." Daz shot him a look. *Quit while you're ahead.* It didn't go unnoticed.

"Okay I think we are just about done here, now listen both of you, do not breathe a word of this to either of those two out there. Number one, I don't want to show their boys up or embarrass the DCI. Two, I'm positive whatever it was that was stuck underneath that drawer is the only reason our man came back here. Why else would he take the trouble to fly a couple of hundred miles and go through all this trouble to get it? It's obviously linked to what he has been doing in some way. All we have to do now is find out what, and where the fuck he's gone with it."

There was a knock at the door to the sitting room.

"Daz, go and see who it is and take your time." Frank quickly removed the rest of the tape from the drawer and put it inside his jacket pocket along with the piece of tape with the clasp and gold flake paint. He replaced the drawer before he and Bob strolled casually into the sitting room.

Daz was stood in the doorway talking to DS McCulloch. She turned towards them as they approached.

"Jayne tells me DCI McAllistair has had a phone call from forensics about the notepad they found in the drawer."

"Sounds interesting." said Frank as he switched off the light and exited the room. He was locking the door when DS McCulloch spoke.

"It is Sir, forensics have done an ESDA test on the top sheet in the notebook that has revealed evidence which could be vital to your investigation. DCI McAllistair has asked them to fax a copy of it over here. He's in the housekeepers office waiting for it now." Frank almost sprinted along the corridor. When it came through he wanted to be there.

DS McCulloch escorted Frank to the office and opened the door to let him in. Daz and Bob went in search of the housekeeper. McAllistair was stood in front of the fax machine wiping the remains of chocolate cake from his mouth with a serviette. *So much for watching his waistline.*

"Thanks Jayne, do me a favour wud'ye, get the drivers tae get their arses oot'side and get they cars warmed up. We're away oota here as soon as Dixon of Dock fuckin' Green back in the office get's his arse in gear and sends this fuckin' fax."

Frank felt sure McAllister ran a tight ship, loved by everyone no doubt. The phone rang, there was a buzz and a click and the paper started to shift through the mechanism. Frank and McAllistair stood transfixed as the old roller type fax machine slowly ground out the paper.

"Fuck this thing is slow, it's gud job we're nae in a hurry eh Frank?"

Frank was not really listening. He had already seen the top few lines on the paper as it rolled out. The machine ground to a halt as the full sheet finally appeared, McAllistair ripped it off the roll and they both looked at it. The Electro-Static Detection Apparatus had detected what had been written on the preceding sheet in the notebook. There were traces of some other writing but the document had obviously been cleaned up a bit. The writing that they were meant to be looking at was there in bold print.

Sharon Byrne R.I.P † Carrickfergus 1980

Elaine Topworth ✓ Redeemed November 2004

Sandra Pollock ✓ Redeemed December 2004

Angela Perriman ✓ Redeemed December 2004

Margaret Smith ✓ Redeemed December 2004

Allison Temple

Barbara Hunt

DCI McAllistair turned to look at Frank. "Any of this mean anything tae ye?"

Frank was in a state of shock. His face had paled and he looked positively unwell.

"Jeezus Christ Frank ye look like ye've seen a ghost, are ye okay?"

Frank responded, just. "That's the second time I've been asked that question today, which way is the toilet?"

In the car on the way back to Tayside Police headquarters Frank rang Barry to give him the news. The phone rang and after several rings switched to his voicemail. There was no way he was going to leave sensitive information in a voice mailbox.

"Barry its Frank, I'll ring you later, ring me if you get this message." He would try again later from McAllister's office. They sat in silence for the rest of the journey.

Chapter 46

Barry fell asleep on the couch in the kitchen and slept like a baby but woke up two hours later with a stiff back and a blinding headache. He got up, put the kettle on and rummaged through the first aid kit for some headache tablets. The coffee and aspirin kicked in instantly and ten minutes later he was sat at his desk feeling better. He picked up a sheet of paper off his desk and stared at the name he had circled in red pen earlier.

Something about the name was still bugging him, but he couldn't quite work out what. He switched on his computer and logged on to the Internet. Several Internet search engines later using the words "Deed Poll" he found what he had been looking for, the website for the London Gazette.

The Gazette, the government's official newspaper, although not on sale to the general public, posts the entire official notices on its own website, including State, Parliamentary and Ecclesiastical notices. Barry browsed through the site for half an hour, ploughing through the information soaking it up like a sponge. The website was full of articles relating to Transport and Planning notices as well as Corporate and Personal Insolvency notices. He skimmed through the additional supplements publishing Honours and Awards, Premium Bond winners and Armed Forces promotions.

Finally he found the bit he was looking for. The London Gazette published the list of people who change their name by deed poll and elect to have it officially enrolled. For this to happen it must first be advertised in the London Gazette then go via "The Royal Courts of Justice" in London and entered into the Enrolment Books of the Supreme Court of Judicature. Barry was surprised to learn that only two percent of people elect to have it officially enrolled.

It was a bit of a long shot, but one worth checking never the less. After several fruitless searches eventually he hit the right link and found what he was looking for. The list of all those who had changed their name and enrolled it with the Supreme Court of Judicature.

The page came up showing 142 notices. He moved the cursor over the scrollbar and worked his way down the list looking for one name. He felt his heart rate quickening as he scrolled his way through each page scanning the list of names. When the name came up he stared at it in absolute amazement. The notice read:

Publication Date: **Monday 01 November 1999**
Notice Code: **1930**

Notice is hereby given of the Deed Poll dated 20 July 1999 and enrolled in the Supreme Court of Judicature on 29 July 1999 by Brian Thomas Murphy of 10 Dyer Street, Salford, Manchester M29 4PL, a British citizen, under section 1(1) of the British Nationality Act 1981, who has abandoned the name of Brian Thomas Murphy and assumed the name of Brian Thomas McBride. Smith & Smithson Solicitors, 20 Tewksbury Street, London W1U 2BJ.

Barry looked back at his sheet of paper; the second name on the list that he had circled in red pen was Brian

Thomas Murphy. Even though the DNA profile had proved to be an almost identical match, Murphy had been eliminated from their enquiries because according to their information he had died a year ago. For reasons they may never find out he had changed his surname from Murphy to McBride by deed poll and enrolled it.

What Barry needed to find out, was whether Murphy had any living blood relations, and if so, who are they? And where are they now? He needed to check the ancestral history records of Brian Thomas Murphy. He was wide awake now and thinking fast. If this information all tallied up he needed to let Frank know. He couldn't wait until the registry offices were open in the morning and couldn't be arsed producing section 23(a) faxes for data protection. He wanted this information now and he knew just the person to get it.

He picked up his mobile phone and scrolled through his phonebook. He found the number he needed, stabbed at the buttons and waited. He looked at his watch, almost eleven pm. It wouldn't matter; the friend he had gone to school with was a complete computer nerd who slept most of the day and was up all night surfing the Internet. The answer phone kicked in, "Shit!" He hung up and pressed redial. After the third ring a familiar voice answered.

"Yes, O Persistent One."

"Jimmy, its Barry."

Jimmy knew already. The rogue equipment connected up to another computer he used to monitor calls to his mobile not only told him who was calling, but also where they were calling from.

"I know, what are you doing still in the office at this time of night?"

Barry thought about asking him how he knew where he was but thought better of it.

"I'm after a favour mate."

He told Jimmy what he was after, but not what for, as if he couldn't have worked it out for himself. He sounded like he was in the middle of something, Barry didn't know what and it was probably better he didn't.

"When do you need it?"

"Well, like *now*, why else would I be calling you?"

"Okay keep your hair on, I'm onto it! Do you wanna hold?" In the background on the other end of the phone Barry could hear the sound of keystrokes being entered at roughly the speed of light. Jimmy was probably going through a keyboard a week if not more.

"Look Jimmy, I know you're good mate but no one is *that* fucking good."

Jimmy sounded insulted. "Give me ten minutes and I'll ring you back. No even better give me your email address. I'll cut and paste what I find minus the links and email it to you. I can't be arsed reading it out over the phone."

By the time Barry had remembered his own email address Jimmy had found the site he was looking for.

"Okay, standby, the email will be with you in five. Speak to you later, Byeee."

Barry thanked him, hung up and checked the time. Five minutes, he thought, time for another coffee. He returned to his desk with his coffee and looked at the screen, the new messages link was flashing.

He opened the email and read the text. It was all a bit irregular with odd fonts and various sizes of text, but it told him exactly what he needed to know. His hunch had been right.

He read through it twice to make sure he had not misread anything and clicked the print icon. The printer in the corner of the room clicked into warm up mode. Two minutes later he had the sheet of paper in front of him. He couldn't believe his eyes, but there it was in black and white.

> Search Criteria: McBride / Murphy, Thomas Brian
> Search results: 15 matches found
> Match 9/15 NAMES: Daniel McBride. Formerly (Murphy)
> SEX: Male. Religion: Roman Catholic
> DOB: 22 February 1965
> Father: Brian Thomas McBride. Formerly (Murphy)
> Mother: Not listed
> Additional NOK: Not listed
> Place of Birth: Carrickfergus Northern Ireland
> Last known Address: Toxteth, Liverpool 8.

Barry was a hundred percent certain the information was genuine. Jimmy had never let him down yet. It could all be officially verified in the morning anyway but Frank would need this information now. The most interesting fact on the sheet as far as Barry was concerned was the location given as the place of birth. Carrickfergus, Northern Ireland. He had the feeling that Frank was going to find it even more interesting. He picked up the phone on his desk and dialed Frank's mobile number.

Chapter 47

The Redeemer got out at Fife main line train station and handed the taxi driver another forty pounds. The driver was more than satisfied with his days work. He drove home with eighty pounds in his own pocket feeling a lot happier than when he had started work that morning.

The Redeemer bowed his head into the wind and walked across the road into the station. Despite having already bought a direct one-way flight ticket to Belfast International from Edinburgh he'd decided it was too risky. He had been lucky so far and although he would have been in Belfast in just under an hour, he was certain if he took the flight he would be detained by the airport authorities and handed over to the police.

There was nothing he could do in Belfast tonight anyway. He needed daylight to complete the final phase of his mission. The train journey would give him time to contemplate his future and catch a few hours sleep. If the police were waiting for him at Dundee station they were going to be disappointed.

The Dundee to London Kings Cross Train would be arriving at Fife in half an hour but he had no intention of going to London, instead he would leave the train at York and catch the connecting train to Manchester. Half an hour gave him just enough time to buy his ticket, get himself cleaned up and into a change of clothes. He paid in cash for a single ticket to Manchester Piccadilly then went to find the washrooms. Checking to make sure no one saw him enter he locked himself inside the larger cubicle for disabled travellers and got undressed. From his holdall he pulled out clean underwear and socks, a pair of casual slacks, shirt, pullover and his walking boots. He carefully folded his other garments into the hold all and took out a small wash bag containing his washing and shaving implements.

Eight minutes later he left the bleach reeking washrooms and stepped out into the fresh chill of the station. As he walked through the foyer he looked up at the huge digital clock in the corner of the station and checked his watch. He had fifteen minutes to spare, enough time to buy newspapers, some food, and a drink to take on the train.

He bought the Daily Record, The Courier and picked up a free edition of The Fife Free Press while he was at it. The train was on time and surprisingly, there were plenty of seats left. Spilling most of his tea from the styrofoam cup along the aisle, he found a seat in the non-smoking section and put his holdall on the overhead rack.

The East Coast Mainline train would take him from Fife to Edinburgh via the Firth of Forth where he would change trains. From there the train would follow the East coast of Scotland to Berwick-upon-Tweed crossing the border into England and south to Newcastle-upon-Tyne. The next stop would be York where he would change trains to arrive at Manchester Piccadilly at a quarter past four in the morning. He planned to get a taxi to Manchester Airport and take the seven thirty am Ryannair flight to Belfast International arriving at twenty minutes past eight.

He closed his eyes and for the first time in a long while he felt relaxed. Within minutes he was asleep. In his dreams he saw green fields, open sea, blue skies and the rough outline of an old stone building.

Chapter 48

At half past eleven Frank, Bob and Daz were sat in McAllistair's office at Tayside Police Headquarters eating fish and chips wrapped in newspaper.

"Ye'll be wanting something tae eat nae doot?" McAllistair had insisted on splashing out to make everyone feel welcome. "The local chippy fries the best fish supper north of the border." DS Mculloch footed the bill.

Frank was shoveling the remains of his supper into his mouth with a plastic fork when his mobile rang. Everyone stopped eating and looked at Frank as he answered the phone with a mouth full of fish.

"DCI Carroll."

"Boss its Barry. I've got something I think you need to have a look at."

Frank paused while he swallowed the rest of his food.

"Boss?"

"Yeah…Barry, sorry about that I was eating…I tried to reach you earlier but only got your voicemail. What's up?"

McAllistair, Bob and Daz finished their food trying their best to look like they were not listening, the suspense was killing them. While Barry was talking,

Frank was making hand signals to McAllistair indicating that he needed a pen and paper.

McAllistair leaned over his desk and handed him a notebook and pen. Frank took it off him and began to write. While he wrote McAllistair didn't take his eyes of him, instinctively he knew something was wrong.

Frank's hands started shaking the minute he'd begun to write and his face was getting paler by the minute.

"Yep... okay Barry got that...thanks...yep wait a minute..." Frank looked at McAllistair and spoke to him.

"I need the fax number for this office and your email address."

McAllistair passed over a card from his wallet and Frank read out the details.

"Alright, thanks, I'll get back to you once I've read it...what?" There was a pause. "No, don't bother waking them yet; you see if you can get some more sleep you sound like you need it."

Franks hand was visibly shaking as he replaced the receiver. McAllistair was already booting up his computer ready to receive the email.

"What are we expecting?" he said looking at Frank. He didn't get an answer.

Frank was on another planet. For the third time that day he felt unwell and looked it.

There was something about this case that made him feel uneasy. The episode in his office, the weird experience of seeing a movie screen showing flash backs from his past. The voices he'd heard, and the one thing which disturbed him most of all, the fact that he'd been so scared of something, it made him piss his pants. If that wasn't enough to convince him, the news he had just heard from Barry was the final proof.

McAllistair was looking at Frank, still waiting for an answer to his question.

"Frank? What is it we're waiting for? Frank answered him; his voice trembled as he spoke. "Unfinished business. Something I'd rather not..." McAllistair's computer pinged as the email arrived.

McAllistair was known throughout Tayside Police as being a hard man, tough as old boots, but when he needed to be, he could be extremely sensitive.

He looked at Frank and asked did he want some privacy while he read the email. Frank was grateful for the level of diplomacy shown by his Scottish counterpart.

"That would be good, thanks."

McAllistair shot a glance towards Bob and Daz. "That includes you two."

They were first out of the office; McAllistair followed closing the door behind him.

Frank sat in McAllistair's chair, opened the mail and read the contents. Instead of sending an attachment Barry had cut and pasted the content of the text straight onto the main body of the email. The bits he'd emphasised over the phone were in bold.

From: E-mail: barry.ferguson@mers.pol.co.uk
Sent: 23 December 2004 23:36
To: DCI Carroll c/o DCI Angus McAllistair
Subject: Re: Telecon 23 Dec 04

Frank,
Please see text below as discussed. Let me know if I can help.
Regards, Barry.

Search Criteria: McBride / Murphy, Thomas Brian
Search results: 15 matches found

Match 9/15 NAME: Daniel McBride. Formerly (Murphy)
SEX: Male. Religion: Roman Catholic
DOB: 22 February 1965
Father: Brian Thomas McBride. Formerly (Murphy)
Mother: Not listed
Additional NOK: Not listed
Place of Birth: Carrickfergus Northern Ireland
Last known Address: Toxteth Liverpool 8.

Frank stared at the text on the screen in total disbelief as his eyes confirmed what his ears had heard earlier. His mind began to race. The reference to Carrickfergus sent shivers down his spine but one thing frightened him even more. The name Brian Murphy was a name he had heard before, but it had been buried in the deepest recesses of his mind for twenty-four years. A name that he had hoped since he was nine years old he would never hear again.

A million thoughts were rushing through his head and deep-rooted memories began to stir. The movie camera was cranking itself up again and the film began to flicker on the office wall in front of him.

Names and places flashed before his eyes with pictures and images of his childhood. Thoughts of his mother and father, his wife, his son, his friends, his colleagues and his job all mixed together swirling around in front of him. His head was pounding and his stomach cramped as the adrenalin gushed through his veins taking control of his body. His mouth dried up, he couldn't swallow and his tongue stuck to the roof of his mouth.

He lowered his head into his hands and felt the beads of sweat breaking out and rolling down his forehead. The bitter taste of acid bile rose to the back of his throat;

he folded his arms together across his stomach as it cramped and heaved. He dry retched twice and reached for the metal wastebasket next to McAllistair's desk.

He heaved again bringing bile and pieces of undigested fish up into his mouth. There was a horrible *bletching* sound as the contents of his stomach forced its way up his gullet and out of his throat. He struggled to breath in between retching as his stomach emptied itself completely. When Bob and Daz came rushing in he was kneeling on the floor leaning over the wastebasket with strings of orange saliva dangling from his mouth. Daz crouched down beside him.

"Fucking hell Frank, are you okay? Do you need a doctor?"

Frank lifted his head and looked at her square in the face. She struggled to understand what had happened to cause Frank to look the way he did.

His eyes were red and full of tears; liquid oozed from his nose and ran down his chin. His lips quivered uncontrollably. He was shaking his head from side to side, whimpering strange noises as he rocked back and forth.

She put her arm around Frank's shoulder, panicking.

"Frank… Frank, what's wrong, are you okay…okay… okay?"

Frank was a million miles away, sobbing his heart out.

"It's okay Ted, sshh… it's okay, it's okay, they won't harm us Ted, they're not going to shoot us, it's okay… sshh"

Seeing the boss in such a distressed state was bad enough, but to hear him speaking like a small child in a strong Irish accent scared the living daylights out of her. She turned around to Bob. "For fucks sake, get McAllistair in here I think we need an ambulance."

Chapter 49

By the time the Paramedics arrived with the ambulance Frank was almost catatonic. Daz and Bob had done everything possible to make him comfortable while they waited anxiously for the ambulance. The Paramedics seeing the state of shock Frank had gone into attached a saline drip to his arm.

Minutes later the ambulance set off with blue lights flashing and sirens screaming taking Frank to Ninewells Hospital in Dundee. McAllistair took Daz and Bob in his own car; he had no trouble keeping up with the ambulance. When they arrived, McAllistair handed Daz the keys to the car.

"Just in case you are needing it later. I'm away hame; I'll get a taxi, its only aboot ten minutes fae here. I'll see ye in the morning, you've got my card if you need me." They shook hands with the surly DCI who they had come to like in a very short space of time.

At the hospital Daz and Bob sat in the waiting room for three hours anxiously waiting an update from the doctors. Twenty minutes later the door opened and a consultant walked in to deliver the news.

"How is he Doctor?" enquired Bob.

"He's fast asleep and stable for the time being. His blood pressure is down and his heart rate is back to normal. We've given him some strong sedatives and he is on a saline drip to bring his fluid levels up. He was totally dehydrated. There was some evidence of kidney and liver malfunction mainly because of the severe lack of fluids. This caused high toxin levels in his bloodstream, which combined with the massive dump of adrenalin is what caused the problems. Your colleague must have received quite a shock to cause him to react the way he did. I've never seen anyone go into such a state without any kind of physical trauma."

Bob wanted to update Hilary on Frank's condition but was not sure how she was going to take the news. "So how long do you think it will be before he's discharged? When will he be able to go home?"

"That depends on what he's going home to," replied the doctor. "If he is able to rest he could be well enough to be discharged sometime possibly tomorrow afternoon, pending further results from the blood tests of course."

Bob felt uncomfortable at the mention of blood tests. "When will we be able to see him?" he asked.

"We need to keep him in under observation and see how he is when his fluid levels are back to normal. You should be able to see him by lunchtime tomorrow. He's certainly not in a fit state to return to work, it could cause a relapse. I'll be able to give you an update in the morning. Meanwhile, I suggest you two get some sleep; you look as if you could do with it. If you'd like to follow me?"

They followed the doctor out of the waiting room into the corridor. "We have a room empty next to your colleague with a single bed in it; one of you will have to take the couch." He left them outside the room and disappeared towards the A&E department.

"Daz, you take the bed, go and get your head down for a few hours. I'll take the couch, I'll make a few calls and let everyone know how he is." Daz yawned, thanked him and opened the door to the room next to Frank's.

Bob pulled his mobile out then realized where he was. He headed for the reception desk on the ward instead. "Mind if I borrow your phone mate?"

The porter recognized the Liverpudlian accent. "Aye, as long as ye bring it back."

Bob was in no mood for piss taking. He flashed his badge at the night porter.

"Is that meant to be some kind of joke mate?"

The porter suddenly found something incredibly important to do and left Bob to help himself to the phone. He managed to reassure Hilary that Frank was going to be fine and convinced her that there was no need to make the journey up to Dundee.

His next call was to Barry. "Sorry about the time mate, but I thought you would want to know the latest in case the Chief Super contacts you." He gave him the news, and then feeling incredibly tired went off to find the couch.

***

Two hundred miles away *The Redeemer* was on the platform at York station waiting for the Manchester Piccadilly train. His flimsy jacket was totally inadequate and he felt bitterly cold. He looked out over the track in front of him at the streetlights lining the road outside the station. In the last ten minutes the first few flurries of snow had begun to fall and a light dusting of snow lay over the roofs of the houses and shops.

No doubt the children would be excited when they woke to see the snow outside. It was Christmas Eve and the weather forecasters were due to take a fall because they had predicted the odds against a white Christmas at 50/1. He just hoped the snow hadn't spread as far as Manchester Airport.

Chapter 50

Friday 24 December Christmas Eve 2004

Bob lay down on the couch and fell asleep to the sound of Daz snoring her head off. Fully clothed he slept like a log for three and a half hours. He woke up needing to go to the toilet. The room was dark except for the small amount of light from the corridor creeping through the blinds. He looked across the room to the bed where Daz lay still fully clothed fast asleep, her mobile phone still in her hand.

He lowered himself off the couch, slipped into his shoes and crept quietly towards the door. He stepped out into the corridor closing the door carefully behind him. He walked the few feet along the corridor to Frank's room and stopped by the window to look through the blinds. From the light in the corridor he could make out the shape of his boss fast asleep in virtually the same position he had seen him in a few hours earlier.

Suddenly reminded of the urgent need to find a toilet he wandered off down the corridor to find one. He didn't like hospitals at the best of times, for a start he knew there was a mortuary somewhere in this building; a lot of people who came into hospital didn't make it out again, at least not on their own two feet anyway. He couldn't help the feeling that hospitals are even spookier at four in the morning.

Fluorescent strip lights triggered by motion sensors flickered into life as he crept along the deathly quiet corridor. Somewhere in the darkness ahead of him a radiator pipe groaned under the water pressure sending a shiver rattling down his spine. Returning from the toilet a few minutes later feeling not a lot better, he was about to open the door to the room where Daz was still asleep when he heard a clicking sound in the corridor.

He turned to see what the noise was. Standing a few feet away was Frank with his shoes in one hand and his jacket in the other.

"Fuck me Boss," Bob said in a loud whisper, "You put the shits right up me there, what the fuck are you doing out of bed?"

Frank looked serious, he spoke hurriedly. "Bob we need to get out of here. I know where he's going and what he is going to do. If we don't get a shift on we'll be too late. Where's Daz?"

Bob pointed to the door in front of him and continued whispering.

"She's in there asleep...but you need to...Boss you can't...the doctor says you need to..."

Frank was in no mood to argue. "Bob, trust me I'm fine, never felt better. Now shut the fuck up and go and get Daz."

Bob was about to open the door, when the light went on and the door opened to reveal Daz rubbing her eyes. It took a second to register.

"Boss? What the..." Frank cut her off.

"Never mind Daz, come on I'll explain later on the way to the airport. We'll need to call a taxi."

Daz held up the bunch of keys given to them by McAllistair.

"No need Boss, McAllistair lent us his car...but are you sure you're alright?"

Five minutes later Frank and Daz were climbing into McAllistair's Audi A4 parked in one of the spaces reserved for consultants in the car park. Daz turned the keys to the ignition, floored the accelerator and revved up the engine to try and get some warmth through the car's heating system.

Frank was in the back seat searching through his address book on his mobile looking for a telephone number. Bob was outside freezing his balls off trying to remove half an inch of frost off the windows with a credit card. By the time he had just about cleared it the first few flakes of snow began to fall.

The sound of Daz revving the engine had alerted the attention of one of the patrolling security guards who came wandering across the car park shining a Maglite torch straight into Bob's eyes. "And jest what the fock d'yer think yer doo'n sonny boy?"

Bob had been waiting for an opportunity like this and wasted no time in taking it. He flashed his badge. "Detective Constable Bob Turner, Merseyside Police, Major Incident team, and *A'am conduct'n a murrder enquiry here.* So get that fuckin' torch out of me face before I ram it up your fuckin' arse."

Frank wound his window down to see what was keeping Bob and saw the uniformed guard covered in snowflakes behind the flashlight.

"DCI Carroll, what's the problem mate?"

"Err nae problem officer, I was just askin yer man here..."

Frank wound his window up telling Bob to get his arse in the car before they got snowed in. Bob climbed into the car muttering to himself, "Fuckin' jobsworth, piss me off."

By now the snow was falling so hard Daz had the windscreen wipers on double speed, with the heater on full blast trying to stop the snow from settling on the windscreen.

Deciding it was probably not a good idea to ask the security guard for directions, they pulled out of the car park with absolutely no idea which direction the airport was in. Daz took potluck and steered the car in the direction of what looked to be the shortest way into the city.

They pulled up at the first crossroads with the traffic lights on red. Theirs was the only car on the road and the snow was already two inches deep causing the wheels on the car to spin as they pulled away from the lights. Frank finally found the number he was looking for and spoke to the helicopter flight control officer at Dundee Airport.

The good news was that their helicopter could be ready in an hour. The bad news was that due to expected blizzard conditions all aircraft were grounded until further notice. Frank passed the news on to Daz and Bob in the front of the car.

"Okay Sterling, you can take it easy, there are no flights in or out of the airport for at least a couple of hours. Besides I don't want you trashing the DCI's car when we've only just met him."

Bob turned to Frank and passed him the half litre plastic bottle he'd filled up from the water cooler in the hospital.

"Drink boss?" Frank took the bottle off him, screwed the lid off and downed the entire contents without pausing for breath.

"Cheers Bob."

Bob looked at Daz. "I think he's feeling better."

They approached the next major crossroads and could just about see through the flurry of snowflakes the sign with directions telling them Dundee Airport was six miles away. As they drove on through the city, the world outside the car began to look like a scene from a winter wonderland. Driving through the snow it took them an hour and twenty minutes to cover the six miles.

At half past six when they reached the airport it was still pitch black outside and the snow was at least seven inches deep and getting deeper by the minute. They cleared the security gate and drove into the airport following the reverse route that McAllistair had taken them the previous night. They left the car under a sheltered area next to the helipad and went to find the portakabin where the crew were resting.

The open steel stairway led them to a makeshift portakabin supported on a steel girder framework. Frank knocked on the door and the three of them stepped inside. The pilot and navigator were still asleep in an adjacent room but the flight officer was awake and waiting for them.

"Morning Sir, doesn't look too good does it?"

"No it doesn't, what's the latest weather forecast?" The flight officer picked up a printout off his desk.

"We received the last update about an hour ago, according to this there is a severe weather warning affecting all regions North of the border. The situation is not expected to change for at least another two hours."

Frank looked at his watch. "So that's around about nine o clock before we'll know if we can get airborne?"

"Well, we might get news earlier than that; I get an updated forecast on the hour so if there's any change I can let you know."

Frank picked up a sheet of paper and a pen from the desk and started scribbling something. When he finished he handed the paper to the flight officer.

"Give this to the pilot. I want a flight plan approved for that destination as soon as possible."

The flight officer took the paper and went to speak to the pilot. Daz was stood next to the window looking out over the airfield when the flight officer returned.

"It looks to me like it might be easing off," she said, to the flight officer. "Any idea what the forecast is in England or how far south the severe weather warning reaches?"

The flight officer picked up his report, lifted the page and looked at the second printout. "The met boys are saying that the front which is causing the snow is spreading North Eastwards from the Pennines so I guess somewhere around Yorkshire."

Frank took a seat in the corner of the room and took his wet shoes off.

"Oh well, as long as we can't fly anywhere neither can McClelland or McBride or whatever his fuckin' name is. We may as well make ourselves comfortable. Bob any chance you might be able to rustle up some food I'm starving."

Bob was pleased to see Frank was back on form. "I'm not surprised Boss, you left your fish supper in DCI McAllistair's office last night."

"Yeah I know. I really must apologise to him for that, and to you guys. But as far as I'm concerned the less said about that little episode the better. I know what caused it and I know who is going to pay for it.

I've finally got the chance to lay something to rest forever, something I'm not proud of I'll admit, but I'm not about to let Jack Frost or Father flaming Christmas stop me from doing something I should have done a long time ago."

Bob left to find some food. The incident in McAllistair's office would never be raised again. Bob returned twenty-five minutes later with egg and bacon burgers for everyone including the flight officer. In minutes they'd finished eating and were all asleep except Daz.

Over an hour later, she was still the only one awake sat at a table by the window, mesmerised by the constant snowfall. She thought about what had caused Frank to react the way he did after reading the email from Barry. Whatever it was, he appeared to be over it and he wasn't going into details. She wondered what was on the piece of paper Frank had given to the flight officer. No doubt all would become clear in the course of time.

She folded her arms on the table to rest her head and was beginning to doze off when her mobile started vibrating across the table. She checked the caller display.

"Hi Barry, what's the weather doing down there mate?"

Barry sounded wide-awake and agitated. "Daz, listen there's been a development down here. McClelland, or should I say McBride as we now know him, caught a flight from Manchester airport to Belfast International. It landed about twenty minutes ago. I contacted Belfast Immigration and the Belfast International Airport Constabulary to alert them but they were too late, he's cleared arrivals and he's nowhere to be seen. "

Daz looked across at Frank still fast asleep on the sofa.

"Okay, I'll let Frank know the score, he'll probably ring you back in a minute."

Barry sounded confused. "But... I thought the Boss was taken ill and he's in hospital?"

"He did, and he was. He sort of unofficially checked himself out a couple of hours ago. We're at Dundee Airport; all aircraft have been grounded because of the blizzard. Listen Barry, the Boss appears to have fully recovered from whatever it was that freaked him out, but don't worry, Bob and I are keeping a close eye on him.

We're waiting for an update on the weather to see if there is any chance we can get airborne with the chopper. I take it there's no problems weather-wise down at your end then?"

Barry was still coming to grips with the fact that Frank was out of hospital.

"No, none whatsoever, we had a light fall overnight but it had melted by this morning, why what's it like there?"

She looked out of the window; the snow was definitely easing.

"Well it's not so bad now, looks like its easing off, but its like a scene from bleeding Narnia outside on the runway, must be two foot deep at least in some places. Listen, thanks for the update; I'll wake Frank and let him know. Speak to you later."

She hung up and went to the small galley next door to make some tea before she woke Frank and Bob with the news.

Back in Liverpool Barry brought Mark up to speed with the news about Frank's remarkable but unofficial recovery. Mark had come straight in to work as soon as he heard what had happened. Barry rang Hilary to give her the official half of the story. *Frank was feeling a lot better.*

While Daz was making the tea the flight officer told her that he had woken the pilot and the navigator, all three of them were going to the air traffic control offices to submit a request for the flight plan to be approved pending the continued improvement in the weather.

She returned from the galley with three mugs of tea and placed them on the table next to the couch where Frank and Bob were asleep. She gave Bob a nudge and then woke Frank.

Frank sat up with a bit of a start, saw the tea and then saw Daz.

"Cheers Daz, what time is it?"

"It's just gone eight thirty Boss, listen I've got some bad news and some good news, first the good news. It looks like the snow is finally stopping."

Frank sat up and looked out of the window. "And the bad news?"

"Barry just rang me on my mobile. McBride is in Ireland. Landed about half an hour ago. Barry tried to alert the authorities but he was too late. There's no sign of him."

Frank took the news a lot better than she expected.

"No problem, I know exactly where he's is going, and if we can only get out of here we'll be there to nick him. Where's the flight officer?"

"He's with the pilot and the navigator; they've gone to air traffic control to get the flight plan approved."

Ten minutes later everyone was wide-awake and looking out the window for signs of activity on the runway. It was getting lighter outside and for the first time the snow looked like it had stopped. Frank was on the phone speaking with officers from the Police Service of Northern Ireland (PSNI) asking them to contact Belfast International Airport Constabulary and the Belfast Harbour Police. He wanted these two small specialised forces to work together in conjunction with the PSNI. He asked them to standby for further instructions and then hung up.

Next he rang Barry and stuck to the essentials. They were flying to Belfast as soon as they got permission to take off. He had just put the phone down when the helicopter crew returned from the air traffic control office. As they walked through the door they looked at Frank and gave him the thumbs up signal.

"Get yourselves well wrapped up we're leaving, we can take off in twenty minutes."

Frank was the first down the open metal stairway from the portakabin with Daz and Bob still putting their coats on following close behind.

Chapter 51

The Redeemer checked to see that nobody was following him as he walked through the arrivals lounge and out through the exit to the pick up and drop off area outside the airport. The area was busy with courtesy buses, private cars, mini-cabs and taxis all loading luggage into the back of them. No one paid him any attention as he walked across to the line of black mini-cabs parked along the pavement.

He walked up to the first cab in the queue; the driver was sitting with the window down smoking a cigarette reading The Belfast Telegraph. When he looked up and saw he had a fare he quickly extinguished his cigarette and started wafting the smoke out the window with the newspaper.

"Morn'n Sir, jump in." he said in a strong Belfast accent.

He climbed into the back, put his holdall on the floor of the cab and fastened his seatbelt. He had previous experience of taxi drivers in Ireland. The driver started the engine. "Where will ye be off to sir?"

"Belfast city centre please, anywhere I can find a dry cleaners, somewhere that does a one hour service if possible."

The driver set off with no idea why someone would step off a plane and the first place they would want to go to was a dry cleaners.

"So have ye bin anywhere nice?" asked the driver, making polite conversation.

"No, just over to Liverpool visiting some friends." The irony of what he'd said struck him almost as soon as he had said it.

The rest of the journey was made in silence. Twenty minutes later the taxi driver was weaving his way through the city centre traffic like Ayrton Senna starting from the back of the grid, showing total disregard for anyone else using the road other than his fellow taxi drivers.

After a scary few minutes the driver pulled his cab up on a double yellow line at the corner of Howard Street and Donegall Square. On one side of the road was the ornate and magnificent building of Belfast City Hall. On the opposite side, between rows of shops was a dry cleaners. The Redeemer looked out of his window and read the sign, *Churchill's Exclusive Dry Cleaners.*

The driver reset the meter. "There you go sir, I think ye'll be finding what yer looking for. That'll be fifteen quid." The Redeemer paid the money without tipping him feeling fairly confident he was being charged too much for the fare anyway.

Inside the dry cleaners the lady behind the counter smiled politely as he walked in. "Morning, what can I be doing fer you sir?"

He unzipped the holdall and removed the crumpled robes from inside. In the clear light of the shop he saw for the first time just how soiled his cassock was as a result of his fall back at the Abbey. He hadn't noticed it earlier, but the dried sweat stains and a tiny smear of dried blood were clearly visible on the white collar.

"Had a bit of an accident I'm afraid, do you think this will come out?"

"Oh dear Father, you know you really should be more careful, what on earth were ye doin t'get yerself in such a mess?" *If only she knew.*

"It's a long story I'm afraid, listen I am willing to pay extra if you can have it ready in an hour."

"Oh don't you be worryin yerself bout that Father I'll have it ready fer ye in no time at all. I can do it while ye wait if ye'd like? Would ye like a cup of tea?" she asked smiling.

He politely declined the offer and gave her twenty pounds. "Thank you very much, I'll be back in an hour." He left the shop and went to find something to eat.

In the last forty-eight hours he had paid for everything in cash. He wasn't sure if he used the cash machine the police would be able to trace him via his credit card number. If they had discovered his true identity by now he felt sure they would have a way of tracking his movements.

He decided if he needed more cash he would get it at the last minute, giving them less time to trace him if they were. He checked his wallet, he had just enough left to get himself a late breakfast and a coffee from a diner further up the road on Donegall Square.

Inside the diner he ordered a toasted scone with a cup of tea, picked up a copy of yesterdays Irish News from one of the empty tables and sat in the far corner away from the window. The news headlines were all about various political organisations, one side ranting on about global warming, damage to ozone layers and singing the praises of alternative energy sources, while the other side was claiming wind farms were causing havoc and killing unsuspecting bird life.

Exactly one hour later after reading the newspaper from front to back he'd found nothing that concerned him. He left the rest of his loose change as a tip and went to collect his dry cleaning.

The woman had been as good as her word. With his freshly cleaned and pressed robes covered in plastic on a coat hangar he went to find somewhere to get changed. He walked the half mile or so along May Street, down to Cromac Square and turned along East Bridge Street to the Central Railway Station. He withdrew £200.00 from the cash point in the foyer, then went into the men's toilets and locked himself inside a cubicle to change.

Relieved to be out of the smell of urine in the toilets he went to the left luggage and put his holdall in one of the empty storage lockers. Before he locked it he opened the small zip compartment inside the holdall, retreived the locket and chain and placed them inside his trouser pocket.

He'd intended to catch another taxi to Carrickfergus, but instead he bought a single ticket from the automated machines near the entrance to the station. He stood on the platform and looked at his watch, it was five minutes to ten, his train was due at five past. With any luck his journey would soon be over and his mission would be completed.

Chapter 52

Forty-five minutes after the pilot gave the thumbs up signal inside the portakabin, the helicopter was still sat on the helipad waiting for clearance to take off. The pilot had switched off the engine to conserve fuel. The snow ploughs were out clearing the runways while the air traffic controllers were juggling a number of inbound aircraft round in a circle in the airspace above Dundee airport.

Frank, Daz and Bob were still sat on board the helicopter freezing their bollocks off. Frank was considering going back inside the portakabin and using the phone to ring the PSNI and the Belfast Harbour Police telling them to standown. If he wasn't going to be there for the arrest of McBride, he wasn't happy about someone else doing it after all he and his team had gone through.

He leaned forward in his seat and shouted to the pilot. "Any news?"

The pilot shook his head. "Last I heard was twenty minutes or there about."

Frank strained his head to look out the opposite window and saw the bright orange flashing lights of the snowploughs in the distance. They were alsmost done. Several minutes later they heard the thunderous roar as the first of the circling aircraft emerged from the deep grey clouds. As the undercarriage of the Boeing 747 airbus touched down on the runway, enormous clouds of snow were blasted into the air from the twin jets of the aircraft.

It looked as if it had landed in deep water causing a huge splash and for a moment it disappeared altogether. Before it re-emerged at the end of the runway the next aeroplane was already poking its nose through the clouds. Frank couldn't help but admire the people working in this industry and decided that no matter what wages they were on, he wouldn't have their job for a gold clock. *But then they would probably say the same about his job.*

For the next half an hour a succesion of aircraft landed on the runway with the blast from the engines finishing the job for the snowploughs.

As the last one cleared the runway the pilot turned towards them. "Fasten your seatbelts we're off."

There was an uncomfortable moment as the frozen ignition struggled to spark the helicopters engines into life. To everyone's relief they heard the high pitched whining sound as the engines fired up and the aircraft started to vibrate as the props began to turn. Frank checked his watch for the umpteenth time. McBride had landed in Belfast just under two hours ago. The flight to Belfast would take about an hour and a half, it would be half past eleven before they landed. He just hoped they wouldn't be too late.

The chopper took to the air and disappeared amidst the snow laden clouds over Dundee airport. Bob was fidgeting in his pocket to remove something that was digging in to his leg. He pulled out a bunch of keys and hung them in front of Frank's face making hand signals and gestures describing a car. Frank was reading his lips.

"Oh fuck, I've still got McAllistairs car keys."

Frank returned the message with his own hand signals roughly transcribing something that sounded like *banker,* and took the keys off him.

The helicopter was having a tough time and seemed to take ages clearing the clouds. It was being buffeted and jarred about in the gusting winds. The flight officer was reading charts and had a serious look on his face. Frank got his attention and used more hand signals to ask if everything was okay. The flight officer held up five fingers on one hand and stuck his thumb up on the other.

Sure enough five minutes later the chopper cleared the clouds and broke through into brilliant sunshine. Everyone relaxed and sat back doing their best to enjoy the rest of the ride.

As they flew in a South Westerly direction the clouds became less and gaps started appearing below them. Ian and Bob looked out the window and saw huge expanses of ground below them covered in a blanket of white. The peaks of the Pennines rolled off majestically into the distance as they cleared Cumbria and the Dales into Lancashire.

It was almost as if someone had drawn a line through the counties of Lancashire and Cheshire, as the landscape below them changed from white to green and eventually to the familiar suburban towns around the outskirts of Manchester and Liverpool.

As the temperature rose, the pockets of ice built up in the nooks and crannys on the helicopters windscreen melted. Rain began pelting them from all sides. Through the rain they could just about see the murky grey colour of the Irish Sea as the wind whipped up the waves producing silky white tips of froth and spray. Half way across the Irish Sea they saw the coast of Northern

Ireland getting bigger by the second, it was the first time Frank had seen it in twenty four years.

The pilot somehow managed to claw twenty minutes off the flight time and at Franks request was radioing ahead for permission to land at Belfast City Airport instead of Belfast International. Frank had thought long and hard about asking the pilot to land anywhere North East of Carrickfergus to save time, but he knew if they did, and McBride was anywhere nearby, he would see the helicopter and abort his plans. There was no telling where he would go next and they could end up losing him forever.

They came in low over the shipping lanes flowing out of the Belfast Lough to Liverpool and Stranraer. The Southern coastline of Carrickfergus was to their right and Frank twisted himself round to try and get a clearer view. He pointed out of the window attempting to indicate to Daz and Bob where ultimateley they would end up.

***

The thirty minute train journey from Belfast Central Station felt like it was taking hours, stopping at seven sub stations on route. The Redeemer got off at Clipperstown (NIR) Rail Station, one stop before Carrickfergus. From here it was only a stone's throw to his final destination. In the distance he saw the ancient castle rising above the Marina of Carrickfergus waterfront.

He looked along the coast road for flashing blue lights or officers patrolling with dogs on the lookout for him. They weren't here yet but he felt they were on their way. He set off in the direction of the Marine Highway.

Walking at an increasingly faster pace he saw the coastal marshland less than a mile away. It would take him twenty minutes, half an hour tops before he reached the Keep. The raw chill of the wind howling in across the Lough was stealing his breath and beginning to slow him down. He could feel the sweat beginning to roll down his face, and the inside of his shirt. Somewhere in the background above the noise of the wind he swore he could hear the distant sound of a helicopter. They were coming for him.

Chapter 53

The pilot brought the chopper in above the helipad on the outskirts of Belfast City airport. Frank looked out the window and saw the three unmarked police cars waiting on the tarmac. They unfastened their seat belts ready to exit as soon as the chopper touched down. The flight officer was poised by the door and slid it back as soon as he felt the wheels touch. Frank, Daz and Bob moved towards the door.

"Good luck sir."

Frank shook the flight officers hand. "Thanks, tell the pilot, he did a great job."

The three of them leapt out onto the tarmac and sprinted under the rotating blades of the chopper over to the waiting cars. Uniformed officers from PSNI stood together with members of Special Branch District Command Unit (DCU) from Carrickfergus. Frank ran up to a senior looking officer waiting by the front car and reached out his hand.

"I'm Detective Chief Inspector Frank Carroll; these are my colleagues DC's Vasquez and Turner."

The senior officer shook his hand and introduced himself. "I'm the DCU Commander, Chief Inspector Victor Molyneaux. Welcome to Ireland Frank. Before we go there's someone who I think you should meet."

"Sorry Victor but I don't think we've got time to..." Before he could finish, the rear passenger door of a black Vauxhall Omega opened, a man got out and walked towards him.

"TED! What the..." The two of them threw their arms around each other and embraced one another like long lost brothers separated at birth.

The fact that Frank had addressed him by his christian name did not go unnoticed. Least of all by Daz, who was finally beginning to get some idea why Frank had been so secretive. Whatever the connection between them was, nobody cared, but judging by the emotion on Frank and Ted's face, what ever it was, there was deep respect.

Ted whispered in Frank's ear as they held on to their embrace. "I know why you're here Frank. There's no way on God's earth I was going to let you do it alone. Let's get it over with."

Deep emotions brought a lump to Frank's throat as he spoke. "Thanks Ted, Thank you, you are a true friend. Come on we need to go."

Frank, Ted and the Chief Inspector climbed into the Omega. Daz, Bob and the remaining officers filled up the two Vauxhall Astras behind them.

Gravel and loose tarmac spun beneath the wheels as the drivers floored the accelerators. Two police motorcycles met them at the exit gates. The cars followed in convoy as the riders cleared the route out of the city onto the A2 Belfast Road.

Frank insisted that no weapons or dogs were needed for this operation, sirens were to be switched off and blue lights would only be used to alert other traffic of their approach.

With the police outriders in front, the cars travelled at high speeds swiftly leaving the city behind them. For Frank and Ted, the sight of Carrickfergus looming towards them brought back memories of happy times they had shared together. Times they had played as kids' young and innocent, totally oblivious of the pains the future would hold for them.

Their happy memories of childhood had been snuffed out of existence, buried by the events that unfolded in the summer of 1980. Twenty-four years later, it had taken the acts of a direct descendant of the perpetrator to uncover them.

Chapter 54

The Redeemer climbed the fence and made his way through the waist high grass onto the patch of waste ground in front of the Keep. He looked across to the place where his father had raped and murdered a fourteen-year-old girl by the name of Sharon Byrne.

Twelve feet of water protected his fathers secret from the rest of the world, a secret that was about to be revealed. The girl, or at least her remains were still here lying at the bottom of a flooded room in the darkened ruins of the old Keep.

The boys who had been with his father could be forgiven for their part for they had been weak and afraid. Now was not a time for being weak and afraid, now was a time to repent and reflect, to pray for forgiveness for himself and his father. He needed to repent for what he had done to the women he had tracked down in Liverpool and for causing the death of a man he had never even met.

His mission had been borne out of anger for his father and the guilt he had inherited when he died. He had deceived Father Maloney and Father Francis who had befriended him, trusted him, shared their food and shelter with him. He felt deeply remorseful for the unholy acts he had committed while pretending to be a messenger of the lord. Surely no man or divine god could forgive him for what he had done, for he had been the messenger of death and the deliverer of evil.

He held on to his crucifix with one hand and took the locket and chain out of his pocket with the other. It felt as if both of them were burning in his hands because he had no right to hold them. Surely what he was about to do now would go someway towards paying for his sins, whatever his penance may be, he was willing to pay for it, even if it meant he paid for it with his life.

He walked the final few yards to the front entrance to the Keep. It was even more overgrown than his father had described it. He looked down at the ground in front of him and wondered, how many people had walked this path before him and entered the Keep for the last time. He knelt down in front of the door at the spot where his father had extinguished the life out of Sharon Byrne. He clasped his hands before him, lowered his head and prayed.

***

The trio of police cars preceded by the two motorcycles screeched to a halt in the lay by where McBride had climbed the fence. One of the cars escorted by the two motorcycles was dispatched a mile beyond the Keep with orders to intercept McBride if he attempted to escape. With Frank and Ted leading the way, Daz, Bob, plus the DCU Commander and two of his officers followed the route that McBride had gone less than two minutes before. They reached the fence surrounding the clearing at the edge of the waste ground and looked towards the Keep. Less than a hundred feet away McBride was kneeling down in front of the entrance praying.

Frank instructed the two uniformed officers from the DCU to stay behind the fence line and move around the back of the Keep in case McBride made a run for it.

Frank looked to where McBride was kneeling, he was holding his hands up to his face, his whole body shuddered as he sobbed uncontrollably. In that moment Frank almost felt sorry for him as a wave of compassion swept over him. He looked towards Ted and could tell that he was feeling the same way. They turned away, briefly speaking out of earshot of the other officers before Frank turned to Bob.

"I want you and Daz to wait here with the Commander, Father Maloney and I are going over on our own." Bob and Daz nodded that they understood but the Commander looked uncomfortable. The three of them had no idea what was about to happen, but whatever it was, it was something that Frank and Father Maloney needed to do alone.

Frank and Ted walked slowly to where McBride was kneeling. As they approached, McBride oblivious that any one was watching him, got to his feet and raised his arms into the air. In his hands were the gold crucifix and locket. McBride let out an almighty cry. "Please, God, forgive me for I have sinned."

Father Maloney crossed himself and shouted to McBride using the name he had affectionately used as a friend. "Andrew, it's me, Father Maloney, and in the name of the Lord I forgive you."

McBride turned his head towards him. "I'm sorry Father. I have something that belongs to someone who died here and I have come to return it."

McBride turned away and disappeared through the doorway to the Keep. Ted sprang forward first, like a startled gazelle being chased by a lion. Frank felt as if the blood inside his veins had turned into molten lead and poured into his feet. He was rooted to the spot, his brain was telling him to run after him but his legs were having none of it. In his mind he saw himself and

Ted as children playing their favourite game of "Who Dares Wins." But unlike in the game where they came running out of the scary place, Ted was running in to it. He opened his mouth to shout after him, he felt his lips mouthing the words *Ted come back, please come back*, but nothing came out. His eyes were wide open staring into space and then everything in front of him faded and turned to black.

The old-fashioned cinema screen unfolded before his eyes and the same movie he had watched on the ceiling of his office began to flicker in front of his eyes. He heard a young girl screaming and the sickening thud-thudding sound as the boy who raped her was beating her.

"Right, away yez go boys, who's next?"

The screaming faded and now he could smell the stench of whisky, he felt the warm sour breath laced with nicotine on his cheek. *"No fucker is gonna kill no fucker, d'yez here me all right?"* He heard another boy's voice, the voice of the one who threatened that their families would be murdered if they told anyone of what they'd seen.

He felt a sharp pain in his hand and looked down to see the blood trickling down his palm from where Ted had cut him with the penknife. Then the sound of his own voice. "I swear, that I will never ever tell a soul what I have seen."

Their oath of silence...Ted... *Ted!* The film abruptly rolled to stop and his vision cleared, focusing now on the entrance to the Keep. *Ted...*

From somewhere nearby he heard shouting, there were screams coming from deep inside the cellar. He ran. As he leapt through the entrance to the Keep the drop in temperature hit him as the dank musty reek of age and rot flowed out of the darkness. Taking his life in his hands, he cleared the first flight of stairs into the cellar two at a time. His lungs filled with the stale musty air as the blackness engulfed him.

Deep below him he heard splashing and gasping sounds, the last throes of an almighty struggle.

"TED! Hold on I'm coming" A single desperate voice answered him.

"Fraa…ank help me I'm…" The voice was cut off as the splashing sounds of water choked it. In a wild panic Frank threw his back against the wall and sidestepped his way through the darkness. The sounds of struggling and splashing were getting fainter. He moved away from the wall with his arms spread out in front of him searching through the cold black air. He stopped and listened for a second, the sounds had stopped.

In desperation he threw himself forward in a leap of faith towards the direction he thought was right. All of a sudden he was running in mid air, arms and legs flailing like a stuntman falling out of a window from a tall building. For a split second it felt like he was running through outer space and he thought he would keep going forever. Then his right foot hit the ground and slipped over the edge of a step.

There was a snapping sound as his ankle ligaments tore away from the bone in protest at the sudden unexpected impact of the full weight of his body bearing down on it.

His ankle gave way and his leg folded beneath him like a collapsing deck chair. The knee of his left leg crashed into the wall to the side of the steps and his body lurched forward. Instinctively he lifted his head to try and avoid the inevitable contact with the floor. It was his chin that hit first, forcing his head to snap backwards as his jawbone fractured. He brought his arms up to try and protect his head from any further collisions with the rough concrete. He continued to roll, his body bouncing, flipping over and over until at last he hit the bottom.

He lay there on his back staring into a space so dark he felt like he had been buried alive. He had no idea how many steps he had fallen down but one thing he did know was that he was at the bottom. From distant memory he knew the oak wooden door was not more than a few feet away. He could hear ripples of water still lapping against the walls inside the room after the struggle between the two men.

Apart from the sound of his own breathing, the rippling water was all he could hear; no voices, no shouting, McBride and Maloney were under the water. He had to move. He rolled over onto his front and lifted his head trying to ignore the excruciating pain in the back of his neck. He crawled on his hands and knees towards the oak doorway summoning every last bit of his strength. He sucked in as much air as he could force into his lungs and launched himself head first into the water.

The cold shocked him as he went under swallowing mouthfuls of the sickly black water. He surfaced choking on the filth and gasping for air. The foul tasting water was thick with silt that had settled on the bottom for years, some of it got into his lungs; it felt like they were burning from the inside. His stomach reacted violently to the sludge he had swallowed making him vomit.

He tried to steady himself, treading water while he took another deep breath. Kicking hard he raised himself above the water as high as he could and then flung his whole body forward and downwards in an attempt to submerge and swim to the bottom. He tried using his arms in a breaststroke like fashion to propel himself further into the icy black depths below him. Even in his state of shock and panic he could feel that his legs were still above the surface and were kicking into fresh air. He bent his knees to his chest and pulled harder with his arms. He pulled again and felt he was moving slowly downwards.

Finally his legs gained some purchase through the water and with a final pull he reached the bottom. His hands slipped through the layers of silt on the bottom and hit the concrete floor. He opened his eyes but it was pointless, like trying to see through paint.

He spread his arms out as wide as he could using a sweeping motion to feel along the floor. His right hand bumped into something soft and he closed his fingers around it pulling himself closer to it. He wrapped his arms around it and felt up and down it with his hands. He felt a shoe, he had hold of a leg, but he didn't know who it belonged to.

His lungs were screaming for more air but he knew if he surfaced now he may not have the strength to get back down to the bottom again. He pulled himself hand over hand and worked his way up the body. Now he could feel two bodies locked together with their arms wrapped around each other in a deathly grip. He tried to heave the both of them off the bottom but only succeeded in turning them over along the bottom.

The effort weakened him so much that he almost lost his grip. He had to know which body belonged to Ted and which one was McBride's. He knew they were both wearing almost identical clothes…and then in an instant it struck him…there was a difference…McBride had taken his gold crucifix cross from around his neck and held it up in his hand before entering the Keep, Ted must still have his on.

He groped frantically for the head of each body and felt for the collars of each one. He was letting air out of his lungs and water was working its way between his lips into his throat making him gag. He was losing consciousness and he felt an almost uncontrollable urge to breathe in. He was about to give up when he felt the slightest touch of a chain between his fingers.

He let go of the other body and used his hand to feel around the chain until his hands touched the unmistakable shape of the cross. He grabbed the body under the armpits and used the weight of it to bring his legs underneath him in a crouched position. Then with what little strength he had left, he pushed himself upwards.

The bodies must have torn free from each other because all of a sudden the one he was holding felt much lighter. He kicked his legs trying to propel himself in the direction of where he thought the surface was. He had no idea if he was going up, down or sidewards. Lights were going off inside his head like flashbulbs; a face appeared in front of his eyes. It was McBride's. He opened his mouth to let out a scream. There was no air left inside his lungs to make the sound. Thick icy sludge sucked itself into the vacuum of his lungs. In his mind he could hear himself shouting,

"Save Ted, please save him." As he slipped into unconsciousness he saw the blue lifeless face of Ted. Then he passed out.

Chapter 55

By the time Daz and Bob reached the front entrance to the Keep, Frank had already disappeared through the door and was nowhere to be seen. They had run after him as soon as he'd chased after Ted, but once inside they had no idea which way to go. So they took the most obvious route and ran up the stairs straight in front of them. They quickly searched the building two floors up, nothing, frantically they raced back down to the entrance.

The DCU Commander was stood with the other two officers inside the doorway waiting for them. All five of them began to make their way carefully inside the Keep until, in the almost total darkness they could just about see the stairs leading down to the cellar. Not knowing where the stairs led to and seeing how dark it was, Bob made a command decision.

"Right, we need torches before we go in any deeper, there's no point in us all rushing down there if we can't see what we're doing."

He asked the Commander if there were any torches in the cars. Before the Commander had chance to answer, one of the uniformed officers spoke up.

"I'm positive there's at least one in the boot, there's probably one in each of the other cars as well."

Bob turned towards the darkened stairs and shouted down as loud as he could.

"FRA...AANK! FRANK can you hear me?" The only sound that came back was the eerie echo of his own voice.

"Right, Daz and I are going to make our way down. Inspector you stay here in case anyone comes up and we don't see them. You two get back to the car, one of you bring the torch as quickly as you can, one of you get on the blower. I want an ambulance and paramedics here like yesterday, and while your at it, radio for the other car to get here with the torches, we're gonna need all the light we can get."

The Inspector waited at the top of the stairs while the officers ran to get the torches. Bob and Daz carefully made their way down into the cellar, feeling their way through total darkness taking several minutes to reach the bottom. They spent what seemed like ages wandering around in the dark moving one foot at a time, stumbling into walls and tripping over stones and debris in the cellar. They tried talking to each other, and holding on to each other at arms length, anything to get their bearings. It was an impossible task.

Just as they thought they were too late they heard shouting from somewhere above them. A light appeared from the top of the stairs. One of the officers came down into the cellar shining his torch. Bob and Daz were stood in the far corner of the cellar, lit up amidst a cloud of dust and algae spores floating all around them. It was like a scene from *The Blair Witch Project*. The officer was gasping and wheezing in between breaths as he spoke.

"The other officers will be here any second with more torches. The ambulance is on its way...ETA three minutes." He was struggling to catch his breath in between words. "I've also… alerted the Air Ambulance and the Fire Brigade just in case."

Bob was holding his hand over his eyes trying to regain some vision after the initial blast of light from the powerful Maglite torch temporarily blinded him.

This was the second time that day someone had shone a torch in his face, but he was more than pleased to see this one.

"Good, give me the torch, we need to find where they went to and quick."

Between the three of them they located the next flight of stairs leading to the sunken room and made their way down. As they arrived at the bottom they heard shouting and footsteps of the other officers arriving with more torches. Somewhere in the distance they could hear the sound of sirens wailing.

Bob shone the torch around and saw the wooden doorway to the flooded room. He leaned inside the arched door and shone the torch sweeping the surface with the powerful beam, but all he saw was the cloudy green muck swirling three inches below the surface. He knelt down to try and get closer to the water's edge holding the torch as close to the surface as possible. Daz was stood right behind him.

"Can you see anything?"

"I can't see… Shit!" He jumped back from the water as the back of a head cleared the surface of the water and began to sink almost as quickly as it had appeared. Bob reached out, stuck his arm into the water and grabbed whoever it was by the collar. He heaved, frantically struggling against the dead weight of the body in the water. Gradually he saw who it was.

"DAZ, ITS FRANK! Give us a hand. Someone get the paramedics down here NOW!"

Bob and Daz knelt side by side dragging the body through the water towards them. As more of the body broke the surface another head appeared. Between them they separated the two bodies while the other officers helped heave them out onto the floor in the cellar. Daz and one of the DCU officers were still giving mouth-to-mouth resuscitation when the paramedics arrived and got to work.

Ted was the first to show any signs of recovery; as soon as the Paramedics were sure he was breathing they carried him out on a stretcher, another Paramedic continued attending to Frank. There was a pulse, just. The paramedics maintained the resuscitation process on Frank as they carried him out of the Keep to the waiting ambulance.

Within minutes the Fire crews arrived. After assessing the scene they kitted up two men with masks, oxygen Cylinders and regulators. Carrying huge underwater lamps they dropped into the water inside the sunken room. It only took a minute before they surfaced. They had recovered the body of McBride. He was dead and there was nothing they or the Paramedics could do to revive him. As they laid him out on the floor inside the cellar, in one hand he was still clutching a chain with a gold locket shaped like a heart. In his other hand he was holding on to something round and covered in green slime. It was the skull of Sharon Byrne.

***

The Paramedics were almost at the ambulance when Frank opened his eyes and tried to sit up. He burst into a fit of hacking and spluttering as he tried to get his first full lung full of fresh air. He spewed a black smelly mixture of water and stomach acid all over the stretcher. He felt as if he had only just surfaced from the water in the cellar.

The Paramedics turned him on his side just in time, as Frank was sick again, coughing up half his lungs. By the time they had got him into the ambulance he had recovered and spoke in hoarse whisper. There was one thing he wanted to do before they took him away in the ambulance. He looked like shit and they were insisting that he go straight to hospital but he flatly refused. The Paramedics wrapped him in a foil blanket trying to at least protect him from getting hypothermia.

With the help of Bob and Daz supporting his weight, Frank was able to get out of the ambulance. The Paramedics followed keeping a close watch on him. Outside it was already getting dark and it was cold, wet and miserable. Uniformed officers were sealing off the area with crime scene tape. His ankle hurt like hell but he fought through the pain as Bob and Daz half carried him to the lay by where they had parked the cars.

He saw the DCU Commander issuing instructions to other officers from the fire crews as they discussed the recovery operation to retrieve the remains of Sharon Byrne from the bottom of the Keep. He heard the wailing sirens as one of the ambulances disappeared in the distance taking Ted to hospital. *Thank God for that.*

He turned to Bob. "Give us a minute."

Bob and Daz left him alone and went to talk to the DCU Commander. Frank limped his way into the middle of the Marine Highway and looked out across the Belfast Lough. He turned and looked up the long slope towards Carrickfergus then closed his eyes and smiled. In his mind he saw the vision.

The sky was bright blue and the sun shone high in the sky. He felt the warm wind on his face and his eyes watered with the tears streaming off his face. His bike was freewheeling down the hill; *to him* it felt like he was going a hundred miles an hour.

EPILOGUE

It was Christmas day in Belfast. Frank and Ted were in a private room at the Royal Victoria Hospital close to the city centre. A string of visitors had come and gone bringing messages of goodwill and some even brought presents. Amongst the visitors were Chief Superintendent Bright and Father Francis. Father Francis had cadged a lift from Liverpool with the Chief Super and was waiting outside with a few visitors from the local parish, one of who was an old school friend of Ted's. There were hugs and floods of tears as they embraced each other.

To Frank's absolute delight they had brought another surprise visitor along for the ride, Detective Chief Inspector Andy Williams looking the picture of health no less. Andy shook Frank's hand as he officially told him that his promotion to DCI was permanent. Frank wished him a long and happy retirement, but Andy had even better news to tell him. Hilary and Cram would be here within the hour.

The visitors finally left and Frank and Ted had just eaten a traditional Irish Christmas Dinner with all the trimmings. They were almost drifting off to sleep when Ted asked Frank a question.

"So what willyer be doin' with yerself next Frank?"

Frank thought for a second and smiled. "Well, I've found somewhere, where they make a fantastic chocolate cake, and at this time of the year the weather is perfect for Christmas so I might go and stay there for a while." He looked across to Ted in the bed a few feet away who was chuckling to himself.

"I'll see if I can arrange it for you Frank. Besides, I believe you've still got something that belongs to someone up there? Maybe it would be nice to deliver it to him in person." Ted held up his hand.

In it was a set of car keys. Frank grinned and closed his eyes. In his dreams he was on a sledge sliding down a hill with Cram clinging on tightly behind him, and everything was just... fine.

Author's Note

As a first time Author I have tried where possible to be as factually accurate in relation to practices, procedures and geographical locations. 'Immaculate Deception' has been four years in the writing and I would hope that anyone with local knowledge of Liverpool would relate to the locations as described in the book.

I have had a lot of co-operation from Merseyside Police and the coroner's office as well as 'forensic' input from doctors and professors. So any mistakes are entirely the fault of the author. Obviously the storyline for the book is totally fictitious; the characters as described are made up and not meant to relate to anyone in real life.

Oh, and by the way, to the best of my knowledge there isn't an eighth floor in Canning Place!

Lightning Source UK Ltd.
Milton Keynes UK
20 January 2010

148846UK00001B/4/P